"Though it's hard these days to feel sympathy for investment bankers and stockbrokers, Vonnegut makes his irreverent protagonist someone we can root for as he pursues crooks who use the redemptive language of hedge funds to hide financial malfeasance. A promising debut."

—*Library Journal*

"Norb Vonnegut's *Top Producer* begins where *Liar's Poker* and *The Bonfire of the Vanities* left off and puts an electrifying spin on the winner-take-all culture of Wall Street. Turn to the first page and plunge into the shark-infested waters of high finance and greed."

—Brent Ghelfi, ITW Award-nominated author of *Volk's Game* and *The Venona Cable*

"A timely read as Vonnegut opens the kimono exposing the intricate cause and effect of finance and murder. He shares his well-earned insights and literary acumen in a manner that entices the reader to reach out for the next chapter. A must for all investors wishing to avoid the next Bernie Madoff!"

—Joe Grano, Former CEO UBS/PaineWebber

TOP PRODUCER

NORB VONNEGUT

St. Martin's Paperbacks

This is a work of fiction. All of the characters, organizations, and events portrayed in this novel are either products of the author's imagination or are used fictitiously.

TOP PRODUCER

Copyright © 2009 by Norb Vonnegut.
Excerpt from *The Gods of Greenwich* copyright © 2010 by Norb Vonnegut.

Cover photograph
© Latrisha Ann Large, Newark Ohio / latrishasphotos@yahoo.com

For information address St. Martin's Press, 175 Fifth Avenue, New York, NY 10010.

Library of Congress Catalog Card Number: 2009012731

ISBN: 978-0-312-38830-0

Printed in the United States of America

St. Martin's hardcover edition / September 2009
St. Martin's Paperbacks edition / January 2011

St. Martin's Paperbacks are published by St. Martin's Press, 175 Fifth Avenue, New York, NY 10010.

10 9 8 7 6 5 4 3 2 1

For Mary, Wynn, and Coco.

You bring me joy every day.

Mary, it was Friday night—not Saturday.

ACKNOWLEDGMENTS

Thank you for reading *Top Producer*. It was a long journey from idea to publication. Writing this novel was like chartering the *Queen Mary II* inside my head. And I must tell you, the late-night parties rocked.

So many people contributed to this book. Caroline Fitzgibbons and Tad Smith referred me to my agent. Their introductions to the media world were significant gifts, especially for a rookie author. Caroline and Tad, I will always be grateful for the way you cheered me on from the start.

Scott Hoffman is an outstanding agent. He is my friend and relentless advocate from Folio Literary Management, the agency he cofounded. Scott's business and editorial counsel is always wise. He works with talented people, like Kate Travers, the marketing director at Folio, and Celeste Fine, who promoted *Top Producer* around the world.

Scott paired me with Pete Wolverton of Thomas Dunne/St. Martin's Press (SMP). Pete edited *Top Producer* and made it a much, much better book. It is a privilege to work with Pete and his colleagues: Sally

Richardson, Tom Dunne, Andy Martin, Matthew Shear, John Murphy, Dori Weintraub, Matt Baldacci, Katie Gilligan, Monica Katz, Sarah Melnyk, and Liz Byrne. Special thanks to Hector DeJean, a terrific publicist at SMP who fielded my bazillion e-mails with can-do enthusiasm.

My great friends—Jon Ledecky, Tony McAuliffe, Scott Malkin, Dewey Shay, Tim Scrantom, Mark Director, Peter von Maur, Peter Raymond, Brooks Newmark, Eugene Matthews, and Chris Eklund—help me understand the world every day. Without our good times together and their appreciation for what makes people tick, I could not articulate the thoughts of my fictional characters. I owe additional thanks to Jon's mother, Berta Ledecky, for encouraging me to write for as long as I can remember.

For many years, Cam Burns, Matt Arpano, and I worked as a team and managed money for wealthy families. I learned so much about financial services from Cam and Matt. And while the observations in *Top Producer* are all my own, I will forever be grateful for their sound judgment and market savvy.

Top Producer includes several Polish expressions. I don't speak a word. Kuba Kierlanczyk, while a high-school sophomore, translated text for early drafts. Thanks, Kuba, dude. Malgorzata Marjanska guided me with the jargon. I highly recommend her Web site, at www.thepolishtranslator.com.

What is a book without lawyers? Thalia Cody reviewed the SEC law and suggested an important plot point. David McCabe fielded questions about trusts and estates. Adam Snukal reviewed the contracts that keep me out of trouble.

Jon Orseck helped with passages about derivatives. Jay Coleman offered insights into I-banking. Michael Liebeskind guided me on important financial topics. Michael Roberts explained the Hollywood angle. Jack Bourger and Selena Vanderwerf spread the word and introduced me to the American Foundation for the Blind, an organization that expands possibilities for people with vision loss. Matt Harrington and his outstanding team taught me how to work with the media.

Other friends, who advised or helped in some way, include: Bob Poirier; many, many champions with the American Diabetes Association; Ryker and Tina Young ("Maui Maui"); Jenny McAuliffe; Shari Director; Gwill York; Emily Benedek; John and Suzie Edelman; Jordana Davis; Bob Grady; Marlon Young; Bill Sorensen; and Tracy Chesman a.k.a. "cheesechick" on Twitter.

Over breakfast several years ago, Mark Vonnegut described writing as the "family business" in his home. Mark, who delivers keen insight in the most amusing manner, was so right about the experience. Great thanks to: Marion Vonnegut, my mother and first fan; Micki and Jack Costello, Buni Vonnegut, and Chris Nottingham; Wendy and Joe Vonnegut; and Andy Graves. My dad could not be here. But he was the role model I needed to get out of bed every morning at five A.M. and start writing.

Nightly dinner conversation at home creates great source material. My children each possess wry humor that found its way into the novel. Thank you, Wynn and Coco. You are my inspiration. There would be no *Top Producer* without Mary, my wife and love. She encouraged me. She read the novel a thousand times, cutting, cursing, and chuckling with every pass. She made the good guys better, the bad guys more evil. She kept me going and tolerated my insane hours. I can only say, "Thank you, sweetie."

There is one absolute truth I have learned as a first-time author: No voyage is complete. No story is worth telling. No book is worth writing, unless someone reads it. Thank you for reading my book.

I hope you enjoy *Top Producer*.

CHAPTER 1

Six weeks ago I was a rising star at a white-shoe investment bank and brokerage firm. I was Babe Ruth on my way from Boston to New York City, John F. Kennedy connecting with crowds during the presidential elections. The markets were rocking during the first half of 2007. And it seemed clear that one day I would become a titan of finance, a fixture on the business pages of *The New York Times*.

My job is the occupation formerly known as "stockbroker." But it has been years since anyone called me that. "Stockbroker" sounds oily. *Glengarry Glen Ross*. The word makes clients twitch. Even brokerage houses, institutions that profit from legions of smiling, dialing, cold-calling robotrons, cast about for less unctuous titles. Stockbrokers are "investment professionals" over at Goldman. Morgan Stanley can't decide whether its people are "investment representatives" or "financial advisers." Another competitor is toying with "private bankers." After eight years in the industry, I have grown numb to all the angst.

I focus on a different name. Wall Street calls its most

successful salespeople "top producers." Think of us as rainmakers, the folks who butter the bread. We are a brash bunch at the office. We have opinions about everything and say what we want, for we understand three axioms about our industry.

One: Investors hire advisers with strong points of view. The more impassioned our convictions, the better.

Two: As long as we generate revenues, bosses tolerate our quirks and leave us the hell alone.

Three: Wall Street firms pay ridiculous money to top producers. And that, my friend, is a beautiful thing if you've ever been poor.

I was a top producer, the captain of a cramped cubicle rigged with a twenty-one-inch flat-screen monitor and an even bigger television hanging from the ceiling. Around my desk the stacks of investment research often crested five feet before toppling like dominos into nearby aisles.

Who needs space to make money?

I managed ideas, not clutter. My job was to cut through all the market chaos and sniff out the truth. Wall Street coughs up so much investment phlegm. If I wasn't on the phone guarding clients, "my guys" to use the industry vernacular, I wasn't making money. Bold, opinionated, you bet. I had all the answers and then some.

On hedge funds: "Would you let someone play Vegas with your money and give them twenty percent of the winnings?"

On McKinsey's alumni, the ex-consultants infiltrating the ranks of Wall Street's management: "Fucking revenge of the nerds. One day, those people will suck our industry dry of testosterone and everything good."

On money management: "Wall Street is the only place in the world where thirty seconds swing ten million dollars into place. Try buying real estate for the same amount and you'll grow old as lawyers negotiate the fine points."

Finance was fast. It was furious. And I thrived on the frenzied pace. I had broken into the big leagues of capitalism and brought my "A" game to the office every day. So I thought. The last six weeks changed everything. My world unraveled the night Charlie Kelemen hosted his wife's birthday bash in the New England Aquarium. Best friend, savior, a man who wore Brioni suits the way sweet Italian sausages split their fatty innards over open flames—that was Charlie Kelemen. He did so much for me. He did so much for all his friends. I still can't believe what Charlie did to us.

The signs were all there. We should have seen it coming.

CHAPTER 2

"No, Grove. It's not happening," Charlie argued over the phone, his voice firm.

I just had to persist. And now I live with the guilt. "The aquarium is the perfect place to surprise Sam."

"Won't happen. I'm hiring a yacht to cruise around Manhattan. It's romantic. It's glamorous."

"It's boring. Been there. Done that."

"But the aquarium is in Boston," Charlie objected.

"What do you care?" Whenever I argued, my faint Southern drawl intensified. "You almost live there now. You're always visiting your in-laws on Beacon Hill."

"Sam's parents would rather fly here. They love New York City."

"Trust me. Boston gives them home court advantage. They can help with the preparations. Besides—"

"Besides what?" he interrupted.

"It's the only way to surprise Sam. She'll never suspect Boston. You know how she is."

"A card-carrying snoop." He chuckled with a touch of Truman Capote in his voice. His nervous laughter signaled fading resolve.

"Everybody knows she's a *snoop*." Repeating key words was a proven sales technique. By emphasizing "snoop," I was selling hard, employing all those time-tested skills of a top producer.

"What about all our New York friends?" Charlie asked without conviction. His objections were dropping like Custer's men at Little Bighorn.

"Charlie, you could fill the aquarium with your friends from Boston. But we'll all come from New York. Tell everybody a road trip is the only way to keep Sam's party a surprise."

"You're right," he agreed, his surrender complete. "I like it."

That was how it all started. That was how I helped my short, squat friend with the humongous head plan his wife's ill-fated birthday party.

The Giant Ocean Tank at the New England Aquarium soars four stories high, contains 200,000 gallons of salt water, and hosts about 150 different kinds of creatures from the sea. The names of its marine inhabitants attest to the fertile imaginations of oceanographers. The "Horse-eye Jack" and the "Scrawled Cowfish" suggest rustic Montana ranches rather than gilled beasts from the murky abyss. The "Sergeant Major" and "Blackbar Soldierfish" hint at distant military campaigns during the height of British imperialism. Some monikers refer to guns, like the "Permit" and the "Sargassum Trigger-fish," a nasty little creature prone to biting the staff during feedings. Taken together, these names paint an exotic world thriving under the sea's endless cover.

Or perhaps they foreshadow dangers from the deep. There are three "Sand Tigers," two males and one female. These sharks, each with three thousand spiny teeth arranged in eight jagged rows, undoubtedly reign as the tank's scariest residents. Their fierce eyes betray the absence of souls, black pupils floating in yellow-gray irises. To them, every vision is a potential meal. No matter how often biologists feed *Carcharias taurus*, they cannot suppress the sharks' natural instinct to hunt. Smaller fish sometimes disappear, victims of endless appetites.

I can spend hours gazing into the saltwater prism from every angle and depth. The wide, ever-rising footpath corkscrews round and round the Giant Ocean Tank all the way to the surface. Fish of every shape and color slowly circle the monstrous Caribbean coral, sometimes breaking ranks from their languid order to flip here or paddle there. They are my Svengalis from the sea. They whisk me from the day-to-day chaos of my world, away from the hoot and holler, break-ins, and other communication tools with names that hint of Wall Street's violent discourse. Ordinarily, I can lose myself in the tranquility of the tank's infinite views as finned creatures keep time to a silent beat only they can hear.

But not on Sam's birthday that Friday night in mid-July. By 8:45 P.M. the cavernous aquarium rocked from laughter and jazz and the randy vibes that accompany endless tides of cocktails. Men in black ties scoped out the cleavage, their keen eyes probing one chest after another. Women in evening gowns knocked back cosmopolitans, their libidos rousing from alcohol and the dance floor's musky scents. I doubted anyone else in the crowd had been celibate for the last eighteen months. The jostle and the noise, however, made it impossible to dwell on this dark thought. The five hundred voices inside the atrium roared like coastal thunder on a stormy night.

There was one constant among the conversations. At Charlie's parties, always a bacchanalian mix of liquor and music, guests inevitably dropped their guard. Squeezing through the crowd, I overheard it all that night. In no particular order, with no particular focus, the conversations played like sound-bite medleys from reality television.

"Don't look now, but the duct tape on her boobs is showing. . . ."

"Three more drinks, and we're out of here. . . ."

"Did you hear about Burkie? He wore a baseball hat right after getting Botoxed, and now he has permanent ridges on his forehead. Looks like a fucking Klingon. . . ."

"I bet that redhead is going commando. . . ."

"Her dress is so last year. . . ."

"Another Botero butt . . ."

"Blonde at twelve o'clock. I need my wingman. . . ."

When I finally reached the bar, a tall brunette with great bangs ordered a frozen margarita and told her friend, "Jill, you look fabulous. How did you ever fit into that dress?"

"Colonic irrigation," Jill whispered into the din. "Speaking of which, I really need to find the ladies' room."

Too much information. Jill scuttled past me with purpose, her singular focus betraying the gotta-go shuffle known to all ages. She had been oblivious to my eavesdropping.

Great Bangs, however, caught me red-handed. She smirked once and then let me off the hook. "Hey, Red," she said, referring to my strawberry-blond hair, "I'm free Monday of next week. If that doesn't work for you, we can make it Tuesday, Wednesday, or Thursday." She wore a strapless royal blue evening gown with a plunging neckline. The cut made me wonder what was holding everything up.

I struggled to say something witty, but my brain failed to deliver. No brilliant repartee. No charming chow mein. Instead, I flashed my most winsome smile.

Great Bangs, undeterred, sipped greenish froth through a straw. Her large brown eyes held mine with the promise of an excellent evening. Maybe more. The look said, *Step up to the plate and swing for the fences.* Really tempting. But even after eighteen months, I wasn't ready.

Frankly, the penguins made better conversationalists than me. In the vast reservoir surrounding the Giant Ocean Tank, they all joined the chatter. The little blues squawked that their smelt was too fishy or their sardines too salty. The African penguins cajoled passing humans to exercise civil disobedience. "Throw us snacks," they demanded in penguin-speak. "Throw us snacks." The rockhoppers gossiped about their neighbors and griped about getting fat. All three breeds pummeled the staff with incessant orders. "We could use a few lounge chairs down here. And bring some rum cocktails while you're at it. Maybe a Frisbee or two." Like the party on the landing above, there was no symmetry on penguin beach, just kinetic revelry for the joy of life.

At 9:15 P.M. the band's lead singer tapped his microphone and called us to attention. His black hair looked like it had been styled with a garden tool, possibly a rake but more likely a weed whacker. "We're turning things over to our host," he said, slurring his words with hazy musician cool.

From every nook and cranny of the New England Aquarium, five hundred people searched for Charlie Kelemen. At five-six and 230 pounds, Charlie waddled more than he walked. No matter. Friends and fans overlooked the layers. His star persona would have done justice to the lankiest matinee idols from the 1950s. We became silent as he approached the microphone.

The penguins, conversely, saluted his arrival with raucous cheers. Charlie's rocking gait, black trousers, and white dinner jacket made him look like their reigning alpha male. The penguins whooped. They hooted. They hailed Charlie and hollered, "More snacks, Master. More snacks."

Charlie blushed, either from the exertion of walking or the realization he was on center stage. Cherubic and pink, he radiated charm and glowed with good-natured warmth. "Thank you," he said. "Thank you for celebrating Sam's birthday tonight. I know it was a total surprise."

He panned a *Yeah*, *right* expression for the crowd,

and laughter reverberated through the cavernous room. No doubt she had found out. Everyone agreed Sam was a snoop.

The fish, circling methodically in the tank, distracted me. A large stingray wove through the water with an undulating motion. A portly grouper followed. Its fat, permanently pursed lips looked like a collagen experiment gone awry.

"Sam, where are you?" Charlie squeaked. "Come over here, sweetie."

The crowds parted. We found Sam. Jet-black hair, cobalt blue eyes, and creamy white skin, she had the coloring of a Siberian husky. Tonight Sam wore a light green gown that ballooned into a bulb over her toned, tight legs. The silky fabric, petals stitched from the Garden of Eden, offered a refreshing alternative to the funereal black shades of most formal garb.

Earlier, Sam had laughed about her outfit. "Grove, I feel like a cabbage. But you know Charlie."

"He loves to decorate you."

With that, Sam fussed my bow tie into shape. "Mr. O'Rourke," she started coquettishly, "you're thirty-two. You're handsome. You've got sweet little hips."

"Thanks, I think, Mrs. Kelemen."

"All the girls are talking about you," she continued. "I won't be happy unless you ask somebody out on a date. Here. Tonight. You have your orders."

Now, with the overheads dimmed, a lone spotlight celebrated Sam's approach. Girlfriends pecked her cheeks as she strode to the stage like Angelina Jolie collecting an Oscar. Men whistled. And from the Giant

Ocean Tank, creature-like shadows splashed across our faces. No doubt Charlie had hired top-notch professionals to arrange the lighting. He had a flair for the dramatic.

"Tonight," Charlie continued, "a special guest has joined us from the teeming bazaars of Turkey. Her name is Neylan, which means 'Fulfilled Wish.'" Charlie pronounced the words lasciviously.

All through the New England Aquarium, five hundred people chanted in unison, "Woo-hoo!"

"Before Neylan performs," Charlie said, "I need the men in the audience to help me set the right mood. Where are you, Crunch?"

The Kelemen family hairdresser, six-one and buff, emerged from the shadows just as Sam found her place next to Charlie. Crunch, scrutinized by five hundred partiers, pushed a hand truck loaded with two huge boxes piled on top of each other. He parked and winked flirtatiously at anyone, male or female, who dared to catch his eye. His red-sequined dinner jacket glittered brazenly under the spots.

With flair and an air of mystery, Charlie reached into the top box and pulled out a red fez made from the same sequined material as Crunch's dinner jacket. He inspected it at arm's length, gingerly treating the hat like a priceless relic from an ancient crusade. He donned the fez, positioned it with a rakish tilt, and warned the crowd, "No cracks about *Casablanca* please." He really did look like a short version of Sydney Greenstreet.

Crunch sneaked up on Charlie from behind, reached his red-sequined arms around the wide girth, and patted

the fat man's titanic gut. Almost as though choreo-
graphed, Charlie pulled a burlap-colored burka from the
second box and backhanded it to Crunch. The stylist
quickly donned the burka and raked his fingers, open
like sideways Vs, across the eye slits. First the left and
then the right.

The crowd guffawed. The cultural reference made
me queasy, but it was classic Charlie. He pushed to the
edge and then some.

"Ladies," Charlie called, "these burkas aren't for you."
He paused and waited for his words to take hold. "I want
each of you to put one on your man. Let's see how they
feel." With that statement Charlie won every woman's
allegiance in the aquarium. Crunch reached into the
boxes and rapid-fired burkas into the crowd. I nabbed
one for myself.

"Ladies," Charlie continued, "these are for you." The
two men reached into the other box and pulled out more
fezzes. Again, they tossed the gear to the guests. Sam
donned a fez and watched in bemusement.

"Now, if everyone will step back," directed Charlie,
"we'll invite Neylan to get started. I need a seat for Sam,"
he said to no one in particular. Alex Romanov, a hedge
fund manager with lights-out investment returns, delivered a chair and gestured for Sam to sit.

The lead singer with the big hair returned to the
spots. He shooed Charlie and Crunch away, while other
band members semi-circled Sam from behind. With the
sultry swagger of an accomplished musician, or practiced tequila drinker, the leader rumbled, "One, two, a
one, two, three." Then the band took us to the Middle

East and jolted our ears with staccato instrumentation, the kind found in Turkish nightclubs that serve curried goat.

Neylan absorbed the spotlight. She beamed from the center of its dazzling arc. The belly dancer became one with the light. Against the blackness that shrouded the rest of us, she soaked in every ray and emitted a few photons of her own. With her arms raised high in a cathedral point, or mosque turret, Neylan invited the crowd to savor the vision. She dared us to let our attention drift. She glowed with the supreme confidence of a performer who had long ago perfected her ability to dazzle audiences and beguile men.

The pose certainly beguiled Jason Tropez, an aging sultan of the hedge fund industry. He ogled every inch of Neylan. He forgot his wife, the stately sexagenarian at his side. He forgot his mail-order mistress from the Eastern European escort agency. The worst-kept secret money can buy, Anastasia had been prancing near the bar earlier that evening. Right now, neither woman mattered. Tropez burned bright with desire for the belly dancer.

Put on your burka, and spare us the lust, I thought.

Neylan erupted. She shook her belly and hips hard. Little waves of fatty flesh rippled from side to side, like surf that crashes against a sandy beach before retreating to the sea for reinforcements. Neylan scooted straight for Sam, rotating her hips this way and that. It was the dance of the suffering stomach.

Thirty years ago when big-breasted women had hips, *Playboy* might have featured Neylan. She embodied the meaning of "voluptuous." Big butt, bulging belly, and bouncing boobs, all three jiggled just a few inches away from Sam's pert little nose. Neylan shook with the intensity of a jackhammer. Her skimpy bikini, fashioned from gold coins and allure, jingled like two pockets full of loose change.

Fun, but fucking weird, I decided. What had possessed Charlie to hire her for Sam's birthday? Belly dancers were a guy thing.

At first, Sam laughed and played along. She toasted Neylan with a full glass of wine but did not drink. Instead, Sam's head bobbed to the rhythm of gold coins and floppy cleavage. No doubt she learned more about Neylan's anatomy than was necessary. As the crowd began to roar, Sam's face grew beet red. Her quixotic grimace asked, *What do I do now?*

"Have a drink," I answered under my breath. But Sam stared in embarrassment, unable to hear my advice.

Charlie's expression, by contrast, surprised me. He glowed with satisfaction, a man relishing his control over the crowd. He watched the audience and seldom bothered to look at Neylan. Not that she cared. She flopped backward and forward, shook her coins, and reached around to caress the back of Sam's neck. Some members of the audience gasped, but most cheered as Neylan tried to seduce Sam with her dance. Crunch, of course, joined in.

I wondered what the fish saw as they peered through their walls. With our burkas, red fezzes, and be-coined boobs quivering out of control, we must have been a curious sight. I half expected the little monsters to stop swimming and press their fish faces up against the glass for a better view. They seemed agitated. The parade of controlled circles had given way to perturbed bursts of motion. They zigzagged around the aquarium in quick flashes, as though trying to catch the light flickering from Neylan's blinding bikini.

Eventually, Neylan and Crunch chased Sam's self-restraint. She rose from her chair, snatched a pink chiffon scarf from a nearby friend, and sashayed into the human ring like a gypsy. Sam reached the scarf around the outside of Crunch's leg and pulled it through the inside of his crotch. With a coquettish expression and a roll of her shoulder, she mouthed words no one heard but we all understood: *Oh my.*

From somewhere in the crowd a voice bellowed, "Take it off."

The guests, captains of finance and bedrocks of philanthropy, cast their inhibitions aside. Charlie's parade of stiff drinks, from martinis to fruity rum concoctions, had taken control. "Take it off" became the universal, audience-wide chant, though it was unclear who was to disrobe—Neylan in her coins, Crunch in his sequins, or Sam in her cabbage outfit.

Charlie had disappeared from the spotlight and was nowhere to be seen. Odd. It was not like him to step aside. But he had created another masterpiece, and I suspected he was about to unveil his coup de grâce. It would be just like Charlie to emerge from the shadows wearing the robes of an oil sheikh. The image made me smile.

For no particular reason I noticed Great Bangs. Her

eyes shone wide with anguish, her face a mix of horror and bewilderment. I looked over at the dancers, thinking their performance had generated the distress. The three wiggled their butts and bellies, hardly the cause of such anxiety. I returned to Great Bangs, and it became clear. She was not staring at the dancers. She was staring at the Giant Ocean Tank.

And she screamed.

CHAPTER 3

Great Bangs's panicked shrieks snapped my head back to the Giant Ocean Tank, and I saw the most curious thing. Charlie. Fat, waddling Charlie, framed against the Horse-eye Jack, the Sergeant Major, and the other toothy sea monsters searching for adventure in their monotonous confines. They inspected him and darted away. Their agitated motions reflected light throughout the tank and made me forget the flashes from Neylan's dazzling coins. The living coral reef, home to sea barracudas and moray eels, loomed large and bizarre just behind him.

Only, Charlie wasn't standing outside the tank. He thrashed deep inside it, underwater and engulfed by the briny liquid. He flailed. He struggled. As he gasped for oxygen, air belched from his mouth and bubbled toward the tank's surface. Charlie beat his arms futilely, desperate to break free from the synthetic sea's drowning clutches.

Stunned, I tried to yell, "Get out," but my vocal cords failed. What was he doing? Five minutes earlier, I thought Charlie had disappeared to change. He was not wearing the robes of an oil sheikh, though. Nor had he donned a swimsuit. He was still wearing his tux. The jacket and fez had disappeared. The starchy stiffness of his shirt had given way to the water's wavy motion.

A rope, knotted at Charlie's right ankle, stretched from an industrial stainless-steel trolley. It looked like a caterer's serving table. Only now, the trolley served as a makeshift anchor. It pulled Charlie down, down, down, dragging him inexorably toward the sandy floor of the Giant Ocean Tank. This spectacle was no stunt. Something had gone bad. Way bad.

Though I had lost my voice, Great Bangs never lost hers. "Do something!" she bellowed. Her screech cut through all the din of the great room: over the band, over the crowd, and over the penguins. Great Bangs pointed toward Charlie with one hand. She covered her mouth with the other. The screams burst through her fingers. She screamed and screamed and screamed.

The revelry stopped. Charlie's drunken guests turned away from Neylan and Crunch and searched for the source of Great Bangs's distress. Her outsized blasts had given birth to a stadium wave. It took only seconds for the crowd to focus on the Giant Ocean Tank.

The band stopped playing. Neylan stopped jiggling. Crunch stopped clowning. And Sam froze. We were five hundred strong. We were five hundred united in horror, watching without believing. Even the penguins stopped yammering. Perhaps they sensed the anguish of their alpha male. He reigned supreme no more.

Charlie sank deeper and deeper, his breath running out. The stainless-steel cart grazed a Sand Tiger, which sent the shark surging through the water, its tail whipping furiously left and right. Through the water and glass, Charlie's face looked pudgy and bloated. His expression howled for help.

I scanned the crowd for a member of the staff and found a woman wearing the aquarium's blue-gray uniform. Pale and thin, she looked more helpless than the rest of us.

Instinctively, I muscled through the crush of gawking people. They rubbernecked. The surreal vision, Charlie Kelemen sinking to the bottom of the Giant Ocean Tank, paralyzed them. I cut left and dashed along a concrete path that spiraled to the tank's surface. Five seconds had elapsed since Great Bangs's first scream. It seemed like five lifetimes.

Do something, I told myself. A half step behind, Alex Romanov joined my pursuit. We had no idea what we were chasing. We had no time to think.

Charlie sank ever more. Over my shoulder I saw Romanov stop and spread his hands out against the glass. He stretched them wide and peered up into the unforgiving abyss, trying to decide what next. For a moment he looked like he'd been crucified. But we needed more than a religious gesture from a hedge fund manager to save Charlie. I felt powerless. I started running up the path again, drawn to the tank's surface. It was the only point of entry. It was the only place to fish Charlie out.

As Charlie plunged, he blinked in my direction without comprehension. Panic and waning oxygen wrecked his reasoning. I saw him look at Romanov, and just for a second Charlie appeared to regain his senses. He

stopped thrashing. His face turned resolute. He wrestled
with the knots that secured the cord to his ankle. But
his movements remained jerky, his struggles in vain. I
noticed plumes of red liquid billowing from his arms
and the tops of his hands. They spread in eerie red-
chocolate clouds that fouled the otherwise clear water.
I wondered how he had cut himself.

It all happened lightning fast. I raced up the pathway,
racking my brain for a solution. Romanov drew level
with Charlie, who had grown frustrated from his losing
battle against time and knots. He no longer controlled
his lungs. My best friend, the man who had saved me,
edged closer toward his own death.

Water can be so refreshing. The way it cleanses cotton
mouth after too much liquor. The way it rinses off the
salt and perspiration from 120-mile bike rides.

But water can be damning and unfamiliar. As water
passes the larynx, drawn by alveoli panicking from the
lack of oxygen, some victims cough or swallow the fluid.
They cannot fight their natural instinct to breathe. The
body's desperate confusion, driven by the need for air
when only water is available, leads to laryngospasm. The
larynx and throat constrict, preventing any more water
from filling the lungs. Or air. Nothing is worse than
drowning.

So they say.

Charlie flapped his arms desperately with gasps of violent motion. Against the cart's weight, he made no
headway toward the surface. He floundered without

hope. His wild, lashing gesticulations only scared the fish.

Some of the fish.

The Sand Tigers did not scare. Far from it. Charlie's frenzy aroused them. The cloud of blood whetted their hunger. It stoked their lust for food and revived their visceral instinct to kill. The aquarium's biologists still had no antidote for the vital fluid's opiate impact.

A seven-foot Sand Tiger whizzed through the water. She lunged at Charlie's arm, three thousand teeth crunching and snapping and gnawing even before contact. She hit. She turned and twisted, working to wrench Charlie's limb from his body. *Carcharias taurus* failed. But that arm hung uselessly at his side. A new plume of blood poured from his body.

The crowd gasped. Someone shouted, "Call nine-one-one."

A second shark, almost nine feet in length, barreled into my hapless friend. Clearly in pain, Charlie surprised me. He fought back, oblivious to the rows of serrated teeth. He bludgeoned the shark's gills with his good arm. He threw hammer punches, again and again. The bloody spectacle, man versus shark, immobilized Romanov and me. We stopped running.

The Sand Tiger shot away in a herky-jerky motion. Sharks feel blows to their gills the way men feel kicks to their balls. The first shark, the seven-footer, attacked again and avenged her mate. She whisked through the water, opened her mouth wide, and slammed into Charlie's stomach. His gut was a fat, juicy target of massive opportunity. Then she retreated, smug and victorious.

Something chunky and red flopped through the white shreds of Charlie's shirt. The mangled gobs looked vital. Intestines, kidney, liver, maybe all three, I couldn't be sure. Charlie reached for the clumps and tried to push them back inside. He moved in slow motion, suffering from a lack of either oxygen or blood. The wound disappeared in the clouds, his life pouring into the water.

From outside the tank I recognized agony. Bile welled inside my throat. And I dry-retched. The crowd screamed, men and women alike, everyone horrified by what they saw. Someone puked the real thing. A sickly smell filled my nostrils, making me dry-retch even more.

The third shark, the biggest of the three, blasted through the water like a guided torpedo. The sight stopped me dead in my tracks. I forgot the nearby nausea. The Sand Tiger held his mouth high and wide, a wizened old veteran of feeding frenzies. His urine-yellow eyes flashed absolute evil. All the guests in the hall froze like deer in the headlights.

He struck.

Charlie's magnificent, humongous head disappeared. Gone. The same beefy belfry that had spawned all the self-deprecating jokes about Cossack ancestors. Gone. The shark's wide jaws crowned Charlie's cranium with ease. Gone.

Without breaking stroke, the shark shot forward, leaving extension cords of vertebrae and arteries where head and neck had once been. He gnashed and gnawed. He chewed the skull with reckless abandon, the way a dog savages a bone. Charlie's remains descended to the base of the Great Ocean Tank under the weight of the attached food cart. The other two sharks circled back and struck the headless torso again and again.

I dry-retched. Someone cacked over the backs of the crowd. It must have been a woman. Burkas would have checked the spew from men.

Deep inside the tank, Charlie's severed arm sank to the sandy base. A moray eel, hidden in that beautiful if man-made coral reef, shot out and pulled the arm into its cave. The eel, an ugly fish with a spiny-toothed sucker mouth and skin resembling snot, struck repeatedly at the hand. Between assaults, Charlie's wedding ring flickered in the light.

I scanned the halls for Sam. No luck. She was lost somewhere in the panicking swarm, somewhere among the stench of fear and vomit shrouding the aquarium.

CHAPTER 4

Over the weekend Charlie's bizarre death made every newscast in the country. CNN. Fox. You name it. One guest had taken a camera phone to the party and, with remarkable presence of mind, taped the feeding frenzy. All day Saturday and all day Sunday, I heard: "An unsettling story from Boston. Charlie Kelemen, noted philanthropist and member of the hedge fund community, was eaten Friday night by three sharks at the New England Aquarium. Film at eleven."

It got worse. Some jerk uploaded the clip onto YouTube, where it immediately became a "featured video." By 3:47 P.M. on Sunday there were 450,467 hits. One was mine. Alone in my condo on Central Park West, I brooded over the horrific images. They were almost impossible to believe, and I found myself flipping to a happier collage of memories.

There was that black-tie benefit held in the Waldorf last January.

"Listen up," Charlie commanded his dinner partners. "I want to know who pees in the shower." With mock gravity he raised his right hand, as though to swear an oath, and poured a fabulous Côtes du Rhône with his left. He gazed into every face around the table. His big, brown eyes goaded us with a look that said, *You can tell me.*

The weight of Charlie's playful stare produced results. One stunning young divorcée, with enough cleavage to bury that bottle of wine, revealed, "I'm Jane, and I pee in the shower."

Almost on cue, the handsome investment banker to her right confessed, "I'm Henry. And I pee in the shower." It started a chain reaction around the table.

"I'm Sam."

"I'm Crunch."

"I'm Grove. And I pee in the shower." In this manner Charlie Kelemen convened the first session of Shower Pissers Anonymous.

He had a gift. Successful and irreverent, Charlie made his friends laugh. There were times when his wit doubled us over. The abdominal spasms hurt until we came up for air. We howled at Charlie, at ourselves, and at the affectations of a society that glorified money, beauty, and youth. Ironically, the world seemed lighter around our fat friend who filled rooms with his outrageous remarks as much as his porcine waistline.

Charlie's joy was infectious. We laughed with him, no matter how coarse his wit. Impervious to his blimp of a head and whale of a gut, he made us dismiss our own flaws. It felt good not to worry about what we ate or whether we had said the right thing. It felt good to join Charlie's embrace of the two most satisfying words in the English language: "Fuck it."

* * *

After the shark attack, I could no more say "Fuck it" than compete in the Tour de France. There were too many questions. How did Charlie's arms and hands get cut in so many places? What about the cart tied to his leg? Who would do such a thing? It made no sense. Charlie had no enemies.

And Sam. What about Sam? I worried about her all weekend. She never returned any of my phone calls.

Message one: "Sam, I'm crushed. Please call me." No response.

Message three: "I want to help." No response.

Message six: "I'm starting to worry." No response.

Even under the circumstances, it was not like her to avoid me. We were too close, friends since college. She had been Sam Wells then. We met at one of those Harvard-Wellesley mixers that invariably married two ingredients: loud, pounding music and "fit-shaced" co-eds buzzed on precoital cocktails. Sam and I never dated, but we stayed close all four years. It had probably helped that Sam and my girlfriend were roommates and best friends.

Hell, I had lived with Charlie and Sam for six of the last eighteen months. Un, Deux, and Trois, their three dachshunds named for the restaurant on West Forty-fourth Street, treated me like family. I walked the dogs far more than Manny, and he was the family's driver and all-purpose runner. All of a sudden, it felt like I was cold-calling my best friend's widow.

Late Sunday night NBC reported that Boston police had closed the New England Aquarium indefinitely. It was a crime scene. The anchor added, "Police will be contacting all guests, who numbered about five hundred people."

"To pick sharks out of a lineup?" I asked darkly and without humor, knowing that the real culprit had two legs.

Who the hell did Charlie piss off? How long will it take the police to reach me? What am I missing?

By 11:30 P.M. Sunday I was still agitated by Friday's events. But it was time to sleep. The markets closed for dead presidents but not for Charlie Kelemen. My alarm would sound at 5:30 A.M., the opening bell for another week at the office. From previous experience, I knew my professional life offered plenty of hiding places from grief.

CHAPTER 5

Sachs, Kidder, and Carnegie (SKC) is a boutique investment bank specializing in mergers and acquisitions. Our headquarters are located in New York City at 610 Fifth Avenue. Inside, the ceiling-high windows overlook a skating rink to the west and Saks Fifth Avenue to the east. We have offices in London, Paris, Singapore, and Hong Kong. There is talk about opening a branch in Rio.

SKC was born in 1991. We are a young organization. But the company name creates images of greatness from America's financial past. The allusion is by design. Percy Phillips, the founder and CEO, wove the surnames of economic legends into a corporate identity. In the process he also ignored the facts. Samuel Sachs and Henry Kidder were never business partners. They competed against each other in the late 1800s. Andrew Carnegie made more money in railroads, coal, and steel than he ever made selling bonds in Europe. No matter. The coined name rings of Wall Street's triumph.

Competitors say, "SKC is nimble and ferocious, a force to fear." I regard my firm as the ultimate meritocracy. We produce. Or we pack up and go elsewhere. Nobody coasts and survives at SKC. Our corporate culture prizes aggressiveness and rewards those who go for it. Damn the consequences.

Sometimes I wonder how SKC ever became my professional home. It differs vastly from the genteel place where I grew up. Change tilled suspicion in South Carolina. And ancestry, rather than performance, conferred opportunity. My dad once quipped, "Charleston is a city distinguished by three hundred years of history uninterrupted by progress." He was right back then. People tell me things are different now, but it is impossible for me to comment. I have not been back to Charleston for some time.

Eight years ago I graduated from Harvard Business School and started as a broker in the Private Client Services division of SKC, "PCS" for short. I manage $2 billion for sixty-five families today, a business that easily nets me seven figures every year. It is an amount I never fathomed while chasing fiddler crabs and scratching mosquito bites as a kid.

It is also axiom number three in action: Wall Street firms pay ridiculous money to top producers.

I love the feverish energy of PCS. At any given moment we scream into our phones. Or we scream at each other, jabbering and gesticulating with two or three people on hold. Almost everybody chews hangnails or fidgets with Hacky Sacks, our nervous tics sweeping through low-rise cubicles like bacterial plagues on the march. The commotion, the consequence of financial greed and highs from coffee, Cokes, and candy bars, can be downright scary to the untrained eye. But to me it is a shot of pure adrenaline.

There's nothing like Wall Street's constant flow of ideas, some good, some bad, and some so toxic they must originate in Chernobyl. Clients pay me to be vigilant. My guys know all the dirt: the public doughnut company that spent as much time cooking the books as it spent frying the batter; the CEO who threw a party with ice sculptures that pissed vodka; and the analysts who publicly extolled companies while privately bashing the same piece-of-shit stocks. My guys hire me to watch their backs. Sure, they grumble about the fees. But I keep their money safe, and they know it.

There's no telling what's out there.

PCS has been especially important on a personal level. During the past eighteen months, the daily regime of sensory overload monopolized all my waking moments. I dissected thousands of investment pitches, wrangled with other advisers trying to poach my clients, and steered great fortunes through the mud and muck of money management. The action, Wall Street's spiderweb of greed and conflict, obscured my wretched memories from that black night in New Haven.

SKC gave me the capacity to cope. This world of ambition, the overlay of lunacy, administered a potent painkiller over the last eighteen months. When my best friend died last Friday, I knew just what to do. I was a veteran patient in the care of PCS.

At 7:15 A.M. on Monday I hurried through the "boardroom," our tongue-in-cheek nickname for the open-plan workstations. I passed Scully, the world's loudest stock jockey, and turned right near Bagwell, who wore a different pair of suspenders every day. I continued straight at Casper, ghoulishly white and known for clipping his nails compulsively. Even at that hour Casper's semirhythmic *plinks* were already reverberating across the room and sabotaging the appetites of those eating breakfast at their desks.

Frank Kurtz, our boss, barreled out of his office and caught me in the aisles. "Grove," he said in a voice already charged from coffee and a cigar, "I want to bounce an idea off you."

"Sure, Frank. What's up?" Like every other adviser on the floor, I distrusted Frank, regarded him as another overhead line item from the layers of management. Behind his back, we all called him the "Monthly Nut."

"Percy intends to re-brand our division," Frank said. "Goldman, Morgan, Merrill, they all called themselves PCS at one time. The name's a commodity."

"Okay," I said, thinking this conversation could wait until after my first cup of coffee.

"McKinsey recommended we call ourselves Global Wealth Management. Tell me what you think. Gut reaction. What's the first thing that comes to mind?"

"Bathhouses."

"Huh?" he asked. With the skinny legs of a ballerina and the bull torso of a weight lifter, Frank teetered slightly. "Where'd that come from?"

"Acronyms, Frank. GWM is the acronym for Global Wealth Management. Tell the knucklehead from McKinsey to read *The Village Voice*. GWM is how gay white males in search of love identify themselves in classified ads."

"Shit," he muttered, and let me go. "I need to call Marketing."

Axiom number two in action: As long as we generate revenues, our bosses tolerate our quirks and leave us the hell alone. Top producers can say almost anything and get away with it.

En route to my desk, it was impossible to avoid Patty Gershon. She had short black hair, Ferrari-red lipstick, and an angular but pleasing nose. Patty was an outstanding adviser, a cagey student of the capital markets, but way too aggressive for my taste. She "jammed product," our vernacular for selling hard and saying anything to turn a buck.

Patty also doubled as a powerful magnet for every woman in the office with something on her mind. She sat at the epicenter of "Estrogen Alley," my term of endearment for the cluster of women working in her vicinity. Their cubicles were loud and raucous, no topic taboo. Male endowment, feminine hygiene, and the havoc that childbirth wreaks on women—way too much information flowed within earshot of my desk.

"Hey, O'Rourke," she called, the only person who ever addressed me by my last name. Patty was wearing a sharp Giorgio Armani suit. At forty-three she still flaunted her body, a successful joint venture between her personal trainer and a skilled plastic surgeon.

"Lady Goldfish," I replied in kind. Goldfish eat their young, and Patty was predatory. She won all her battles, the inevitable ax fights that erupted over wealthy prospects, through a fearsome combination of guile, decibels, and threatening comments about prejudice in the workplace. Fortunately, she never quite grasped the hidden meaning of her nickname. Patty thought it was a character from *Finding Nemo.*

"What do you call a two-hundred-and-thirty-pound philanthropist?" she asked.

I blinked, never expecting Charlie's clip to become source material for Wall Street's dark humor. But every topic was fair game, no matter how unkind or distasteful the material.

"Bait," she answered. "What do you call a friend that gets eaten by three sharks?" This time she stared at me intensely, in order to build anticipation.

"I give up."

"Chum."

I walked. Patty was clueless about my friendship with Charlie. She had no idea about my suffering. Advisers hid clients from colleagues. For all the esprit de corps at SKC, we worked in silos. We never knew when someone would leave the firm and become a competitor.

"Wait," she insisted. "I've got more. What do you feed a shark with indigestion?" I knew better than to respond. When Patty spoke, she ran all her words together without breathing. Every sentence became one long, extended word. Her syllables grew spontaneously like cancerous cells that kept splitting and splitting. It was impossible to interrupt politely. I waved good-bye over my shoulder and closed fast on the last few feet to my desk. "Don't you want to know?" she called after me.

Some other time.

Annie and Chloe were manning our phones. Both my assistants looked downcast, their expressions troubled. Charlie had been their friend, too. He sent flowers on their birthdays and chocolates whenever the spirit moved. He constantly asked Chloe, a single mom, about her daughter. And he teased Annie, two years out of college, about her relative youth. All three of us were still in shock.

Annie ended her conversation abruptly, "Gotta go," and bear-hugged me before I could sit. She was slender and tall at five-nine. I felt the sweet weight of her head on my shoulders, the ticklish brush of golden blond hair, and the fullness of her breasts against my chest— simple affection without the complication of romance. In that moment it felt good to work with her, to call Annie "my friend."

Perhaps I savored Annie's touch a little too long. A hush gathered over Estrogen Alley. With Patty and her gang gawking, Annie and I broke gently. "I can't talk about it just yet."

"Me either," she agreed in a voice that lacked the usual spark. Annie returned to the phone, rubbing me on the back as she moved away. Chloe continued with her conversation, her eyes dark pools of blue melancholy.

My first inclination was to wake up Ray Ranieri. I'd probably start the call with something pleasant, something snappy and to the point, something like, "Fuck you, numb nuts." It would go downhill from there. "Radio" Ray—"Radio" being shorthand for "Radioactive" and a reference to the nuclear waste he sold—was a bond trader on the high-yield desk. Last Thursday he had dumped crappy bonds at a crappy price on me, and it still pissed me off. This morning seemed like a good time to continue our argument. Deep inside I knew the real reason. The ensuing squabble would put Charlie Kelemen out of my mind for a while.

Fights erupted every day over trades. And in our world of unbridled conflict, bond traders equated courtesy with naïveté. For prophylactic reasons it helped to come out swinging, to start all conversations with "Fuck you." Otherwise, the traders would smell easy prey and price bonds too high. Not on my watch. Not with my clients.

Two degrees from Harvard made no difference. I had sold out and become a word whore. A foul, fucking, four-lettered lexicon marked me as a wizened veteran of the capital markets. Wall Street was one of the few places on earth where a severe case of Tourette's syndrome might go unnoticed. "Dickhead" and "asshole" were the favored terms of endearment in every shop, from Goldman to Merrill to SKC.

Sitting at my desk, waiting for domestic markets to open, I doubted my resolve to spar with Radio Ray. My computer snoozed in silence, still no sign of the craggy stock charts and blinking tickers that would flare up when trading began. I called Sam. And of course, the answering machine picked up.

Message eight or nine: "I'm worried, Sam. If you don't call, I'll swing by your place and bang on the front door until you answer." I immediately regretted the words. They sounded insensitive and way too combative.

The recovering Catholic in me craved to confess. The message I never left: *Sam, the aquarium was my idea. I'm sorry.*

I called Cliff Halek next, my closest friend at the firm and the head of Derivatives. Medium height, rounding, and balding, Cliff was brilliant. Summa cum laude from Princeton. Weekend computer geek. He had a knack for reading the markets. Cliff could always tell when arbitrageurs or hedge funds were building positions. SKC recognized his genius. Halek made Managing Director at age thirty, a first in our firm.

"Cliff," he answered on the first ring, his raspy voice the casualty of a career on the phone. His colleagues in Derivatives called him "the hoarse whisperer," a tribute to the guttural tones.

Brevity was a time-honored tradition on Wall Street. A one-name greeting spoke volumes. It said in effect, *I'm really fucking busy. So quit screwing around and get to the point. Time is money, and I'm not here for my health or your small talk. Now, what do you have?*

"It's Grove."

"Oh shit, I've been meaning to call. That guy on the news was your buddy. Right?"

"Yeah, Charlie Kelemen."

"I'm sorry. Did he have family?"

"No kids. His wife has been a friend since college."

Cliff recognized grief in my voice. "Grove, go home and take care of yourself. Or go see Kelemen's wife and take care of her."

"I can't reach her. All I get is the answering machine."

"Then give her some space. The press may be hounding her."

"But—"

"But nothing. I need to fly. Sorry. Dinner tonight at our house. Lacey and I will see you around seven-thirty." That meant no earlier than 8:15. "Foster misses you. We won't take no for an answer." He spoke with a rat-tat-tat cadence, and then he was gone.

Dial tone. There was no chance to argue. Cliff hung up without saying "good-bye" or "get fucked." I took no offense. That was Wall Street. Testosterphone, our clipped conversations cut short by urgency and the next dollar, was acceptable etiquette. Extra words cost money.

Lacey was Cliff's wife, charming and five months pregnant with number one. Foster, their Australian terrier named for the beer, was a legend on Wall Street. Several years ago, Cliff rigged up a web camera to keep tabs on their pooch. Whenever the phone rang, Foster would trot into the bedroom and lick the phone, the camera, and most everything in sight. The fish-eye lens made Foster look like forty-five pounds of wet doggy tongue.

Unfortunately, Cliff shut down "Foster Cam" several years ago. Word of the site had spread. And for a while, traders from every shop on Wall Street were conference-calling Cliff's home. They usually bet how many rings it would take Foster to appear on camera. It all ended when an equity guy from Goldman Sachs spied the Haleks' maid reading *Cosmopolitan* on their bed. Cliff decided enough was enough.

* * *

Noon and no word from Sam.

I waited all through lunch. It was the usual circus. Couriers from kitchens across Manhattan arrived in the lobby. Our assistants met them downstairs and returned with almost every food under the sun: ten-topping pizzas, hamburgers with blue cheese and sautéed onions, curly fries that had grown flaccid from the trek, five-alarm jalapeño burritos, Tabasco buffalo wings, General Tso's chicken swimming in Madame Chang's sesame sauce, flat dogs with cheese grits, and spicy garlic meatball subs. No one ordered sushi. It had to be greasy. It had to be caloric.

One-fifteen and still no word.

By 2:30 P.M., PCS reeked of discarded food. The greasy, garlicky remnants now coagulated in open cardboard boxes piled high in the rubbish. The disparate cuisines, growing rancid by the moment, waged war on everybody's nostrils. The stench was overwhelming.

I had not touched my salad and wondered whether to pitch it. Annie interrupted the deliberations. "Grove, Alex Romanov is on your second line."

Why is he calling?

Romanov was not a client. We saw each other at Charlie's parties from time to time but shared nothing in common other than the markets. When they were closed, I bicycled. He sparred in an amateur boxing league. Or he hang-glided. Or he raced his Porsche at a track on Long Island. Anything for a rush. But "the next Warren Buffett," a title he owed to *BusinessWeek,* never phoned.

"Sam asked me to call, Grover."

"Is she okay?"

"She's pretty torn up," Romanov replied, his voice soft but powerful nevertheless. "She's with her parents. And yes, she's okay, Grover."

"I'm still sick about what happened."

"We all are, Grover."

It bugged me when people used my full first name, especially three times in as many breaths. Condescending. Now was hardly the time, though, to reprimand the next Warren Buffett. "I've been trying to reach Sam since Saturday."

"She told me. That's why I'm calling. Services start at St. Joseph's on Wednesday at ten o'clock. Gotta hop."

"I'll be there," I answered to dial tone. For all my petty thoughts about "Grover" three times over, I was glad Romanov had called. Sam was okay.

At 3:35 P.M. I called it a day. The Dow Jones Industrial Average had dropped steadily since the open. It was down 87 points, primarily because one of the pharmaceutical companies had pulled a promising drug from development. My portfolios, laden with medical stocks, had suffered. But I was oblivious. My head was not in the game, the death image of Charlie still clear in my mind.

On the way out I heard Patty hammering a client: "Bobbie, listen to me. IBM. Did you hear that name? IBM is on sale. On sale, Bobbie, on sale." She pounded her fist on the desk and then waved the same hand wildly. "You won't find bargains like this in Filene's Basement."

Too pushy, I thought. *Not my style.*

Ever vigilant, Patty spied me leaving prior to the market close and made a big show of checking the time. She covered the mouthpiece of her receiver and shouted for all PCS to hear, "Thanks for coming in, O'Rourke."

What's she want?

Patty's attention made me suspicious. We never spoke. Like me, she was a top producer. Like me, she was one of the department's biggest moneymakers— though not the biggest. I still had her. It probably bugged the shit out of her.

No matter. We focused on business and avoided distractions, Gershon's intensity the stuff of legends throughout PCS. She was forever telling the younger stockbrokers, "Think golf. This business is not a team sport." But Patty had initiated a conversation in the morning. Now she was breaking from a client to speak again. Top producers don't do that.

I smiled, gave Lady Goldfish a thumbs-up, and headed for the elevators.

Somewhere over the din, the last thing I heard that afternoon was Casper. He was hard at work again.

Plink. Plink. Plink.

CHAPTER 6

On Wednesday Monsignor Byrd presided over services, first at St. Joseph's Church in Greenwich Village and later at Woodlawn Cemetery in the Bronx. At times I had found Charlie a touch ungodly around his parish priest. He dubbed him "the Bird," and it seemed to me a one-fingered salute was no way to describe the good father. But that was Charlie.

Monsignor Byrd overlooked these transgressions. "Charlie Kelemen gave more than he got," he told the red-eyed congregation inside St. Joseph's hallowed halls. His praise gushed nonstop, the eulogy flowing like a dime novel from Horatio Alger's pen.

There was good reason. Charlie overcame every kind of adversity. When he was three, his father had abandoned the family for a floozy named "Jackpot Jane." Charlie's mother died a few years later, leaving him in the care of an ancient aunt. The skinny little boy, curly brown hair and big white teeth, somehow scraped together enough money to attend Providence College. He graduated with honors.

Shortly after returning his mortarboard and gown,

Charlie joined Barclays Bank. He was already a portly young man. Good news: He met Sam in the training program. Bad news: Banking proved way too harrumph harrumph. That was when Charlie founded the Kelemen Group, a money management firm that invested in hedge funds.

The business proved perfect. Through his philanthropic largesse, Charlie knew scores of the über-rich. He also possessed uncanny market instincts, a personal LoJack for finding hot hands among hedge funds. As Charlie married wealthy investors with his portfolio of talented money managers, he never looked back. He grew richer and fatter every day.

For a brief moment during the eulogy, Monsignor Byrd sounded more like a ringside announcer than a Catholic priest. "Last Friday we took a gut punch," he lamented. "Charlie Kelemen taught us one of life's great lessons." The good father was referring, of course, to the prosperity that accompanied Charlie's selfless altruism. My best friend was always charging off to help the sick, the needy, and the emotionally frail.

Or maybe Monsignor Byrd was prepping mourners for the collection plates at Mass. We numbered more than 250 inside the church: bankers, hedgies, and ad executives from Madison Avenue. Alex Romanov, whom Charlie called "the Mad Russian" rather than the next Warren Buffett, joined Annie and me in our pew. Betty Masters and Susan Thorpe came to grieve. So did Crunch, who arrived with hairdressers from each of his three salons. St. Joseph's offertory plates promised prime pickings for a parish priest on the prowl.

Flashes of wealth were one thing. Fragile souls were another. Among the mourners were divorcées coping with betrayal, widows drifting in their private seas of desperate solitude. One high-strung I-banker, recently emasculated by a pink slip, was fretting whether he would ever see seven figures again. Charlie Kelemen— caretaker, guardian, champion—had rescued scores of emotional strays. His friends, in turn, embraced his largesse and became a personal posse. Dealing with the loss of their leader, they appeared shaken and weak.

Who picked up my friend and threw him over the Giant Ocean Tank's guardrail?

In a pew off to the right, Lila Priouleau stood well over six feet in black stiletto heels. Perhaps the most notorious woman ever to walk Harvard's campus, she had been one of three in Sam's rooming group at Wellesley. More than most, Lila owed Charlie eternal thanks.

The Priouleau family had seldom asked anyone for help. What was the point? In the late 1980s *Forbes* estimated their fortune at $120 million. The family owned vast real estate and media interests. Their car business, whose advertisements always included goofy jingles with "Priouleau prices" in the refrain, made them famous throughout Atlanta.

Lila's regal bearing confirmed the privilege of her childhood. Unlike many tall women, she carried herself with the perfect posture of a Soviet-era gymnast. Shoulders back, chest thrown forward, she was Nadia Comaneci plus twelve inches.

The salesmen in the family's Mercedes dealership

had noted Lila's confident curves, the graceful lines. They referred to her jutting breasts as "hood ornaments." But never to her face. She would have slapped their shit.

There was a time when Lila lost that magnificent posture. She bent under a torrent of withering abuse from Hurley, husband and ex–football star from Yale. At first, the beatings were verbal. Later, they became physical. No one noticed the warning signs from Atlanta's perfect couple: quick tempers, raised voices, and innuendo that things in the bedroom sucked. No one spotted the ugly purple welts spreading under the cover of Lila's blouses.

No one but Charlie. During a business trip to Atlanta, he smelled trouble and confronted Lila in private. Her bruises made him wince. He informed Cash, Lila's father, and then used his considerable powers of persuasion to prevent the Southern gentleman from killing his son-in-law.

Charlie also referred Cash to a top-notch gumshoe from Baltimore. The detective caught Hurley red-handed with another woman. Graphic photos made the divorce settlement a one-sided affair. Charlie, intuitive and coldly calculating, probably saved the Priouleau family millions.

"Come to New York," Charlie soothed Lila. "The change will do you good."

He was right. Away from Hurley, away from the verbal and physical abuse, she recuperated. She had almost forgotten how to have fun. But Sam and Charlie made sure that Lila, now a single mother in New York City, had plenty to do. There were innumerable dinners and theater outings, so many new art exhibits to see. Lila regained her dignity and stood straight again.

She also exacted the sweetest revenge. Eighteen months after the divorce became final, Hurley returned to the Yale Bowl, where more than sixty thousand fans had packed the stands for the Dartmouth game. During halftime, the school celebrated its gridiron greats. The honorees included the wife-beating bag of runny squirrel shit. He ranked fourth on Yale's list of all-time leading rushers.

Hurley never heard cheers that crisp autumn day in New Haven. As a lone biplane circled low over the stadium, the crowd's raucous laughter robbed him of all glory. Trailing the plane was a long banner that read: "Hurley has a small dick."

The crowd guffawed. The frenzied Yalies chanted at the top of their lungs and the peak of their IQs, "Small dick. Small dick." That was how the ex-fullback became an all-time joke and ex-legend.

No one understood the power of public humiliation more than Lila Priouleau. She had good reason, having learned her lesson as an undergraduate at Wellesley.

Lila was standing with her father now, silently thanking Charlie like the rest of us. Non-Catholics, the Priouleaus watched curiously as Monsignor Byrd consecrated the Communion hosts. Cash had flown in from Atlanta to pay his respects, and I wondered what he was thinking. Perhaps Cash sensed my interest. He caught my eye and nodded, no doubt aware that Charlie had once come to my rescue.

Up to that point of the funeral, I had given a wide
berth to Sam. It was not clumsy sensitivity holding me
back. It was self-preservation. When Sam turned to take
Communion, it proved impossible to avoid her glassy
blue eyes any longer. Tears, visible even through a black
veil, streamed down her cheeks.

There are no words for what she is feeling.

Our eyes locked with immediate intimacy. With sorrow. With memories of the last time death had touched
both our lives. That was eighteen months ago. A police-
woman, her eyebrows etched high in a worried expression of permanent surprise, had said, "Mr. O'Rourke,
I know how tough this is."

CHAPTER 7

With those words the officer led me inside a refrigerated New Haven morgue. There were two stainless-steel gurneys in the center of the frigid room, a covered body on each. One adult. One child.

I prayed the Our Father a million times, hoping for a miracle. I pledged never to miss Mass again if only God had somehow spared my family. Evelyn was my college sweetheart, my wife, my lover, my rock, my friend, the generous woman who had given me Finn, our daughter. I longed to hear our four-year-old's peals of laughter.

Charlie's posse recited the Our Father in St. Joseph's now, a grim reminder of how my frantic prayers had gone unanswered in New Haven. A trucker had fallen asleep while driving his eighteen-wheeler just outside the city. Evelyn and Finn died instantly in the ensuing crash, their bodies disfigured by the impact and the jagged edges of disintegrating vehicles. The memory stung, and I shook uncontrollably inside the cavernous church as Annie took my arm.

Not until the funeral procession arrived at Wood-lawn did I regain my composure. The rain probably helped, in part because it camouflaged my tears. As the posse laid Charlie to rest, the clouds buried the sun and suppressed the hot mugginess of July in the Bronx. For a while I savored the air's moist breath. It smelled fresh, the scent of cut grass at dusk. I gave thanks for overcast skies. Bright sun had always tested my fair complexion. With the mild temperatures, however, it seemed my best friend had couriered one final act of comfort from the heavens.

That was Charlie Kelemen. He was always there. He was the one who forced me to pick up the pieces after Finn's and Evelyn's deaths. He was the one who insisted I move into Greenwich Village with him and Sam. It took me six months before I could function on my own.

Thank you, Charlie.

Sam helped. She opened their home to me, the broken guest, while soldiering through her own grief. Evelyn had been her college roommate and best friend, Finn her goddaughter.

During the graveside services Sam reminded me of the Wellesley student from over a decade ago. Charlie's death, it seemed, had sanctioned a full-scale retreat. There was no hint of the bright, fire-engine red lipstick she had taken to wearing. Her black dress was unremarkable. It looked like a sack.

Nor did I see her signature jewels, like the cluster earrings made from marquise and pear-shaped diamonds or the blue-green peacock brooch fashioned from diamonds, sapphires, emeralds, and at least one black opal. Perhaps Sam's necklace of black pearls would have been more appropriate. But none of the baubles, all gifts from Charlie, were anywhere in sight.

She only wore the jewels to please him.

She had never been showy at Wellesley. She was too much of a Yankee. Frugal to the core.

Crunch, subdued and fidgeting with his wraparound sunglasses, studied Sam intently. Except for the sergeant major stripes sewn across the chest of his black slicker, he looked like a mortician standing and dripping next to Monsignor Byrd. Crunch must have seen something change in Sam's demeanor, for he suddenly rushed to her side.

Sam buried her face against his chest and, without the slightest hint of a warning tremble, began to rock from spasms of grief. Crunch steadied her, the power of his arms evident even under the slicker's vast rubbery folds.

I wished it had been me comforting Sam. I berated myself for not getting there first or even second. Like Crunch, Alex Romanov had moved more quickly. He gently grasped Sam's shoulder from behind. His reassuring touch proved just the right antidote, for her shudders stopped. I resolved never to mock the next Warren Buffett again.

Sam, though surrounded by her family and Charlie's posse, never seemed more alone. She had given up on her umbrella. The rain ran off the sides of her hat, like water off a tile roof with no gutters. It gushed onto her black trench coat, carelessly open. She no longer cared about getting soaked.

Charlie was gone. His sealed mahogany casket, eerie

in its finality, reminded me that Evelyn's and Finn's caskets had also been closed. The parallel, between my best friend with no head and my wife and daughter with disfigurements that haunt me still, made me sob. Annie took my arm for the second time that rainy day.

Lost in my grief, I floundered in a sea of personal disbelief. Charlie's murder, the spectacular carnage in front of five hundred people, made no sense. It was all too bizarre. Something more conventional would have been so much easier: gun, knife, or even defenestration. But why?

Everybody loved Charlie.

I would later learn that almost everyone—Sam, Romanov, Crunch, Lila—had moved beyond denial. For their own reasons they were each struggling with a more vexing question.

Did one of Charlie's business deals go bad?

CHAPTER 8

Had Charlie's death threatened a merger or bond offering, our I-bankers would have attended his funeral en masse. Not so much to mourn or pay their respects. It would have been to kick-save their fees, the holy grail of finance.

There were no pending deals. Charlie's money management firm, insanely lucrative, was too small for our bankers to notice. The capital markets thundered forward Wednesday without Annie and me.

Well, almost.

Chloe ran the desk and fielded all calls. Among them, one came from a CEO named Thayer. Another came from Sutherling, a sandy-haired energy banker with a bourbon-on-rocks voice. His team had just edged out the empty suits at Morgan, and we were on a six-month countdown to take Thayer's company public. Through Chloe, Sutherling insisted I meet with the CEO and pitch him on SKC's wealth management capabilities. She dutifully scheduled an appointment for Thursday, good timing for Thayer, who was here on business from the West Coast.

Crappy timing for me. I had planned to visit Evelyn's and Finn's graves in Rhode Island that day. *Need to spend more time with the family,* I thought in a black moment at Charlie's graveside.

I also had professional misgivings. Many regarded wills, durable powers of attorney, and the other tools of mortality as my industry's response to Ambien. Not me. Estate planning was the single most important topic to discuss this far in advance of an IPO. Thayer could save a bundle in taxes by establishing trust accounts. It was my job to describe the benefits and outline his options. One problem. The financial side of death was hardly my favorite topic at the moment.

How do I keep my shit together?

Deferring the meeting was not an option. Thayer's net worth would total something north of $100 million after the offering. Appointments with that kind of wealth were too hard to win.

Plus, there was Sutherling to consider. Investment bankers were notorious for drop-everything mentalities. Putting Thayer on hold would piss off Sutherling, not a winning strategy. Bankers could shower anyone with referrals, not just me. And my PCS colleagues would rip out drills and interrupt root canals midway to meet with someone of Thayer's net worth.

One hundred million is size, real size.

Thursday morning came all too soon. The police had left a voice mail for me sometime the previous night. Distracted, underprepared for a meeting, I couldn't deal with them. I sat in one of our mahogany and leather conference rooms, smiling at Thayer and considering where to begin.

Ordinarily, prospect meetings all started the same way. We would two-step the small talk. It took about ten minutes to circle the dance floor, me probing for common interests and gauging personal chemistry.

Next, I would produce inch-thick pitch books stuffed with glossy exhibits and assorted propaganda from the firm's marketing library. The presentations could be tailored to specific needs. There was no end to our choice of topics. Zero-cost and put-spread collars, portable alpha, bond durations, or correlation coefficients—we had something mysterious for everyone. SKC's graphs looked great, and our lingo sounded smart.

Unfortunately, there had been no time to assemble a pitch book. Nor had I persevered through my grief and researched Thayer's company. That was a problem. It was more important to connect in Thayer's comfort zone, his area of expertise, rather than mine. The reason: Outside of New York City, America distrusts Wall Street. What do you expect with the subprime mortgage fiasco?

No pitch book. No preparation. That Thursday morning, I felt "nekkid." For all the meetings through the years, for all the business won and asses kicked over at Goldman and Merrill, I still suffered from butterflies when meeting new prospects. All-star athletes often barfed before big games. First meetings with wealthy prospects brought the same anxiety, even to top producers.

One hundred million is size, real size.

Perhaps Thayer sensed hesitation, the sure sign of a newbie, for he dispensed with pleasantries. He attacked. A thin, fit man with a shock of black hair, he looked at me impassively through rimless glasses. Glancing at his watch, he announced, "You have forty-five minutes."

You scheduled the appointment, I thought to myself.

"Plenty of time," I replied, glad the game had begun. The butterflies disappeared in that instant. They gave way to the confidence that accompanies practice and years of training. Slick pitch books and exhaustive research were never a substitute for experience anyway.

Thayer saw nothing different. He wore the kind of face CEOs pull out of the closet when unimpressed. "There's no one joining us?" It was more accusation than question.

"No."

"At Goldman Sachs, a dozen people met with me. Same thing at Merrill, Morgan, and Lehman. Your competitors fill the room every time with portfolio managers, stock-hedging teams, even their chief strategists." Thayer had mastered the fine art of putting people on their heels. He drummed his fingers on our conference table.

"If head count is important to you," I replied calmly, "half the firm will join us. But it's not what I recommend during a forty-five-minute meeting."

"Forty now." *Zing.* "Don't you want me to understand your firm's capabilities?" *Zing.* Even in his chair, he lorded over me like a boxer who had just decked an opponent.

"The problem with a roomful of suits," I countered, "is they trip all over each other trying to sound clever. No one listens. I can't understand what's really important to you if everybody's competing for air time." *Zing*.

"I like that," Thayer mused. Sometimes a simple jab changed the dynamics of a meeting. "In fact, your bankers told me all I need to know about SKC," he continued, warming to our discussion, ceding ground. "I'm more concerned about what to do now. My money is tied up in private stock, and once we go public, there won't be much time to evaluate advisers. I have a business to run."

"Do you have children?" That question was the one I feared, a sure segue to financial topics involving death. I had to ask. It was my job.

"Two. A daughter, she's eighteen. Her little brother is fifteen."

"How do you feel about taxes?"

"Four-letter word."

Time for a war story, the sure way to establish myself as a seasoned veteran. No one with money ever volunteered to serve as a tackling dummy for stockbrokers starting their careers.

"Several years ago," I began, "one of my clients put thirty percent of his stock into a grantor retained annuity trust. At my suggestion he made the contribution prior to going public."

"A grantor what?" Thayer asked, taking notes on a pad from SKC's conference table.

"GRAT for short. In any event, thirty percent of his

holdings were worth a million dollars while the company was private. The stock took off after the IPO. That same thirty percent equaled fifty million when we sold."

"You just set the bar for my deal," he said, salivating over the appreciation. "What was the point of the GRAT?"

"The CEO paid nothing in gift taxes."

"What about capital gains taxes?"

"He still paid those. But here's how the numbers worked. After capital gains taxes on the sale, the CEO had forty million left. The money was inside the GRAT and outside the estate. Had he died and left the forty million outright to his kids, his estate would have paid around sixteen million in taxes." I paused for my words to sink home and then added, "Not now."

Thayer blinked once, then again. "You saved him sixteen million! Bet he genuflects when you meet."

"Sometimes the most important decisions are the ones you make before investing the first dollar."

Thayer took off his glasses and cleaned them absently with his tie. "Do GRATs take much time to draft?"

"You need a trust and estate lawyer. I work with the best."

"Good," he replied. "Now, what else should we discuss?"

Thayer stayed more than forty-five minutes. Two hours later I wrapped up with my signature line: "My job is to bring you the best of Wall Street." Heavy pause. "And to protect you from it at the same time." There was nothing better than a hard edge to seal a deal. Skeptics sounded shrewd and battle tough.

Thayer did not commit. Nobody with $100 million

ever signed paperwork at the first meeting. But he said all the right things.

I should have been elated. New prospect. Strong start. More money on the horizon. Don't get me wrong. It wasn't the money driving me. My motivation was more about the game, helping clients, crushing competitors, winning over and over again. I understood why Roman warriors poured salt over the ruins of Carthage. One day I hoped to pour salt on Goldman Sachs.

The thrill of a new prospect, however, was lost on me. In the aftermath of Charlie's funeral, I wondered whether he had left his affairs in order. That's the problem when three sharks surprise someone in front of five hundred horrified people. There's no chance to study what-if scenarios with your financial adviser. Charlie was not a client. Never had been. He was my friend. And that was it.

So much for winning over and over again.

Charlie was also a professional. He knew all the tricks, possessed all the tools to take care of Sam, who had not worked for years. No one ever wants to deal with mortality, though, unless there is a reason. And that reason, in my experience, was children. Kids were always the catalyst to deal with difficult decisions. Kids got parents off the dime. Even though the Kelemens had no children, Charlie was way too obsessive about details. He would never leave Sam in the lurch.

He was a control freak about money.

CHAPTER 9

Gloom is no path to becoming a top producer. Or staying one. My career is all about making happy, no matter what the day brings.

Your sales assistant fresh out of college takes an order "to cover" 20,000 shares and buys call options with a $25 strike price instead of selling them. Four months later, you discover 40,000 shares in the client's account because the stock ran past $25 and forced an automatic purchase. In effect you bought 20,000 shares at $25 instead of selling them, but now the stock has collapsed to $21. With mounting horror you realize there is a $160,000 error, 40,000 shares at $4 each, and you will eat the expense because stockbrokers pay for trading errors out of their own pockets. That's when a client calls and asks, "How are you?"

"Awesome."

Your legal department reviews documents for a zero-cost collar, a hedging technique that will enable your client to avoid catastrophic loss on 2 million shares and retain additional upside. The stock is highly volatile, and as you wait the excruciating wait for Legal's okay, the shares fall below the limit price at which you are authorized to transact. To your chagrin, the trade evaporates and with it the opportunity to pocket $300,000. That's when a client calls and asks, "How are you?"

"Awesome."

Three sharks eat your best friend. When you seek comfort from your wife, you remember she is dead, too. Thinking you can find solace at the office, you instruct clients about estate planning but realize your daughter is gone, your family no longer exists, and you have no personal need for the techniques you teach others. That's when a client calls and asks, "How are you?"

"Awesome."

It's like I tell the PCS newbies: "Depression and our careers don't mix, especially when you talk to clients about their portfolios. You need a strategy to stay upbeat."

On Friday morning Annie's blue-green eyes blazed with excitement. I knew that look—happy, irreverent, the glint of a born troublemaker and loveable rogue. Annie had no clue, but she was my secret sauce in an ongoing quest for optimism. She made me laugh.

"Boss, did you hear what happened to Scully?"

It was 7:40 A.M., the hour when Wall Street research vied with gossip for mind share. Inside PCS the clashes were no contest. Scandal, hearsay, scuttlebutt, the unthinkable, and the sordid always prevailed. Associates gathered around coffee machines to report the latest sexual trysts. Brokers swapped bar stories rather than stock ideas. And herds of young women invariably thundered into the bathrooms, driven more by chitchat than bodily need. Somewhere, someplace, Annie had scooped a story.

I had been listening to John Dewey broadcast over the squawk box. A cable analyst known for his Texan aw-shucks hyperbole, Dewey declared Microsoft was trading "cheaper than sunscreen in a snowstorm."

Give me a break.

I focused on Annie, wholly taken by her perfume as she rolled up a chair. "What happened to Scully?"

"Strip club." Annie smirked. She knew those two words would pique my curiosity.

Other than being a serial suck-up and the world's loudest stockbroker, Scully was far too priggish to make the grapevine. He worked late and avoided the impromptu bar binges. Like so many other suburban fathers, he knew little about how his wife and four daughters spent their weeks.

"Scully's too smart to expense anything." Submitting tabs from a no-no bar was the surest way to get fired.

"That's not it," she replied. "The client paid."

"Okay," I drawled in the precise time it takes to say, "What do you know?"

Annie understood my intonation perfectly. "His assistant told me everything. He drives Jeanie up the wall, you know."

"Got it."

"Apparently, Scully has a huge client from Denver. The guy flew in yesterday morning, and they spent all afternoon behind closed doors reviewing the portfolio."

"Bet the poor guy's ears took a beating." Four walls

and the world's loudest stockbroker—it struck me as cruel and unusual punishment.

"Don't interrupt," Annie admonished. "After dinner, the client says he wants to go to a strip bar in Times Square. Scully freaks out. He's afraid somebody will recognize him."

"But agrees to take one for the team."

"Exactly," Annie continued. "The client insists on sitting right up front. And Scully drags his heels, trying to look as small as possible, when he sees the dancer onstage."

Annie rose from her seat and retreated five steps. She turned and walked toward me, swinging her waist and swooshing her hips like a stripper. Both arms were bent at the elbows and raised over her head.

Nice body English.

"Something about the dancer looks familiar," Annie said three struts into her walk. "But Scully can't place her." Annie frowned momentarily to imitate deep concentration.

How many women can tell a story about a strip bar?

"The dancer, however, knows Scully right away. She takes one look at him and covers everything up." Annie folded her arms in an X over her own chest.

"I get the picture."

"She runs offstage screaming something in Norwegian."

"How do you know it was Norwegian?"

"She's Scully's au pair."

"No way."

"Apparently, the girl was disappearing every night

around eight-thirty until the wee hours of the morning. She was so good with the kids that his wife didn't say anything. And Scully gets home late. He always thought the au pair was in bed."

"What did the client say?"

"Oh, he's pissed. A bouncer threw them out of the bar. The girl was hysterical."

"I would have paid to see that."

"It gets better. There were two police outside, and the bouncer complained to the cops. Big ruckus, you know how loud Scully gets. A few reporters showed up at the scene, and now the *New York Post* may run a story."

"With SKC front and center," I noted.

"Not to mention Scully and the client," Annie replied. "I wonder what their wives will say?"

We both laughed, and Annie's face warmed with the pleasure that had exited my life. For a long, lingering moment, I considered inviting her downstairs for coffee.

No, I told myself. *Annie works for you. She's eight years your junior.*

I decided to ask anyway. It had been months since I last met a woman for a cup of coffee. And yesterday had been tough, talking to Thayer, teaching him the financial side of death. I could use Annie's company. And it was important to venture out. The Scully story, working like a tonic, seemed to release unwanted memories. My career was taking hold again, distracting me from my past. Annie, PCS, and a new prospect—it was all good in that moment.

The phone rang, however, and robbed me of my opportunity. I never asked Annie. The interruption reminded me that things would never be the same. There was no going forward or moving on. There would always be something to suck me back inside the world of Charlie Kelemen.

CHAPTER 10

"May I speak with Grover O'Rourke?"

"Call me Grove."

I've always wanted to say that.

"Mandy Maris here." She sounded energetic and commanding.

"How can I help?" I looked at my watch and signaled Annie to wait a second.

"Well, you could buy me a cup of coffee," Maris replied, outgoing, all butter and charm.

You're keeping me from one now.

"I understand Charlie Kelemen and you were close friends," she continued.

"Okay," I said, hitting the brakes, "maybe you should introduce yourself, Mandy Maris."

Annie sensed a prolonged engagement and returned to her desk. In our business we never knew when a new opportunity, or problem, would surface.

Damn.

"I'm with the *New York Post*," Maris explained. "I'd like to ask you a few questions."

Not this.

"Hang on," I said, and transferred Mandy Fucking Maris to SKC's Department of Public Relations. I didn't warn her, just punched the transfer button, keyed in the internal extension, and bam, punched the transfer button again.

It wasn't a proud moment. Force of habit or Broker 101, advisers learned never to speak with reporters. There's nothing but downside. The press terrified me, sort of a Pavlovian response from eight years of brainwashing.

The phone rang instantly, leaving no time for me to second-guess my rudeness or for Maris to dial back. "Heard you were in the office yesterday," Cliff Halek whispered in his gravelly voice. "I thought you were going to Rhode Island."

"Graveside referral from the bankers. Literally." Sometimes I hated my BlackBerry.

"Big sitch?" he asked, using SKC's shorthand for "situation."

"IPO. My guy's got a hundred million dollars in stock." There it was, the word "guy." Consciously, I had already closed Thayer and moved him from prospect to client. Subconsciously, I was trying hard to flip into the swagger-speak of finance. It wasn't working, though. No enthusiasm in my voice. No "awesome."

"Don't forget your starving pals in Derivatives," Halek teased, always asking for the order. A $100 million block of stock offered a hedging opportunity for his team. He was also testing me. He heard something foreign, none of the kick-ass bravado of a top producer.

"It's early, Cliff. Six months to the IPO. Six months

of banker's lockup. Who knows when the corporate windows will open? I bet it's eighteen months before he can trade."

"Got it." Changing the subject, he probed, "How was the funeral?"

"Decent eulogy, but I wish Monsignor Byrd had wrapped it up sooner."

"Catholics have it easy. Just be glad you don't sit shivah. That's seven days."

He chuckled. I didn't. We both had better things to do than make small talk and listen to me bitch about a Catholic priest. New ideas swept through the trading floors during morning hours, the busiest time of day. Cliff had broken from his daily grind, however, to check on me.

"Do you need to be in the office?" he ventured.

"It's the best thing." I knew what he meant. A good friend, he sensed something amiss. "Trust me."

"Something wrong?"

"It shows?"

"Yeah."

"The *New York Post* just called. They're researching a feature on Charlie Kelemen."

"What'd you tell them?"

"Nothing. I just hit the transfer button to our PR department."

"Good answer," he said. "But you knew it was only a matter of time before the press called."

"Yeah, I know."

"Have you spoken with the police yet?" Halek continued.

"A detective named Michael Fitzsimmons called Wednesday. I left a message for him late last night."

"Glad to see your sense of urgency," Halek chided playfully.

"NYPD." I paused. "One-hundred-million-dollar guy." I paused. "You make the call." It was hardly a close play at second. There had been plenty of time to phone Fitzsimmons. The reality: After the funeral I was in no shape to handle a discussion about Charlie with anyone.

"I bet NYPD has a mile-long list of questions for you."

"What's to tell? Charlie was a stand-up guy. Whoever tied the cart to his leg was a sick fuck."

"You may know that sick fuck."

"I doubt it. His friends loved him."

"Somebody didn't."

"Tell me what you think about the market," I said, flipping into work mode, avoiding Cliff's rock-solid logic.

"Oil prices are spooking the hedge funds," he replied. "The hedgies are convinced the Dow will correct ten percent, and they're asking my desk to lever the short trades."

By "lever," Halek meant "magnify." The D-boys could invent products that lost 20 percent of their market values if the markets fell 10 percent. The shorts would be thrilled because they made money in collapsing markets.

"Good info, Cliff." His insights always made me better on the phone. "My guys will be lining up for bonds."

"Ah, security."

*   *   *

There is no such thing as the "securities industry." The term is oxymoronic, emphasis on "moronic." There is only pace, the rush for money and the frenzy of combatants, the distractions from memories eighteen months old.

Wall Street is all about angst. My contemporaries fear everything. We fear the loss of clients. It happens all too often. We fear that others have better information. Somebody wants to sell what we want to buy. We fear the Securities and Exchange Commission and the other regulators who govern us. We fear risk. But we fear running in the middle of the pack even more. So we take risks. We fear our wagers will look stupid and talking heads will expose our follies within seconds. Wall Street may be about "swag," the best word I have ever heard for money. It may be about ego and hormones and the glory of betting big and being right. But it is fear that makes us who we are. I worry about my clients and pray they never succumb to our schizoid mind-set.

Fear is one thing. Greed is another. Everybody has an agenda. There are no exceptions.

Patty Gershon stopped by my desk around ten A.M. When she used my first name, I knew something was up.

"Grove," she said, "I came to apologize."

Chloe whipped around from her terminal to face us. Annie, her blue-green eyes wide from disbelief, studied Patty suspiciously.

"For what?" I asked.

"Those bait jokes. I'm such an ass. Charlie Kelemen was your friend."

"How'd you hear?"

"Kurtz told me. Grove, I'm really sorry."

"Forget it, Patty. No harm, no foul."

"Always the Southern gentleman," she said. We both smiled. Cheer replaced remorse in her brown eyes, and our truce was complete.

"Lady Goldfish" may be too harsh.

"What do you like in these markets?" Patty asked, changing the topic.

"Bonds."

"Besides bonds."

"BRICs," I replied, using Wall Street's acronym for the fast-growing economies of Brazil, Russia, India, and China.

"I like Jack Oil," she countered, eager to weigh in with her opinion. The company sold high-tech drill bits to oil producers like Exxon and traded under the ticker symbol "JACK."

Taking the bait, I said, "It's a good company."

Setting the hook, she replied, "And I heard you cover Jumping JJ."

Josef Jaworski, the CEO of Jack Oil, was my biggest client. He became "Jumping JJ" during his company's initial public offering. When one of Fidelity's market mavens nodded off during a road show presentation, Jaworski jumped up on the conference table and danced an Irish jig to rouse the somnolent investor. The nickname Jumping JJ soon spread through money management circles.

JJ's offering worked beyond everyone's wildest expectations, including his own. He had already diversified half his position in Jack and still owned 2.3 million shares worth $190 million at $83 per share. Not bad for an emigrant from Poland.

"Who told you Jaworski is a client?" I immediately suspected Kurtz, our boss, the department's "Monthly Nut."

"JJ did."

I almost coughed up my liver.

"We met at a party last weekend," Patty explained. She leaned in close, too close, close enough to share buttonholes, close enough to flash her plastic surgeon's handiwork. "We hit it off."

"How is JJ?" I asked, trying to sound calm but feeling my heart pump faster.

"I bet I can help you with him." There it was, the beginning of a fight. Lady Goldfish was angling to share the economics on my biggest client.

"We have a good working relationship," I said, trying to defuse her interest, "but let me think about it." It was important that she save face. There were no rewards for fighting with Patty.

"You know where to find me, O'Rourke," she called out breezily on her way back to Estrogen Alley.

When Patty was out of earshot, I called JJ to assess the damage. Jumping JJ and I enjoyed an excellent rapport. But we disagreed on some basic investment strategies, like the need for safety in his portfolio. He found bond discussions worse than scraping dead flies off flypaper. It was possible that Patty had sabotaged my market advice. It was also possible I needed another axiom.

Four: Top producers are paranoid. Otherwise, we never become top producers.

"Hello," Jumping JJ answered on the first ring. That one word signaled something was wrong. JJ never picked up the phone. Ginger, his ace assistant, screened all calls. And Jaworski's inflection usually resonated with power, the vocal mix of sarcasm and remnants from a lingering Polish accent. Think Jack Nicholson from Warsaw.

Not today. That "hello" sounded limp. Now was no time to probe about Patty.

"What's wrong?" I asked.

"Jestem udupiony," he replied.

"What's that mean?"

"It's Polish for 'I'm fucked.' "

"That's no good."

"You know Ginger, right?"

"Of course. How could I forget?" His personal assistant was a model of corporate productivity. She also distracted every male within fifteen feet. JJ once convened a male-only meeting on her behalf. He instructed the men of his office to stop ogling her *cycki*, which was Polish for "boobs."

"Ginger resigned yesterday," he said.

"You're kidding." I wondered how JJ could function without her. "What happened?"

"Over the weekend we put in a new phone system."

Where's this going?

"Okay?" I said aloud.

"The phone mail burped."

"It what?"

"It burped. Ginger was having an affair with a married guy in our office," he said.

"How do you know that?"

"On Wednesday night the guy left a fifteen-minute voice mail for her. Apparently, they had just broken up. He asked Ginger to take him back."

"I still don't understand how you know this."

"Our cutting-edge phone system forwarded his message into everyone's voice mail."

"Oh shit!" I exclaimed. "Everyone heard it?"

"All eight hundred and thirty-seven of us. All our offices around the world."

"What did he say?" However aghast, I could not help but indulge my prurient curiosity.

"The guy dictated a sequel to the *Kama Sutra*," JJ replied, the Polish accent reverberating through his words. "'Ginger, I'll get on my knees and do this. Ginger, I'll spank you and do that. Ginger, I'll teach you stuff they haven't figured out in Hollywood.' And so on."

"Fifteen minutes is a long time to talk dirty into an answering machine." I never really understood the whole phone sex thing.

"It wasn't all sex. He sniveled, too."

"Sniveled?"

"'Please take me back,'" JJ mocked the man with a whiney, Polish-accented voice, or Eastern-bloc Jack Nicholson. "'I'll leave my wife for you.'"

"Asshole."

"You're telling me. My inclination is to fire him if he doesn't quit."

"Why haven't you?"

"Lawyers."

"Gotcha."

"Hey, listen," JJ started, switching subjects, "I can't talk about my shares right now." I had been urging him to sell some Jack, maybe even hedge, anything to get safe. He had no idea that Patty Gershon, not derivative trades, had prompted my call.

"Whenever you're ready, JJ." There was no point in discussing Patty. JJ's abrupt change of topic telegraphed his need to end the call.

As soon as I hung up, Annie said, "Sam Kelemen's here to see you."

"Is she all right?" I asked, alarmed.

"She's fine." Annie nodded. "But hurry up. She needs you."

"What do you mean?"

"Trust me. It's a girl thing."

CHAPTER 11

Companies start their sales pitches in reception areas. We have a competitor headquartered on West Fifty-seventh Street whose lobby views are stunning: the emerald foliage of Central Park from sixty stories high, the refined elegance of Manhattan's eclectic architecture, and the structural majesty of the George Washington Bridge off in the distance. The company is telling investors, *We're prosperous and rock solid. Work with us and you will be, too.* I would sign papers just to look out their windows. That reaction is precisely what they want.

Inside PCS we lack a rarefied view of New York City. Only four floors above Rockefeller Plaza, we see the grotty instead of the grand. Our windows overlook peripatetic swarms, perhaps a few media executives from NBC, but mostly map-toting tourists who push through the congested streets and haggle with choleric sidewalk vendors over fake Louis Vuitton handbags. We see shoppers who struggle with the weight of their booty, dazed as much by their reentry into the crowds as by the disturbing realization of what they spent at Saks and the other self-indulgent stores encircling us. Even from our perch, it is clear that crowds avoid the homeless as though the perfume of urine and living on the streets is somehow contagious. We see society's success coexisting uneasily with its failure, the mixed results hardly the foundation for a responsible corporate message.

But make no mistake. We start selling immediately. Clients realize SKC is different from the moment they arrive. Our lobby, neutral walls appointed with splashy paintings by emerging masters, has no seating. There are no chairs or couches to give the dogs a break. The reason is simple. Our clients do not wait. We greet them when they arrive.

Our corporate message: *We're here for you.*

I hustled into the reception area and found Sam. She sagged. Her head drooped. Her arms hung listlessly. Bent, dispirited, she looked defeated. Even those marvelous Siberian-husky eyes appeared gray and unremarkable. Sam did not speak. Nor did she did make eye contact.

She seemed at odds with the orientation of our reception area, her background colors misplaced in the foreground. Sam wore the urban, neo-Gothic garb of a freshly minted widow: black jeans, black ribbed top, no earrings or necklaces from her cache of bangles, and the ultimate heresy for a kid from Boston, black Yankees cap pulled low. Behind her, the paintings danced in a conga line of dazzling colors against the PCS walls. It should have been the other way around, the bright colors out in front.

Charlie would have gagged at Sam's ebony mono-
tones, and frankly, her appearance distressed me as well.
For in Sam I found my reflection from eighteen months
ago—despair, melancholy, a face without hope. That
night in New Haven began my new life, the one I now
hated. A voice inside my head, the homunculus from
hell, punished me every day with one unanswerable
question: *Where were you when it counted?*

Eighteen months later I still cursed the truckers that
menaced I-95. And myself. If only I had caught the earlier flight from Miami to LaGuardia. If only I had said
no to that extra martini with my client. If only I had been
the one driving to our beach house in Rhode Island.

Sam and I shared too much death: her husband, my
friend; my wife, her friend; my daughter, her goddaughter. During our undergraduate days of vodka and
academic enlightenment, we had never anticipated how
sharks and truckers would one day entwine our lives in
shrouds of darkness. Perhaps through osmosis, Sam's
depression suddenly welled up inside me.

Our lingering clasp, the clutch of body against body,
invited curious stares from visitors round the reception
area. Earlier that week Annie and I had drawn similar
stares from Lady Goldfish and her unholy spawn in
Estrogen Alley. There was more to be gained from holding a woman, it seemed to me, than the uneasy sensation
of being on exhibit.

As Sam trembled against me, unsuccessful in her
attempts to stifle the sobs, I said, "Let's grab a conference room." We walked. And I cradled Sam's waist,
acutely aware of her need to be held. I had been eager

to speak with her after the party, all those phone messages. Presented with the opportunity now, I doubted the right words would come.

"I'm sorry to surprise you like this," she volunteered.

"Come on, Sam. You know better," I whispered gently. With the meat of my palm, just under the thumb, I wiped a tear from her cheek. "I've been worried sick about you."

"I know."

"I've been trying to reach you all week."

"I know."

Sam was monosyllabic. I was one big knot. Humor, my standby for releasing tension, was no help now. It was hardly the time. Ever since Charlie's funeral I had agonized over what to say, how to soothe my friend from college, a woman who had pulled me back from the brink.

"Sam, I've been through this," I said, helpless and frustrated. "I wish I could say something to make you feel better. But I never heard the words myself, and I doubt they exist. Just tell me how to help. I'll drop everything, any time, any place."

"I need to ask you something." Sam trembled.

Her eyeliner had smudged, but she still looked every bit the Siberian husky. Those blue eyes. That black hair. With my thumb this time, I wiped another errant tear from her cheek.

"It's weird," she added, her voice quivering from fear or hesitation or both. "Maybe it's a favor."

"Name it," I replied, empowered by Sam's request for help. "What can I do?"

"I'm not sure where to start."

"Just spit it out."

"I feel so stupid," she confided uneasily.

"Come on, Sam. It's Grove, remember? I wrote the book on stupid."

"Charlie handled all our money," she began. "Every dime, every dollar, went into the Kelemen Group."

CHAPTER 12

In finance lingo the Kelemen Group was a "fund of funds." Charlie invested in hedge funds and charged an annual fee of 1 percent on assets. He also kept 10 percent of profits. If the portfolio grossed $10 million, his shop earned $1 million in participation fees. Not a bad payday.

The company was nothing if not successful. Crunch once told Charlie, "If I had your money, I'd burn mine."

There was no need. My friend, the fat man with the lean childhood, torched cash. He spent freely, almost drunkenly, flashing and flushing and frivoling away his funds as though the markets would always cooperate. During lavish nights in New York City, Charlie picked up tabs without fail. Dinner for ten at Le Cirque or tickets to the hottest shows on Broadway made no difference. He paid for everyone and everything with crisp hundred-dollar bills. I never saw him use a credit card. Not once.

At times the gaudy display made me uncomfortable. But Charlie told me to lighten up. "Sales 101, Grove. Gotta spend money to make money."

The marketing budget may have been boundless. In all other ways Charlie ran a tight ship. Modest office on Broadway. Basic computers. No flat-screen televisions tuned to CNBC or Fox Business. The Kelemen Group never hired MBAs to cull through market-neutral or long-short funds. Nor were there teams of quant jocks building 10,000-line Excel spreadsheets that optimized the right mix among convertible-bond, event-driven, and other money management styles. There were just two employees at the Kelemen Group, Charlie and his fifty-something receptionist named Martha.

"Size doesn't matter," Charlie once explained. The comment was no joke. It was the cornerstone of his investment philosophy. "Access to the best managers is what's important."

He was right in one sense. The best hedge funds enjoyed more demand than supply. Drawing on provisions from Section 3(c) of the Investment Company Act, hedgies minimized regulatory oversight by limiting the number of their investors. As a consequence, top-performing funds became the Studio 54s of finance. They granted admission or turned away investors from the performance-hungry crowd. Hedgies based their decisions on what people brought to the party—like the size of their checkbooks or whether investors could drive investment performance through industry knowledge.

Charlie celebrated this supply-demand imbalance. "We get into the funds you can't."

He used the extravagant parties and charity benefits to build relationships with elite money managers. And it paid off. "For years," Charlie often said, "my company has been generating twenty percent after fees. Like clockwork." It never surprised me when hedge fund legends, Alex Romanov or Jason Tropez, showed at Kelemen functions. Both had attended the ill-fated party at the New England Aquarium, Tropez with wife and mistress in tow.

Charlie rejected analytical tools like Sharpe ratios. "Excess return per unit of risk," he mocked, "give me a break. Math works in the rearview mirror. All the analysis in the world won't tell you when a manager is about to suck."

Due diligence was neither heavy nor light at the Kelemen Group. It was unorthodox. Competitors ran numbers trying to identify hiccups in investment strategies, whereas Charlie tried to burrow inside the heads of his managers. "It's how we make money and keep investors safe."

During the countless Kelemen soirees, I observed Charlie's knack for ferreting out information. He knew when husbands or wives were having affairs. He could detect subtle behavioral twitches, doubt in their speech, the way they fiddled their fingers. He knew who was struggling with their career, who was suffering from substance addiction, and who was hiding some deep, dark secret. Charlie knew the closet sexual preferences among New York's beautiful people, even the kinky things that reached well beyond the straight-versus-gay question, spankings to wit. He knew who farted at black-tie parties, and he carried matches just for those occasions. He knew where emerging artists found their inspiration, be it Picasso or Monet, and he knew whether anyone had left home in too big a rush to brush. Charlie saw, felt, smelled, heard, and tasted everything.

He just knew stuff. I had no doubt that he brought the same powers of reconnoitering to investment decisions. Sometimes with a few glasses of wine under his belt, Charlie would take a long pull from his glass and say, "You can't kid a kidder."

"At least I think all our money went into the Kelemen Group," Sam said. "Do we keep an account with SKC?"

"You're kidding, right?" It was not one of my more ambassadorial questions.

"No, Grove," she barked. "I'm not joking." And for the first time in my life, I bore the chill wrath of those Siberian-husky eyes.

"Believe me, Sam. I tried to sign you up as clients. I thought you knew."

"No."

"I told Charlie to pull a few dollars out of the Kelemen Group. I'd put it into bonds, something safe. But he said it would screw up our friendship."

"Charlie said that?" Sam asked in disbelief.

"I told him it would screw up our friendship if you didn't invest with me."

"What did he say?"

"Doesn't matter. There's no account at SKC. I let it drop." In my profession it was important to know when to back off from friends.

Sam's eyes softened, and trouble replaced the blue

ice. "How long will it take to pull money out of the Kelemen Group?"

"It depends. Who's the executor?"

"I don't know."

"What do you mean?" Money was my turf. My professional instincts were taking charge, chasing the overhang of sorrow.

"I'm not sure we had a will."

My eyebrows arched, but I said nothing.

Sam noted the reaction. "What good was a will?" she stammered defensively. "We don't have kids." She bit her bottom lip, perhaps an unconscious mechanism to hold back tears.

Just as I feared. Kids are always the catalyst. They get parents off the dime.

"Without a will, it may take a while to pull your money out of the Kelemen Group." I spoke softly but professionally. Now was no time for an emotional response. "The timing depends on ownership. If Charlie owned everything, the state courts will decide what to do with the assets."

"I spoke with Ira yesterday." Ira Popowski was New York's most preeminent trust and estate attorney. For nine hundred dollars an hour, he counseled clients how to die with their affairs in order. His rates provided good reason to live longer.

"But you don't have a will?" I objected, confused by the revelation.

"His firm filed the paperwork to create the Kelemen Group."

"Gotcha."

"He knows nothing about the operations, just that the company was an LLC. And it was in Charlie's name. He offered to help."

"Good, we may need him." It was time to take charge. "Have you called the accountant yet?"

"Crain and Cravath audits the Kelemen Group. I left a message yesterday."

The joys of small audit firms.

"Good start," I said. "What about your personal accountant?"

"Like I said, Charlie handled everything."

"You don't know your accountant?"

Sam shook her head no, and in that instant a more immediate concern struck me. "Where's your checking account?"

"Chase."

"How much do you have?"

The question hit a raw nerve. Sam hesitated and said, "Charlie deposited money into a house account every week. We used it to pay miscellaneous bills."

"How much, Sam?"

"You won't laugh?" she asked hesitantly.

"Of course not. Just tell me how much."

CHAPTER 13

"Six hundred, give or take."

"Okay, then. We can work with that." Sam had prepped me for a modest number. But not that low. Hopefully, my faint Southern accent hid what I was really thinking.

You mean $600,000, right?

"Didn't you hear me, Grove?" she demanded. "All I have is six hundred dollars. That's it."

Sam could not buy lunch for six hundred dollars. The Kelemens had sallied through life with no pretense of fiscal restraint. A party here meant a $50,000 bauble there, or some modest such trifle. There was always a reason to dine at the most expensive restaurants or decorate Sam in the latest haute couture.

"What's a girl to do without her Birkin?" Charlie once observed, referring to his wife's five-figure handbag.

Don't get me wrong. Sam never wallowed in Charlie's benders of conspicuous consumption. Not at first. She endured it. She was, after all, the product of a frugal Yankee childhood. It took years for Charlie to wear her down, years before she stopped resisting every time her husband uncorked his vintage bottles of excess.

"Come on, Sam," Charlie hollered. "We have to go." The Kelemens had been married about a year. The four of us were convening inside their apartment before heading to a party in the Hamptons.

Moments later Sam appeared in a crisp blue blouse, designer capris cut just right, and espadrilles. It was a simple look, but flattering and fresh and right for the season.

"You're not wearing that," he declared, somewhat aghast. "Not to a tented lobster picnic, for Chrissakes."

Sam trooped back to her closet and reappeared moments later in a short, almost sheer, safari-style shift, the perfect foil to her runner's legs. She pirouetted in her bare feet, sarcastically to be sure, but she looked stunning in the wisp of a dress. No doubt, Sam would turn heads.

"Better." Charlie nodded approvingly.

"I'd rather wear shorts and a T-shirt," she said. "Don't blame me if the claws shoot lobster juice all over my dress."

"What about the shoes?" he asked, ignoring the wisecrack, sending her back to the closet with Evelyn close behind. To me he boasted, "I found that dress at Bergdorf for forty-three hundred dollars."

"You picked it out?"

"That and most of the other good stuff in her closet."

After a few minutes Sam returned in a pair of flats that appeared ordinary, nothing special. Charlie believed otherwise. "A woman needs her Chanel," he crowed.

"I'd be so much happier in fuzzy slippers," she replied, indifferent to the fashion statement on her feet.

Charlie ignored the wisecrack. "Come with me," he told Sam. "I know the perfect pièce de résistance."

The two disappeared. I turned to Evelyn and asked, "What's the big deal with the flip-flops?"

"Those flip-flops," she explained, "probably cost four figures."

"Are they air-conditioned?"

"I love Charlie," Evelyn confided in a hushed tone, "but he would drive me fucking nuts." She reconsidered almost immediately. Upon spying the pièce de résistance, Sam's chunky cord of pearls, Evelyn admitted, "Maybe I could get used to it."

Charlie appraised Sam head to toe—the stylish haircut, the pearls, the $4,300 shift, and the four-figure flip-flops. Approval filled his eyes. Exasperation filled hers. Awkward discomfort filled ours.

"Now we're ready," Charlie pronounced in triumph.

Those tiffs ended years ago. Sam settled, however grudgingly, into Charlie's big lifestyle. Over time she even embraced the parade of personal services. My Yankee friend never missed her weekly sessions with Gilberto, the family masseur, or Dagmar, the therapist who had once been a dominatrix. The basics with Crunch, five hundred dollars every other week, seemed downright reasonable. Of course, the pedicures, the highlights, and the facials, even the bikini waxes, were all extra at the salon. All it took was money.

Time to cut back.

Charlie's tangle of overhead would take weeks to unwind. Manny, the full-time driver, was almost family. How could Sam fire him? The home-delivery cleaners were mission critical. How could Un, Deux, and Trois survive without their fresh woollies? What about food? Every trendy kitchen in New York City had delivered takeout feasts to the Kelemens' Greenwich Village apartment. Sam could no longer heat a can of Boston baked beans if somebody fired the burners for her.

I know. During my six months in the Kelemen household, she botched any dish that required a stove. It had seemed impossible to ruin bacon, eggs, and grits, Sam's one concession to my Charleston roots. Somehow, some way, she torched anything and everything over flames. Even the dachshunds winced at her cooking.

Charlie Kelemen's widow now faced a daunting challenge: survive on six hundred dollars until further notice. Her eyes filled, and she turned to hide the tears. "I'm scared, Grove." Money fears were picking at her thoughts like a carrion bird.

Sam teetered on the verge of insolvency. Sure, the cash-flow crunch was temporary. When we liquidated the Kelemen Group and its portfolio of hedge funds, Charlie's estate would yield plenty of money. Problem solved.

Not so fast. Redemption clauses would drag out the process. Hedgies often locked up investors for months, even years, before redeeming capital. The ungainly exit provisions were known as "Hotel California" clauses, a reference to the last line of the Eagles hit. It might take months, maybe more, to liquidate the portfolio, gather the incoming cash, and then distribute funds. Sam, like the rest of Charlie's investors, would have to wait for her money.

What will she do in the meantime?

Sam could never ask her parents for a bridge loan. They were crusty New England clams. The ignominy, the contrition, would be too much. Helen Wells, Sam's mother, would rant and rave as though her daughter's profligate spending had single-handedly destroyed generations of Yankee-codger values. "Damn it, Samantha, what were you thinking?"

"Come on, Sam," I said, wheeling my chair over, clasping both her hands with mine, forcing the Siberian-husky blues to make contact. "We'll sort this out. I promise."

"I don't have the stomach to wind things down at the company."

You have no choice.

"It would break Charlie's heart," I replied, trying to empathize. "He put everything into the business."

Sam nodded.

"You both did," I added quickly, acknowledging their team effort. Sam had always been at Charlie's side. "Why don't I try the auditors again? The annual reports will make things simple."

"Why's that?"

"They'll list the hedge funds where the Kelemen Group invested. Once we know the funds, we can send in redemption notices. I'll help you coordinate things."

We sat awkwardly, uncertain what to say, Sam thanking me with her eyes. She finally broke the silence. "You've always been rock solid, Grove. Evelyn was so lucky to get you."

Please don't say that.

"Do you have your checkbook?" I asked.

"What?" She looked confused. "Are you billing me for your time?" she asked impishly as she rifled through her Hermès handbag.

"For laundry," I teased. "Your tears soaked my shirt and took all the starch out."

Sam's eyes sparkled. In that brief moment she reverted to the confident woman who had rescued me from personal hell.

"Just give me a blank check."

Sam handed me a check and mumbled darkly, "Nothing over six hundred dollars, please."

"Save your money for lunch."

"Lunch?" she asked, puzzled.

You can't buy lunch for six hundred dollars.

I said nothing but wrote "Void" across the check.

"What are you doing, Grove?"

"I'm wiring you some money. You can pay me back once we unwind the Kelemen Group." Sam started to resist, but I cut her off. Touching her full lips with my index finger, I warned, "Don't say anything."

"But—"

"Zip it."

She squeezed my hand, kissed my cheek, and grabbed the conference room door. "Thank you," she whispered, choking back the emotion. For the briefest moment, I thought Sam might kiss me on the lips. She pulled back, disappointing me to be honest, and added, "There's one other thing. Do you mind calling Betty Masters?"

"No problem. Why?"

"She called yesterday and asked about the Kelemen Group. I'm really not sure what to tell her."

"She was an investor?"

"Seems that way. We entertained so many people, I could never tell who was what. She sounded anxious."

"Leave it with me."

Sam and I walked through the reception gallery to the elevators, saying nothing. Silence between two people ordinarily distressed me. I always felt a need to fill the void. Not now. We held hands, and it felt right. We had weathered so much together.

Finally, I spoke. "We'll get your money out of the Kelemen Group, Sam. We'll find missing investment accounts, no matter where they're hidden. And I'll be there every step. You can bank on it." As Sam disappeared onto the elevator, all dressed in black, Charlie Kelemen's killer was the last person on my mind.

CHAPTER 14

What the fuck was I thinking?

"You can bank on it." I actually said that. Where would I find the time to unearth hidden bank accounts, liquidate the Kelemen Group, and discover what Betty Masters wanted? Where would I start? I had a day job. I had a business to run.

I'm no Dick Tracy.

Charlie never revealed much about his wealth. He just spent it like a rummy. He never disclosed much about the Kelemen Group. He just bragged about investment returns. Like most money managers, Charlie guarded the secrets of his success. Even with friends.

I had overpromised Sam and knew better. Nobody on Wall Street guarantees results. We equivocate. That's what we do. That's why we print ten pages of disclaimers in every research report.

Back in the boardroom PCS rocked with adrenaline. The buzz of activity reminded me that top producers focus. We can't turn our backs on the markets or our competitors for a moment. Oil prices had fallen $6 in the last forty-five minutes. Nigeria, according to the rumors, was breaking ranks with OPEC. Someone, maybe Zabelskas from Goldman Sachs, had reported the country would increase production 25 percent. The DOW was soaring, up 223 points.

It wasn't advice I heard on the way to my desk. It was the cha-ching of stockbrokers punching their cash registers and ringing up commissions. Our guys always buy on the way up.

The loudest broker, Scully of megaphone mouth, boomed into his receiver with palpable glee, "We're making money, buddy."

He bugged the ever-living shit out of me, never a hair out of place, never a wrinkle in his crisp white shirts, just way too loud. He had built his clientele through "assmosis," the time-honored practice of absorbing sales leads by sucking up to management. There was no love lost between Scully and me. We were all competitors inside PCS.

Patty Gershon waved away two women loitering in Estrogen Alley. They fidgeted something fierce, apparently anxious to share the latest gossip. Patty ignored them and berated a client instead: "You'll buy next time I tell you to buy. Right, Henry?"

At my team's trio of workstations, the telephone consoles blinked brighter than Vegas lights on New Year's Eve. Incoming calls. Several lines holding. Traders reporting executions. Dozens of Post-it notes mottled my computer terminal, a Rorschach collage of urgent communiqués and flashing stock tickers. Ordinarily, this was my kind of day, chaos my thing.

Halek's name appeared on my phone's LCD. "Let's discuss Jack Oil," he said.

Cliff was a born moneymaker. He always called with good ideas, and we had spoken many times about Jumping JJ. Two-point-three million shares of an $83 stock commanded attention everywhere. But that "burping" phone had distracted JJ, and I knew it would be a waste of time to discuss a trade. "Not today, Cliff."

"Vols are pumped," he reported, pushing to continue the discussion.

I understood immediately. "Vols" referred to volatility, one of the variables used to price zero-cost collars. Net, net, Cliff was saying, "Market conditions are perfect for JJ to hedge his shares and eliminate the risk of his stock crashing."

"JJ won't focus," I replied. "He's up to his ears in personnel problems."

"Understood," Halek conceded.

"Glad you called anyway," I said. "Sam Kelemen just left my office. She's in trouble."

"How so?"

"Charlie put all their money into the Kelemen Group," I started. "Sam has no liquidity. She's down to her last six hundred dollars."

"Life insurance?" he pressed hesitantly, not believing his ears. "No bonds or cash somewhere on the side?"

"Nothing," I confirmed. "She even asked if I had opened an account for Charlie."

"I don't buy it," Halek observed cynically. "Any bonehead keeps cash on the side."

"She's terrified, Cliff."

"The whole Kelemen thing's pretty fucking weird if you ask me."

"You got that right," I agreed. "Ever since the funeral, I've been wondering who tossed Charlie in the tank. Now Sam and the money. It's a shit show."

Cliff paused, and for a moment I thought we had been disconnected. During our rapid-fire banter he seldom held his tongue. He finally said, "Hey, Grove," and waited for my undivided attention.

"Yeah."

"Charlie's not your concern."

"That's cold."

"Just practical," he countered. "Charlie's dead. You can't do anything about that. Sam Kelemen has the problem. Is there any chance she wants to run the Kelemen Group?"

"Didn't ask," I replied, kicking myself for the oversight. "But I doubt she has the stomach."

"Then focus where you can make a difference and help her wind down the company. Leave the detective shit to the cops."

Detective shit, I mused.

"That aquarium stuff is bad biz," he warned, "maybe dangerous." Halek hopped before I could respond. "Gotta go," he announced, leaving me with a dial tone and discomfiting wisdom.

There was no time to dwell on his words. My phone was ringing nonstop. Von Maur, our securities lawyer, asked for an update on Jumping JJ.

"Forget it," I advised. "He's not trading today."

Fletcher, a client who had just sold his auto parts

business for $50 million, was on my second line. "Can I afford a ten-thousand-dollar case of wine?" Money was so new to him.

"Only if we share a bottle, Fletch."

Annie, Chloe, and I fielded other calls by the dozen. We made more of our own, and I addressed the usual questions that accompanied strong trading sessions.

"Should I buy?"

Me: "I wouldn't. That stock is trading at twenty times earnings but growing ten percent annually. Over-priced in my book."

"Should I sell?"

Me: "Let's move fifteen thousand shares today. That leaves us with thirty thousand. We'll still be thrilled if it continues to run."

"What's this stock trading at?"

"How about that one?" And so on. The level of activity was unusual, and I found myself buried deep inside the securities business.

Wall Street generally yawns on Fridays during the summer. Clients disappear. The most powerful money managers board helicopters in the morning and retreat to the Hamptons, where the square footage of their palatial estates grows faster than the portfolios they manage.

For almost everyone else, lunch serves as the starting gun to bolt and beat the weekend traffic. Traders and brokers, the rank and file of the capital markets, abandon their Aeron chairs and proprietary trading screens for weekends at the Jersey Shore or other retreats. It's a wonder their pell-mell breaks for the elevators don't produce more casualties.

Upon occasion, resignations break up the Friday ennui. Brokers resign on the last day of the week. Competing firms offer fat checks for advisers to leave and take clients with them. The payments can be huge, as much as two times total fees and commissions over the last twelve months.

"Remember all the good things I said about my old firm? All the stuff about great money managers and outstanding trade executions? I was wrong. The old firm sucks. Can't compete with the new shop. Trust me."

It's a tough sales pitch.

So what. For the right amount of money, some brokers will say anything. Those knuckleheads trace their genealogical roots back to the world's oldest profession. They're "in the life," as streetwalkers say. Those brokers give guys like me a bad name.

Parade-like pageantry, however modest, accompanies every resignation. Security guards, wearing metal name tags fixed to their uniforms, escort departing brokers to the front door. The brokers wave to their friends, who are now competitors. Like conquering heroes, the defectors gloat over the seven-figure paychecks waiting across the street.

The currently loyal salespeople stop what they are doing and gawk, wide-eyed, silent, and hungry for more money, more assets, and more recognition. They wonder if their bosses will favor them with a few juicy accounts to defend.

* * *

True to form, the early frenzy of that Friday dissipated. A spokesman for Nigeria denied any rift with OPEC or increase in his country's production. Oil prices recovered. The market sold off 60 points from the early highs. PCS advisers began to leave.

By one P.M. I had returned all client calls and cleared the Post-its from my desk. No word from Detective Fitzsimmons. That was just as well. Unfortunately, the receptionist took a message when I dialed Charlie's auditors.

Accountants like early weekends, too, I reminded myself. *I should have phoned Crain and Cravath sooner.*

My in-box required immediate attention. It had become a towering stockpile of M-bombs: management memos about compliance changes, sign-up sheets for management outings, personnel changes affecting management org charts, and sales productivity articles circulated by management. The requests for information never ceased.

"Who are your top ten clients?"

"Are you on the verge of winning any new business?"

"How can you increase revenues ten percent, twenty percent, or more?"

The paperwork was one fucking nightmare. Rather than fill in the blanks, I opted to send a headache back to my boss. Why empower dysfunctional corporate behavior? "Annie, do me a favor," I whispered.

She leaned forward, all ears, that conspiratorial smile.

"Spread the word I have ten dollars on Patty Gershon

resigning this afternoon." It was Friday after all, the traditional day for changing shops.

A gung-ho accomplice to any mischief, Annie cocked one eyebrow and grinned wickedly. She reigned supreme among the gaggle of PCS sales assistants, mostly women in their midtwenties en route to graduate schools. They worked hard, gabbed constantly, and punctuated every other sentence with the exclamation "Shut up!" It would not take long for Annie's whisper campaign to coax Frank Kurtz from his office. Soon, he would start sniffing around Estrogen Alley to assess the rumors about Patty himself.

Chloe was still on the phone. More accurately, the phone was still on her. She sported a prodigious headset. Two massive bowls crowned her ears and obscured much of her short brown hair. The headphones belonged to a different time and place, perhaps the landing strips of World War II rather than the crazed commerce of Wall Street.

Would you wire seventy-five thousand dollars from my account to Sam Kelemen? I mouthed the words and handed her Sam's voided check. The numbers at the bottom contained details necessary to route funds.

We communicated all the time like this, Chloe locked in deep conversation and me using hand signals to communicate instructions. I dared not speak aloud. Otherwise, the mouthpiece on her jutting boom would broadcast my words to someone else. Chloe had an uncanny ability to speak with several people at once. The skill made her invaluable.

Underneath the headset, Chloe's forehead furrowed

into long extended lines. Her eyes dilated. Her expression, a mix of gatekeeper and surrogate mother, challenged me. "Are you sure?"

I nodded yes with my most commanding face.

In all honesty the external conviction belied internal Ping-Pong. Spontaneity, the thought of wiring $75,000, was never my thing. Bucks had been sparse during childhood, hard to make as an adult. That was my left brain.

But this was Sam. She needed me. I owed Charlie. I had given my word and overpromised on the deliverables. "You can bank on it." Neither of the Kelemens had blinked about my six-month stay in their town house. That was my right brain.

The phone interrupted the match. Three short bursts indicated an internal call. Ordinarily, we regarded this special tone as the frightful harbinger of incoming M-bombs.

Frank Kurtz's name appeared on all three of our LCD displays, and I thought Annie would kick off her heels and dance. She swiveled round in her chair and stopped yakking into the receiver. She flashed a blinding mouthful of pearly whites, a shit-eating grin for the ages. "Mission accomplished." Triumph rang in her words.

"Damn, you're good," I congratulated Annie while punching the talk button to greet Frank. Her gang had delivered.

"What'd you say?" Frank bellowed, his voice frothy, bold, and robust, a stein of good cheer.

Frank was not a large man at five-eight. He just seemed big. Thanks to a daily regimen of lifting weights and quaffing red wine, Frank had bulked his torso into oversized, almost comic proportions. His hard-packed belly, an uneasy détente between muscle and fat, dwarfed the skinny, spindly, spider-like legs underneath. He exuded physical strength when he spoke, his thunderous voice jostling the thin office walls. His words were another matter. They never fit the physical presence. They regularly betrayed indecision underneath.

"Damn glad you called," I replied, working quickly to mask the praise intended for Annie. "I need to ask you something."

"Me first," Frank objected. "Have you heard anything about Patty?"

"You mean about her leaving?" It was easy to bait Frank.

"Oh shit," he snorted nervously. "I was afraid of that." He was already fretting over his bonus.

"Forget it, Frank. It's a cheesy rumor. She's not going anywhere. You've been too good to her."

"You think?" he asked. Puffed-up pride replaced his flaccid inflection. Come-and-go bravado superseded his fear.

"I'd bet your next referral on it. Nothing happens today after four P.M. Mark my words."

"Done," Frank bellowed with confidence. "If you're right, you get the next I-banking lead." Banker referrals made it easy to meet wealthy executives who had sold their companies or taken them public. Warm introductions could make a broker's career at SKC. "Now, what's on your mind, Grove?"

CHAPTER 15

"May I swing by your office, Frank?"

Sam Kelemen was on my mind. The day had slowed. The markets had lost their chaotic urgency as money people switched from price-earnings ratios to weekend plans. And I needed to discuss a few things about my best friend's widow.

Kurtz, I hoped, would offer guidance. Not about time management. He was the Monthly Nut after all. He reminded me of the tidal-creek catfish from my youth, all mouth and no brains.

But Frank had worked with all sorts of stockbrokers for twenty-plus years. He had seen everything, run into the train wrecks that turned the press yellow. He had survived. That's 90 percent of the game. I knew how to investigate the Kelemen Group. I hoped Frank could show me where to look for Sam's missing accounts. Top producer or not, I had no idea where to start.

Like sales managers at all brokerage firms, Frank Kurtz served as a cheerleader. His job was to build revenues. Kurtz also functioned as top cop, the first defense against churning, unauthorized trading, or similar transgressions. He ensured his stockbrokers adhered to the SEC, NASD, CBOE, NFA, and CFTC, not to mention all fifty state regulators like the BSR in New Hampshire or the DOJ in Delaware—the latter not to be confused with the federal Department of Justice. Taken together these governing bodies equaled NFW, the acronym for No Fucking Way Wall Street could trade in peace.

Frank's dual roles required the wisdom of Solomon. If he was too strict, revenues would dry up and salespeople would bitch to our CEO. If he was too lenient, we would read about the fallout in *The Wall Street Journal*. The media always reserved space for sensational stories about rogue brokers and their dupes. Either way, Frank Kurtz's job was on the line.

Frank's office juxtaposed good and evil. There was a papal blessing on one wall. It vaguely resembled a diploma, except for the autographed head shot of Pope John Paul Umpteen mounted within the frame. Though the pope epitomized everything good, his photo regularly evoked the worst in Frank and me. We debated who had been the altar boy from hell and compared childhood stories about torquing off nuns or chugging wine when the priests weren't looking. As fellow Catholics we sanctioned each other's irreverence, past, present, and presumably the future. And that was the good wall.

On the wall behind Frank's desk hung a collection of celebrity photos: Frank shaking hands with Andrew Fastow, Frank clinking wineglasses with Bernie Ebbers, and Frank sharing cigars with Dennis Kozlowski. The gallery, a murderer's row of financial corruption, reminded PCS advisers how quickly fortunes change. The photos perplexed us. We wondered if our boss was a human divining rod for Wall Street's miscreants.

Frank rifled his thinning black hair, a comb-over on the come, and scratched the nape of his neck. "You're sure about Patty?" he asked, his tanned face a mass of furrows and other calling cards from life on Wall Street.

For a moment I appraised Kurtz carefully, steadily. With a flat palm facing him, I waved my hand through the air. The motion was slow and circular, almost theatrical. "Relax, Frank."

"What the hell was that?"

"Jedi mind trick," I said. "Gershon's not going anywhere."

Frank sighed, ready to move on but still not convinced. "Do you want a cigar?" he asked, opening his humidor to display dozens of well-preserved stogies.

About as much as a barbed-wire enema.

"No thanks," I said.

"They're Cuban," he bellowed, enthusiasm in his voice, surprise over my refusal. "Cohibas." The thin walls of his office had begun to reverberate. Frank always exuded the most power when he discussed his two favorite topics, red wine and Cuban cigars.

"Not my thing. But thanks."

"Suit yourself." Brief awkward pause. "What's on your mind?"

"Sam Kelemen."

"Who?"

"She's my friend's widow, the guy at the New England Aquarium."

"Oh, right," he said, "I'm so sorry. Her name threw me."

"Short for Samantha."

"Got it. What's the issue?" he asked, fussing with his cigar cutter, a double-blade guillotine.

"Sam's tight on cash," I explained. "Charlie invested everything in the fund of funds he founded."

"How much did he manage?"

"Not sure. Probably two hundred million dollars or so."

"Small shop," he observed. "And not our problem. We don't lend against funds of funds. No liquidity." Having forestalled a margin request, Frank severed the head of his Cohiba.

"I'm not here to discuss a loan."

Frank pursed his lips. He ran his thumb and forefinger their entire length, as though zipping a plastic freezer bag. Everybody in PCS had seen Frank do the "shut up and listen" one time or another.

"Forget the Kelemen Group," I said. "It may take time, but Sam will get her money out of the company."

"Right," he concurred, pleased to be off the hook for a loan, curious what I wanted.

"She asked if Charlie had opened an account here."

"Did he?"

"No."

"What's the issue?"

"In eight years, Frank, I've never heard a widow ask about hidden accounts."

"Goddamn goofy," he agreed. Over on the walls, John Paul bounced at his blasphemy. Fastow, Ebbers, and Kozlowski held their ground. Kurtz then added, thoughtfully, only half in jest, "Husbands hide mistress money all the time."

"That's different," I said. "Sam Kelemen has a grand total of six hundred dollars in her name. Nothing else."

"Why are you screwing around with six hundred dollars, Grove? We're in the high-net-worth business. Remember?"

Anyone else would have let that crack slide. It was a soft jab, nothing more than an example of the mouth-to-mouth combat that characterizes our industry. No harm, no foul. Right?

Wrong. Top producers don't back down from over-head line items. I stared at Frank hard. My eyes bull-dozed his skull, told him to get fucked, though I said nothing. Let none of the sweet drawl from the saccharine South slip over my lips. Never explained my need to protect Sam as a way to atone for Evelyn and Finn.

Where were you when it counted?

"Sam is my friend," I replied, suppressing my anger. "Nothing else matters."

Kurtz tasted bitterness in my words and averted his eyes. He acted like a man who had witnessed something feral and reckless in an old colleague for the first time. So I thought.

"There must be a system for locating lost accounts,"

I continued. "Can't we plug a Social Security number into a database somewhere?"

"Grove," he ventured cautiously. "We've both been in this biz a long time."

Uh-oh. Lecture.

"We both know financial institutions would never agree how to store personal information or protect privacy."

"I'm double-checking, Frank. I had to ask."

"No, you didn't," he countered, his force catching me by surprise. "If I were you, I'd keep my distance."

"Why's that?"

"For one," he counseled, "stuff shows up when people die, skeletons, mistresses, investments. All the things they tried to hide while alive. Let it play out."

"What else, Frank?"

"You don't want to hear it."

"Go ahead. It's okay."

"You don't need the distractions. Know what I mean?"

Yeah. You're worried about your bonus.

"Let me worry about my time, Frank. It's never been a problem before."

"Suit yourself," he said at first. Then he reconsidered. "I'm asking you to back off, Grove. Somebody whacked Kelemen. I don't want you stepping on the wrong pile."

Just clean the dog turds off your soles and move on.

"Won't happen, Frank," I replied vaguely, before straightening John Paul on the way out. It seemed the good Catholic thing to do.

Back at my desk I hit the speed dial to Ira Popowski.

Reaching him on the first try seemed unlikely. We often played phone tag for days before connecting, the victims of busy schedules and competing demands for time. Ira billed about $5 million in annual fees to his clients, a big practice for a trust and estate lawyer.

"Ira Popowski," he barked into the receiver, answering on a half ring, clearly expecting someone else.

"That was friendly." The name, Popowski, sounded powerful. It rang of aggression and brutish intellect, desirable traits in a lawyer. "Ira, this is important."

He recognized the gravity of my tone. "I thought you were my conference call. What's up?"

"I've been speaking with Sam. By any chance, did you ever draft a will for Charlie?"

"I tried."

"What do you mean?"

"He always put me off."

"Shit."

"There's always something more important," Ira explained dispassionately.

"So what happens if he died intestate?"

"The state laws of New York take over, and assets in Charlie's name go to Sam. It's relatively straightforward."

"Except for one thing."

"Which is?"

"Everything's tied up in the Kelemen Group. Sam doesn't know whether they have any other investments. I thought you might."

Silence. Ira replied in an even, measured tone, "What do you mean, she doesn't know?"

"Just that. Sam knows about one checking account with six hundred dollars, but that's it. Charlie handled everything."

"She called yesterday. She didn't say anything about that," he remarked, sounding harried all of a sudden. "Grove, my conference call just started. If Sam needs help, I'm in."

"One other thing."

"Quick," he urged.

"Your firm set up the business. What about the fund itself? Offering documents, prospectuses, the stuff people get when they invest?"

"I pitched for the business," Ira replied, a wistful tone in his voice.

"Charlie didn't hire your firm?"

"Said we were too expensive." Then Ira was gone.

I sat for a moment and grew angry. Not at Ira's abrupt sign-off. We both struggled with the exigencies of time and the tyranny of deadlines. Our exchanges had always been blunt, with a clipped rhythm unto their own. Two Ivy League graduates unable to complete sentences. Two guys competing over who could hang up first.

It was Charlie who pissed me off. His lack of planning was completely out of character. He had been fastidious, so painfully absorbed with the details of life. Why had he dropped the ball? He left Sam nothing but a stack of trouble.

And Sam. She was smart, perkier than a closet full of alarm clocks. She had grown confident during their marriage. Yet she had avoided the one topic every couple discusses—money. What was that all about?

Not important. She needs help.

I dialed Betty Masters. To my dismay, the answering machine picked up. There was no choice but to leave a message. "Grove O'Rourke here. It's short notice, but I'll be in New Paltz tomorrow. Are you free for lunch?"

Underneath the two computer monitors on my desk, galaxies away from the charts and all the scrolling headlines, Evelyn and Finn smiled at me from a photo. That brisk fall day had dabbed rosy hues across their coffee-and-cream skin tones, a gift from Evelyn's Portuguese ancestors who had landed in New England generations ago. The ocean breeze mussed their hair in a way no artist, not even Crunch, could replicate. Their brown eyes sparkled like exotic jewels. The background of coral beach boulders magnified the warmth of their happy smiles. Every single day of my life now, I longed to return to that afternoon together. Especially on Fridays.

It was almost four P.M. As soon as the market closed, I would leave the hallowed halls of PCS, no loitering, not even for a second with my weekend at the ready. Friday evenings started in Central Park with my cycling club. We rode eyeballs out and hurt at the finish thirty-five miles later.

Afterward, it was takeout from Shun Lee, my favorite Chinese restaurant. Half a dozen spring rolls, a mountain of pork-fried rice, and a whole carton of Szechuan crispy beef. I always scarfed down dinner in front of some cable movie classic. It was a wonderful way to end the week.

It was for shit. I dreaded weekends. I had yet to date

anyone and hid from loneliness by cycling, scouring *Barron's* from cover to cover, or hanging out with Sam and Charlie. One of my antidotes for self-imposed isolation was gone now, and my thoughts turned cynical. There was a new way to fill those empty stretches.

Find Sam's money. Avoid Charlie's killer. And think long and hard about what to tell the Monthly Nut.

My discussion with Kurtz had triggered an unintended consequence. He made a request that I had no intention of honoring: *"I'm asking you to back off, Grove."*

That's trouble.

For all my axioms, top producer this, top producer that, I still recognized one unassailable truth. Kurtz was the boss. It didn't pay to ignore a direct order. Especially not in public.

Somewhere in a distant cubicle, Casper toiled over his fingernails. Or maybe he had moved on to his toenails. He should have left long ago, but it seemed his clippers were keeping time to my deliberation.

Plink. Plink. Plink.

CHAPTER 16

The next day I tried hard to enjoy the drive to New Paltz. With the top down on my Audi, *The Best of Johnny Cash* blared over the highway noise. There had been a time when I loved to push the speedometer up over ninety, even a hundred miles per hour. Not now. Those days disappeared with an eighteen-wheeler outside New Haven. I traded speed for July sun and "Folsom Prison Blues."

My thoughts inevitably returned to Charlie Kelemen. Locating hidden investment accounts, I feared, would take forever. Kurtz had only confirmed the obvious and even suggested patience. *"Let it play out."*

Whatever happened to your sense of urgency, Frank?

Charlie's fund of funds seemed like a more reliable way to recoup money for Sam. The Kelemen Group was out in the open. The auditors would make things simple. And I could speak with Charlie's investors to gain their input. Today's visit with Betty, one of the investors, was step one.

My cell phone rang and interrupted Johnny Cash.

"Bet you can't transfer me this time," a familiar voice observed, a touch triumphant and self-congratulatory.

Mandy Fucking Maris.

"How'd you get my cell number?" I asked, more impressed than annoyed.

"I'm a reporter. It's what I do," she explained. "Now why don't you help the world remember Charlie Kelemen the right way?"

What's that supposed to mean?

"Mandy," I finally said, extending my phone far to the left, "you're breaking up." At sixty-five miles per hour, the oncoming wind made for great static.

"Stay with me, Grove."

"What's that? Mandy? Are you there?" I hung up, miffed by her persistence.

That woman won't give up.

I felt like pond scum for hanging up on her. But nobody ever declared victory after talking to the press. My last trip to New Paltz had been far less complicated.

"The world just doesn't make hippies like Abbie Hoffman anymore," Evelyn remarked wistfully.

We were visiting New Paltz for her cousin's wedding, glad for the weekend escape ninety minutes north of New York City. One of Evelyn's English literature friends from Wellesley had described New Paltz as a "classic hippy town stuck interminably in the 1960s."

Damned English majors. Normal people never used phrases like "stuck interminably." Evelyn and I half expected to find head shops on every corner, women clomping down the streets in clogs, and gaunt men wearing faded jeans and tie-dye shirts. We looked everywhere for henna tattoos and accoutrements of social discord on loan from another era.

The town disappointed on its advance billing. None of the guys sported ponytails. And head shops? Give me a break. Instead of hookahs and roach clips, the clapboard stores of Main Street housed kitchenware and athletic goods. New Paltz probably hadn't seen Panama Red and the good shit for twenty years.

Evelyn and I cracked up as we looked for radicals. They were either extinct or had taken refuge in the more rugged parts of the nearby wilderness. Once we reached this conclusion, our conversation turned to more pressing matters. We speculated on how our lives would change once the baby arrived. Evelyn glowed from the sweet stew of hormones and girl juices marinating Finn. My wife never looked more beautiful, swollen belly and all.

Betty Masters had never been a hippy. She belonged to the rubber-chicken circuit of black-tie philanthropy. She wore conventional white pearls, gallons of Chanel perfume, neutral silk blouses, and trim linen suits in season. Denim was out of the question. She rarely drank but occasionally sipped wine spritzers during visits to New York City. Whenever chatter edged toward contentious topics, Betty steered clear—with one exception.

She despised her ex-husband. She called him "the unctuous, low-life miscreant that abandoned us." He was "a vile failure of a man . . . a jar of Vaseline with legs." She insisted his middle name was Shithead. Other divorcées in Charlie's posse referred to their mistakes as "the ex." Not Betty. She used his full name, Herb Shithead Masters, every time.

Herb was the classic deadbeat. He vanished after the divorce became final and could have been running a Mexican bordello for all we knew. It was as though there had never been a marriage, except for one thing. They had a son. His name was Fred. He had Down's syndrome, and his father failed to make even one child support payment. Herb ranked lower on the food chain than organic vermin living inside the assholes of runt maggots eating turds from the bowels of syphilitic billy goats.

Ask me how I really feel.

Betty would have agreed. She seethed with anger, stayed bitter over the way a father had forsaken his son. She loved her boy. She built a careful life, one under the radar, just for Fred.

Outside her Victorian cottage, the house swaddled by steep hills and delicate birch trees, Betty broke from gardening and waved hello. She looked much like Jackie Onassis, the same jet-black hair, sparkling eyes, and re-cherché bone structure. The two women could have been twins, except that Betty's face was wider and darker. Her high cheekbones suggested faraway roots.

"How was the drive?" Betty flashed a smile that would have ended hostilities in the Middle East.

"Nothing like a convertible on a beautiful day," I said, patting the Audi's hood.

"I hope you used your sunscreen."

Why do women always say that?

When we kissed hello, our cheeks padding like fluffy pillows, the sweet scent of Chanel nearly smothered my olfactory senses. "Please let me buy you lunch."

"Don't be silly," Betty replied. "We settled all that."

Betty had insisted on cooking. "I make a mean cheeseburger," she boasted over the phone after we finally connected. "Best garlic dill pickles north of the Mason-Dixon Line." It took me all of three seconds to concede.

Now, after the drive, the prospect of a home-cooked meal appealed more than ever. I was tired of eating out. The culinary one-upmanship among New York City's restaurants had become tedious. I longed to hang out in somebody's house with a glass of wine and music in the background, no waiters buzzing the aisles for tips. "You sure it's no bother?" I asked again on her front lawn.

"I'm thrilled for the company. Besides, I want you to meet my boy." He had just emerged from the front door. "Fred, come say hello to Grove."

Short and stocky, the kid wore a Yankees hat with the bill pointing far right. He appeared to be in his late teens, and as Fred walked toward us with a slightly pigeon-toed gait I recognized Betty's features peeking through his flattened nose and upward-slanting eyes. He carried an aluminum bat with his left hand and squeezed a fielder's glove under his arm.

"Hello," he said, shaking my hand but looking away with a wan smile. Like me, he found the whole ritual of introduction awkward.

"You wouldn't happen to have a baseball buried in

that glove?" Sports have long been the world's greatest icebreaker. I had not thrown a baseball in six years, not since breaking my collarbone during a cycling race. But the equipment beckoned like an old friend.

"Softball," Betty clarified.

"Wanna play?" the boy asked eagerly.

I looked to Betty for her okay. She smiled radiantly. "Throw underhand and be careful," she warned. "Fred tags the ball every once in a while."

"Come on, Fred. Let's see what you got."

Betty walked inside and called over her shoulder, "I'll call you boys when lunch is ready."

I had no idea what to expect. Fred lined up in front of my Audi. The car was not my first choice for a backstop, but our game was slow-pitch.

What's the harm?

"Okay, tiger. Here comes the heater."

My first pitch was awful, below the knees and away. Fred swung with a huge, lunging golf shot around his ankles. He missed and observed, "Not a good pitch." The ball rolled past him and bounced innocuously off the Audi's rear tire.

The next pitch sailed outside again, but high this time. Once more Fred reached with his bat and missed. "Not a good pitch," he repeated. The ball thumped against the rear door. No dent.

On the third try I concentrated hard and lobbed the perfect target of opportunity. The pitch floated straight down the middle like an inflatable beach ball, its arc perfect.

To say that Fred tagged the pitch would be an

understatement. The softball exploded from his aluminum bat like the shell of a howitzer. A metallic clang shattered the neighborhood's silence with the perfect blend of body torque, bat velocity, and an enlarged sweet spot. The projectile shot at my head. It whizzed through the air at fifty miles per hour. The speed seemed more like two hundred miles per hour given the short distance between us.

I hit the deck. Butt first in a heap. The blast missed my head by inches.

Fred looked at me, his expression uncertain yet satisfied. "Good pitch," he commended. I chuckled at first. But my uneasy relief gave way to belly laughs as Fred snickered.

Betty had been watching from the window. She flew out the front door, her panic palpable. "Are you okay?"

"Nothing that a cheeseburger and a glass of wine won't fix."

"I told you to be careful," she scolded playfully, realizing no one was hurt. "Fifteen minutes more," she added, and scooted back into the house.

"Okay, tiger," I said to Fred, "let's see you try that again."

He waggled his bat with big-league swagger. Fred missed a few pitches. But mostly he connected. Pop flies rained across the yard like fungoes during fielding practice. I caught a few, had no chance at most, and remembered for fifteen glorious minutes the joys that accompany summer softball. Pride being what it is, I hoped Betty did not watch all my errors through the kitchen window.

Our impromptu game of swat and fetch the soft-ball proved the perfect prelude to lunch. I was starved. Betty piled mushrooms, fried Vidalia onions, and fat slices of crispy bacon on top of the burgers. She laced pickles throughout the pile and used Muenster cheese to glue everything together. Bright red tomatoes, which will never see the inside of any burger I eat, garnished the plate right where they belonged. When Betty served strong coffee and chocolate-covered potato chips for dessert, I was happier than a dog with two tails.

Afterward, Betty had an agenda all her own. "Fred, why don't you play video games," she said. "Grove and I will take care of the dishes." The boy disappeared into the other room, clearly delighted to avoid the chores. She turned deadly serious. "Grove, I need your help."

"But *I* called *you*," I replied, confused by her comment.

"Yeah. Yeah. You're here because of Sam. I think you can help both of us."

Danger, Will Robinson.

People tussled all the time over money. Sam and Betty might clash one day for reasons not yet apparent. Instinctively, I flipped into top producer mode and started to probe, went on the offensive. "Sam said you invested with Charlie?"

"He had the Midas touch," Betty replied, flashing her 150-watt smile. "Where else could I get returns over twenty percent and stay safe?"

Twenty percent returns are never safe.

"Charlie knew how to make money," I acknowledged, avoiding the temptation to debate financial risk. "How much did you invest?"

"I don't have much money," she said, almost apologetically. "Not like your clients, Grove. My interior design business pays the bills, but sometimes jobs are slow. That's why we live in New Paltz rather than New York City."

Betty had not answered my question. She fiddled with a pearl earring, suddenly uncomfortable with our discussion. It was classic money angst. Outside a fifty-mile radius of Wall Street, polite company veered away from discussions about "how much."

"It's your money," I countered, trying to put Betty at ease. "You earned it. And I know you're saving for Fred. That makes it a fortune." Planning for children with special needs was always a challenge. I hoped my reference had not crossed a line.

"Thanks, Grove," she sighed. "It was two hundred and fifty thousand dollars. I had complained to Charlie about my mutual funds. The returns were pathetic."

"And he offered to invest your money?"

"He waived his minimums," Betty said, sounding matter-of-fact. "The Kelemen Group has a one million minimum, you know."

Charlie was a rock star of sales.

Betty was the client. She almost sounded thankful my best friend was managing her money. It should have been the other way around.

"Charlie was a good guy," I said, mentally chastising myself for the cynicism, remembering my six-month stay with the Kelemens. "You know what he did for me."

"We all have our Charlie stories," Betty empathized.

"Several years ago, Sam and Charlie commissioned me to decorate their house. That job saved my business."

The Kelemens' town house defined opulence—aged tapestries from Europe, the finest rugs from Turkey, and antique furniture from Asia. Their vibrant palette contrasted with the more soothing colors of Betty's home. "They spared no expense."

"Charlie picked out the paintings, but I did everything else. It was a huge job. He didn't even care about my fees." Her eyes moistened. "It was like he sponsored me."

"That was Charlie, our man from the Medici."

"I sold my funds the moment he offered to help, wrote a check that day."

Too bad she didn't wire the money. I could have gotten banking details for the Kelemen Group.

"I was taking control," she continued, "doing the right thing for Fred."

"You're a good mom."

"Oh, please," she demurred, shrugging off the praise.

"By any chance did you ever get an annual report for the fund?"

Audited statements, with a schedule of Charlie's hedge funds, would be enough to get started. The list would guide Ira Popowski for his work with state-appointed executors. Together, they could start the tedious process of redeeming investments. The list would also give me a head start on the auditors. When they called back, I could ask whether Charlie had made any changes to his roster of managers.

"I keep my statements," Betty replied. "But I probably tossed anything over a quarter-inch thick."

"Nice filing system," I laughed.

"I'm not kidding," she countered. "Before Charlie, my broker buried me with paperwork."

"Tell me about it. Our compliance is a nightmare at SKC. What did the Kelemen Group send?"

"Quarterly statements. One page."

"Sweet."

"Let me check my files," she offered, and started to stand. "Maybe I kept the annual report."

"Tell me something first."

"Grove, you sound so serious." She sat and quickly filled my wineglass as though to accentuate the point. Maybe it was self-defense.

"I'm curious about your call to Sam."

Betty smiled her dental blizzard.

"Why did you phone the day after the funeral?" I immediately regretted the question, artless, a touch confrontational. "I'm not trying to be combative. I just want to understand. Sam said you sounded uneasy."

"I was. I still feel like a jerk for calling so soon."

"Forget it. The Kelemen Group has obligations to its investors. Believe me, Sam understands completely."

"I know how things are in small companies," Betty remarked.

"You run one yourself."

"Right. There's not much backup. Sam probably needs to sort things out for the Kelemen Group." Betty traced a line on the table with her finger. "And I need to make sure my investment is in order."

"Absolutely," I agreed, choosing my next words carefully. "Sam is tending to the Kelemen Group." That was true. "Unfortunately, Charlie never brought her into the business. And now she's building her knowledge about the corporate affairs from scratch." Also true. "I'm sorting things out with the auditors and her estate attorney." More true than not, but worth a trip to confession.

"I feel so much better, Grove."

And I need to see Monsignor Byrd pronto.

My intent had been to show confidence, outward calm while gathering facts. It had been unnecessary to overstate my progress or inflate the meaning of Popowski's words, "I'm in."

"About those financial statements."

"Oh, right. Let me check," she replied, rising from the table. She noticed my glass, still half full, and asked, "Is the wine okay?"

"Perfect. It's just that I have to drive back to New York City."

"I know two hundred and fifty thousand is not much money in your world," Betty said as I rose. "But it's everything to Fred." She sounded hesitant, doubtful about her right to talk finance with a top producer.

"Stop. It's real money."

"I'll be right back," she said, and disappeared to find the paperwork.

I cleared the remaining dishes from lunch. The white wainscoting from the sunroom continued into a large, inviting kitchen filled with white appliances. The cupboards, with their see-through glass panels, were finished in antique white. Everyday wear and tear had created a patina that said *aged elegance*. Evelyn would have loved Betty's home. Finn would have loved the yard.

Betty reappeared and handed me a quarterly statement. "My home office is a disaster. Let me keep looking for the annual report. I'll call you."

"If you find it, great. If not, no big deal." I glanced at the sheet for a moment. Her $250,000 had grown to over $300,000.

Nice.

"Grove," Betty said, summoning my attention, "there's one other thing."

"Which is?"

"Charlie agreed to be Fred's guardian if anything happened to me. I need to find someone else now."

For the slightest instant it seemed Betty was asking me to take the job. She had several sisters, though, and I decided the request would be far too impulsive. Down's syndrome raised the stakes. Betty would be more careful.

"I'll help any way possible. Where's Fred?"

Several minutes later, after a hug and a handshake good-bye, I left New Paltz feeling queasy. The sour sensation had nothing to do with indigestion. My best friend, Mr. Detail, had failed his wife. Strike one. Now he had left a single mom feeling anxious about her son's welfare. Strike two.

Ease up. Liquidating the Kelemen Group will fix everything.

Yeah, right. The image of Betty and Fred waving

good-bye haunted me all the way back to New York City. The stakes had grown beyond Sam Kelemen's six hundred dollars and Frank Kurtz's instructions to mind my own business.

CHAPTER 17

At the frightful hour of five A.M. on Sunday, I focused on a more immediate issue than Charlie Kelemen's big mess. My problem was "bed suck." That's a cycling expression. It occurs when warm racks yank riders back under the covers and refuse to let us train. Right then and there, a swathe of luxuriant sheets was beckoning me to stay.

Only today, I was neither training nor about to succumb. Our club sponsored races every other Sunday during the summer, seven loops around the Central Park oval for a total of forty-three miles. The starting guns always sounded at six A.M. sharp.

We had a race. There was something exhilarating about the torturous cramps and spectacular crashes. Trash-talking among testosterone-laden rivals made racing a must. That Sunday I arrived at the starting line wide-awake with twenty minutes to spare.

It took the elite cyclists, the human lungs on steroids, less than two hours to kick my ass. My results were statistically good, tenth in the field of 124 cyclists. But a furious paceline had drained everything during the first

42.5 miles. I had no gas in the tank to contest the mad dash at the end. It pissed me off. I always wanted to win.

After the race I grabbed a twenty-ounce coffee and a slab of cinnamon crumb cake from Starbucks. The coffee and crumb cake were appetizers, barely enough to carry me through a steamy shower in my fifth-floor condominium. Given the hard riding, I had but one mission. Stuff my face with home fries, smoky sausages, cheesy three-egg omelets, and stacks of banana pancakes all in one sitting. There was a bacchanalian food orgy of 9,600 calories just ahead. It had the makings of a perfect day.

I was mistaken.

Jorge, the building's tip magnet and doorman of perpetual good cheer, buzzed my apartment before I could hop into the shower. "Mr. Grove, there are two policemen here to see you."

"You're kidding," I replied, thinking Sunday was an odd time for them to visit. No one had called, either.

"They showed me their badges." He sounded antsy, like he was pleading for me to bail him out.

"Send them up."

Moments later a pork-butt fist pummeled my front door and shattered the morning's tranquility. The thunderous knocks angered me. They were hardly necessary given Jorge's advance warning.

"Wait a minute," I hollered on the way to the door.

One of the officers stood six-four and weighed at least 275 pounds. His size shut me up fast. He looked like 9,600 calories all day, every day. The other policeman resembled an upright ferret with deep-set eyes. The two wore rumpled sport coats, their shirt collars open and Windsor knots flying half mast. It was not yet nine o'clock on a Sunday morning, but both men looked exhausted. They flashed their police badges in unison, a kick line of "cop cred."

The leviathan, curly brown hair, blue eyes, and ruddy face, announced, "I'm Detective Michael Fitzsimmons, and this is Officer Mummert. We're with the Boston Police Department." He spoke with a classic Boston accent, broad vowels and *r*'s on sabbatical. His torso bulged, a weight lifter's non-neck and a barrel chest capable of holding a few scuba tanks inside.

Fitzsimmons's gut jutted over an ornate brass belt buckle. There had to be a bar story. Maybe some hapless mechanical bull had collapsed under the officer's weight.

"Boston Police," Mummert echoed. He even sounded like a ferret.

"Why Boston? I thought you guys were NYPD."

"Boston has jurisdiction over this homicide," Fitzsimmons explained. "We're working in New York for now."

For a moment I stood my ground in the doorway. "You didn't return my call on Friday."

"Sorry," Fitzsimmons apologized. "We have a long list of people to interview. We tried your office on Saturday and left a message. We tried here, too, but no one picked up."

He was right. I had not turned on the answering machine, probably a Freudian thing that dated back to Evelyn and Finn. A message had been my first hint of tragedy. "Mr. O'Rourke. This is Officer Rizzo from New Haven. Will you call me please?" Answering services, even on my mobile phone, had been a source of apprehension ever since.

"But you're here on a Sunday?" I persisted.

"Like I said," the leviathan replied, "we have a long list of people."

I led the officers through the foyer past my bicycle, a carbon and titanium Colnago leaning against the wall under old photos of Bernard Hinault and Jacques Anquetil. Hinault had won the Tour de France five times and earned the nickname Le Blaireau (the Badger) because of the animal's reputation for never allowing prey to escape. Anquetil, another cycling great, hammed for the camera with a podium girl under his right arm.

"We need to ask you about Charlie Kelemen." Fitzsimmons rolled his head in an exaggerated orbit, as though to punctuate his sentence. The resulting cracks, bone against bone, made me wince.

"I assumed as much."

We huddled around three stools in the kitchen. Ordinarily, I would have done the Charleston-hospitality thing and offered them some coffee. Only I was starved now, consumed more by hunger than curiosity. Forty-three miles on a bike will do that.

"Got any coffee?" Fitzsimmons asked.

Oh, great. They're settling in.

"Yes," I replied, not offering to brew any. I really wanted to eat pancakes with bananas and maple syrup. None of that imitation crap, either. Only real maple syrup from Vermont.

"Make mine regular."

Talk about pushy.

"How about you?" I asked the ferret.

"Yeah, regular." Mummert's nose twitched.

From six years in Cambridge I knew "regular" meant cream and two sugars.

"That guy looks familiar," Fitzsimmons said, and pointed to a cyclist's photo overlooking the island counter.

"Familiar," Mummert agreed. "I never forget a face."

"Greg Lemond. First American to win the Tour de France."

"Why's he scowling?"

"He was a guest at my last dinner party," I joked.

Fitzsimmons blinked without smiling. He said nothing. Joe Friday plus 125 pounds. Officer Mummert, sunken brown eyes, pointy nose, small teeth, swallowed saliva or something, his Adam's apple bobbing up and down from the motion of peristalsis. He said nothing. Joe Friday minus 125 pounds. My audience had given me the hook.

"That's Lemond after he completed a stage in the Tour de France. He's grimacing," I explained, "because he had ridden thirty kilometers with diarrhea oozing down his legs."

"Why'd he do that?" Fitzsimmons asked, more curious than disgusted.

"Sometimes you can't stop."

"The diarrhea?" Fitzsimmons asked, amused by my unclear reference.

"Funny."

"Gives a whole new meaning to 'gotta go.'" Fitzsimmons cocked his head to the right with a crack. He cocked it to the left with another.

I hate when people do that shit.

Mummert fidgeted, not interested. His eyes darted round the room, visually clearing my condominium from force of habit. His wrinkled sport coat looked like it had seen action as a pajama top.

"How well did you know Mr. Kelemen?" Fitzsimmons asked.

"Best friend."

"Any enemies?"

"He pissed off a Yalie named Hurley once. But that's it."

"Lila Priouleau's ex," Fitzsimmons confirmed.

The due diligence impressed me. "You spoke with Lila?"

"What do you think about Hurley?" Fitzsimmons shot back, taking command, not answering my question.

"Total loser. Beat his wife. But I doubt he killed anyone."

"Why's that?"

"The guy's a wuss. We haven't seen him in years."

"You're a bright guy," Fitzsimmons observed.

I hate when people start that way.

"And the victim was your best friend. You must have suspicions about someone."

"Charlie was a human Rolodex," I said.

"Short and boxy?" Mummert interrupted.

"That too. He knew everybody, more people than

me, and that's saying something. All my friends loved Charlie Kelemen."

"Somebody didn't." With that comment, both cops began firing questions. They barely waited for my response to each round.

Fitzsimmons: "How long did you know the victim?"

Mummert: "What do you know about his work?"

Fitzsimmons: "Who were his closest associates?"

Mummert: "Where'd you get your Southern accent?" Clearly, no topic was taboo.

Fitzsimmons: "Did you see anything strange at the aquarium?"

"Well, yes," I replied. "There were two hundred and fifty men wearing black tie and burkas."

Mummert: "Do you remember anyone pushing a stainless-steel cart?"

Fitzsimmons: "Where were you when Mr. Kelemen fell into the tank?"

Mummert: "Was he drinking?"

Fitzsimmons: "Did you notice anything unusual before the party?"

I had watched my share of *Law & Order* reruns. The questions sounded routine. Mummert, however, probed the more personal issues. I didn't like it. "Nice place," the thin officer observed in low, guttural tones. "Big for a bachelor." He shifted on his stool.

"Widower," I corrected, and held up my left hand to display the wedding band. Inside, it read: "Grove, you are my truc love. Evelyn."

"Sorry," Mummert apologized. "There aren't family

pictures anywhere," he observed, "just all these guys with bikes."

"I keep the photos of my wife and daughter hidden. Tough in an empty house." Both police raised their eyebrows at the mention of "daughter."

Months after the accident on I-95 North, I quarantined all memories of Finn and Evelyn. Their feminine scents had clung relentlessly to the closets and drawers. Their photos, scattered everywhere, filled me with longing. I stuffed girl things—clothes, jewelry, the whole shebang—into Finn's bedroom. So began the somber diaspora of self-preservation. There was no other way to cope. My picture at work, Evelyn and Finn at the beach, was the only one out.

Every few months Charlie suggested I donate Evelyn's gems to charity. "Here's how I see it. Evelyn was all Yankee. Frugal. Practical. Logical. You probably have four hundred thousand dollars' worth of stones there. Take a tax deduction. Evelyn would approve. It's cash in your pocket. Giving it to another woman would piss her off."

"Another woman, Charlie? I can't even think about a date."

"Yeah, yeah. There will be a day," he replied dismissively. "I can take care of the jewelry, the receipts, all the crap you need for the IRS. I know the right guys on Forty-seventh Street."

"I don't know, Charlie."

"What's not to know?"

"I'll think about it."

"That's all I ask. But don't you ever bitch about your taxes to me."

The opportunity to bitch at Charlie about anything was long gone. Evelyn's jewelry box still sat on the nursery bureau, still full, the issue still unresolved.

Mummert, Fitzsimmons, and I sat. We said nothing. We breathed the miserable air. Fitzsimmons finally interrupted the moment. "How would you describe Mrs. Kelemen's relationship with her husband?"

"What do you mean?" I asked, genuinely puzzled.

"They seem like an odd pair."

"Really odd," Mummert agreed.

"He was fat," Fitzsimmons continued, "and she is . . ."

"Smoking hot," I finished for him. "You're a big guy, Detective. How's your love life?"

Fitzsimmons, a powerful man unaccustomed to rebukes, backtracked. "I don't mean to offend you." He opened his palms and tilted his head to the side. His words soothed, but his body language said, *I know the thought's crossed your mind.*

"Charlie worshiped Sam."

"What about her?"

"What do you mean?"

"Was Mrs. Kelemen faithful?" Fitzsimmons clarified.

"She never misses Mass."

"That's not what I meant," the big man snapped.

"No shit. I have no idea."

Fitzsimmons tilted his head to the left, and his neck crackled like cereal. "Listen," he snorted. "I have a murder on my hands. I have a victim with lacerations up and down his arms and a serving cart tied to his leg. I have a fish tank full of ripe chum. All the blood sends three sharks into a feeding frenzy, even though this particular species never attacks humans. Until now. I have a nation that watched the whole incident on the evening news, and they're horrified. They want answers. No one asked for another low-budget sequel to *Jaws*. Least of all me. I have a boss harassing me. Twenty-five years on the force and he's never seen anything like it. He wants to know who turned your friend's head into a burger. And everywhere I go, people tell me how great Charlie Kelemen was. 'A saint. No enemies. Salt of the earth.' I have zero leads. Count 'em. I have a distraught aquarium staff. They're still suffering from nightmares about what happened on their watch. The mayor and the governor both want answers. One of our senators is calling for a national hearing. At this rate, it won't be long before I'm a regular on *Meet the* Fucking *Press*." Fitzsimmons paused to breathe. "So tell me, Mr. O'Rourke. How was their marriage?" His eyes drilled mine.

It was my turn to snap. "Is she a suspect?" I demanded angrily.

"Who isn't?"

"Sam Kelemen," I barked, rushing to her rescue. "We all saw what happened. She was up to her eyeballs with a belly dancer when Charlie appeared in the tank. There must have been five hundred people watching."

"I'm trying to understand the background," Fitzsimmons pressed. "So I'll ask again. Was Mrs. Kelemen involved with anyone else?"

"No way," I snapped. "Not in a million years. Sam adored Charlie. She's a mess. And she has no money."

"No money?" Mummert mumbled.

"You don't know?"

"Know what?" both officers replied, an unintentional chorus.

"She has money," I backtracked, "but it's all tied up in his business. She's illiquid."

"Insurance?" Fitzsimmons asked.

"Charlie didn't believe in it. Most people in my business don't. Besides, there's plenty of value in the Kelemen Group."

"What do you know about the business?"

"Not much. Charlie ran a small fund of funds. I would guess about two hundred million in assets."

"What's a fund of funds?" Mummert asked.

I'm never going to get those pancakes.

For twenty minutes more I described Charlie Kelemen's wealth and his Midas touch. I explained the Kelemen Group's business, doing my best to avoid the technical stuff like alpha and other measures of performance. Charlie knew every hedgie in town, wined and dined them all. It was the sum total of my knowledge. It seemed like nothing.

When we finally finished "Fund of Funds 101," Mummert headed for the door. He was anxious to leave. I was anxious to see both officers go but asked, "Is it possible for me to get access to Charlie's office?"

"What for?" Fitzsimmons replied.

"I'm helping Sam wind down the Kelemen Group. I'd like to look through his files."

"Won't happen," the big officer refused, "not until we tie up this homicide." Fitzsimmons retrieved a business card from the folds of his jacket and scrawled a 212 number on the back. "Thanks for your help. If you think of anything, give us a call. Just do me a favor, and don't interfere with our investigation." Mummert said nothing. The two left. No "good-bye." All business.

In the empty silence of my apartment, I realized a pattern had formed. Cliff Halek, my friend, my confidant, had started it. At least I trusted him. Kurtz followed. Now it was the police. Everybody was telling me to back off Charlie Kelemen's affairs. I had not heard so much rejection since my first days of cold-calling eight years ago.

En route to the shower, at last, I noticed the door to Finn's room was ajar. It always remained shut, a lid on my memories. Summer humidity sometimes sprung the door and released the lingering scents of mother and daughter. In that whiff of an instant my resolve magnified tenfold. Sam Kelemen. Betty and Fred Masters. It was clear what was necessary.

I don't give a shit who objects.

CHAPTER 18

It was seven-thirty Monday morning. I sat at my desk, concentrating hard and nursing a tasteless cup of coffee. Betty's statement showed her home address in New Paltz and Charlie's business address on Broadway. Two lines recorded her investment. The first read: "The Kelemen Group Fund of Funds, Series B: $307,931."

Solid return on $250,000.

The second read "A Class of the Kelemen Group Master Trust."

Legal fingerprints all over that description. If Popowski's firm didn't do the work, who did?

The phone rang. It was Halek. "You awake, Grove?"

"Not only awake, I have good news for you."

"Which is?" he asked, somewhat startled by my early-morning energy.

"I spoke with my mom over the weekend. She says Catholics are letting Jews into heaven."

"Great. Tell your mom that Jews are letting Catholics onto Wall Street." Halek never missed a beat.

"Nice."

"Jack Oil," he said, shifting to business. "I'm about to do you a favor."

Favor?

The mere mention of Jack always made me perk up and pay attention. It was JJ's company after all. He was my biggest client, a guy important enough for me to put everything else on hold. That included Charlie Kelemen and his unfortunate stew.

Macbeth's witches can take a number.

"I'm all ears, Cliff."

"Is JJ going to hedge?" he asked.

"No clue." Cliff was not one to pressure for a trade. He had posed the same question on Friday. Here it was Monday, the market not yet open, JJ probably not in the office, and Halek was dragooning me for a trade. Not his style. "Why do you ask?"

"You may lose that business."

"How's that?"

"You know the drill," he replied. "No borrow, no zero-cost collar."

"Shit." Cliff had just spoken volumes.

JJ owned $190 million of one stock. *That's risky as shit.* The markets can cut share prices 60, 70, or 80 percent in seconds. If Jack Oil crashed 50 percent, for example, JJ would lose $95 million. That's why I wanted him to hedge.

A zero-cost collar would insure JJ against losses greater than the first 10 percent. Of the $95 million loss, JJ would eat the first $19 million. That's 10 percent of $190 million. But with SKC's hedge in place, my firm would pay him $76 million. That's $95 million minus the $19 million. JJ limited his downside and avoided catastrophic losses.

He could have avoided all risk simply by selling his shares. But JJ was bullish on the stock and wanted to retain upside. Typically, we could structure a trade that gave him appreciation equal to the first 20 percent. If JJ's position increased 20 percent to $228 million, therefore, he kept every dime. It beat selling if you were a CEO betting on your company's future.

Anything over $228 million belonged to SKC. That upside was valuable to my firm. Selling it was valuable to JJ. By trading some of his upside for downside protection, he never wrote a check to cover the insurance. That's why we call these derivatives "zero-cost collars."

I'd take that trade all day long. A risk of down 10 percent for upside of plus-20 percent.

There was no alchemy in a zero-cost collar. If SKC agreed to insure JJ's position, we would borrow shares of Jack Oil and sell them short. In effect, we hedged our own obligations as the stock collapsed. Our gains would fund the payments to Jumping JJ.

There was only one problem according to Cliff. "No borrow, no zero-cost collar." Shares are seldom available to borrow in unlimited quantities. Many factors affect the supply. Who owns the shares? How volatile are they? Has demand consumed the available reserve? The reason made no difference. If SKC could not borrow Jack, we would never collar JJ's stock.

One other thing. There are no visible commissions

in zero-cost collars. We don't explain the inscrutable mechanics of "delta hedging." But make no mistake. Costless collars contain plenty of cha-ching. This is Wall Street, not church.

We charge high prices for downside protection— one dollar when a reasonable price is ninety cents. We pay low prices for upside participation—one dollar when the fair market value is $1.10. The dollars zcro out so clients don't see our profits. But missing a big collar, assuming JJ authorized it, would cost me a few hundred thousand dollars in earnings.

That was the least of my problems.

"What's the issue with the borrow, Cliff?"

"It's tight," he replied.

"That's nothing new," I countered. "There aren't many lenders under normal circumstances."

"The lenders are the same," he explained. "There may be a trade that forces my desk to borrow all their available shares."

"Is the demand from hedge funds?"

"No." He paused before answering, "Inside PCS."

"Who?"

"You know I can't answer that." It would have been inappropriate for Halek to discuss another broker's business.

"Cliff, listen to me. Jack Oil's major shareholders are all institutions. Fidelity. Vanguard. Major hedge funds. To my knowledge there's only one client of PCS with a major position in the company. That's JJ. I cover him. And he's not ready to hedge."

"The issue isn't who," Cliff shot back. "I don't know who the client is. Don't care. The issue is the borrow. There's someone with a competing interest. If JJ wants to trade, he needs to get off the dime."

"You're right. Thanks. I'm still curious who the broker is."

"Figure it out. I've said too much already."

The realization struck me like a falling piano. "Gershon's been sniffing all over Jack Oil."

"You didn't hear it from me," Cliff replied.

What the hell is she doing?

CHAPTER 19

By the time Cliff and I finished, the research analysts had updated their stock opinions with one of three ratings: "buy, sell, or we don't have a fucking clue."

It was eight A.M., five minutes before the start of our firm-wide Strategy meeting. Chloe waved from her desk, already plugged into that monstrous headset, already advising clients what to make of Wall Street's indecision.

Annie beamed, light tan, golden-blond hair, starched white blouse. "How'd you do in the race?" she asked as I rose to leave.

"Tenth out of one hundred and twenty-four," I reported, neither pride nor apology in my voice.

"Got your ass kicked? You're not putting on weight, are you?" She patted my stomach playfully as though patrolling for paunch.

"Hey now."

"No middle-age mush," she concluded. Approval registered in her voice. "Wouldn't pay to lose the six-pack."

"I'll make a note."

"Tough love, Boss. Tough love."

* * *

Upstairs in our auditorium I checked e-mails and fidgeted with my BlackBerry. Scores of colleagues from every division, Investment Banking to Global Capital Markets, filled the rows. More and more women had joined our firm through the years. But they were still the minority.

Patty Gershon's cream-colored Chanel stuck out like a sore thumb among the drab business suits. Her signature Ferrari-red lipstick, bright and glossy, said, *Look at me.* She sat next to Sutherling, the energy banker who had referred Thayer. The two laughed and waited for Strategy to begin. They were clearly enjoying each other's company, Lady Goldfish glomming onto the banker who had given me a $100 million referral.

She's pumping him for leads.

I looked away, avoiding the temptation to stare. Several rows up, an especially dense cluster of bald men caught my attention. They looked like a rack of worried cue balls, tapping into their BlackBerrys, fretting about the week ahead. Ordinarily, the sight would have been amusing. Not today. Patty was bugging the shit out of me, my mood growing worse by the minute.

She's outflanking me with Sutherling.

Our four hoary strategists—global, domestic, fixed income, and economic—would begin soon. Every Monday they predicted the market direction for the upcoming week. From a top-down perspective, their conclusions generally parroted the analysts who preceded them: "buy, sell, or we don't have a fucking clue."

What's your game, Gershon?

After watching Strategy for eight years, I can report with absolute conviction that "smart money" leaves much to be desired. SKC's panel discussions—ego fests of Malthusian magnitude—often disintegrated into verbal sparring sessions, heavy on one-liners, light on facts. Our four pallbearers of market gravitas would clear their throats with annoying regularity, quip about each other's false teeth, and suck the room clean of all oxygen.

Otto Galbraith, SKC's resident perma-bear, opened discussion the same as always. He forecast Armageddon with one of his trademark wisecracks: "The market is going to hell in a Prada handbag."

The room sputtered with nervous laughter. The cue balls punched their BlackBerrys, all thumbs blazing. Barely cracking a smile, I glanced back at Patty.

What's your interest in Jack Oil?

Gershon edged closer to Sutherling, her hand holding the back of his seat, not quite touching his shoulders. He was divorced, his marriage the casualty of late nights and countless business trips to the oil fields of Texas. Patty was divorced, too, her failed marriage the stuff of shudders, a grim reminder there are worse things in life than eighteen months of celibacy. The mother of three, she was knocking out a big career in an environment where middle-aged white guys still retained a chokehold on power.

Cut her some slack.

Unfortunately, there was only one logical explanation for Patty's interest in Jack Oil's borrow. And with it, all my charitable instincts dissipated.

You better not be talking to JJ about a collar.

Patty would never pitch my client so overtly. Even Kurtz, the boss with no backbone, would shut her down. Wall Street's managers resolved coverage disputes through simple questions: Who opened the account? Who got there first? Any revenues yet? Patty would never win that argument. She knew it. I knew it.

Pay attention to Strategy.

Otto was my moneymaker. I ordinarily listened to his advice and wrote down every word, though not for the reasons he thought. Whatever he recommended, I did just the opposite. If he said, "Buy pharma," the abbreviation for pharmaceuticals, I shorted the sector with a vengeance. When he said, "Sell," I backed up the truck.

Gershon has no chance with JJ.

There are plenty of cynics among stockbrokers. Glib analysts have burned all advisers at one time or another. There was more to my investment style, though, than simple disenchantment. Through the years, our chief economist had crafted an almost unblemished track record for being wrong.

Otto on Google in 2004: "Management's untested. I doubt the stock ever trades over its IPO price." Google went public at $85. It's over $500 now.

Otto on oil in 2005: "Crude prices will range between forty and fifty dollars a barrel for years." It crossed $70 this summer. It's headed higher, as best as I can tell.

Otto on Wall Street last year: "Two thousand seven will be a banner year for financial services." Right now, banks and brokerages are grappling with billions in bad assets from the subprime mortgage fiasco.

Never one to be daunted by personal error, our chief economist preached doom and gloom throughout the greatest bull market of the twentieth century. Had I listened to his advice, my clients would have bolted long ago. In fairness, Otto got it right once. As early as 1999, he forecast the burst of the technology bubble. He labeled his most infamous publication "The Coming Rupture of Dot-comdom." An unfortunate image if you ask me.

It bothered me that SKC's chief economist was such a steady and reliable contra-leading indicator. But clients loved my portfolio returns. We laughed and agreed, "It's a beautiful thing."

As Otto spoke, I glanced at Patty and happened to find her appraising me. She winked once, blew a Ferrari-red kiss in my direction, and turned her attention back to the panel discussion. Afterward, I didn't hear another word my moneymaker was saying.

There are times when every top producer needs to rally, even from Gershon-induced funks. Monday morning was one of them. Slipping out of Strategy a few minutes early, I returned to the fourth floor. Frank Kurtz, with support from SKC's entire chain of command, had asked me to lecture a class of freshly minted MBAs.

It was hardly "teaching." My job was to tell war stories before our rookies began cold-calling in earnest.

"Open their eyes," Kurtz had said. "Get them jacked up so they hit the ground running."

Do I look like Tony Fucking Robbins to you?

Frankly, I had never expected to teach at SKC. Top producers did not tutor. We stalked bazillionaires and ate what we killed. It would have been a career-limiting gesture, however, to send "no" all the way back to the CEO. I willed myself to suck it up and forget Lady Goldfish, to forge ahead with my class.

Zola Mancini, a newbie with a monster personality in a modest package, caught me in the hall leading to the classroom. She stood about five-five, though I was uncertain about her exact height. She always wore heels and moved with seductive grace, a practiced swish of the hips that made it impossible to tell where athletic legs ended and Gucci heels began.

Those legs made some men whip their heads around in double takes. Others focused on the shirts that bunched at her breasts. For me it was Zola's black hair. A thick shock of kinky curls consumed her head. It was as though the hair follicles had exploded. Silky streamers of unruly locks ran wild across her dark, exotic features.

Today an enormous bandage covered one ear. Even under her mop of hair, layers of gauze bubbled out for the entire world to see. "What happened to your ear?"

"I had plastic surgery." Zola smirked whenever she spoke. A wisecrack lurked round every sentence.

"Since when do ears need bodywork?"

"Stretched asshole," she said, holding her hands six inches apart, palms facing each other, a nonverbal gesture indicating size.

"Nice mouth," I snorted. Good thing I had not been drinking coffee. I would have kecked caffeine all over the place.

Zola's eyes twinkled, delighted by my reaction. "Hey, my earrings stretched the lobe out of shape. The hole was gross." Her expression was half smirk, half smile, and total killer.

Source material for obsession.

"So what are we learning today?" Zola continued innocently.

"Asset protection," I replied. "Prenups, offshore trusts, ways to avoid gold-digging litigation raptors. And with your mouth, Zola, you'd better pay close attention."

"Don't worry about me, Sensei. I can hide my money in Swiss bank accounts with the best of them."

To this day I have no idea why Zola's comment returned me to the horror of that night in the New England Aquarium. Perhaps it was her bandaged ear rather than the reference to the Swiss bank account. But in that moment, the world ground to a halt. I forgot Zola and the class of newbies waiting expectantly. On the brink of a personal epiphany, I even forgot Lady Goldfish and her unholy spawn. I thought only about Charlie Kelemen and his last few minutes alive.

The killer tortured him.

The gashes. The cuts on his arms and legs. The psychological terror of a makeshift anchor tied to his ankles. The killer abused Charlie, both mentally and physically, long before the sharks ground his viscera with their rows of serrated teeth. Charlie's spectacular death, five hundred people watching him shovel gak and guts back inside, had been a cover. The extravaganza overshadowed true intent.

The killer wanted information.

Maybe Charlie kept all their money in a Swiss bank account. Maybe he kept it closer to home. Whatever. Somebody filleted Charlie's arms and legs on the edge of the Giant Ocean Tank, tortured him with pain greater than a thousand paper cuts. Why? To make him talk? To locate his money? Did the Kelemens possess a vast fortune far greater than I realized? The über-wealthy hired bodyguards all the time. Charlie didn't. Maybe that was his first and last mistake.

When Charlie didn't talk, the killer tossed him into the tank, frustrated in his attempts to find any money, frustrated just like me. Or maybe Charlie confessed everything. His assassin found the money, and now it was long gone. At least the killer couldn't steal Sam's money from the Kelemen Group. Court oversight would ensure an orderly return of all proceeds to investors.

Warnings from Halek, Kurtz, and Boston's finest suddenly seemed less panicky. More reasonable. They were right.

The killer wants the same information I want.

"Hey, Sensei, you still with me?" Zola snapped me out of my reverie, as we both entered the classroom. There were twenty newbies—ready, waiting, starry-eyed, fearless. They smiled enthusiastically, anticipating both wisdom and war stories from a top producer. I blinked once, twice, searching for words, struggling to extract myself from the nightmare of the New England Aquarium.

"Listen up, numb nuts," I directed, returning to the present. "Let's get started on asset protection."

CHAPTER 20

"Hey, O'Rourke."

Class had ended, and I was returning to my desk. Patty's voice cut through the rowdy din of brokers as they counseled clients and tongue-lashed traders. Mondays were always busy. Close on my heels, Gershon pierced Scully's deafening decibels and made me forget Casper's pestering plinks. Those two words, "Hey, O'Rourke," exposed my position deep behind the enemy lines of Estrogen Alley.

Stay cool. Don't betray Halek. Not a word about Jack Oil.

I went the ambassadorial route as we continued to walk. "Nice haircut." Goldfish or not, Patty deserved the compliment. Her short, stylish locks would trigger double takes among the chic set of Parisian nightclubs. My strategy was simple. Throw out an olive branch. Avoid confrontation. Call Jumping JJ the second she's gone.

"Did you hear about Frank?" she asked.

"No, what happened?" I asked, instantly alarmed by the tone of her voice.

"Kurtz is fine. The client has a problem."

"What do you mean?"

"Hunting accident. Frank shotgunned a guy's hand over the weekend. Another Dick Cheney."

"That's awful."

"You got that right, O'Rourke. I bet the client pulls his account."

"That's not what I meant."

"Whatever. Have you given any more thought to Jumping JJ?"

"Not much," I lied. Truth be told, I wouldn't share a heart attack with Patty Gershon, let alone a client.

"Hey, Boss," Annie interrupted, "Mandy Maris is on your first line."

My world erupted. Had I been in Italy, that nation would have forgotten Mount Vesuvius. Snatching the receiver from its cradle, forgetting Gershon and my team, I exploded, "What is it you don't understand about no? If I were drawing my last breath on earth, I wouldn't talk to the press."

Maybe it was the trick of a veteran reporter. Maybe it was simple anger. Maris counterattacked. She never cowered. She disemboweled my oversized ego, a flaw shared by every top producer. "Alex Romanov is helping my story every way he can. That's why he runs a hedge fund and you're just an employee who can't fart without company approval."

"Good. Talk to Romanov." With that I slammed down the phone.

"Who was that?" Gershon asked, wide-eyed from the mini-explosion she had just witnessed. Annie and Chloe both blinked with surprise.

"It's a long story, and I don't have the time."

"We should talk," Gershon cooed, touching my shoulder, trying to ease the tension.

"Patty, JJ's account is open. There's no way I'm splitting economics." My words surged, direct and to the point.

"Your relationship may not be as deep as you think."

"What makes you say that? You just met JJ at a party."

"We spent forty-five minutes together," Patty countered. "You'd be surprised what a girl can learn."

"Such as?"

"He has two-point-three million shares of Jack Oil you haven't hedged."

"That's public record, Patty. I'm not impressed."

"You can't borrow enough shares to collar JJ's stock," she persisted. "It's too tight."

Only if you're competing for borrow, Gershon.

"Plus," she added before I could speak, "he won't go for it."

I flipped. "How do you know what JJ thinks? Have you been calling my client?"

"Of course not," she soothed. "Let's just say, I've done my homework."

Talk about condescending.

"I want to bounce an idea off you," she added.

"Okay, Patty," I said, doing my best to project bored resignation. In reality, she had piqued my curiosity. "What's on your mind?"

"Not here," she replied coyly. "Not where everybody can hear. I'm running to my daughter's recital in a few.

I'll swing by your desk tomorrow, and we'll grab a conference room." I recognized the sales tools of a top producer: mystery, suspense, and the hint of good things to follow.

Am I being played?

"Great," I said, no conviction in my voice. For a moment we lingered, then parted abruptly.

"Keep an open mind, O'Rourke," Patty coaxed, positive thinking through and through.

"Annie, any calls this morning?"

"Sorry about Mandy Maris," she replied, not answering the question. The force of my eruption had apparently surprised her, too.

"It's not you," I said. "I have this thing about the press."

"Betty Masters called," she reported, relieved, now addressing matters at hand.

"Oh?"

"She needed our fax number."

"What for?" I asked, suddenly optimistic.

"She said something about audited financial statements for the Kelemen Group. Apparently, you wanted them. She has them."

"Out-fucking-standing. By any chance, did Crain and Cravath call?"

"Who?" Annie asked.

"I'll take that as a no. They prepared the financial statements Betty is sending."

"There's one other thing," Annie said.

"Give me a few minutes. I need to call JJ right quick."

An unfamiliar voice answered at Jack Oil. "Mr. Jaworski's office."

"It's Grove. You must be JJ's new assistant. Is he there?"

"May I tell him what this is in reference to?"

Every stockbroker has heard that line before. It's the age-old screen for phone solicitations, annoying when you're building a book, a breeze when you're a top producer. "He knows me," I replied. "And you will, too."

"Grove," JJ boomed into the receiver thirty seconds later, "how's my stock?"

"Up a half on above-average volume. That's one reason I'm calling. When can we continue our discussion about collaring?"

"Next week," he replied. "I'm buried. And honestly, I'm lukewarm on the concept. I don't like anyone shorting my stock. Even if it's to hedge me."

"Who told you about shorting?" I asked. "We hadn't gotten that far in our discussion."

"I met one of your colleagues at a party about ten days ago."

"Patty Gershon?"

"That's her," he replied. "She's explained the whole kit and shebang." JJ, ever the Eastern European emigrant, still butchered our idioms from time to time. "She's smart, Grove."

She eats her young, JJ.

"There are plenty of smart people at SKC," I said, "and Patty's right. Collars require us to short. But I'd like to discuss the technique at your office with your general counsel present."

"Call me next Monday," he replied. "We'll put something on the calendar." Then he added, "You said 'one reason.' What's the other reason you called?"

"It can wait," I replied. JJ had already addressed my other reason for calling—Patty Gershon. She crossed the line. She advised my client. She interfered and undermined me in the process. Had she been a guy, I would have kicked whatever the liposuction had missed.

Patty's chair in Estrogen Alley was empty. Already gone, I noted. One more call to make.

"Crain and Cravath," the receptionist answered on the second ring.

"Grove O'Rourke here. Who handles the Kelemen Group?"

"I need to check. May I get your number, Mr. O'Rourke? We'll call back."

The joys of dealing with small audit firms.

"Please do. We've left at least two messages already." Sam on Thursday. Me on Friday.

Hanging up the phone, I called over to Annie, "Didn't mean to cut you off."

"Sam Kelemen phoned. She has big news."

"What? Tell me." My mood immediately brightened.

"She wouldn't say."

"Did you tell her I'd call back?"

"No." Annie grinned fiendishly. Her eyes danced with mischief. She spoke no further.

"That's it? No?" Annie pushed my buttons with the best.

"Not exactly. I took a few liberties with your schedule."

"Such as?"

"You're having dinner with Sam at Live Bait. Tonight at six-thirty. I told Sam to meet you there. And I promised you won't be late."

"I see." Even though our team used a group calendar on Outlook, I arranged all my own appointments. But Annie's decision pleased me. In a voice balanced unsteadily between feigned exasperation and delight, I asked, "Is there anything else I should know about my schedule?"

"Yes." She grinned. Her eyes sparkled. Annie knew more about flirting than Bobby Fisher knew about chess.

"And that would be what?" I asked with my hand on my hip in mock exasperation.

"You're taking Chloe and me out for drinks before."

"What about her kids?" Chloe was a single mom. The child-care question came to mind first.

"Don't worry. Chloe's parents have them tonight."

"Well, aren't you two enterprising. May I inquire what the occasion is?"

"Well, Boss, it's like this. I promised Sam you'd be on time. Check. We'll get you there. Then there's this other matter."

"And that would be?"

"We the jury find you guilty of working the team too hard."

"Little lady," I replied in my best impersonation of John Wayne, "out here, due process is a credit card." The Duke had nothing on me.

CHAPTER 21

Live Bait would not have been my first choice for dinner. But Annie had insisted.

"Lighten up, Boss. It's a girl thing."

The ramshackle restaurant reminded me too much of Charleston. Of my legacy growing up with SOBs. Of the cliquish Southern bluebloods who delighted in shabby-chic watering holes. I never quite grasped their affection for Big John's on East Bay Street. Appointed with items rejected by eBay, the bar was little more than an outhouse with a liquor license. And here in New York City, a similar dump was thriving near the corner of Twenty-third Street and Fifth Avenue.

With Charleston in my past, I would forever consider myself an outsider in any social setting. Unlike my family, scions of the Holy City had lived in the same neighborhoods, sometimes the same houses, for generations. They banded together in loose cartels that dominated the city's DNA. They argued politics nonstop, like whether to unfurl Confederate flags atop government buildings, and occasionally drank too much at oyster shucks when nightly ocean breezes failed to chase the daily haze. They bucked change and distrusted outsiders. They waged war on progress from their homes south of Broad Street, the posh part of the peninsula, while their brick and stucco houses waged war against time and the ravages of termites. Their sobriquet, SOBs, was a geographic reference to South of Broad rather than bastard bloodlines, and they decreed that families live in Charleston for one hundred years before achieving the hallowed status of "local."

That one-hundred-year rule excluded my family. We had emigrated from an Air Force base nestled in America's heartland of Knob Noster, Missouri. We did not have Southern names like Cooper, Ashley, or Palmer. We had family names, like Grover, that would forever betray our status as foreigners. We did not speak like locals. We spoke like Air Force mutts, our accents amalgamated from my father's posts as far away as Clark Air Force Base in the Philippines.

I tried to assimilate, at least some in voice. It took months of SOB osmosis, immersion therapy akin to Berlitz, before I lapsed into the soothing rhythm of syllabic expansion and turned one-syllable words into two. Boat became "bow-at," and with time "eggs" morphed into something that sounded like "a-igs." I even stopped using the letter *R*, my twenty-five-letter alphabet a harbinger of later years in Cambridge, Massachusetts. When I said the word for "balcony," it came out "poach." And I perfected the Southern verb conjugations of syrupy deference, mastering new tenses like "might could." To my everlasting horror, I once asked a woman during high school "if we might could go to the movies."

Sam could have dated anyone at Wellesley. She was smart and athletic, her body toned from varsity track. There were hundreds of introductions, hundreds of Harvard guys locked in male perma-heat who came sniffing. She didn't care. Until Charlie Kelemen waddled into Sam's life, courting and *Cosmopolitan* made her teeth hurt.

Our dinner hardly qualified as a date. We were two friends. We were meeting to drink wine and compare notes. I owed Sam an update of my progress. Apparently, she had her own agenda.

What's the big news?

At precisely 6:45 P.M. with shrimp poppers and several glasses of wine under our belts, Chloe and Annie said good-bye. They left me to wait for Sam among the vinyl-covered chairs and Formica tables circa 1950, underneath the ceiling tiles that sagged precariously. A hard sneeze would have shaken the pressed tin loose. Perhaps the bric-a-brac littering the walls, too. Annie had laughed at the old bait freezer in the back. "Blood-worms" was stenciled on one end, "marriages performed" on the other.

Sam arrived twenty minutes later. For all her many gifts, she had no sense of time. It would have been just like her to burrow into some project and forget about dinner. Evelyn and I once set Sam up on a blind date during college, and she failed to show. Later, mortified, apologetic, she explained, "I fell into one of my art history books and forgot. Sorry." In some ways Charlie's absolute control over family finances made complete sense. She never would have paid the bills on time.

The sweet pucker had returned to Sam's lips since last Friday, the sparkle to her eyes. Her skin glowed, and her black hair glistened. Opting for a plain black top, she had already abandoned Charlie's penchant for flamboyant attire. Simple fashion suited her.

"How was your day?" she asked.

"Dear," I said, finishing the sentence.

"Huh?"

" 'How was your day, dear?' That's the expression."

"Oh, stop it. I'm curious."

"I told a reporter to get stuffed, got into a fight with a colleague named Lady Goldfish, and FedExed a rubber chicken to a prospect. All in all, I'd say it was just another day at the office."

Ask me about the reporter.

"Why the chicken?"

"To snap a guy out of his funk. He wants to be a client, but he's dragging his feet. Won't make a decision."

"And your FedEx sends the right message?" Sam asked, smiling wryly.

"Well," I said, measuring my words, "a rubber chicken seems more politically correct than hot dogs. I almost sent him a package of weenies."

"Oh, stop it," she repeated, laughing now. "It's a wonder you have any clients."

"Hey, whatever it takes. In my profession everything works. And nothing works."

"It's sweet that Annie arranged for us to meet here," Sam said, changing the subject. "Did she know the four of us were regulars?"

"Probably not. She said Live Bait is a 'girl thing.' "

"Beats me," Sam observed on behalf of girl things everywhere.

"Annie said you have news, right?" Without thinking or stopping to listen, I rapid-fired a second question: "Do you want a bottle of wine with dinner?"

"Yes and no." Sam glowed, and I decided she had never looked more beautiful. Or maybe my drinks were taking their toll. Maybe I needed to slow down on the sauce.

"What's that mean?"

"It means yes, I have news. And no, I don't want any wine."

"Okay?"

I had never seen Sam drink to excess. Or go without. Nobody could teetotal around Charlie. Or could they? I remembered Sam's birthday party. Surrounded by guests and nose-high with Neylan's navel, Sam had toasted the belly dancer with a full glass of wine. Sam never drank that night, not even a sip.

Now Sam's remarkable blue eyes taunted me. She offered no clues. She gave no hints. When it finally hit me, disbelief first, then exuberance, I raced round from my side of the booth and squeezed Sam and cheek-kissed her and announced in a voice raspy from the rounds, "What a gift."

She pushed me away. "What are you talking about, Grove?"

"You're not pregnant?" My face turned scarlet, and I felt every bit the jackass.

Sam showed no emotion. Her expression was a mask, stoic and inscrutable. After an eternity plus some, she decided enough was enough. "Gotcha," she relented, and hugged me back. "About two months."

Relief coursed through my veins. "Cute," I replied, savoring her joke.

"Grove," she countered, at once teasing and coquettish, "you've always been so gullible."

"Do you know if it's a boy or a girl?"

"We haven't peeked." Sam quickly corrected herself, "I haven't peeked."

With those words, the room's déjà vu grew dark. No Charlie. No Evelyn. No Finn. One simple substitution, "I" for "we," had turned our old haunt strangely foreign. Sorrow tunneled through our thoughts like worms in a morgue.

Doesn't take much.

Sam's smile faded, mine too. Neither of us knew what to say. A CD blared woefully in the background, a woman singing the blues about her rotten life with six no-count husbands.

Bet you're no picnic, lady.

The singer sounded convincing. Too many cigarettes. Too many tumblers of cheap scotch. Our waitress finally rescued us. Sam ordered catfish. I ordered chicken-fried steak in honor of Charlie.

There was that time when he could not choose between Plantation Gumbo with Andouille Sausage and Robert E. Lee Chicken-Fried Steak. Charlie ordered both and chased the dueling entrées with a side of honey and butter sweet potatoes over marshmallow dirty rice, collard greens with ham hocks, and at least one pitcher of beer. He almost finished with two scoops of chocolate ice cream buried under slices of butter-fried sugar bananas. But later he asked if there were any cookies to accompany his Kahlúa. Evelyn and I had watched the entire gorge-o-rama in disbelief.

I broke the silence first. "You guys had been trying for a while?"

"Not too long," she replied. "The fertility drugs kicked right in. And wham bam, hello, Sam." She sounded rueful and happy, both at once.

"Maybe it was all that hard work," I offered helpfully.

"It's a tough job," Sam agreed.

"But somebody has to do it," I finished on cue.

"Do you miss your girls?" Sam sounded fearful, hesitant to compare her future to my past and present. She was really saying, *What will I do without Charlie?* At least that was my translation.

I measured my response, summoned every ounce of compassion in my psyche, and lied. "Time makes it pass."

Total bullshit.

"What do you miss?" she persisted.

"Evelyn's mocha skin." With that, eighteen months of grief gutted all self-control. "I miss her brown eyes and the way one sat just a little higher than the other. I miss Finn's bed, how all three of us crowded together and read stories every night. I miss spooning with Evelyn when we retreated to our room afterward. I miss the things that bugged me while Evelyn was alive, her command mode, the way she scheduled every detail of her life. I miss Finn's colds, the times when she was snotty and utterly miserable and I had to prod her to finish bowls of broth. I miss her peanut butter diapers. I miss Evelyn's smart-ass mouth. You know what I mean? My little girl was developing a smart mouth of her own, and I wish Finn had lived to catch up with Evelyn. I would trade everything to get them back. I'd give anything to walk my daughter down the aisle some-day, to grow old with my wife and hold her hand again."

Tears streamed down Sam's cheeks, making me re-gret my outburst. "I'm scared," she confessed, shaking against my chest. We sat for a long time. When our waitress arrived with dinner, Sam avoided eye contact and refused to come up for air. Head down, she planted her nose in the crook of my shoulder.

Our twenty-something waitress, trendy and borderline Gothic, assessed Sam for a moment. Then she scowled at me. When Goth Girl finally turned, a Kilroy tattoo peeked over a black thong that soared high above tight jeans. Shabby chic. She whispered to another waitress just loud enough for me to hear, "The shithead probably dumped her."

"Men suck," the second woman agreed. "I usually like redheads, but he's way too manorexic for my taste."

Every New Yorker has hair-trigger opinions.

By and by, Sam relaxed her vice grip and blinked away the tears. The scent of Cajun fare wafted up from the plates. The ambrosial aromas filled our nostrils and Sam focused on her catfish.

We made light talk. I told Sam stories about my grandfather, the first Grove, the one who had thrown dice for his cigar store in Chicago. She updated me on the adventures of Sadie, her cousin and the family groupie who had stalked Bob Dylan for years. Charlie, Sam, Evelyn, and I used to laugh our heads off about that one. It took some time, but the gloom faded and our good memories prevailed.

Of course, I couldn't leave well enough alone. Five or so glasses of wine had turned my right brain into a mosh pit. Booze didn't justify the next question, though. At times I simply asked the most unfortunate shit. "You know about the *New York Post*, right?"

"They're running a story," she confirmed.

"It sucks, if you ask me."

"You hung up on that reporter, Maris I think?"

"Force of habit," I replied. "How'd you know?"

"I told her to call you."

CHAPTER 22

"So that's how Maris got my cell number." I had been curious ever since she interrupted *The Best of Johnny Cash* en route to New Paltz.

"She phoned the day after the funeral," Sam explained, reaching over and finding my hand. Her depth of emotion, her simple touch, they roused me. "I can't talk about Charlie yet."

"Maris called more than once?" I already knew the answer.

"Last Saturday. She said you're a jerk."

Are you there?

Anger mushroomed inside me. Not at Mandy Maris; she was doing her job. Not at Sam; she needed help. Mentally, I blasted myself for botching her care package. What had I done?

Hung up on a reporter three times.

"I'm sorry, Sam. I should have handled things differently."

"Forget it, Grove." She squeezed my hand more tightly.

"I have this thing about the press," I added, growing more penitent by the moment.

"It's under control," she soothed.

"What do you mean?"

"Alex Romanov deals with reporters all the time. I told Maris to call him."

"No wonder," I muttered aloud, remembering her crack about hedge funds.

"No wonder what?"

"Maris mentioned Alex this morning."

"Really?" This time Sam apologized. "I'm sorry, Grove."

"What for?"

"I thought she would stop calling."

"Sam, it's not important." Now we were clutching each other's hands. "There's only one thing that matters. That's for me to help sort out your finances. Whatever it takes."

I paid the bill, tipping Goth Girl too much from force of habit. She glowered anyway, remembering Sam's tears. Goth Girl's expression said, *Don't you dare break up with a girl in my bar again.* If only she knew. Sam and I exited Live Bait, deserting the spicy Cajun smells that had whetted appetites and fed our memories.

Outside, New York City greeted us with pungent odors of a different sort. What was it about hot muggy nights in July that released the street's toxins? Twenty-third and Fifth reeked like a pissoir, though I doubted dogs had been responsible for the acrid aromas.

So many homeless. Such a rich city.

Garbage from surrounding restaurants already lined the streets. The late-night exhaust fumes almost made me grateful for yellow cabs combing the streets for fares. The occasional shrieks from their horns reminded me I was mistaken.

Funny location for a competitor.

Credit Suisse's New York headquarters sat off to our right, on the other side of a small park. Sam took my arm and snuggled close. She felt vulnerable, almost needy. The contact flipped a switch, her body against mine. Her perfume reminded me of all those weekends when the Kelemens had been tonic for my loneliness.

Don't drag Sam down with your shit, I told myself.

"Let me walk you home."

"You sure?" Sam asked. "It's a hike." She was right. By foot, it would take about thirty minutes to reach her brownstone in the Village.

"Maybe we should cab it," I conceded, wondering how best to please Sam. "You're walking for two after all."

"I'm pregnant. Not crippled," she scolded playfully. "What is it with all you guys?"

Why "guys"? Why plural?

We squeezed against each other and joined Manhattan's relentless foot traffic, beating our way through the shadowy streets of the Flatiron District. My feelings confused me. It wasn't desire I felt. Not for my best friend's wife. The emotions weren't dark, nothing like jealousy over Sam's baby, envy because I had lost Finn.

Perhaps I was savoring the forgotten pleasure of

companionship. Sam's touch warmed me inside, reinforced the wine's rosy afterglow. I prized her friendship even more. It had been so long since I had spent any time with a woman, one on one.

Unsure of my feelings, certain of my obligations, I retreated to Switzerland. Money was safe. I could always talk about money. "Betty Masters said hello. I saw her over the weekend."

Sam stopped. She looked into my eyes with an odd combination of warmth and surprise. "You drove up to New Paltz for me?"

"I made a day of it."

"Thank you," she said sweetly, squeezing my arm. "How'd it go?"

"I told her where we are. That I'm helping you unwind the Kelemen Group. That I called the accountants and your lawyer."

"My lawyer?"

"Popowski. Ira said he would sort out probate with the state. He can help in ways I can't."

"Thank you," she repeated, appreciation clear in her tone. "Did you hear from the accountants?"

"No."

"Me either," Sam sighed, worry now in her voice.

"It's the summer," I soothed. "Everybody's on vacation."

Pisses me off they haven't called.

"Do you know the names of anyone on the audit teams?" I asked.

"Crain or Cravath," Sam suggested logically.

Duh.

"We don't need them quite yet," I said, trying to save face.

"What do you mean?"

"Betty found a financial statement for the fund. It will list the hedge funds where Charlie invested. We'll start redeeming, one by one."

"Are there many?"

"Don't know. Betty hadn't faxed anything by the time Annie, Chloe, and I left."

"Do we even need the auditors?" Sam asked.

"Absolutely. Their info is more current."

"I would love to wrap up this whole thing," Sam announced. "My parents are investors, too. They're starting to ask questions."

Charlie's body isn't even cold.

"Too bad I can't go through Charlie's office."

"I know," Sam agreed. "There's tape all over the place. The cops pulled out the servers, the answering machine, the works." Sam paused and added, "But they overlooked one thing."

"Which is?"

"I have Charlie's laptop."

"Why didn't you tell them?"

"Why didn't they ask?"

Inside the Kelemen brownstone Sam poured me a steep shot of limoncello. The alcohol and sugary lemons chased the aftertaste of Cajun spices. It also saved Sam from my Live Bait breath as we huddled silently on a taupe sofa in the family room. Un, Deux, and Trois licked my hands with a vengeance, hoping to root out the source of chicken-fried-steak scents, and Ray Charles belted out "Georgia on My Mind" in the background. I sipped the syrupy liqueur. We were all happy, dogs included.

Eventually, my arm draped around Sam. There was no special significance. We held each other like siblings rather than young lovers yearning for more. The dachshunds watched intently. All three sat tall on their haunches, vertical hot dogs defying the laws of physics.

I surveyed the exposed brick walls and twenty-foot ceilings. The bones of the room dated back to the late 1800s, to a time when people and money had poured into Greenwich Village. Architects would never again design residences with six-foot stained-glass windows. Nor would they fill homes with chiseled marble fireplaces from Milan or staircases carved from West Indies mahogany. The crown molding was anything but symmetrical. Carpenters had whittled it to look like vines from overgrown rain forests, like jungle creepers triumphing over people in the age-old war to dominate the environment. The effect was spectacular.

Charlie's karma enveloped us. He had commissioned the whimsical glass chandelier, shaped like an enormous octopus, for $25,000 just as he had commissioned a fourteen-foot painting. The painting's abstract explosion of swirling reds, textured blacks, and earthy oranges could easily have overwhelmed the room. Instead, the gargantuan canvas complemented the faded hues of a $125,000 Oriental rug that graced wide wooden planks.

Charlie believed the artist to be the next Picasso.

"That painting cost a quarter million," he told me once, "but I can sell it for double."

To my eye, the artist was a con artist armed with a brush and a sack of paint. "Hit the bid," I had advised.

That was trading lingo for, "Take the offer."

Charlie scoffed and shook his head, sure of his cunning. "Grove," he admonished, "stick to your numbers and leave the art to me." He was right. He always made money on collectibles.

Sam poured me another shot of limoncello and placed it on the coffee table, a hand-painted Indonesian antique. The colors, once bold, had mellowed through the centuries. "Grove, I can't thank you enough."

"You know me, always searching for a good meal."

"That's not what I mean. I can't keep the money you sent."

"I don't expect you to keep it. The money is a loan. Besides, I've been thinking."

"It's about time." Sam's playful smile stirred the limoncello inside me.

No matter the late hour, I intended to cover one last idea. "I can arrange a home equity loan, enough to tide you over until we liquidate the Kelemen Group. Or find accounts. Whatever comes first."

"You're kidding, right?" Her words were less question, more accusation.

"What do you mean?" I bristled. "Seventy-five won't last forever." Then I realized Sam was worried about her credit. She had not worked a day during their marriage. "How much is your first mortgage? Maybe we can get you approved with a low loan to value."

"We rent. We don't own."

"No way. You spent at least a hundred thousand dollars renovating this place."

"We have an option to buy the building. We can always get our money back."

Her admission stunned me. Not knowing what to say, I changed course. "No insurance on Charlie, right? I told the Boston police he didn't believe in it."

"You got that right. Insurance torqued him off."

"Everybody in finance thinks they can earn better returns elsewhere."

"That's one reason," Sam agreed. "But I think the medical requirements made him sensitive. Charlie hated the way doctors told him to lose weight."

It wasn't obesity that got him.

"I went through our safe," Sam continued.

"I'm glad you double-checked."

"I was actually looking for jewelry," she explained, "not insurance documents. Frankly, that's another problem. My good jewelry isn't in the safe. The everyday stuff is there. But my expensive things are gone."

"The black pearls?"

"Gone," she replied.

"That peacock thing?"

"Can't find it.

"The necklace with greenish sapphires and emerald-cut diamonds?"

"It would have been perfect with my dress at the aquarium. I first missed it that night."

I realized Sam had not worn her magnificent jewelry either at the funeral or during her visit last

Friday. "You know, there's something that's been troubling me."

"Troubling you," she snorted. "They're my best jewels."

"Well, that's just it. You can't find your jewels. And you only have six hundred dollars in your checking account."

"Not anymore," she said thankfully.

"You know what I mean," I replied. "Did it ever occur to you that Charlie might be hiding something? Or something from someone?"

"What makes you say that?" she asked. The three dachshunds scratched about in the kitchen, defending their turf against some unknown menace.

"A few things. Like asset protection. Sometimes people hide their money to protect it. And there's common sense. Charlie wouldn't put every cent into an illiquid investment."

"I don't get the connection to the six hundred dollars."

"If Charlie hid the jewels," I explained, "maybe he hid your investments."

Sam brightened. "It's possible. He handled everything."

"Just a theory." It was important not to inflate Sam's expectations. "No chance somebody stole your jewels, right?"

"The thought never crossed my mind. Charlie had a key. I have a key. Nobody else has a key, and there were no indications of forced entry. I don't understand why Charlie would move our things."

"Did you tell the police?"

"What would I tell them? That Charlie stashed my jewelry somewhere and I can't find it? Nobody broke into our apartment."

"You should tell them anyway. Maybe somebody forced Charlie to move your stuff."

Neither of us spoke for a moment. I remembered Fitzsimmons's question and broke the silence with the courage of limoncello and the unfortunate candor that had destined me to a career outside the United Nations. "You don't suppose Charlie was having an affair?"

"No way."

"What makes you so certain?"

"Where would Charlie find a better piece of ass?" Sam eyed me playfully. During college she never would have joked that way. It was only through Charlie's tutelage that Sam learned to play the nymph and skirt the bawdy edges of male lechery.

She had a point. They were an odd couple. Sam was buff. Charlie was buffet. I swallowed hard, considered Sam's comment carefully, and slurred, confident of my charm, "It truly is a come-hither ass, Sam, approachable and well balanced, with tannins that would appear to reward those with the patience to wait. I anticipate a crisp, full-bodied, and strong finish that one should savor through the years. Do you have any more limoncello?"

"Grove, I'm cutting you off." With mock outrage she added, "And stop talking about my tannins."

"Probably a good idea." Suddenly, my little outburst annoyed me. "I'm cutting myself off."

Stupid. Stupid. Stupid.

"I had fun, Grove."

The tribe had spoken. It was time to go. "Me too, Sam."

"Let me get you Charlie's laptop. Maybe you can find something. I couldn't get past the password."

The dachshunds raised hell as I left. All three hot dogs tried to crowd through the front door, drawn by their desire to sniff and pee and rip into the night. Their commotion stopped me from hugging Sam a proper good night.

"Hey, Grove," she called after me.

"Yeah."

"Thanks."

"Whatever it takes, Sam."

Five minutes later the world started to spin. I sat in the back of a cab enduring the glare of Manhattan's streetlights, stomaching the mayhem of a wine and limoncello drunk. All the way back to Central Park West, I brooded over new reversals of fortune. No jewels. No title to the real estate. No insurance. No clue. There was only one consolation.

Charlie Kelemen's laptop sat by my side.

CHAPTER 23

Wall Street is a morning business. Preparations begin long before trading opens on the New York Stock Exchange. *The New York Times, The Wall Street Journal,* even the *Financial Times*—brokers and traders read at least two of these publications prior to seven-twenty every morning. That's when proprietary research meetings start at most shops.

I am not a morning person and have the results from personality tests to prove it. Much to my dismay and counter to the advice from Harvard Business School's job coaches, I wake long before sunup and begin a self-engineered transfusion of caffeine. I soldier through the periodicals, but it takes time for the brain to engage after five or six hours of sleep. I speak in monosyllabic grunts that linger well into the morning. They temporarily mask my Southern accent and stifle the soothing sounds of syllabic expansion.

Those first few hours of consciousness, essential to understanding the markets and analyzing their direction, sabotage an otherwise perfect career choice. Like Sisyphus pushing a boulder up the mountain, I struggle to make research. I fall back and repeat the same brutal ordeal Monday through Friday.

Hangovers don't help.

That Tuesday my alarm clock buzzed at 5:30 A.M. My head throbbed like an open wound disinfected with limoncello. I turned the alarm off, fell back asleep, and straggled into the office long after research had ended. It was around 8:45 A.M. when Patty Gershon greeted me with her stupid joke: "Thanks for coming in today, O'Rourke."

"You need new material, Patty."

"We need to talk," she shot back.

"Let me get settled," I said. "How about this afternoon?" I meant after the close. I would learn later, in the most unfortunate way, that Patty Gershon understood something else.

"Now is better. I need to ask you something."

That woman can steamroll concrete.

"Patty, what don't you understand about me getting settled?"

"You sound gravelly, O'Rourke. Big night?" Hangovers commanded respect in my industry. Throaty voices served as the Purple Hearts of Wall Street.

"What's the question?"

"Do you know who Eva Braun is?" It was not a test. She had no clue.

"Of course," I replied.

"Will you tell me?"

"Just Google her, Patty." Wall Street people are bankrupt when it comes to history. Through the years I had grown accustomed to the dearth of knowledge. But Patty's question floored me. She was Jewish. She should have known the name of Hitler's mistress.

"The server's been down all morning. No Internet access." She nodded at the computer I was carrying, Charlie's laptop, as though to emphasize the tyranny of technology glitches.

"Why do you ask?"

"My mom," Patty replied, "said I remind her of Eva Braun."

In the history of the universe, there had never been a more contemptuous remark between mother and daughter. Hiding my outrage, I asked, "Did you guys have a fight?"

"How'd you know?" Patty asked, her forehead furrowing.

No Botox.

"Lucky guess," I lied. "Something in your voice, maybe."

"So who is she?" Patty persisted.

"During World War Two," I started, summoning every ounce of statesmanship in my body, "Eva Braun consorted with the Axis leaders on a regular basis. Some considered her a great beauty. Others regarded her as a controversial figure because of the company she kept." It seemed likely my explanation would hold up, even if Patty checked later. "Your mother," I added at my ambassadorial best, "probably wants to reconcile."

Confession time.

"Thanks." She called after me, "This afternoon, O'Rourke."

* * *

In the adjacent cubicle, Annie was just finishing a conversation as I began the day at my desk. Our low, open-plan partitions made for easy communication, good visual and verbal access. They also eliminated privacy. Fights between spouses, job offers from competitors, ED and other medical setbacks—everybody knew everybody's affairs. Literally.

"Last night was great," Annie said into the receiver. "Love you too."

She's seeing somebody.

"Oh, Boss," Annie crooned, stretching out the two syllables, not in the Southern way but more in the singsong way of a woman with gossip on her mind. "Tell me about last night."

"What's to tell? Great to see Sam. Probably drank too much."

"Didn't notice," she croaked huskily, mimicking my hangover rasp. "Want me to order a bacon, egg, and cheese?"

"Who's better than you?" I confirmed.

Ordinarily, Annie would have swiveled around in her chair and dialed the deli downstairs. She lingered, though. She appeared hesitant.

Did I miss something?

"What's the news?" she asked.

Curious?

"Sam's pregnant. Two months. So don't say anything."

"That's wonderful." She brightened, but for only a moment. Her warm smile faded. "I think." No doubt

Annie was considering Sam's future—pregnant, widowed, and broke save for my $75,000 wire.

"The baby's a gift," I reassured Annie.

"Sam must be scared." Fiddling with her golden blond hair, Annie added, "You're a good friend."

This is awkward.

"Any calls?" I asked, changing the subject.

"Halek. You need to call him."

She's distracted about something.

"When don't I call Cliff?"

"Today's different. Congratulations are in order."

"Promotion?" Cliff Halek was SKC's smartest man, after all.

"Nothing like that," she said. "You know how he hates Goldman." It was more statement than question.

"Of course."

"Remember the *Wall Street Journal* article last Friday?" she asked.

"Which one?"

"The one where Goldman's head trader bragged about eating everybody's lunch. Merrill, Morgan, SKC, all of us."

"Saw it," I acknowledged. "The guy's a bonehead."

"Cliff knows him. Says he's a jerk. He sent the ultimate 'screw you' to their trading floor."

"Which was?"

"One hundred pizzas," she answered.

"Sounds more like a gift."

"There are all kinds of pies, Boss." Annie's blue-green eyes gleamed. She temporarily forgot whatever was troubling her. She was a born storyteller, a natural raconteur. I think Annie found joy, some kind of inner peace, from spinning yarns or delivering dénouements.

"Okay?"

"These pies were made with garlic anchovies, ripe Limburger, and fried onions. Every last one. Halek stank up Goldman's trading floor. The pizzeria even threw in some liverwurst."

"That's disgusting," I said, feeling more alert now, warming to the day. It was too bad Ponce de León never found Wall Street in his quest for eternal youth. Few people in our industry ever matured past adolescence.

"His note was short."

"Typical Halek."

"All it said was 'Eat this, Goldman.'"

We both chuckled. But there was something about Annie's vibe. It still troubled me.

What am I missing?

"Annie, is there something on your mind?"

She hesitated for a split second and said, "No, Boss."

"You sure?"

"Absolutely." Pause. The moment dallied before passing uncomfortably. "I have that fax from Betty Masters."

"Out-fucking-standing."

Annie wheeled around, picked up a fourteen-page fax from her desk, and handed it to me. "I'll be back with that bacon, egg, and cheese."

"You're the best."

Something's bothering her.

I made two mental notes. One was to speak with

Annie later. The other was to congratulate Halek. His pizzas were the best "fuck you" I had ever heard. Right now, I needed to work. Make a few phone calls. Follow up on some prospects.

Yeah, right.

Curiosity was killing me. I rifled through Betty's fax, the audited financials we had discussed. On the first page, Crain and Cravath summarized their findings: "In our opinion, the financial statements present fairly, in all material respects, the financial position of the Kelemen Group Fund of Funds, Series B (a class of the Kelemen Group Master Series Trust)."

Thank God I'm not an auditor.

The net assets number on the next page, $320 million and change, proved anything but tedious. Charlie ran a bigger operation than I thought. If the fund returned 5 percent, his performance fee would total $1.6 million. Last year, however, the market was up over 15 percent. If Charlie kept pace, he earned about $4.8 million.

Nice.

I leafed through the Statement of Operations, thumbed past the Statement of Cash Flows, and paged into the Notes to Financial Statements—expecting to find a schedule of investments somewhere. What I found annoyed me. Nothing. No list of investments. Not a damn thing.

It's got to be here somewhere.

It wasn't. Note two, "Significant Accounting Policies," explained the absence in the standard, if stultifying, vernacular of dweeb-speak: "The Fund records its investment in the Master Fund at fair value. . . ."

Translation: Betty did not invest in the so-called Master Fund. She bought into a different vehicle, which provided capital for the Master Fund. In turn, the Master Fund invested in outside hedge funds. Accountants dubbed this setup a "master-feeder" structure.

Revenge of the nerds.

Note two continued: "Valuation of investments held by the Master Fund is discussed in the Master Fund's financial statements and accompanying notes. . . ."

Translation: There was no schedule of investments among these papers. I held Series B financials. I needed Master Fund financials. Betty had faxed the wrong thing. Who could blame her? She got lost in FASB, short for the Financial Accounting Standards Board. Their reporting conventions made sense to auditors. For everyone else, they equaled the Bermuda Triangle.

Looking at Charlie's laptop, I muttered, "You don't make anything easy, bud."

CHAPTER 24

The Windows operating system, tediously slow, stopped cold at the dialogue box requesting a password. I tried "PC" and "Providence" for Charlie's academic institutions. No good. I tried his birthday, then Sam's. No good. I even tried the names of the dogs—Un, Deux, and Trois—employing a dozen different permutations. Still no good.

I need a geek to hack in.

Annie delivered the bacon, egg, and cheese along with a bottle of Advil. "Take two and call me around eleven A.M." She never admitted something was bugging her. But I could tell.

"Pizza" and "Bolognese" and Charlie's other favorites did not work. The Windows dialogue box came up empty. Nothing.

That was when the phone took over. Betty Masters called first. "Did you get my fax?" she asked.

"Thanks. I was just about to call you."

"What's with the voice?" she asked.

"A few drinks last night."

"Sounds like you left your vocal cords in a shot

glass." I imagined Betty's 150-watt smile and started fumbling around for my sunglasses.

"Cute. I was just looking at your fax. By any chance did you receive a second financial statement from Charlie? There should have been two."

"I don't think so. I'll check again."

After we hung up I typed "fundoffunds" as one long word into the Windows dialogue box. Nothing.

Alex Romanov, the self-appointed patron saint of lights-out performance, called next. "I'm glad you're helping Sam," he said. "Would you fill me in, Grover?"

The question rankled me. Maybe it was Romanov's intonation, condescending, dictatorial, irritating to a hangover. Maybe it was his success, annoying the way he always gloated about triple-digit returns.

Halek often predicted Romanov would blow up. "Risk will get him. You can't deliver three digits without stumbling. Some time, some place, I don't know how. I just know it always happens."

Whatever the reason, I reacted to Romanov the way every finance jock handles would-be alpha dogs. "Do you know anything about probate?" I sniped, pleasant enough in tone, but already knowing the answer.

"Not much," he admitted.

I smiled, savoring first blood in the clash between two well-hung egos circling in the wild. "There's really not much to report."

"But," Romanov continued, "I have legions of lawyers on deck."

Translation: "More money than you, so don't pull your probate crap on me."

He paused to let his words register. "Call me later this week and let me know about your progress."

What was that all about?

I typed "jerk" and "butthead" into the dialogue box. Nothing.

Fitzsimmons phoned next. He picked up where he left off on Sunday. "This fund of funds," he said, "did you ever refer any clients to Charlie Kelemen?"

Danger, Will Robinson.

"Why do you ask?"

"You're a stockbroker," he replied. "It's what you people do, right?"

You people?

"Before I can introduce clients to money managers, SKC investigates them," I replied. "We have teams of people who review investment styles and operational procedures. I won't recommend any manager until we complete our due diligence."

"I thought that's what the victim did," Fitzsimmons replied. "You know, the due diligence."

"He did. But just as Charlie investigated his hedgies, we would investigate the Kelemen Group."

"Got it," Fitzsimmons said. "The victim—" Fitzsimmons started.

"Would you stop calling him that?"

"Mr. Kelemen and you were close."

"Best friends," I agreed.

"That's my point. You never referred any of your clients to him?"

There's some top producer in Fitzsimmons. He pushes until he gets what he wants.

"What is it you want, Detective? Do you have some reason to believe I made a referral? And if so, why the fuck is it important?"

"We're exploring all angles," he barked back.

Evasive.

"Don't tell me you never talked shop," the officer argued.

Just before Christmas last year, Charlie and I were savoring pulled-pork sandwiches and Pinot Grigio at Virgil's Barbecue on West Forty-fourth Street. "Why don't you join me at the Kelemen Group?" he asked. "You've got a great book. And I need people to grow the business."

"Charlie, I don't know what to say."

"Just say yes," he encouraged. His perfectly white smile, the product of repeated bleaching, could have closed any other deal at that moment. "Grove, in this world there are pleasers. And there are takers. You and I are pleasers. We'd make one helluva team."

I put down my glass of wine and gazed at the backs of my hands. They looked frail. In a low voice I made a subtle reference only my best friend would understand. "I'm not ready yet."

"Don't give me that crap," Charlie snapped. His smile vaporized.

The outburst, so sudden and hostile, made my eyes go wide. But I recovered. "Might be a good time to back off, pal." That was Charlestonese for *Get out of my face.*

Charlie charged into dangerous territory, indifferent to my warning. "This isn't about New Haven."

"I'm telling you, Charlie—"

"It's something else," he spit, speaking over me, dogging me with his uninvited insights. A look of comprehension flared in his eyes. "You're afraid. That's it?" he asked rhetorically. "You don't have game. You're starting to believe all that conservative crap you feed your clients."

Charlie's words hit their mark. He knew. For all my external bravado, "Wall Street this" and "Wall Street that," he knew. I had stopped taking chances since the wreck outside New Haven. Played everything safe. He knew. His insight made me feel weak and compromised, anything but a titan of finance. Salvaging my dignity, I said, "Let me think about it."

"Yeah, whatever. Get the check," he bristled. I had never paid for a meal with Charlie before. Pulling out my credit card, I could feel the sting of his disappointment. Our lunch ended abruptly, the friction atypical.

He had all but forgotten a week later. Sam and Charlie invited me for Christmas dinner, and the topic of joining forces never surfaced. To the best of my knowledge, he never told anyone about my secret fears. He never betrayed me. He just picked up the checks, including mine, and let the good times roll.

"Of course we talked shop," I told Fitzsimmons. "But I never referred any clients."

"Strikes me as strange," the big man observed, skepticism seeping through his voice.

"That's because you're a cop," I retorted. "I can't

recommend money managers without my firm's okay. Compliance would have a cow."

"How would they find out?"

"Doesn't matter. It's not worth the risk."

"Why's that?" he asked.

"SKC doesn't have a fee-sharing agreement with the Kelemen Group. I couldn't get paid."

"There's something we all understand," Fitzsimmons remarked dryly.

"Why are you asking me about referrals?"

"We need to understand his financial ties," the officer explained.

"Me too," I agreed wistfully, without thinking.

"What's that mean?"

My second line buzzed. "Unless there's something else, Detective." I stopped right there, didn't say another word, sounded assoholic even to myself. The message was clear.

Get off my phone.

"We'll be in touch," Fitzsimmons promised, and clicked off. I regretted not telling him Charlie's laptop was sitting on my desk. But our conversation, the recollection of lunch at Virgil's, gave me another idea.

I typed "pleasers" into the Windows dialogue box. Didn't work. When I tried the singular and typed "pleaser," however, Windows opened and chugged through the litany of start-up procedures. It was all I could do to keep from whooping at Gabby, the PCS receptionist, who was on my second line.

"Grove," she said, "Mr. Crunch is here to see you."

"Crunch? Tell him I'll be right out."

"No can do," she replied.

"Is there a problem?" I asked.

"That depends on how well you know him," she said. "He's on his way back now."

I wonder if he's missing any money.

CHAPTER 25

Through the years Wall Street has grown more tolerant of homosexuality. Acceptance never broke from the gate, however, during the early days of rah-rah machismo. For every step forward, there were two steps back. Plenty of finance goons perpetuated prejudices as they plied their trade. "Queers, fags, butt bandits"—gay bashing was once a loathsome mainstay of our culture.

Forbearance has picked up steam recently. Most firms sponsor sensitivity seminars and outreach recruiting. SKC and all the investment banks send people to speak at leading business schools whenever, wherever there are gay symposiums. Efforts appear to be working. At some shops it's almost "in" to be "out."

For all the success, I doubt my industry will ever become the national showcase for open-mindedness. Our unspoken convention is slightly more progressive than "don't ask, don't tell." It's okay to ask. It's okay to tell. It's career death to show. Wall Street has zero tolerance for effeminate behavior.

It would be a colossal mistake, therefore, to describe Crunch's PCS debut as anything less than spectacular.

That Tuesday morning, amid the power-money setting of leather trim and tiger-maple paneling, every broker on the boardroom floor gaped. Every pair of eyes trained on the hairdresser as he walked toward my team.

It's hard to say why Crunch attracted so much attention. He wore loose chinos and a white oxford, sleeves rolled to the forearms. He worked out. That was clear. The shirt and pants seemed ordinary, though, no trace of the inner queen that surfaced sometimes at parties and only when Charlie was in the room.

Maybe my colleagues were inspecting his black Ferragamo shoes and matching belt. The signature Double Gancini hooks were striking against the weathered cotton, but the departmental fuss surprised me.

Those buckles look like horseshoes.

Or maybe the Versace sunglasses, perched high atop Crunch's shoulder-length hair, made PCS do a double take. I knew one thing. People were gawking.

Crunch knew, too. Cocksure, confident, he invited attention and ignored opinion. He was onstage, savoring the stares, determined to make them last. He clutched a red folder in his left hand.

Crunch was born Marion Michael Morrison in honor of John Wayne's real name. At the time, his parents were paying tribute to the Duke and the flicks they loved. They never expected their son would one day become a real-life John Wayne as a member of the Army's elite Delta Force.

After leaving the Army, Marion Michael Morrison let his black hair grow long and legally changed his name. When he met people for the first time, he often repeated the same introductory lines: "Call me Crunch. One name works. It's like Cher or Madonna."

Crunch now fashioned thin wispy strands, survivors of the baldness wars for scalp supremacy, into flowing manes. He changed mousy brown colors into locks of sunshine. He fretted over every snip and brush stroke. Through his chain of three salons, he created the world's most elegant coiffures. Every aspiring hairdresser in New York City yearned to work for the master.

Crunch's military bearing had softened. He was happy and affable, out with everyone. We saw hints of the Delta Force every now and then, like his 101st tattoo and the occasional show of army boots, but Crunch concentrated on his life as a stylist. He pretended to abandon all worries.

The truth lay elsewhere. Crunch regularly suffered a broken heart, about as often as his salons bikini waxed their patrons. Every affair spawned new runs of misery and melodrama. That was where Charlie entered.

Crunch told Charlie everything. The stylist recounted his steamy trysts. And Charlie patiently listened to stories that all ended the same: "My partner left me."

Barreling past my outstretched hand, holding the red folder, Crunch hugged me hello. He made smoochy sounds with Annie as they touched both cheeks, European-style. She noted the top three buttons of his shirt were undone. "Nice pecs, Crunch."

"They're real," he replied.

Chloe, deep in conversation underneath her monstrous headset, waved a subdued welcome. Crunch would have no part of it. He stretched the left audio bowl from the side of her face and whispered something in her ear. She was glowing crimson by the time he returned the cup.

My colleagues watched from every corner of PCS. Crunch could have been a client. Nobody said a thing; nobody, that is, except for Scully. He blew a discreet kiss in our direction.

"Have a seat, Crunch." I gestured to a small guest chair on the side of my desk. "How'd you get past security?"

"Somebody was leaving, and I slipped through the glass doors."

"What did our receptionist say?"

"Told her I'd be just a minute."

"Probably not a good idea."

"I'm so impatient," he professed, undeterred by my comment. "You know what I'm saying?"

"What can I do for you, Crunch?"

"You sound awful."

"Sam and I had a few drinks during dinner."

"She asked me to stop by later during the week."

"Good to keep her busy," I replied. "She'll get lonely in that house." I knew from experience.

"I brought you a present," Crunch said, bunching his shoulders and acting delighted as he handed me the red folder. It was hard to believe this man had ever killed anyone. He had no visible scars, no visible malice, nothing other than the 101st tattoo hiding beneath his sleeve.

"Grove," Annie interrupted. "Lila Priouleau is on line one."

Ordinarily, I would have picked up the phone. A good friend, Lila was a great prospect. Curiosity about Crunch's visit won out. "I need to call her back."

"Don't you dare hang up," Crunch scolded. With lightning-fast moves from the old days in Iraq, he snatched the receiver from my desk. "Hello, girl," he boomed at Lila. "I have just the right stocks for you."

A label on the red folder read "MRI Capital," Alex Romanov's hedge fund. At a party once, Charlie told the Mad Russian, "The corporate name's a little subdued."

"It's easier to name rug rats than companies," Romanov reasoned. "There are a million little Johnnys. But only one Cerberus." Romanov was referring to the private-equity fund named for a mythological three-headed dog that guarded the gates of hell.

You're single. What would you know about naming kids?

Romanov was right on one level. Hedge funds had ballooned in number from four thousand to eight thousand through the years. Each one needed a name. The metaphor-hungry hedgies christened their shops after trees, mountains, and architectural elements. They scooped up seafaring expressions, not to mention all the Greek and Roman gods. They rifled through most heroes, leaving only the dregs of mythology. The name Satyr Capital was still available for good reason. The ancients often painted priapic satyrs roaming the woods with massive erections, okay for Viagra ads but probably not the right image for lords of finance.

"MRI like the medical device that scans for problems?" I had asked Alex, avoiding any reference to Mad Russian Investments.

"Exactly," he replied. "We look where others don't."

As I thumbed through the red folder now, Crunch yakked with Lila. "You should buy some Coach," he advised. "They make the cutest handbags." He cupped his hand over the receiver and announced, "I'm working it."

"You go, Crunch." Leafing through the papers, I found a prospectus for MRI Capital. There was also a printout listing its portfolio of stocks.

Interesting.

Crunch hung up with Lila before I could review MRI's positions. No time to discover the secrets behind Romanov's king-sized returns. "You're all set," the hairdresser proclaimed happily. "You need to send Lila the paperwork to open an account."

"Nice work." Crunch had asked for the order, something I hadn't done with Lila in eight years.

"She wants Coach, Tommy Hilfiger, and a little Saks," he continued, "but no, repeat after me, absolutely no Wal-Mart. You know what I'm saying?"

"You're the best," I praised. "What's with the folder?"

"Charlie left it at my salon."

"Did he forget it?"

"No, sweetie," the hairdresser sighed. "He didn't want to lose it."

Don't call me sweetie.

"Was he worried?" I asked.

"He didn't want to leave it in a restaurant," Crunch explained. "Charlie was always forgetting things."

"Couldn't Sam put the folder in her purse?"

"She wasn't there. We were scheming about burkas and fezzes, you know."

"Got it," I said. "Why give the folder to me?"

"You'll know whether it's important." Crunch added hesitantly, "It's probably junk."

"Did Charlie ever say if he invested in Romanov's fund?"

"Sweetie," Crunch exhaled, "we never talked business. I have no head for figures. The kind on paper, that is."

"You seemed to be doing just fine with Lila's portfolio."

"Yes, and you can buy me a thank-you cup of coffee downstairs," he said, "and tuck me in a cab, too."

"You got it, brother." We were comrades in arms, one adviser to another, however impromptu.

An early lunch crowd had packed onto the elevator, including the last person I wanted to see. Scully wore a navy blue suit, yellow Hermès tie, and starched white shirt. There could only be one explanation for his full head of perfectly combed hair. Gel and a blow dryer. He said nothing, spared the elevator from his deafening decibels, but grinned shit-eating smug from ear to ear. The mocking smile, the meatball face, Scully winked at me as though to ask, *Who's the fruit?* He made one mistake. He thought Crunch, a man who had once scanned windows and doors for snipers, wasn't looking.

The events that followed started subtly. The doors closed. Scully inched slightly to the left, carving out some body space, distancing himself from the hairdresser as best as possible in the tight quarters. Crunch looked straight ahead and said nothing, eyes fixed on the doors. He, too, inched left. Left toward Scully.

On the third floor, two people exited. Three boarded. Scully flattened against the elevator wall. Crunch leaned against him and violated the body space, perhaps the body parts, of the world's loudest stockbroker. From the corner of my eyes, I watched Scully's growing distress.

His brow is damp.

On the second floor, one person boarded. There was no more room in the elevator. Nowhere for Scully to creep. Crunch tilted even more, squeezing across the plane of good taste, crushing white oxford against navy blue suit. When the doors closed, I thought Scully would burst.

He did. "Get off me, man," Scully exploded. He twisted his body and shook his shoulders in the crowded little compartment. With his left fand, he tried to shove Crunch back.

In that split second Delta Force skills reminded me of bicycling. Once you learn, you never forget. Crunch moved quickly but casually, almost like covering his mouth to yawn. He snatched Scully's mitt with his right hand, stifling the thrust as suddenly as it had started. "Whoa, big boy," Crunch declared.

The doors opened on the ground floor. People spilled into the corridor. There had been a flash of motion in the elevator. They knew something was wrong.

Crunch clamped Scully's hand with the detached authority of a shop vice. Squeezing. Crushing. Squashing. Scully's face turned white. His knees began to buckle.

How's he do that?

"No, Crunch," I said, seeing Scully wince, his brow filling with beads of perspiration. "It's okay."

Crunch straightened Scully's tie with his left hand—silver ring on the middle finger—and eased the death grip of his right. Delta Force operative or stylist, he gently mussed Scully's gelled hair and smiled. "Have a good day, sweetie."

Then Crunch turned to me. "Forget the coffee," he said. "My work is done."

The incident bugged me. But I returned upstairs to Charlie's computer and the red folder. Frank Kurtz was right.

Stuff shows up when people die.

CHAPTER 26

After a bang-up lunch of Coke and two more Advil, I stopped trading. No more calls to clients. My mouth tasted grim, cottony like I had swallowed a Dust Bowl from the 1930s. For a moment I deliberated over what to examine first, the red folder or Charlie's laptop. The choice proved a no-brainer. Romanov's investment secrets could wait. I slid the red folder away.

Sam and Betty come first.

One tap of the return key woke Charlie's computer from its sleep. Guessing "pleaser" had been lucky. That password never would have worked inside a large brokerage firm. SKC required a minimum of eight characters with at least one number and one capital letter, tough sledding on Wall Street. Our vocabularies seldom progressed past four-letter words, five at the outside.

Where to start?

PCS did not host a wireless connection. But our area intercepted a number of wireless signals, two from adjacent buildings and another from inside SKC. Of these transmissions one connection was unsecured, no password necessary. Clearly, the source company operated outside the securities industry. Their laissez-faire approach to privacy would never fly inside an investment bank and brokerage.

Their Internet connection came in handy. It was the only way to check personal e-mails. SKC's computers restricted access to accounts on Yahoo!, Google, or any of the other e-mail providers. Management was forever explaining, "Outside e-mail accounts make us vulnerable to viruses."

The filters bugged the shit out of me. SKC, the ostensible pride of free enterprise and unfettered capitalism, reminded me of Red China. They had their Internet restrictions. We had ours. Using my personal laptop, I had often pirated into that wireless connection. Charlie's Outlook mailbox indicated there were 661 unread messages.

Another day in the life of a finance jock.

Unlike the e-mails that flooded my computer on a daily basis, Charlie's traffic consisted mostly of junk. The subject lines included "Lose 30 lbs in 45 days . . . Rid your colon of toxins . . . Big savings on the little blue pill." There were plenty of mass forwards, friendly-fire spam from friends containing patriotic diatribes, chain prayers, tips about health, and bitchy jokes about spouses. Apparently, Lila Priouleau needed to weed her distribution list. At least two of her forwards hit Charlie's in-box over the weekend.

Who reads this crap?

Like the MRI file, Charlie's e-mails could wait until later. I'd cull through the 661-strong onslaught after work, even though the prospect troubled me. Reading them felt voyeuristic.

Sam. Betty. Fred. Get over it.

For now I clicked on the Outlook calendar. An appointment with "Nurse Pinckney" caught my attention. It was scheduled for next week.

Nothing she can do now.

That meeting was unmemorable to anyone else in New York City. Pinckney, however, was one of Charleston's more common and historic names. I absently scribbled the nurse's name and phone number on the back of the red MRI folder.

Enough calendar.

The Windows search tool located a folder on the hard drive titled "The Kelemen Group." Bingo. With Charlie's secrets waiting before me, I fancied myself a master sleuth in the modern era.

Bring it on, Sherlock.

Few people, especially Evelyn, had ever accused me of getting to the point quickly. She had been methodical and verbally sparse, the signature of a true Yankee with Portuguese roots. She had often accused me of "going around Robin Hood's barn" to get somewhere right in front of me. I now longed to tell Evelyn. She would have been the perfect ally to snoop through Charlie's affairs.

My jubilation proved transient. About three thousand files cluttered the folder, the sheer number overwhelming. Most contained self-explanatory names, although some had useless titles like "Miscellaneous." The jumble ranged from Excel to Word to Adobe formats. There were hundreds of electronic missives from money managers, all touting their ability to navigate treacherous financial markets. There were no categories, no color codes, and no subfolders to establish order amid the chaos. Charlie, "Mr. Obsessive" about his attire, had been a complete storage pig on his computer. He dumped all the bits and bytes and electronic shit into one big digital compost heap.

The Windows sort tools offered some relief. I hit the sort-by-name button and scrolled down the alphabetical list. It took forever. Nothing jumped out until midway, an Excel spreadsheet named "Investors." Too bad there was no document that showed Charlie's hedge fund investments. That way, we could contact the funds and liquidate the Kelemen Group. No such luck. Charlie, the quintessential storage pig, probably never synched his laptop with computers at the office.

The Excel spreadsheet listed investors in Series B, no surprise given the name. The posse had bankrolled the fund en masse. Sam's parents invested. After Walter and Helen Wells came Lila Priouleau and her father, Cash. Betty Masters invested. So had Sam's therapist as well as Jane, the busty divorcée who peed in the shower. Several names were unfamiliar, including a guy from San Francisco and one from Chicago. But I knew most and estimated women outnumbered men two to one. Crunch was noticeably absent.

One column showed how much each person had invested. Betty's $250,000 stake was there. Sam's parents had invested over $2 million, and Jane accounted for $1 million. The biggest numbers appeared next to the Priouleaus. Cash had invested $8 million and Lila $2 million in her own name.

Great prospects, I reminded myself wistfully. *Need to take it up a notch.*

The column did not total investments, probably because 25 percent of the cells were blank. There were two possible explanations. Charlie had not received funds. Or he ran out of time. The "last modified" date of the spreadsheet confirmed what I suspected. Charlie was working on "Investors" the week he died.

Good start. But where does the Kelemen Group keep its cash?

That's when the brain-housing group engaged. At my last Harvard reunion there had been a panel discussion titled "Where We Live on the Web." Charlie had probably used Web-based banking for both his business and his personal finances. I still believed he had taken some money off the table. Otherwise, why would anybody torture him?

All those cuts on his arms.

Alone in a cone of silence, oblivious to the antics of PCS, I questioned my old friend, "Where did you live on the Web, Charlie?" Internet Explorer launched, and his home page, *The New York Times*, appeared. It struck me as an ordinary choice, a routine place to start surfing the Web.

To the right of the address line, the drop-down menu showed the historical record of Charlie's surfing sessions. Methodically, I selected the first site on the list, without bothering to look at what it was. Big mistake.

The computer whisked through cyberspace. Up

popped a phalanx of penises, every size, shape, and color. The Web site boasted the best in bears, twinks, and bottoms. It promised the finest videos of men in uniforms or college boys frolicking in their dormitory showers. Gay porn everywhere. The site even blasted music across the laptop speakers. I think it was something by Madonna.

"Charlie?" I stammered inside the din of PCS. It was there, with me suspended in disbelief, that my worst nightmare materialized. From over my right shoulder, I heard the two most terrifying words in the English language.

"Hey, O'Rourke."

CHAPTER 27

I slammed shut Charlie's laptop, buried it underneath elbow and armpit. My face flushed. My throat swelled. Whirling round in my chair, I found Patty Gershon.

For a long humiliating moment, a silent vortex shut out the noise around us. "Hey, whatever floats your boat," Patty finally relented, smirking ever so slightly. "I don't care."

"It's not what you think."

"We need to finish yesterday's conversation," she continued. "But I want you to know. It's okay with me. Really. It's okay. Some of my best friends—"

"It's not like that."

"You can talk to me, O'Rourke."

"You don't understand."

"Those Web sites make for hostile work environments," Gershon observed in a matter-of-fact voice that belied her intent. Wall Street fired people all the time for inappropriate Internet behavior.

Are you threatening me?

"Know what I mean, jelly bean?" she added.

Call her bluff.

"You sound traumatized," I recovered, shoveling something between sarcasm and Southern largesse. "Why don't we walk down to Human Resources? Get some counseling together. You and me, Patty."

"We've got better things to do," she said. "Let's grab a conference room."

"I'd rather talk here." Chloe, distracted by all the commotion, focused on Charlie's laptop. Annie watched Gershon back me into the ropes.

"What I have to say, O'Rourke, isn't for public consumption."

We found an empty conference room, one usually reserved for client meetings. "I'm taking you over the wall," Patty proclaimed, pompous and self-important.

Translation: "I'm disclosing confidential information about a company. During the foreseeable future, you cannot trade the stock or advise others about its prospects." Patty's words tasted like sour milk. I-bankers were the ones who juggled inside information. They took advisers over the "Chinese wall." Not stockbrokers.

"Are we in Banking now?" I had all but forgotten Charlie's gay porn.

Patty ignored my sarcasm. "The CEO of Brisbane Oil Services is a client," she said. "He wants to buy Jack Oil."

"Did he tell you?" I already knew the answer. No fucking way. CEOs rarely confided their buyout plans to personal advisers, no matter how close the relationship. Patty might say something that jeopardized the deal. Even worse, she might accidentally tip someone who traded on the inside information. CEOs feared nothing more than unfriendly visits from the SEC.

"Let's just say," she replied, "that I put two and two together."

Happens all the time.

"Why are you telling me?" I asked.

"Let's work together." She leaned forward and wrapped her hands around my balled fists. The gesture was not sexual. But it was intimate.

"Work on what?" I objected. "Your guy needs bankers, not brokers. Go talk to Sutherling." He handled mergers and acquisitions all the time. Sutherling would know what to do.

"I did."

That's why they were so chummy during Strategy.

"Great. You'll get a nice referral fee from Banking."

"Not so fast," she snapped, recoiling, her hands abandoning my balled fists. "Brisbane uses Morgan for all its banking. SKC's play is to represent Jack Oil."

"And I'm supposed to deliver Jumping JJ."

"I can if you can't," Patty retorted, confident and borderline smug.

"Why doesn't Sutherling call me directly?" I asked.

"Because I'm driving, O'Rourke. I figured out Brisbane's interest in Jack. I alerted Banking. And I'm the only one who knows all the players, including JJ."

The vein in my forehead almost burst. "You spent forty-five minutes with JJ and fucked up any shot I have at collaring his stock. What'd you tell him anyway?"

"Are we back to that?" It was Patty's turn to sound sarcastic. "You don't get JJ at all. He won't collar his stock, O'Rourke. You're missing all the cues here, pal."

"And you've got the finesse of a gorilla in heat. There's a right way and a wrong way to describe the trade to a CEO."

"There's no way," she interrupted. "I checked with Halek. JJ can't hedge Jack Oil. The borrow is for shit. Besides."

"Besides what?"

"Halek priced out a collar. JJ can get about twenty-seven percent upside, maybe twenty-eight if he's lucky. My guess is that Brisbane will pay a fifty percent premium. Your collar, O'Rourke, is a stupid trade."

She does her homework.

"Patty, let me explain this in terms even you can understand."

We heard a knock on the conference room door.

"Come in," Patty called.

It was Casper, AWOL from clipping his fingers. "Can you guys keep it down?" he asked. "My client and I can hear you in the conference room next door. Grove, you're louder than goddamn Scully."

"Sorry, guy," I apologized. Casper closed the door and returned to his meeting.

Patty and I returned to our brawl. "Gershon," I said in measured decibels, "you've got a hunch, nothing more. No facts. No direct confirmation from your guy at Brisbane. You don't know jack."

"Funny."

"No pun intended. I wish I had a dollar for every time somebody puts two and two together and comes up with some half-assed banking idea."

"Sutherling wished he'd thought of it," she replied coolly.

"So what. It's a good idea. You're smart." I had to give on that issue. "But JJ is my client. I've known him for six years, Patty. Six years."

"You finished?"

"Not yet. There's no fucking way I'm splitting economics with you just because you gave Banking a heads-up. JJ uses Goldman for these deals anyway. He's not hiring our bankers just because you spoke with him for forty-five minutes. Give me a break."

"You finished?" she repeated.

"I'm not splitting economics, Patty."

"You know those forty-five minutes? Those forty-five minutes you keep discounting? I did something you'll never do."

"What's that?" I asked.

"Spoke to him in Polish," she replied nonchalantly. "I'm fluent, O'Rourke. Did JJ ever mention how proud he is of his Polish roots? He gave a million bucks to the Polish-American Society. He funds a scholarship for kids of Polish descent."

"Six years, Patty."

"Let me explain so you understand," she said, parroting my earlier dig. "SKC stands to make ten million dollars in fees from the deal. Maybe twenty million dollars. That's more money than you can generate in

ten years with JJ. I'm Sutherling's best shot. No other
bank can bring a native Polish speaker to the table.
And you know Sutherling. He hates Goldman as much
as anybody."

"What do you want?" There was no resignation in my
voice. I was still gathering facts, though one outcome
was clear. If Gershon delivered a $20 million banking
assignment, I would lose Jumping JJ as a client. SKC
would assign coverage to Lady Goldfish.

Sensing her advantage, Patty began outlining her
demands. "A onetime referral fee from Banking won't
cut it," she stated. "That's what, a half million? Chump
change. I want sixty percent of all the money management fees with JJ."

"Fuck you."

"Fuck me?" she laughed. "No. Fuck you, O'Rourke.
A twenty-million-dollar banking fee means I decide
the split. I'm not sure you deserve a dime over thirty
percent. But I like you, O'Rourke. And I'm feeling
charitable."

"Let's see what Kurtz has to say," I bluffed.

"Be my guest," she shot back. "He's already salivating over this year's bonus. Our division refers a twenty-
million-dollar banking assignment and the boss looks
good."

The hit-and-run was now official. I felt like my face
had been plastered against the chrome grate of a Mack
truck. But Patty, mother of three, was no eighteen-
wheeler. She had outhustled, outthought, and outma-
neuvered me in the battle of interdepartmental spin. I
had no idea what to say.

Patty finally broke the silence. "Grove, you look ashen. You okay?" she asked disingenuously.

"*Jestem udupiony,*" I muttered, remembering JJ's words from when he lost his secretary.

"You got that right," Patty muttered. "Only your accent sucks."

"We need to do the right thing for the firm," I finally said. It was the only thing to say. Gershon would report every word back to Kurtz.

"I knew you'd see it my way," she gloated.

"I need time to think."

"About what?" she demanded.

"I spoke with JJ today. He doesn't want to speak again until next week. He was emphatic."

"Don't play games, O'Rourke. You better not talk to him behind my back." Like every stockbroker, Patty knew the one way to win all turf battles: Get the client on your side.

"Wouldn't think of it, Patty."

Confession time.

"You'd better not blow twenty million dollars in fees," she added.

"Give me until Monday afternoon. I'll tell JJ to meet with Banking."

"I'm on that call," she snapped.

"Not a good idea," I said. "It makes more sense for me to set up a meeting. JJ will wonder why you're on the phone."

"Let me worry about that," she said. "I don't want this deal to get away."

"Me either."

"And there's one other thing, O'Rourke."

"What now?"

"Keep away from those Web sites. I don't want my new partner fired for surfing porn at the office."

CHAPTER 28

The next morning I hunkered down, shelved Patty's politics knowing our fight was far from over, and returned to my day job with no further thought of three sharks, Sam's jewels, or the Kelemen Group. The markets consumed my attention. Radio Ray, who ran the high-yield bond desk, called and pitched the latest from his team's petri dish. Using a bond trader's inscrutaspeak, he offered, "Five million Buckeye five and seven-eighths of '47 to go at six."

Translation: You can buy bonds from an Ohio issuer unrelated to the football team. Each year the bonds pay $58.75, the "five and seven-eighths" Radio Ray referenced. Given market conditions, buyers can purchase these bonds for less than their $1,000 face value and earn 6 percent annually through 2047. Business as usual.

"Too long. I want something that matures while we're all living."

"I like the Florida Dirt Panther Creek five and one-eighths of '13 at six-fifty."

"Better. I can use three million."

"Done."

For the next forty-five minutes I advised clients. That's when Lila Priouleau called. "How are things?" she asked.

"Awesome," I replied, staying in top-producer character even though Lila had been a friend since college.

She hesitated for a moment and whispered with all the sweet syrup of the sunny South, "Get off it, Grove."

"What do you mean?"

"Something's eating you. I can tell."

Lila was right. Evelyn always said her third roommate read me like a book. Maybe it was the Dixie roots we shared. "I learned something about Charlie yesterday, and I'm not sure how to tell Sam."

"Tell me."

"It's complicated."

"Sam's important to me," she argued. "We slept together for three years."

"Hey now." I got the joke. Lila meant the same room at Wellesley, not the same bed. There was nothing funny about Charlie's surfing habits. But I knew Lila's guidance might help me say the right thing to Sam. "It's awkward," I ventured.

"Awkward," she scoffed. "You don't know awkward."

Lila Priouleau was the most notorious woman who ever bussed into Harvard Square. She owed her fame to fifteen unfortunate seconds. Otherwise no one would have known her at Harvard. She rarely visited Cambridge. Few people knew her name. And almost no one from Harvard could identify her on sight. Lila spent all her free time down at Yale with that cretin Hurley.

Her celebrity, however, extended to nearly every graduate program. The future captains of industry at Harvard Business School knew about her. So did the craftsmen of jurisprudence from Harvard Law School. The male policy wonks at the Kennedy School of Government gossiped about Lila as they strolled through the ivy-lined courtyards and mingled with other aspiring diplomats. The creative types at the School of Architecture, those who would one day design the next generation of cityscapes, found artistic inspiration from the steamy urban legend that chased her everywhere.

The notoriety at Harvard began with a sophomore biology class at Wellesley. During one unfortunate lecture, the professor described the composition of male ejaculate. She turned the topic, fun stuff for a room full of young women, into a marathon of tedium. On and on she droned. "Semen" here, "semen" there, "semen" everywhere. The professor's flat delivery and matter-of-fact monotone elicited yawns rather than curiosity.

At one point she dully stated, "Fructose comprises over seventy-five percent of semen."

Lila's hand shot up. "Then why doesn't it taste sweet?" she asked with the earnestness of the entire South in her euphonic drawl.

A hush gathered over the room. The professor, an exceedingly proper and schoolmarmish spinster of fifty or more years, retorted, "Would that be your opinion from field research, Miss Priouleau?"

Lila looked at her classmates. They had all swiveled in their seats to gawk. Their eyes dilated wide with amazement, and their jaws hung slack with surprise.

Lila pondered for a moment. She assessed the attention. As the stunned silence in the room gave way to belly laughs and fingers pointing in her direction, Lila knew what to do. She stood. She excused herself from the lecture. She pranced out of the room, her hips rocking like the haughtiest models from Madison Avenue.

On the way out she heard a woman from ZA, the rival sorority, call out, "You go, girl," and more laughter followed.

By the next day word of Lila's comment had spread all through the grapevine of Wellesley's mafiosi. That was just the start. Given the osmotic flow between campuses and the yakety-yak among girlfriends and boyfriends, Lila's seminal query soon became the stuff of legend at Harvard University.

"Why doesn't it taste sweet?" No doubt later Lila drew on memories from that embarrassing lesson. She understood the sting of public humiliation when she hired a biplane with a banner to circle Hurley at the Yale Bowl.

"You don't know awkward."

That line sold me. I briefed Lila on the gay porn, avoiding any reference to Sam's financial woes. Nor did I tell Lila about Patty Gershon and the events following my unfortunate discovery. They were none of her business.

"Tell Sam," Lila counseled. "She deserves the truth."

"What do I say? Charlie was ambisextrous?"

"That's a start."

"There's no proof. All I have are a few Web hits."

Last night in the relative safety of my apartment, however, I had traced Charlie's Internet history. It contained
nothing but gay porn. There were no bank accounts,
brokerage sites, or answers to the only questions that
mattered.

Who killed Charlie? Where is his money?

"What if Charlie didn't wear condoms?" Lila persisted.

"I don't want to spoil things."

"Spoil what?"

"Sam's pregnant, Lila."

"She's what?"

Mistake.

"Two months. Let Sam tell you."

"Pregnancy doubles the urgency, Grove. You tell her
about Charlie."

"I'd rather get the facts first."

"What will you do? Cull the webmasters and cancel
the charges to his credit cards?"

Charlie never used credit cards.

"I'll speak with Crunch."

"Let's continue this at the gym tomorrow night,"
Lila said. "I want to discuss some business in person."

Nice.

We agreed to take a spin class together. Lila's conversation with Crunch had been a ray of sunshine. Her
account would serve as a beachhead into the Priouleau
family's wealth. So I thought. Her talk of business, I
would learn later, had nothing to do with Crunch's comments about Coach or the other retailers they discussed.

After we hung up, my thoughts returned to the dark

side of the last twenty-four hours. Charlie Kelemen had surprised me from the grave. Best friend, savior, and now a dead father—he had been the king of private eyes, the one who hired gumshoes and exposed Lila Priouleau's ex. Charlie had sniffed out philanderers, rescued wives from infidelity and husbands from cuckoldry. He was the patron saint of underdogs, a fat guy who gave meaning to "good." The image was a joke. Gay was okay. My issue was whether Charlie had cheated on Sam.

Lost in these thoughts, I sat and pressed a thumb against my lips. The pose probably looked catatonic to Annie. "Boss, I'm going to Starbucks," she said. "You want a cup of coffee?"

"My treat," I answered, blinking with awareness. "Chloe, how about you?"

Chloe smiled, nodded yes at Annie, but said nothing. She was confirming a trade execution with our equity desk.

"You're the best," Annie said with no hint of yesterday's moodiness.

"Hey, that's my line."

Snagging a twenty-dollar bill from my outstretched hand, she smirked. "Go back to Grove's world now."

"Aren't you a piece of work?" I snorted.

Annie headed toward the elevators. She wore a short khaki skirt, equal parts grace and sex appeal. The smooth lines. The slinky cut. Chloe caught me looking, rolled her shoulder, and winked in an exaggerated manner that said, *Gotcha.*

My face reddened. Busted. At that precise instant,

Frank Kurtz called. Never in the history of mankind had anyone been so grateful for a phone call from the boss. Kurtz wrecked my relief in all of three seconds.

"Frank," I saluted into the receiver, charming, energetic, the make-happy voice reserved for management.

Chloe giggled behind me.

"I hear you're teaming with Patty on JJ," Kurtz announced, his voice buoyant.

NFW, I thought, and glanced over at Estrogen Alley. Patty was on the phone, locked in deep conversation with her latest casualty.

Kurtz encouraged partnerships. He regularly cited the need for competence in fixed income, equities, hedge funds, and estate planning. No broker could master all four categories. Coverage teams with broad expertise, he reasoned, could advise clients more capably.

I preferred a more cynical explanation—the Judas factor. Kurtz knew joint coverage made it harder for brokers to leave SKC. If I took a paycheck from another firm, Patty would fight tooth and nail to keep JJ's assets. Why not? She would keep 100 percent of the revenues instead of 60 percent. It wasn't partnership. It was betrayal on the come.

"Nothing's certain," I replied.

"What's the problem?"

"Economics for one." Gershon's math sucked. Not including shares in Jack Oil, I managed $200 million for JJ. He was only one client among my sixty-five families. But his portfolio generated $1 million in annual fees, of which I kept $350,000. If JJ sold his company, that total could easily double to $700,000. Except for one thing. Lady Goldfish was demanding $420,000. From me. That's big money in anybody's book.

"What about the banking deal?" Frank asked. From experience he knew better than to negotiate splits between advisers.

"JJ's a prickly guy, Frank. He prefers to keep his personal business separate from his investment bank."

"Says who?"

"JJ."

Frank thought a moment. "We want a twenty-million-dollar banking fee more than a money management relationship," he said finally. "You know it. I know it."

"I'll pretend you never said that, Frank."

He ignored my words, the obvious hostility in my voice. "Banking will be all over my ass if this deal slips away." Frank sounded apprehensive. He needed a Cohiba. Cigars were to Frank what spinach was to Popeye.

"That's crazy, Frank. I'll talk to Sutherling. Gershon may be wrong for all we know."

"Don't let this fee get away, Grove."

He hung up before I could ask, "Is the pope askew?" The exchange left me exhausted. I needed a new axiom to complement the preceding four.

Five: Top producers avoid management in order to conserve energy and make money.

Sutherling, investment banker and work dog, had been in Wichita yesterday. I dialed again, anxious to touch base, anxious to learn what he knew. Lady Goldfish, out of earshot, waved at me from her cubicle. I smiled back.

"I bet you're calling about Brisbane and Jack," Sutherling answered.

"That almost sounds like a cocktail."

"One we both can drink," he agreed.

"How well do you know JJ?"

"We've met. I've never gotten anywhere with him."

"How can I help?"

"Get us in a room together. The sooner, the better."

"That's why I'm calling. I'm boxed out until Monday."

"What do you mean?"

"JJ and I spoke yesterday. He wants to speak on Monday but not before. He's busy as shit."

"If there's a deal percolating, we need to speak now."

Sutherling was right. But JJ was the client. I needed to satisfy both. "Here's what we do," I said, taking command. "Wait fifteen minutes. I'll call JJ's assistant and explain why he needs to speak with you. Then you call. He might take your call. If he doesn't, I'll speak with him on Monday. One thing's for sure."

"What's that?"

"He'll meet with you, if I ask him. Timing is the only issue."

Confession time.

"What about Patty?" Sutherling asked.

"You tell me."

"You guys are covering JJ jointly?" he asked.

"Nothing's certain yet," I said. There was that foul taste again, spoiled milk.

"Look," he said brusquely. "I don't want broker bullshit getting in the way of a big M and A win. Her

Polish may be just the edge we need to oust Goldman.
She's on the team, like it or not."

I had just managed to piss off my best source of referrals from Banking. Not a good thing. "Whatever it
takes," I conceded.

She leaves bodies in her wake.

After we hung up, I called JJ's assistant as planned.
He was in a meeting, but she promised to get him a
message. The phone traffic, so frenzied earlier, had died
down for the moment. I called Crain and Cravath, annoyed they had not returned any of my calls dating back
to Friday.

"Is Crain there?"

"May I take a message?" the receptionist asked.

"Yeah, if I thought it would do any good. Is Cravath
there?" I continued.

"Your message?" she yawned. I could almost hear
the receptionist give me the finger. Auditors would
never make it as brokers.

No service ethic.

"Tell both of them that I'll camp outside their door if
they don't call back by tomorrow."

It was a good opportunity to review the information
on MRI Capital, Romanov's hedge fund. I reached inside my briefcase and pulled out the red folder. It was
one of the last items Charlie had touched while living.

*Maybe I should give the file to Fitzsimmons and
Mummert.*

CHAPTER 29

Bullshit.

No way I was giving the red folder to Boston's police department. Their priority was to find Charlie's killer. Mine was to find Sam and Betty's lost money, something of a tangent to Fitzsimmons and Mummert. Pregnant mother or single mom in need of cash—they didn't care. The homicide investigation came first as far as the officers were concerned.

Never thought I'd be protecting anyone from the police.

The file bulged with MRI offering memorandums. There were also clippings from every major business publication, *Business Week, Forbes*, and *The Wall Street Journal* to name a few. I was still wrestling with yesterday's question to Crunch.

Did the Kelemen Group invest in MRI Capital?

Charlie had been a great salesman. And from personal experience I knew the one factor that united all salespeople. We're suckers for great pitches. My fat friend with the humongous head was no different. He could have worn crosshairs on his back.

Maybe he did.

Alex Romanov knew how to sell. He told *Forbes* magazine, "Some say luck is what separates smart money from dumb. I don't buy it. We do our homework. We don't look for great companies. We look for great value." Sitting at my desk, I could almost hear the Mad Russian pounding the table.

Charlie ate this stuff up.

Romanov possessed the kind of conviction that turned ordinary stockbrokers into top producers. In one article after another, there in bold print, I found axiom number one in action. Investors hire advisers with strong points of view. The more impassioned our convictions, the better. Apparently, the same energy worked for hedgies promoting their funds.

Several years ago *Barron's* invited Romanov to join a panel discussion of small-cap money managers. The magazine described the feature as a variation of its Roundtable stock picks, must reading for investors. By declining, Romanov surprised everyone.

Some hedgies reacted like Marlon Brando had just refused an Oscar for *The Godfather*. Others charged that Romanov was unwilling to share center stage. True to form, he got the last word. "Groupthink," he explained to *Fortune* in an article profiling MRI Capital. "Nobody makes money from *Barron's* tripe."

It was an incendiary remark for a guy with $800 million under management. But Charlie Kelemen savored every word. He highlighted "groupthink" with a yellow fluorescent marker. In the margin he penned two asterisks. Or perhaps they were line drawings of assholes.

He's intense, Charlie. I'll give you that.

In other articles Romanov harangued with the certitude of the insane. He always presented his stock picks with the same signature line: "We are *maniacally* obsessed with value." He never failed to emphasize the word "maniacally."

Romanov really is a mad Russian.

He claimed to own "fallen angels." In classic Wall Street vernacular, "fallen angels" were bonds that had lost their investment-grade credit ratings from the usual suspects among paid professionals. Moody's, Standard & Poor's, and Fitch no longer considered the bonds rock solid, because profits and cash flow had faded at the issuing companies. They now rated the bonds BB or worse—junk.

I took issue with Romanov's use of "fallen angels." MRI Capital owned stocks, not bonds. Romanov invested in small businesses with total market values of $300 million or less. Wall Street called them "micro caps." Sometimes, he even invested in "nano caps." These firms were worth less than $50 million. No one ever challenged Romanov's use of the slang, though.

Tough to argue with triple-digit returns.

In some ways I wished SKC's analysts were like Romanov. We boasted our share of *Institutional Investor* All-Stars. But I feared the best minds had bolted to a land of milk and honey prophesied by the Old Testament—hedge funds.

The draw was simple. Hedge funds paid better. Partners sometimes gorged on Croesus-sized comp because of the fees charged by their funds. Hedgies kept 20 percent of all investment profits, the "carry," with no commensurate obligation to share risk.

Danger, Will Robinson.

The carry rewarded hedge funds for winning bets. It did not punish them, however, for excessive or ill-advised investments. Investors ate the losses, not the managers. As a consequence, hedgies wagered big, the better to goose returns and maximize incentive fees. One hundred million in trading profits, for example, meant the hedgies earned $20 million in their personal accounts.

It's not "the carry." It's hara-kiri.

No matter the divergent interests, investors agreed to the fee structure. The best and the brightest minds of Wall Street mesmerized them, seduced them with the heady allure of better returns. By agreeing to the carry, investors financed the migration of top talent from investment banks to hedge funds.

Nobody gives a shit about 20 percent when you're making money.

Quite by accident, the czars of oversight fed a growing indifference to risk. The SEC, NASD, and other regulatory bodies ruled unevenly. They came down hard on brokerage houses, less so on hedge funds. Prosecution and the specter of jail cast a fearsome shadow over Wall Street's brokerages. Naturally, top talent sought refuge in more benign settings with better comp.

Somebody should keep tabs on the bureaucrats.

SKC employed legions of lawyers just to comply with all the statutes. In more cynical moments, I told clients, "We're really a law firm with a large finance subsidiary."

With less oversight, the hedge funds dealt themselves extraordinary investment powers. They borrowed to the gunwales. They cut side deals and catered to the well-heeled investors with more market savvy. Some offering documents even allowed them to value private securities like motion picture partnerships.

Sure makes the 20 percent calculations more subjective.

For all my cynicism surrounding the industry, I respected Romanov. He had grossed 129 percent last year. He was up 75 percent through July.

Hard to argue with the results.

Forbes estimated Romanov had taken home $30 million through the years. It was no surprise that Charlie befriended him. As a fund of funds the Kelemen Group actively searched for outstanding investment managers, for guys like the next Warren Buffett.

Inside the red folder I found an offering prospectus. The subscription agreements had not been filled out, nothing to indicate whether Charlie had invested in MRI Capital. There was plenty of the legalese, the ponderous and mind-numbing language that dampened the soles of my feet with perspiration. A dozen dog-eared letters added heft to the file. No way would I read them, either. They were yesterday's news, dated market commentaries Romanov had mailed to investors months ago.

Boring.

Rooting through the stacks, I searched for the list of stocks Romanov owned. The printout showed a date two weeks prior to Charlie's death. It seemed strange that my friend possessed anything so current. Hedge funds buried their secrets. Given Romanov's success, he could do what he wanted and tell investors what he chose.

The Mad Russian's investment strategy dominated my thoughts for the moment. Now I possessed a laundry list of the companies he owned. I could generate similar eye-popping returns for my clients' portfolios. Plagiarism, after all, was no sin on Wall Street. It was a requisite for success.

None of Romanov's holdings looked familiar, not one name. I generally bought blue-chip shares for my clients and stayed away from the micro caps. Charlie had circled one name with a red pen, Rugged Computers. Just outside the circles, he had also scrawled "31.12" and "30.11."

Charlie's interest, his scribbles, struck me as curious. He never spoke about individual holdings. He picked fund managers, not stocks. Even with his Midas touch, he often joked, "Don't ever buy my hot tips."

What do the numbers mean, Charlie? Why'd you care about Rugged Computers?

CHAPTER 30

I grabbed a late lunch with Zola, the newbie with the bright mind and bandaged ear. She ate eggplant, couscous, and assorted vegetarian roughage best left to the rabbits. Béarnaise sauce topped my bacon burger, no tomatoes, cheesy waffle fries, and Lipitor on the side.

"We have the Series 7 on Monday," Zola announced.

"Don't screw up," I advised, only half tongue in cheek. Every so often, some newbie blew the exam and washed out of SKC's training program. Proper licensing was the lifeblood of advisers, the Series 7 our equivalent to the bar.

After lunch the phones heated up. It was not until 4:45 P.M. when I came up for air. Gershon left early to attend her daughter's play, her empty chair a relief. I considered how to ask Crunch whether our friend had stepped out on Sam.

Lila Priouleau's words still haunted me: "Pregnancy doubles the urgency, Grove. You tell her about Charlie."

Outside, the hacks were changing shifts. Their roof lights all read "off duty." I managed to snag a yellow cab, but my sense of good fortune was premature. The cabbie from Where-the-Fuckistan ran a red light at the corner of Fifth and Fifty-second and almost clipped a messenger cyclist in the process. We got the bird.

He stopped short at the corner of Madison Avenue, turned left from the right-hand lane of our one-way street, and cut off a Lincoln Town Car. His multicultural disregard for New York's traffic laws provoked angry honks and furious shouts. We got the bird.

Heading up Madison, there were no further turns to make, and it appeared the tricky part was behind us. No such luck. The cabbie weaved in and out of traffic far too fast. He never bothered to signal and never alerted other drivers whether we were bearing right or pulling left. Not once, not twice, but a total of three times we got the bird.

Where-the-Fuckistan finally deposited me at Crunch's salon on Seventy-sixth, and I encouraged him to visit San Francisco. "They pay cabbies top dollar out there."

Like all beauty parlors, Crunch's place reeked, the combo-stench of Starbucks and hair goop. He should have piped oxygen onto the premises. Air-quality controls worked on the space station. Surely they would deliver equal results inside a salon on the Upper East Side. Instead, Crunch tolerated the toxic fumes.

His patrons reminded me of Charleston's swamps. Thick gelatinous masks covered their faces. The black goop looked like pluff mud from the banks of the Ashley, where predatory crustaceans trolled for sea refuse in their daily quest to survive. Several of the customers wore thick white bathrobes and wrapped towels around their heads turban-style. When I squinted just right, the assortment of terry cloth resembled chitinous exoskeletons.

For the briefest of moments I returned to the low-country. Only now I inhaled cappuccino and carcinogenic shit for hair instead of noxious fumes from the paper mill west of the Ashley. And blue peeked through ringlets, not the body armor of little crabs waggling their fearless claws against overwhelming odds.

"Oh my God." Crunch's voice boomed through the salon. He scooted up from behind and whisked me into a stylist's chair. In his black barber's smock, cropped at the shoulders, Crunch looked beefy and severe. His biceps bulged, and I feared they might tear the fading 101st tattoo. His long hair shone with the most brilliant shade of black. The black was almost blue, a hair color that I had seen among Filipinos but never on a white guy from New Jersey.

The crustaceans studied Crunch under the cover of their black goop. None waved their claws in our direction or scuttled defiantly from side to side. There would be no fight to the finish this time, and the peace in the salon pleased me no end.

"Crunch, I—"

"I nothing. You look like a fucking rag bag," he whispered.

"What's that?"

"Army for 'mess.' Now sit still." Crunch's eyes blazed with concentration. One hand explored the nape of my neck, the other the crown of my head. He moved methodically, but roughly indifferent to my growing consternation. He clipped from above, from behind, from everywhere, it seemed.

"I don't need a haircut. I just had one."

Crunch changed in that moment. He transformed into a gay version of Lloyd Bentsen, the late senator from Texas. Solemn and grave, Crunch replied, "I know haircuts, Grove. It's what I do. That's no haircut."

"You think?" I asked, at a loss for words, understanding how Dan Quayle felt during the 1988 vice presidential debate.

"Word," Crunch affirmed with papal conviction.

"What the hell does 'word' mean?"

"It means I'll fix everything, sweetie."

I ignored the "sweetie" and focused on the reason for my visit. "I need to ask about Charlie. Things I'm not comfortable asking."

Crunch said nothing at first. He focused on my locks, tugging and pulling them. He snipped errant strands with casual abandon. After an interminable pause, three hours in dog time, Crunch asked, "Are you a real redhead?" He rubbed my shoulder suggestively. "You know what I'm saying?"

"Knock it off, Crunch. I need you to focus."

"I can't talk about Charlie yet," he sniffed, more of a queen with his mannerisms now. "I'm still in mourning, you know." He fiddled with the collar of his black smock as though pinching back the grief.

"What about my hair?" I asked, backing off, giving Crunch room to collect his thoughts. "I never said what I want."

"Would you tell Picasso how to paint?"

"Well, yes, if he painted my hair. It might come out blue."

"Trust me, sweetie." Crunch squirted shaving cream onto his hands and began lathering my face. The heated barber's foam warmed my cheeks and made my face glow.

Yet I was far from comfortable. Crunch's razor gave me the willies, his previous career the source of my angst. As he scraped the blade against a sharpening strap, the steel-against-leather strokes hissed, *Watch what you say. Watch what you say.*

"What do you want to know about Charlie?" he finally asked.

Crunch's timing sucked. I had never discussed homosexuality with a gay ex-killer from the Delta Force, one brandishing a razor so near my neck. Now seemed the wrong time to start. "Was—"

"Don't gulp," Crunch interrupted, "unless you want your Adam's apple around your ankles."

"Sorry."

"I've had plenty of practice, sweetie. You know what I'm saying?"

That practice is what bothers me.

Deep down I knew better than to worry. Crunch had parked his fearsome skills in the Middle East long ago. I closed my eyes and hoped for the best. "Was Charlie gay?"

"He was married."

"That doesn't answer the question," I replied, opening my eyes.

There was a long, awkward pause. The crab look-alikes chattered in the background. I waited.

"He had his experiences," Crunch said evasively.

"What does that mean?"

"A boy has to pledge, before we accept him into the club. You know what I'm saying?"

"Maybe." The truth was I had no clue what Crunch meant. "Did Sam know?"

"They had issues."

"Will you stop all the cryptic shit? You sound like Dr. Phil."

My angry voice cut through the salon's vapors. The crustaceans eyed us suspiciously. The other stylists stopped clipping and stared in our direction.

I tried to ease the palpable tension in the small room, "Sorry, folks."

Crunch put down the razor and walked to the front of the stylist's chair. Locking onto my eyes, he pushed his face into mine. Too close. It was the same violation of body space, the same kind of intimidation, that had worked so well on Scully. "She knew," Crunch whispered tersely.

I recoiled.

He pressed closer. "Showdown at the OK Corral." No longer effeminate but tense and conspiratorial, Crunch behaved like he was laying bare some deep, dark secret.

He was. The information troubled me. After our dinner at Live Bait, I had asked Sam if Charlie was having an affair. She responded by flirting: *Where would Charlie find a better piece of ass?* Suddenly, her answer angered me.

Just as suddenly, I relaxed. Charlie's betrayal, it occurred to me, had embarrassed Sam. I assumed "experiences" constituted some form of betrayal. The thought made me sad. I wanted to believe in Charlie. I wanted to believe in Sam. They had done so much for me, for each other.

"You didn't hear it from me," Crunch said, looking for stray strands to snip. He trimmed my eyebrows, attention to detail that would have made Evelyn so happy. "You know what I'm saying?"

"Don't worry. I'm Schultz."

"Who?"

"The fat guy on *Hogan's Heroes*. 'Nothing, nothing, nothing.'"

"Oh, sweetie, you need to get out more often." Crunch held up a mirror for me to assess my haircut. "Do you like?" he asked.

"Damn, Crunch. It looks good," I admitted genuinely. "I need to visit more often."

He clasped his hands together by his neck, cocked a hip, and immodestly congratulated himself, "I know."

"There's one more thing."

Crunch leaned forward and violated my airspace for the second time. "Yes?" he said flirtatiously.

Instead of backing away again, I inched even closer and grabbed each of his hands, one in my left and one in my right. The gesture rattled Crunch, particularly the way I riveted onto his eyes. Proximity was his game. He was the one who used drama as a social weapon. He was the one who flinched, though. "Crunch, would you please stop calling me 'sweetie.' You know what I'm saying?" It was one of my more assoholic moments, no doubt.

"That's it?" he asked, genuinely surprised. "That's the one thing?"

"No. I may need your help with Sam. I'm just not sure how."

Crunch pulled back, and I sensed indifference. His reaction seemed odd, more confusing than effeminate. Crunch had been so kind to Sam at Woodlawn Cemetery.

Is that hostility?

"Are you still visiting Sam this week?" I asked.

"Maybe. And don't you dare get me in trouble with her."

The crustaceans would shed their shells soon. I was tempted to wait and see what emerged. Instead, I paid $175, reminisced about the days of $5 haircuts, and exited into the fresh air of New York City.

Back in the open, taxi fumes and humidity now flushing the glue from my lungs and brain, I regretted my jerky comment to Crunch. It made no sense to alienate a resource. Crunch had told me something. I just couldn't figure out what.

You know what I'm saying?

CHAPTER 31

Thursday morning I called Halek first thing. We could always talk, and I needed his input on several fronts. "Don't say a word to Sam," he advised. "Charlie's bedroom choices don't affect anyone now."

Hmm. Lila says tell. Halek says don't.

"That's not the issue, Cliff. Sam joked when I asked if Charlie was having an affair."

"Give her a break," Halek urged. "She just watched three sharks eat her husband."

"She lied."

"Forget it. There's only one way to help Sam and your other friend." Cliff meant Betty Masters. "Wind down the Kelemen Group."

Lady Goldfish was next on my agenda. When I briefed Halek about Patty's power play, he grew agitated. "Fucking harpy," he growled.

It was the perfect metaphor. In Greek mythology harpies were the death spirits that constantly stole food from Phineas's plate. Thinking about Patty's grab for my client, I understood the old boy's frustration.

"You got that right."

"I'm going to Kurtz," Cliff thundered.

"On what basis?"

"We ran numbers and spent forty-five minutes discussing the borrow."

"So."

"I have better things to do than shoot the shit with some gasbag who's lying about a trade."

"She'll eat your lunch, too."

"What do you mean?"

"Sutherling's in her corner, and there's a twenty-million prize. That's not a fight you want."

"Doesn't matter." Halek was boiling now, anger overriding his trademark calm.

"The Monthly Nut won't do a thing," I cautioned. "No sac."

"You got that right." He paused, ratcheting back his wrath. "She'll blow herself up, Grove. It's a matter of time."

You say the same thing about Romanov.

"I'm trying to figure out how to light the match."

"Just do what all advisers do in your shoes." He sounded more cerebral now, the everyday Cliff, the calculating strategy general.

"What's that?"

"Arrange an intervention."

"What do you mean?"

"Get the client involved. Works every time."

"It has to wait until Monday."

"Suit yourself. But ask yourself one question."

"Which is?"

"You think Patty is waiting until Monday?"

I was all set to call Crain and Cravath, yet again, when Annie delivered a fresh cup of coffee. Chloe mouthed the words, *My treat*. She was listening to someone on the phone.

It was clear Annie wanted to gossip. Gabfests were Wall Street's exhaust, the inevitable fumes from our culture of ambition and relative youth. "Did you hear about Gibson?" He was one of the older brokers in the office, a fifty-something guy who lived in Bronxville.

"What happened?"

"He was drinking at the Whiskey Bar last night." That watering hole was a trough for bad behavior. It had spawned numerous office legends, which grew in hyperbole each year as we retold our stories and embellished them with slightly different twists each time.

I know where this is going.

"He staggered out of the bar around one A.M. last night," she continued. "Blind drunk."

"Been there before."

"Not this bad," Annie countered. "He went from happy to ripshit in five seconds flat."

"What was the problem?"

"No cabs."

"What'd he do?"

"Hired one of those horse-drawn carriages, like the tourists get, to take him home. All the way up Broadway."

"That's fifteen miles," I noted, not believing my ears.

"The ride cost him eight hundred dollars," she confirmed. "The guy's a rock star if you ask me."

Just as the day turned better, the pleasures of Annie's stories, it turned worse. "*New York Post* on your second line," Chloe interrupted.

"You're in luck," Mandy Maris announced over the receiver.

"You too."

"Why me?" she asked, taken aback by my response.

"I'm not hanging up on you. I didn't realize it was Sam Kelemen who put you onto me."

"So you'll do an interview?"

"Not sure yet. Why am I in luck?"

"We're not running the story on Charlie Kelemen until the middle of next week."

"What's lucky about that? Anybody but a cobra fucker would leave his widow alone."

Wrong thing to say.

"It seems to me," she replied, ignoring my jab and setting the bait, "I'd want to clear my best friend's name. Set things right. But that's just me."

"What do you mean, Mandy?"

"His investors are starting to worry about their money. The Kelemen Group has no bench strength."

"Are you free early next week?"

"I'm free now."

"Not happening, Mandy. I need to get somebody from our PR department to join us."

Advisers don't talk to the press.

* * *

Patty's chair was empty over in Estrogen Alley. Halek's words still gnawed at me: *"You think Patty is waiting until Monday?"* Perhaps she was sitting in JJ's office right now.

No way I'm calling him before Monday.

Instead, I dialed Charlie's auditors. This time a guy answered. "Crain and Cravath." His voice sounded twenty-something.

"Let me guess," I replied sarcastically. "Crain is at the Jersey Shore. And Cravath is in the Hamptons."

"May I help you?" he asked. He sounded distant and aloof, enough composure to put me over the edge.

"I've been waiting for a return call since Friday," I bristled.

"I'm sorry," he said. "May I take a message?"

"Sure, but first I want your address. Then you can tell Crain and Cravath that I'm camping outside their doors until they speak to me."

"You're welcome to visit, sir. But they won't be here." Ice water coursed through the kid's veins. He was unflappable.

"Why's that?"

"We're an answering service."

I should have known.

"Do you have a number where I can reach them directly?"

"We don't give it out."

"May I speak to the manager?"

"Sure," he replied. "What would you like?"

"To speak to the manager," I repeated, losing patience. "What is it you don't understand about speaking to the manager?"

"I'm the manager. We don't give out client phone numbers. Is there anything else?"

"Forget it." I hung up. Exasperated, I called Betty Masters.

"Grove, it's good to hear from you. How are things?"

"Some progress," I reported. "I'm working my way through Charlie's laptop. The filing system is a mess, but I found a record of your investment."

"That sounds like good news," she replied brightly.

"By any chance, did you find a second audited statement?"

"You have what I have. Is there a problem?"

"I'm still looking for the master list of his funds. And I don't have access to Charlie's office."

"Have you asked the police for permission?"

"No," I admitted. "The lead cop—"

"Fitzsimmons?" she interrupted.

"He's been out to see you?" I asked.

"Both Fitzsimmons and his partner," she confirmed. "Nice men."

"You're kidding, right?" Fitzsimmons was a crusty New Englander, and Mummert was nothing more than his echo.

Sensing my disagreement, Betty counseled, "Just tell them what you want, Grove. You never know."

"Maybe you're right." Thirty seconds later, I reached Fitzsimmons on his cell phone.

"Do you have something for me?" he asked. Right to the point.

"I'm hoping to gain access to the Kelemen Group's files."

"We've already been through this," he replied.

"Is that a no?"

"You catch on fast."

"I thought you were trying to understand his financial affiliations, Detective Fitzsimmons." I remembered how he had grilled me about the referrals.

"What's that supposed to mean?"

"Sam Kelemen has no source of income until she unwinds the Kelemen Group. And Charlie's investors are starting to bitch."

Thank you for that pearl, Mandy Fucking Maris.

"I still don't see why you need access," Fitzsimmons said.

"You interrupted. I need the Kelemen Group's financial statements to start liquidating the portfolio. I'm kind of stuck."

"You're not touching my evidence," he barked. "And what do you mean you're stuck?"

"The files on Charlie's personal computer are a mess. I haven't found anything yet."

Wrong thing to say, the sequel.

"What computer?"

"Charlie had a laptop."

"Why didn't you tell us?" Fitzsimmons growled.

"I was trying to help Sam Kelemen. Betty Masters, too."

"You really are a chowdahhead," Fitzsimmons replied, annoyed no end.

"What's with the attitude? I might be able to help you as well. Finance is my world, not yours."

"Let me worry about that. In the meantime, you're withholding evidence. Where's the laptop now?"

"My office."

"We'll be over in thirty minutes."

"Great," I said sarcastically.

"One other thing," he added.

"Yes?"

"You keep holding back on me. I don't get it. I don't like it. And you're becoming more interesting to our investigation all the time."

We hung up. I should have been scared. Fitzsimmons had all but called me a suspect. I didn't kill Charlie, though, and without guilt I was unafraid. Just pissed.

"Hey, Boss," Annie said.

"Can't talk," I snapped. She recoiled, and I immediately regretted my foul humor. "I need to buy a hard drive. And fast."

CHAPTER 32

The visit from Fitzsimmons and Mummert proved anticlimactic. They impounded Charlie's laptop in our reception area. I returned to my desk without a word about the backup copy on my new hard drive.

The real trouble started that evening. Lila Priouleau and I met at the Reebok Sports Club on Columbus Avenue. Like everybody in their early thirties, she joined a gym to stay fit and stave off the coming onslaught— droopy triceps, love handles, and other cruel tricks of the body. The Reebok Club offered four weight gyms, crack squads of private trainers, and a lap pool. It guaranteed access to the latest and greatest exercise machines.

The club also boasted one of the hottest singles scenes in New York City. From the moment the doors opened, it buzzed with young professionals. Buff men honed their six-packs. Fetching women meditated through yoga and free-weight combos that kept busts up and pounds down. Amid the smell of perspiration and the moist exchange of phone numbers, it paid to look good.

Lila wore skimpy neon yellow running shorts to the gym. Every man with a pulse checked out her legs. Every woman took a long, hard look. I strained not to gawk at Lila's cleavage. Her breasts, like gifts from Botticelli, poured from a black top and cast shadows across a ribbed jersey. Her green eyes, tomato-red hair, and Mediterranean tones completed the pièce de résistance.

Next to Lila I looked piggy. Soiled medical tape held together the remnants of my ancient mesh-and-leather Rivat shoes. Black cycling shorts and a Harvard sweatshirt, cropped just above the elbows and soft from a thousand spins through the washing machine, hardly qualified as haute couture.

The Body Nazis in our spin class favored the spandex billboards worn by professional cyclists. I would never understand why anyone voluntarily chose to wear brands of butter emblazoned across their butts. People should stink when they exercised, not care whether they owned the same rubber-band suits as Mario Cipollini, the great Italian sprinter with movie-star looks.

Our spin teacher was an ex-Marine with a devoted following, the Reebok Club's answer to Gunnery Sergeant Hartman in *Full Metal Jacket*. He tailored "jodie" calls, otherwise known as military cadence, to his indoor cycling classes. At first Lila and I spoke little as we listened to his bullhorn voice.

> *"Biker, Biker, where you at?*
> *Come on out and lose some fat!*
> *Is it whiskey? Is it wine?*
> *Or is it lack of PT time!"*

It proved impossible to stay silent all through the class. Lila and I had not seen each other since Charlie's funeral. After fifteen minutes of hard-core pedaling, she volunteered, "We're moving back to Atlanta."

That's why she wanted to meet.

"Really?" Lactic acid screamed from inside my legs. "Why?"

"For one thing, I haven't found the right guy. And I want Katie Anne to spend more time with her grandparents."

"Well, that's direct," I said. "I'm surprised you moved here in the first place."

"I don't want him to see Katie Anne." Lila wheezed from either exertion or revulsion when she said "him."

"You mean Hurley?"

"No. I mean Osama bin Trailer Trash."

"Won't he still be in Atlanta when you return?"

"Hardly. He can't seem to keep a job." She smirked.

"Why's that?"

"You don't piss off Cash Priouleau on family turf. Let's just leave it at that." Lila's Southern accent could sweeten the thump of a guillotine.

"Got it." Steering toward business, I said, "That's some conversation you had with Crunch."

"He's a riot." She panted as she spoke. Lila's cyclometer registered ninety-five revolutions per minute. Even through the olive skin tones, her face burned red from exertion. "I'm glad we spoke."

"I didn't bring any paperwork."

"I mean about Charlie," she said, pedaling harder.

Ease off the sales pitch.

"Crunch and I spoke about the Web sites . . ." I paused for effect. "And other things."

"It almost doesn't matter," she huffed. "Tell Sam he was gay, end of story. I want to discuss the Kelemen Group."

It was only a matter of time.

"I know Cash and you invested ten million dollars. But that's about all I know."

"You make it sound like a big surprise, Grove."

"What's that supposed to mean?"

"You've known for months."

"Excuse me?" I didn't believe my ears.

"Don't be goofy," she puffed. "You heard."

Alarm bells erupted inside my head. "I learned two days ago, Lila. Your name was on a spreadsheet."

"Hang on, fellow." Lila's voice grew terse. She stopped pedaling. Her wind returned miraculously. "I invested in the Kelemen Group partly because of the letter you sent. It's just business, you know."

"What are you talking about?"

"Our put option?"

I stopped pedaling. "You'd better start at the beginning. I have no idea what you mean."

"Charlie asked our family to invest in his fund of funds."

"Okay?"

"He said we couldn't lose."

"Lila, I know your father invested eight million and you invested two."

"Only because Charlie agreed to guarantee the investment."

"Guarantee?"

"If the value ever fell below the initial investment, Charlie agreed to make up the difference."

"I know what 'guarantee' means. I just can't believe he agreed to that."

"It was Charlie's idea," Lila said. "He said everybody on Wall Street uses put options."

"We do. But you pay for them."

"My dad's was one million, mine two hundred and fifty thousand dollars."

"How's this relate to me? The 'just business' part?"

"We weren't certain if Charlie had the wherewithal to guarantee ten million bucks."

"Okay?"

"That's why Charlie offered to get that letter from you."

"What letter, Lila?"

"You're starting to annoy me, Grove." Her accent no longer sounded sweet.

"What letter?" I repeated, my choleric tone turning the heads of others in the spin class who were trying to listen to the Marine.

"The letter that said 'I have known Charlie for I-forget-how-many years. He maintains an eight-figure account with SKC. We value our long-standing relationship with Mr. Kelemen.' Blah, blah, blah."

"I never sent that letter."

"A signature says you did."

"Can I get a copy?"

"Of course," Lila said. Her face had turned to stone, expressionless and unmoving.

I felt sick. It had nothing to do with exercise. It had everything to do with Charlie Kelemen. I never sent Lila a reference letter. Charlie was not a client. What had he done? I wanted to head over to Woodlawn, dig Charlie out of his damn box, and kick his fat dead ass. Instead of pleading my case, though, I asked questions. Interrogation was the fail-safe mechanism employed by top producers confronting uncertainty. "What would you say if I told you Charlie never banked with us?"

"I'd say SKC has a big problem. What are you telling me, Grove?"

I avoided her question and posed my own. "How come you never mentioned the letter to me?"

"What was the point? Charlie and you were good friends. And we have a letter of confidence on SKC's letterhead."

"I see." My stomach belly flopped onto the small intestines.

"There's the other thing, too."

"Which is what?"

"Charlie paid a two percent finder's fee for new investors."

"You've known him as long as I have, Lila. Why would he pay me anything?"

"You're a broker, Grove. You guys work on commission, and I just assumed—"

"Lila," I butted in, "Charlie never paid me a dime."

Sensing my anger, she repeated, "It's just business."

The Body Nazis were staring now. The ex-Marine bellowed:

> *"He stole whiskey.*
> *I stole wine.*
> *Now we're doing double time."*

CHAPTER 33

My bed has two pillows, soft and mushy, delicious and ductile. They are forgiving lovers, generous and buxom, always willing to nestle in tight no matter how foul my mood or execrable my morning-after breath. They are tender, a faithful blend of cotton and goose down. At night they comfort me with insouciant dreams. On the weekends they beckon me to join them for ménage à trois power naps. The pillows overcome all my objections, and I succumb, the willing guest of gracious hosts.

One pillow cradles my head. The other doubles as a want ad for a new lover, the kind of announcement that appears in the classified wilderness of *The Village Voice*.

WORKAHOLIC STOCKBROKER DESPERATELY SEEKS SINGLE FEMALE WITH SASSY GOOD LOOKS AND DROLL INTELLECT TO MATCH. MUST BE WILLING TO DEAL WITH EMOTIONAL BAGGAGE AND NURSE FRAGILE MALE PSYCHE BACK TO HEALTH.

There has been no guest traffic through my bedroom. No "flow," as Wall Street describes trading activity.

Sometimes the second pillow props my head just a little higher, the better to read. Sometimes it becomes an adult teddy bear, the willing recipient of fetal death grips. It works well with the first. The two pillows are veteran dance partners. They complement each other's moves with grace and fluidity. Together, they whisk me off to a better place.

After seeing Lila I slept for shit. The pillows lost their magic that night. They exposed my flank, left me vulnerable to an incoming salvo of worries. That night my bed was no five-star retreat.

The tortuous turning started at once, tossing, tossing, and more tossing. All I saw was Charlie. His fat head. His goofy smile. His chins waddling and banging against the folds of his neck. His gut hanging over his belt like a silk sack loaded with three-dozen doughnuts. His pudgy man breasts straining against a pink oxford shirt, once crisp from starch but now wilted with messenger bags of sweat riding beneath plump armpits.

What the fuck have you done, Charlie?

From eleven P.M. until 1:07 A.M. I thrashed. I looked at my alarm clock every five minutes or so. I urinated a hundred times. I lowered the toilet seat after every agitated piss. Evelyn would have approved. I raised it every time my peevish bladder beckoned. Raise, lower, raise, lower. I congratulated myself for toilet seat etiquette above and beyond the call of duty, like it deserved the Nobel Peace Prize among married couples. But Evelyn was gone. Raise, lower, raise, lower. I lay

on my side. I flopped on my back. I pulled the covers
over my head like a cocoon. I kicked the sheets down
around my ankles. I plucked goose nibs projecting from
the corners of my second pillow. I took my shirt off. I
put it back on. I played Billie Holiday music. I turned
her off. I opened the window to get some fresh air. I
closed it when the fresh air smelled less fresh and more
like stockyards, ripe from the July humidity. Raise,
lower, raise, lower.

Why'd you forge my name, bastard?

I was pissed. That letter was a sham. I never signed
it. Charlie never opened an eight-figure account with
my firm. That letter would drag SKC through a fen of
litigation if not refuted beyond all doubt.

"Your Honor," Cash Priouleau's lawyers would say,
"our clients invested ten million with Mr. Kelemen.
They paid one-point-two-five million dollars for put
options, securities designed to protect their principal.
That's a total of eleven-point-two-five million. Mr.
O'Rourke's testimonial swayed their investment decision, Your Honor. His company has a market value of
thirty-five billion. It professes expertise in money management. It's only fair this big, powerful, influential
firm with deep pockets reimburse our client for their
losses."

Where'd you get SKC's letterhead, bastard?

Those arguments could cost SKC $11.25 million. In
fact, the Priouleaus might win damages totaling millions more. Pain and suffering and all that crap. Cash
and Lila had not lost any money yet. But who knew
what would happen when we unwound the Kelemen

Group? Hedge funds lost money just like everybody else. The Priouleaus would raise hell if they received anything less than $11.25 million. A messy court battle would cost me my career.

No wonder you got whacked, bastard.

Evelyn knew how to handle these situations. She thought methodically, chewed on facts for days. She developed intricate solutions. She reviewed each step, played out what-if scenarios, and discarded the actions with bad outcomes. I needed Evelyn now. What would she do? I encouraged her to take matters into her own hands.

If you see Charlie, kick his fat ass for me.

At 1:08 A.M. insomnia took the gold. I kicked my pillows to the side and padded to the kitchen. Pinot Grigio and extra-butter popcorn—I punched the comfort food button and channel-surfed through ESPN, *Leave It to Beaver,* and sixteen different versions of *Law & Order.*

Try as I might, there was no escaping Charlie Kelemen's big adventure. Nothing could make me forget the trio of well-fed sharks at the New England Aquarium. Or Sam Kelemen's raccoon tears. Or Lila Priouleau's letter.

Not even Mariska Hargitay.

I needed to inspect that letter and read it for myself. I planned to scrutinize every comma, every colon, every damn syllable. Maybe it would offer some clue, some shred of information that revealed Charlie's game. Or maybe it contained a mistake that proved I was not the author.

Around 1:46 A.M. Ron Popeil distracted me with his pitch for rotisserie ovens. The gung-ho audience chanted over and over, "Just set it and forget it."

Wish I could do that with Charlie's mess.

There were so many people I needed to call—Lila, Frank Kurtz, and especially Cliff Halek. He would know what to do. I considered whether to call Lila's father and drop the bomb on him directly: "That reference letter is a fake, Cash. I don't know what to tell you."

He'll shit. Better to deliver tough news in person.

As Ron Popeil threw in free steak knives for acting now, I toyed with the notion of flying to Atlanta first thing. That way I could look Cash in the eye and convince him the letter was phony. "No way," I finally told Ron after much deliberation. "I need to square up things with SKC first."

Ron didn't offer any advice. He was too busy promoting six easy payments of $16.95 each. Around 2:59 A.M. I crawled back into bed, long one rotisserie oven and a set of razor-sharp steak knives, short one answer to the question troubling me most.

Why did Charlie forge that letter?

Three hours later my alarm clock buzzed, *Get your lazy ass out of bed.* Someday I would flush the damn thing.

This morning I turned it off and stormed into the bathroom, where the mirror flinched and said, *You look like crap.*

Eighty minutes later I paid no attention to our morning research call. None of the money babble registered.

I kept thinking about that damned letter, mentally debated whether 8:30 A.M. was too early to ring Lila. The deliberation proved unnecessary. At 8:23 A.M. the fax machine bleated like a stuck goat. I jumped.

It was Lila. Two pages arrived. She had scrawled "Grove, call me" on the cover sheet. "We need to talk."

Did she speak to Cash yet?

The letter began: "Dear Lila, I have known Charlie Kelemen for ten years." True. "He maintains an eight-figure relationship with Sachs, Kidder and Carnegie." False. "Our firm values the relationship with Mr. Kelemen, who has been a wonderful client for four years, and we hope to assist him in all ways possible." Bullshit. It was signed: "Sincerely yours, Grove O'Rourke, Principal."

What the fuck, Charlie.

Throughout eight years at SKC I had never referred to anyone as a "wonderful client" in writing or otherwise. The phrase was hackneyed and sycophantic. The punctuation in the letter sucked. They could get away with lousy punctuation at Yale or Princeton, but not at Harvard. We separated our coordinate clauses with commas.

The signature was mine. Someone could have scanned "O'Rourke." It would have been easy to trace my name. I was forever sending handwritten thank-you letters to Charlie and Sam. E-mails struck me as a tacky way to say thanks. They were far too convenient to express true appreciation. I always penned thank-you letters on Crane's stationery.

Thank you for dinner, Charlie. Thank you for the

theater tickets, Charlie. Thank you for forging my name, bastard?

There was only one thing to do. I dialed Halek, my go-to guy. He always had a view. I almost shouted his name before he had the chance to answer. "Cliff."

"Yeah?" he asked, unaware what was coming.

It took thirty seconds to describe the reference letter on my desk. When financial disagreements boiled over, lawyers inevitably frisked for the deepest pockets to sue. I could just hear some mouthpiece claim, "Had it not been for the confidence Mr. O'Rourke expressed in Mr. Kelemen, my client never would have invested in the Kelemen Group." Those deep pockets belonged to SKC.

"Go see Kurtz," Cliff ordered.

"I didn't write the letter."

"Doesn't matter. Every bomb makes a mess when it explodes. Do yourself a favor and get out in front of the issue."

Cliff was right. He took a page right out of the Catholic playbook. You go to confession. You spill your guts. You cop to everything, including the time you mooned Sister Mary Loretta in ninth grade. You say you are sorry. You say it a hundred times, each time more penitent than the last. You pray for forgiveness. You hope like hell that Saint Peter remembers when you stand outside the pearly gates one day.

"Cliff," I said.

"Yeah?"

"We'll make a Catholic out of you yet."

"Listen, pal," he scolded, "don't fuck around." Dial

tone. His rebuke left me cold and, frankly, uncertain about our alliance.

Nobody wants this.

At 9:03 A.M. I walked to Frank Kurtz's office and peered through the glass. His door was closed, unusual with just twenty-seven minutes to the opening bell. Issues always surfaced. Frank generally left his door open to either address questions or approve complicated trades.

Not today. He scrutinized one document from the scatter of papers on his desk. When he looked up, he signaled for me to come back later. Get lost. He was busy. Frank never showed backbone.

Unless problems bite him in the ass.

I opened the door and barged inside his office. Bad decision. Frank glared at me over tortoiseshell reading glasses, the voodoo death stare of the undead. His face scowled, *Big mistake*, but he said nothing. The room was more silent than the inside of a coffin.

There was no turning back. "Frank, I need to see you."

"And right now, I'm exercising the self-restraint of Mother Teresa. Don't let the door hit you in the ass on the way out." He stood and swept his right hand to the door, the age-old gesture to get the fuck out of his office.

"Frank, this is important." I stood my ground.

He recognized trouble. "Sit down."

I gave him the fax.

He said nothing for a moment. Then the third degree detonated. "Did I approve this? You said Kelemen wasn't a client. What's going on?"

"I didn't write the letter, Frank."

He looked at my signature and said, "You'd better start at the beginning."

I described the Kelemen Group, the $1.25 million put options, and the $10 million investment. "Lila said this letter influenced her family's decision to invest. The Priouleaus asked for a credit reference. Otherwise, they could not be sure that Charlie's guarantee had any value. He produced this letter, and I think it's a problem."

"No shit, Sherlock," Frank barked. "Did you ever refer any investors to the Kelemen Group?"

He was already evaluating SKC's liability. It was my turn to get pissed. "No, Frank. No fucking way."

"What about your signature?"

"Forged. Or somebody used software to cut and paste."

"What about our stationery?"

"I'm not sure. I keep some at home, and Charlie visited my condo plenty of times. But I'm not sure."

"Is there anything else?"

"Let's be really clear, Frank. I didn't write that letter. I didn't sign it. I think Charlie forged it, and I have no idea what he was doing."

"I get it. I need to hear what our lawyers think. I'm sure we need to get the police involved."

Great. Fitzsimmons and Mummert, the dynamic duds.

Kurtz rose and said, "I told you not to get involved." His body language said, *Dismissed.* It was like a Mafia don had kissed my cheek for the last time.

Back at my desk I called Betty. She answered on the first ring.

"I have a quick question for you."

"No need to hurry," she replied. Betty was always agreeable.

"Did I ever send you a letter about Charlie?"

"That's a weird question."

"Work with me. Did I ever send you a letter about Charlie?"

"No," she said firmly. She paused before asking, "What kind of letter? Should I be concerned? Are you okay?" Her discomfort increased with each question.

I became careful, unsure how much to tell her about my own problems. "Sometimes, investors require reference letters before they put money with hedge funds or other money managers. Charlie never arranged for anything of the sort, right?"

"Grove, that's crazy. Why would I need a reference for Charlie?"

"Not everyone knew him as well as you," I hedged. Internally, I sighed with relief that there was not a second letter with my signature.

"You know," she paused, "in the early 1980s kids with Down's syndrome lived to age twenty-five on average. Most parents outlived the child. It's different now. Kids with Down's syndrome live to fifty-five on average. They're outliving their parents. Charlie understood these issues."

He also understood how to Photoshop signatures.

"In most families the siblings take over for the parents," she continued. "But Fred only has me. Fred would run out of money without better investment returns. Charlie helped us."

For all my cynicism, I felt conflicted when we hung up a few minutes later. Once again Charlie had conducted himself like the quintessential caretaker. I berated myself for doubting him, for turning negative in less than twenty-four hours. But I still cursed him for sending that letter to Lila.

Charlie, how can you save Fred Masters one minute and torch my career the next?

CHAPTER 34

Andy Warhol gets too much recognition. "Fifteen minutes of fame" misses the point. It's not fame. It's shame. In the future we will all weather fifteen minutes of humiliation. Just ask the executives disgraced by broadcast news or the politicians exposed by YouTube, each group starring for reasons other than choice.

Or ask me. Charlie's letter crippled my credibility. It compromised my confidence. I was more of a top preacher than a top producer, lecturing high atop a sanctimonious mountain of righteousness, telling everyone the capital markets were no more than classic confrontations between good and evil.

"My job is to bring you the best of Wall Street and to protect you from it at the same time."

Yeah, right. The notion of me guarding clients was a joke. I couldn't protect myself. I had embraced a cancer, eaten spaghetti Bolognese with a melanoma, and guzzled cabernet sauvignon with a sarcoma. Afterward, my thank-you letters served as source material for Charlie's forgeries. Stupid, stupid, stupid.

My best friend? Fuck him and his fat head. I was

afraid of a forged letter, of lies and secrets to follow. I was afraid of things easily explained, of auditors who never returned my calls. I was afraid of fifteen minutes.

On Wall Street we each have one reputation and a thousand opportunities to destroy it every day. Once a name registers horror, there is no turning back. There is no way to fix the damage and end the flux of unsavory associations.

Dennis Kozlowski. Jeffrey Skilling. Grove O'Rourke.

Financial scandals wreak havoc. We can beat the charges—maybe. We can walk freely among our colleagues—maybe. We can start fresh and allow time to dim the memories. Don't bet on it. Salvaging reputations is like pissing into Hurricane Hugo. The stream boomerangs back at 180 miles per hour. The soil of bad press and tang of yellow journalism stain our careers forever. Unflattering articles never go away. They smear oblivious brokers who happened to be in the wrong place at the wrong time.

Thank you, Google. You will always be there for me in .18 seconds or less. Thank you for sharing all the sordid speculation. You are a credit to the forces of muckraking, with never a complaint, and no gripes about the workload. You deliver all the news fit to print, and some that is not, with tireless and unflagging dedication.

Twenty years from now, Google will still be there for me. I suspect the delivery time will improve to .007 seconds, given the relentless advance of technology. My old friends will be acquaintances by then, their judgments final about my character. They will still gossip behind my back and occasionally search my name to refresh their flagging memories.

"Poor Grove. What was that trouble again?"

My imagination runs wild. I foresee investors losing money at the Kelemen Group. Then I kick myself for worrying.

We have audited financials. There's a reason the auditors don't call.

I foresee the police linking me to the crime at the New England Aquarium. Then I reassure myself with an alibi more potent than innocence.

Five hundred people watched Charlie, Romanov, and me.

Back and forth, logic and alarm, my mind plays tricks. I foresee that article in the *New York Post*, now with a different angle. Mandy Maris paints Charlie's death in graphic detail before proceeding to Sam, the brilliant, if flaky, widow. She discovers Charlie's pet description for Sam, and references to the "Siberian husky" fill the prose. She weaves a tale of sharks and shadows and New York's most philanthropic couple. The money, the glamour, the gory death, they all sell copies of the city's favorite "scambloid."

At the heart of her story, at the core of her intrigue, Mandy Maris emphasizes one key component. Me. She poses leading questions about a top producer from SKC. "Who is this self-made millionaire, Grover O'Rourke? Why did he write that reference letter? Is he just a friend of Sam Kelemen's? He lived with the couple for six months, and she is a striking, if unusual, beauty."

Mandy's editors are too smart to allow slander. Her innuendo slips through anyway. She minces words and vilifies my good name. She injects mystery into her pages and misery into all my waking thoughts. She asks: "Would you trust this man with your money?"

In my mind the *New York Post* runs a honey shot of Lila on the front page. Her olive face is perturbed, her cleavage in full bloom, her pant pockets pulled inside out from blue jeans. The caption underneath the photo asks: "Does Grover O'Rourke know the whereabouts of this woman's money?"

The story debuts everywhere. From the news racks of Grand Central to the vinyl seats of yellow cabs, Lila Priouleau stands before New York City. Where-the-Fuckistan sees my picture splattered across page three and says, "I know that guy." Throughout New York's maze of subways, straphangers in wifebeaters read the article from hell.

The headline fascinates our jittery natives. They all fret about money—making great fortunes or making ends meet. They swig Mandy's sentences like coffee. And they lock the unanswered questions about Grove O'Rourke into their memory banks forever.

I worry what my coworkers will say. The Ten A.M. Ablutions Club bugs me no end. PCS males habitually thunder into the bathroom stalls thirty minutes after the opening bell. Some wait and bitch and complain about the "full house." Those who arrived first slip off their nymph and skull suspenders. Out come the pima-cotton shirts. Down go the pin-striped pants. Their fruity boxers drop like last week's dirty laundry. The "Ablutionists" read their papers in earnest and chatter between the stalls. They debate the markets, concentrating amid the strains and grunts and other concert music from their extended stays.

"Fuck him. And fuck the press," they opine from their porcelain perches. "O'Rourke is costing us money. Our clients don't trust anyone at SKC."

The Ablutionists prospect my guys. It's reasonable retribution, to their way of thinking. There are other factions that join the free-for-all. One splinter group includes Scully. Casper belongs to another. Patty Gershon has a head start on everyone.

Sensing her advantage, Patty goes for my jugular. Her pitch to management is predictable: "We've got a situation on our hands, Frank. O'Rourke hasn't been the same since he lost his wife and daughter. You know it. I know it."

"This thing with Lila Priouleau is a doozy," Frank says, not yet venturing an opinion, his indecisiveness an invitation for Lady Goldfish to strike.

"Call it whatever you like, Frank. O'Rourke's dirty. He went off the deep end. He's probably sleeping with Sam Kelemen. Do you really want him covering a client who invests two hundred million dollars with SKC and keeps another one hundred and ninety-one million in stock here? If you don't assign me the account, JJ will make a decision for you. He'll take his assets to Goldman. Or Morgan. Or Merrill. Get the point, Frank? You want that?"

Jestem udupiony.

* * *

Friday afternoon I was a wreck. Kurtz's casual comment had not helped: "I need to hear what our lawyers think." The business prevention units made every top producer nervous. We're cocky until there's trouble.

By three P.M. the office was half empty. PCS brokers and sales assistants were already hustling off to the beaches. For a moment I hatched my own escape. There was no place like Narragansett on the weekends. The rock beaches. The salty ocean air. The relentless crash of waves eclipsed any symphony Beethoven ever composed. Only I no longer heard their melodic roar.

A seaside photo had replaced the three-hour drive and empty house on the other side. On my desk Finn and Evelyn would laugh forever. They hugged under the dappled sun, the shadow of an autumn day. A white sliver over Evelyn's left lip discolored her rose and mocha skin. I loved that scar, an old softball trophy from sliding into home plate. It marked the fighter, the lover, and the woman I had pledged to honor and protect.

As I stared at the photo my old nemesis reared its ugly head and asked, *Where were you when it counted?* In retrospect, the homunculus probably did me a favor.

The question pissed me off. Grief was no option. Escape, one of Rhode Island's many draws, was no option. Charlie's lies had turned personal. They threatened my career, my reputation.

Dennis Kozlowski. Jeffrey Skilling. Grove O'Rourke.

To understand my anger at that moment, you must understand cycling. During every tight race somebody always makes a move near the finish. It's not any move.

It's *the* move—a short surge ending in glory for one person. That burst makes me crazy. It flips a switch inside, the one that reminds me I fucking hate to lose. There's a certain ignominy to watching a spandex butt cross the finish line first. Somebody else's victory equals joy at my expense. Maybe it was German cyclists who coined "schadenfreude" just for such moments. The move ignites my anger, fuels my desperate sprint to the finish. I don't always win, but in those last few seconds I'm oblivious to crashes or the torture of my sport. I'm angry. I'm feral. My instincts take over, and I don't think. That's how I felt Friday afternoon.

Two share prices were my only hint about Charlie's last acts while alive. I had nothing but gut instinct. Perhaps the Kelemen Group had invested in MRI Capital. Maybe not. But clearly, Romanov and Kelemen had been discussing something prior to that night in the New England Aquarium.

What do they mean, 31.12 and 30.11?

I dialed MRI Capital and ordered the receptionist to put Romanov on the phone.

"He's in a meeting."

"Fish him out."

"I can't do that," she resisted.

"Suit yourself. But don't blame me when he gets all pissy."

Broker 101. Make the gatekeeper doubt the screen.

Thirty seconds later the Mad Russian took my call. "What's so important, Grover?" His words sounded like he might crush the receiver.

"I need to see you."

"I'll get my secretary to schedule something," he replied, his exasperation obvious.

"Now."

"I'm busy."

"Perfect. Let's say the Harvard Club for a drink."

"Excuse me?"

"You're right. Four o'clock is too early. We'll make it four forty-five."

"Grover, I don't know what your game is," he replied. "But it's Friday, and I have plans."

"So does half your neighborhood if you don't show."

"What's that supposed to mean?"

"You can join me for a drink. Or you can listen to my party on your doorstep all weekend. I'm posting an invitation for free pizza and beer on craigslist. A few kegs and people will be pissing all over your poach. Wonder what the neighbors will say."

"Poach?"

"Charleston for 'porch.'"

No might could there.

"One drink," he finally acquiesced.

After we hung up, Annie said, "Hey, Boss, it's okay with me if you scoot out early this afternoon." No doubt she had listened to my half of the conversation.

"Gee, thanks."

"Hey, Boss," she persisted.

"Yeah."

"As long as you're taking off early, mind if I scoot out, too?"

"See ya."

"Who's better than you?" she said, and packed up.

For the first time in a great long while, I had no interest in speculating about Annie's weekend. I wanted answers about two prices, MRI's connection to the Kelemen Group, and why Charlie had forged my name on that damn letter.

CHAPTER 35

The Harvard Club on West Forty-fourth Street gave me home-court advantage and served my pettier need to one-up Romanov. The Mad Russian was not a member. Nor would he ever be a member. His boasts about "triple-digit returns" irked me no end. But he would never sign the neat little chits printed in crimson.

Turn up the South, I told myself. *Less aggression. More courtesy. It's the only way to sniff out info.*

Romanov arrived at 4:45. He wore a beige linen suit, wrinkle free even though the day had run its course. His white shirt still looked taut and fresh against a black silk tie and gold cuff links. I almost asked him not to spill any starch on the crimson rugs and polished floors beneath us.

The Mad Russian was no metrosexual. Still, I wondered how anyone so aggressive could wear French cuffs. He boxed on the weekends. He raced a Porsche. He belonged in sweats, not Ferragamo. I had no explanation for the contradiction and knew little about Romanov's life prior to Wall Street. There were rumors he had driven a cab to pay for college.

Google him later.

We headed for a corner, where Romanov came out swinging: "What's this about, Grover?" The *r*'s in my name rolled off his tongue, creamy rich and buttery smooth, not quite basso profundo, but close. Bottling his voice would put chocolate out of business.

"You tell me."

"I don't have time for games, Grove." His hands looked like massive battering rams, all sinew and knuckles.

Bet I can take him.

"I've been trying to help Sam Kelemen."

"I know," he observed impatiently. "Will you get to the point? CNN version please?"

"We're liquidating Charlie's fund of funds. She needs the money. She's tapped out." There was no need to tell him about my $75,000 wire. "Did Charlie invest in MRI Capital?"

That fast enough for you?

If Romanov answered "Yes," it would be my first positive step toward freeing all the assets locked inside the fund of funds. The flow of money would solve plenty of issues. Sam would not worry about rent. Betty would not worry about Fred. Lila would not worry about $11.25 million. And I would not worry about a letter with my forged signature.

Who says money doesn't buy happiness?

"No," Romanov replied, looking at his fingernails, split and gnarly from action inside the ring. "Charlie asked me to take his money. I said no."

Damn, I thought.

"Why?"

"Too unreliable. The minute there's a bad year, a fund of funds heads for the doors. No loyalty."

One down year and you're toast, pal. Wealthy investors will leave you just as fast.

"The Kelemen Group's interest in MRI strikes me as odd."

"How so?"

"Charlie compiled a large file on MRI. It looked like due diligence."

"Oh?"

"He had a list of your stocks as well as your offering memorandum." The Mad Russian, I suddenly realized, had taken control of our conversation. I was the one volunteering all the information.

The surrounding talismans of the Harvard Club had failed me. I looked at the great warthog hanging on the wall. Its tusks could no longer gore tofu on salad greens, let alone beasts of the wild.

Serves you right.

Romanov spoke, and it sounded as if he were playing a bass violin of vowels and verbs. "Charlie was interested in my companies. Everybody is," he observed as though stating a mathematical truth. "How do you know Charlie had a list of stocks?"

Another question, I observed silently. *He's wringing me for information.*

"I told you. I have his folder."

"I see." Romanov folded his hands and laced his fingers halfway between "here's the church" and "here's the steeple" from the kids' game. He looked tougher than a bag of ball-peen hammers. Those brutish hands. Those split nails. "Grover," he said finally, "why are you telling me all this?"

"Charlie was screwing around." I immediately regretted my choice of words. "I'm not sure what he was doing. But he sucked me into a mess that I'm trying to sort out." The words dissolved into the Harvard Club's rarified air. "I was speaking with Lila Priouleau—"

"The perfect second wife," Romanov interrupted. His eyes flared lasciviously, communicating the feral lust that unites all men. He meant his words to be some kind of common ground—the brotherhood of lechery.

Not interested, pal. I have my ass to save.

"Lila gave me a reference letter with my signature," I explained, not taking Romanov's bait. "Charlie guaranteed her family's investment, and they asked him for credit references."

"You vouched for the Kelemen Group?" he asked, modestly surprised.

"That's just it. I didn't write the letter."

"Then there's no problem," he concluded flippantly.

"Charlie forged my name. I don't know why. I don't know what it means. I don't expect anything good."

"That's a problem," Romanov admitted.

"Great, isn't it?"

"What does this have to do with me?" he asked with the ambassadorial sensitivity of a rogue fart adrift in the UN.

"Probably nothing. I thought you might have some info. There's one other thing, too."

"Which is?"

"Charlie scribbled some notes next to one of your portfolio companies."

"Which one?"

"Rugged Computers."

"What kind of notes?"

"Nothing much. He wrote 'thirty-one-point-twelve' and 'thirty-point-eleven.' They look like price targets."

"Price targets!" Romanov scoffed. "If Rugged Computers hits anything north of twenty dollars, I'll own Bermuda."

"The whole thing?"

"And then some."

"Nice."

"Did you bring his notes with you?" Romanov asked.

"No."

"Can you drop his file off on Monday? I'd like to see it."

"Of course."

Romanov rose from the chair, the movement his unilateral declaration that our meeting was over. "If you don't mind, my weekend is waiting."

"Understood. Thanks for meeting."

Thanks for the third degree, chump.

"Grover," he replied, and waited at the front door.

"Yes."

"If I were you, I'd be a seller of intimidation." Fast as any boxer, he patted my cheek with his open palm, short of a slap but enough to sting ever so slightly. "Some people don't back off. Are we clear?"

The doorman gestured to the exit. He was anxious

to see us leave the Harvard Club. He had seen the Mad Russian's not-so-friendly pat.

You won't last three rounds, bubba.

We left. Romanov headed to Fifth. I headed to Sixth. There was still time to join my cycling club. During the summers, we rode every Friday night. I did my best thinking on a bike. All the pain in my legs and lungs wouldn't be enough that evening to mask what really irked me.

My face stung all night.

CHAPTER 36

Saturday morning, and the July sun drenched my sheets. It beamed across the wooden floors of my bedroom. The bright rays pried open my eyes and toasted my body. Boxers and beard, I scratched my stomach and stretched awake. Just feeling. Not thinking. Savoring the end of warm slumber. Drifting languorously into the day.

Not a chance. Three names ricocheted inside my head. They caromed every which way.

Charlie Kelemen. Alex Romanov. Patty Gershon.

There was no time to lounge in bed. I salvaged a faded polo and khaki shorts from the hamper, camouflaged my bed head with a baseball cap, and hurried over to a Starbucks on Broadway, computer in tow. The line was short, and I armed myself with the barrel-sized café mocha. Staying away from SKC seemed a sound strategy. Gershon often worked in our office over weekends.

Who takes care of her kids?

The "Investors" spreadsheet, now on my portable, had piqued my curiosity from the start. But markets,

clients, and Gershon's play for Jumping JJ kept inter-
rupting all week. They diverted my attention. They pre-
vented me from dissecting cells and discovering the
truth. I had no explanation why Charlie had forged my
name. I had no proof.

My day job might get me fired.

You can't snort Ritalin. But breathing at Starbucks
came close. The air mixed one part oxygen with two
parts caffeine, my preferred cocktail for concentration.
There had been countless distractions at the office. No
doubt I overlooked something important on the "Investors" spreadsheet. Excel allowed users, for example, to
hide rows and columns inside spreadsheets. This feature simplified visuals, made presentations better. Or
it hid clues to Charlie's monkey business. Something
would surface. It was there. Whatever "it" was.

There was just one problem. Alex Romanov dominated all my thoughts. It was that way at the Harvard
Club. It was that way while cycling last night. It was
that way now. Except for his gnarled hands the Mad
Russian had no outward flaws—sartorial grace, chocolate voice, and triple-digit returns. He reminded me of
Scully, never a hair out of place. My instincts screamed
for me to probe further.

Danger, Will Robinson.

Romanov's smug attitude roused my suspicions. Nobody could sustain triple-digit returns forever. Peter
Lynch, Warren Buffett, and other legends of money management second-guessed themselves. The markets made
everyone look foolish at some point, even the wizards.

Maybe it was my ego driving. Romanov's pregnant

tap still bugged the shit out of me. Had we been outside the Harvard Club, that little exchange would have escalated. One thing was certain. Time was running out. Nothing good would come from Kurtz's decision to turn Lila's letter over to the lawyers.

The l word.

Evelyn was forever saying, "Figure out what bothers you, and deal with it." I took her advice and Googled Alexander Romanov and MRI Capital. Charlie's skeletons could wait a few minutes more.

The Mad Russian's family had immigrated to the United States when he was five. He grew up in Brighton Beach, the New York neighborhood affectionately known as Little Odessa. His father worked as a cobbler, and the whole family toiled over shoe leather in the modest store. Alex broke free of his immigrant shackles through hard work and education. He graduated magna cum laude from UCLA before obtaining his MBA from the University of Chicago.

Romanov now ranked among the next generation of finance superstars. He had delivered awesome returns. Investors clamored for entry into MRI, and he usually declined with some flip comment: "No room at the inn." According to Alex, he had blackballed the Kelemen Group just like the others.

Romanov's close was "soft" in my opinion, more marketing than reality. *The next Steve Rubell*, I thought cynically to myself. *Forbes* once estimated there were 946 billionaires across the world. I bet MRI Capital would accept money from all of them.

The Mad Russian certainly attracted a crowd. Many investors possessed foot-washing faith he would make them wealthier. At times it even seemed Romanov bought into the hype. "Everybody loves the way we make money," he once bragged to *Business Week*.

"No ego problem there," I muttered under my breath.

For all his coolness, for all his sophistication and acclaim, Romanov made one decision that bordered on bizarre. He lived in Brighton Beach, hardly the choice of a capital-markets rock star. He eschewed the glitter of SoHo and the vogue of the Upper West Side. No Greenwich country estate for him.

Romanov relished the spoils of Wall Street but preferred the murky dialects and exotic cuisine from his old neighborhood. He traded porterhouse steaks for *vatrushki*, a kind of cheese pie. He adored *salo*, pure pork lard sliced and heaped on slabs of grainy bread. What were days without borscht and shooters? He drank Stolichnaya and regarded other vodkas as third-rate swill.

The Mad Russian also favored Brighton Beach for its views. They belonged more to Eastern Europe than American neighborhoods, especially one so near Springsteen's backyard. Seventy-year-old men, loose white bellies flopping over Speedos, performed leg squats while hoisting medicine balls. Slavic women, glossy red fingernails, gold lamé tops, all heels and attitude, strutted the boardwalks. The look, loosely translated, said, *You can lick the Lappi cheese off our toes.* Alex loved Little Odessa, relished the sights and smells of a community at peace with its quirks.

Amid the *parikmakherskaya*, barbershops to the rest of America, Romanov gutted and renovated an old building overlooking the ocean. He spared no expense. He occupied all twenty thousand square feet, once apartments, and filled the space with relics from the days when Russia was Christian. He became a new-age czar and refused to join hedgies in their more opulent neighborhoods elsewhere.

The first few Web sites told a familiar story. *Forbes, Fortune,* and *Institutional Investors* extolled Romanov's market savvy and meteoric rise from humble beginnings. I knew the legend.

Three pages into the Google hits, I learned something new. Romanov had purchased rights to *The Rocky Horror Picture Show* and planned to remake the movie. The article, posted on a celebrity gossip site, reported the Beastie Boys would dominate the cast. One of them would play Frank-N-Furter. Beyoncé was the inside favorite for the role of Janet Weis, though negotiations were still under way with her agent.

"Huh?" I muttered, and confirmed coffee was in my cup. I double-checked to make sure the article referred to the same Romanov.

The venture struck me as brilliant. How could the Mad Russian miss with this cult classic? How could he miss with hip favorites from the now generation? The venture struck me as moronic. No one could improve Tim Curry's and Susan Sarandon's work in the original *Rocky Horror Picture Show.*

Talk about "style drift." What did Romanov, the hedge

fund manager maniacally obsessed with value, know about Hollywood? Had he told his investors? What made him think he could produce a movie? Away from the chaos and computer screens of Wall Street, finance people could bungle two-car funerals. Something smelled.

For a prolonged moment I stewed about yesterday's meeting with Romanov. Instead of challenging him, instead of questioning investments like *The Rocky Horror Picture Show,* I had rolled over like a Michelin tire. He had been the one asking all the questions.

Not enough homework.

I ordered more coffee. Another barrel. The surfing grew tedious, though, from too many unrelated hits. One plastic surgeon in Miami boasted, "I deserve an Oscar for my outies." Exasperated, I switched to the Kelemen Group spreadsheet.

Forty-five minutes later everything became clear.

CHAPTER 37

I'll go out on a limb here and make a prediction. *CSI: Excel* will never become a television series. Spreadsheet forensics may arouse the number crunchers of Wall Street. Everywhere else our models trigger brain freezes.

Sure, finance jocks look inside cells. But we examine mathematical formulas, not the dietary content of stomachs. There's none of the ugh factor found in forensic toxicology. Nothing to stir morbid fascination. Spreadsheets don't tell whether victims ate chicken burritos for lunch. They just include equations and data, numbers and text. Excel will never disclose whether the pizzas came with anchovies.

Sure, we look for bugs. But not insects. We seek errors in logic: dividing by zero, adding rather than subtracting, and referencing the wrong cells. Sometimes, it takes hours to understand why formulas don't work.

Forensic entomology, by contrast, rouses the macabre in all of us. I call it "better gore through arthropods." The link between murder and insects, like using blowfly larvae to establish the time of death, draws television audiences who would find spreadsheets painfully tedious.

Sure, we use trace evidence. Excel includes a function that points at relationships between cells. Multicolored arrows literally highlight the links. The visuals are excellent. Still, we don't have hair or soil with unusual characteristics, no elements to touch or smell. Our world is digital. It takes time, patience, or both to sort through all the columns and rows.

Inside Starbucks a bucket of body parts could not have distracted me from Charlie's spreadsheet. Now that Kurtz had summoned the lawyers, there was no telling how they would handle the forged letter. Their first duty was to protect SKC. They'd throw me under the bus and wave sayo-fucking-nara in less time than a *CSI* commercial break.

Spreadsheets have been my opiate ever since Harvard Business School. Back then I churned out the models, had one for every class, even Organizational Behavior, which covered soft issues like the importance of wearing thin ties in thin-tie cultures. At SKC I dissected analyst models late into the night and crunched numbers with my eyes closed.

At the moment, I drilled into "Investors." It included five columns: "Name," "Phone," "Address," "Amount Invested," and "Market Value." They resembled telephone directories, not the output from complex mathematical calculations.

Basic stuff.

Charlie had hidden additional columns as I suspected.

Excel's unhide command displayed two. One showed the date of each investor's initial contribution. The other showed redemption dates, if applicable.

Too simple.

Contributions were fine. Funds generally accepted money on the last day of each month, easy enough to plug into a column. The redemptions bothered me. It took forever to get money back. To start the process most funds of funds required notice ninety days prior to quarter end. In practice, notice periods often stretched out five or six months. Instructions on January 15, for example, did not meet the ninety-day requirement for March 31 redemptions. Instead, they triggered a series of payments based on June 30.

Hotel California.

Acting on a "June 30" notice, a fund of funds would alert its hedge funds. The hedgies then calculated their redemption values as well as their fees. They remitted net proceeds back to the fund of funds, which in turn calculated its fees. Toward the end of July, the fund of funds would remit 90 percent of the balance due. Industry standard. The investor, who first gave notice on January 15, still did not have all his money.

"You can check ou . . . But you can never leave."

The fund of funds would release the 10 percent holdback when audited results were complete—April of the following year. This way the fund could adjust its fee calculations in case the hedgies made changes. Fourteen months had elapsed since the investor first gave notice on January 15 of the previous year.

Redemptions were a process, not a onetime event.

Charlie could have entered the initial notice, return of the 90 percent, or the final payment. Clearly, he had not entered quarter ends. March 31, June 30, September 30, and December 31 were nowhere to be seen. The simplicity of the column bothered me. The model did not reflect reality.

I love this shit.

Betty Masters invested $250,000 in February of last year. Her dollar amount appeared in cell C24, and the confirmation made me feel good. It reminded me, however, that I had made little progress since last Saturday. I clicked the cursor onto the $250,000 and discovered the most curious thing. The cell contained a formula, not raw data.

Why did Charlie calculate a number he knew?

I clicked the software tool to trace precedents. This function used arrows to point out other cells that played a role in the equation. To my surprise, one blue arrow pointed to Betty's cell. It started on a cell showing an initial investment of $1.25 million. I did not recognize the name of the investor.

A second blue arrow pointed from Betty's investment to a cell showing $1.5 million. The money belonged to Susan Thorpe, a woman from Charlie's posse, a woman I knew reasonably well. Her $1.5 million was in the redemption column.

Betty had funded on February 28. So had the other investor. February 28 made sense. Funds often used windows to regulate cash flows, accepting new money only on the last days of calendar months or quarters. This mechanism allowed them to calculate redemptions and retain cash, even if the actual payments occurred months later.

The liquidity was valuable. Forced sales could distress prices. Or they could produce ill-timed exits. No fund wanted to sell Yahoo! a few days before Microsoft offered a 62 percent premium to buy the company.

Susan Thorpe had redeemed her money on March 5. I wondered if the incoming cash from Betty and the other investor had funded Susan's redemption. Everybody won, Susan, Betty, the other guy, and Charlie. There was no need for the Kelemen Group to liquidate underlying investments. Everybody was happy.

Everybody except me. I was agitated. Charlie had calculated Betty's investment. It made no sense to use a calculation. Charlie knew she had $250,000. He saw her brokerage statements. She confided in him. They talked about Fred. Charlie studied the boy's needs and signed on as a surrogate guardian. He probably consulted Betty about her taxes. They were too close for Betty's investment to become a calculation. Charlie knew. He just knew.

Susan Thorpe.

A member of the posse, she doubled as a "trace precedent" on Charlie's spreadsheet. What was her link to Betty and the other investor? Susan had redeemed her investment, and I wondered why. Performance had been excellent. She made $500,000 with the Kelemen Group, a 50 percent return.

Nice.

For a long while I pondered the equation. Betty's $250,000. Susan's $1.5 million. The other guy's $1.25

million. Starbucks's tables had already turned over twice. A trendy New York couple with a stroller eyed my table covetously. I gestured for them to come over. The baby burped.

In that instant a terrible feeling gurgled through my own stomach. I hoped it was coffee. But I recognized the sick thud of comprehension. I cleared the table, packed up my laptop, and headed outside to call Susan Thorpe. It was clear Charlie had been raising capital—Betty's money—to make payments. There was no other explanation for the calculation. That's not what troubled me.

The numbers were too neat. Nobody earned an even $500,000 from hedge funds. There were always a few shekels in one direction or another, like $497,631.04 or $523,781.93. There was only one explanation.

Charlie cooked the books.

CHAPTER 38

Susan Thorpe was a sixty-seven-year-old widow. She lost her husband, the chief executive of a pet superstore chain, ten years earlier after he drank too much at a grand opening in Australia. As Duncan Thorpe barfed into the bathroom bowl of his hotel, a deadly venomous Sydney funnel-web (*Atrax robustus*) waged war on his throat. He passed out, as much from the tequila shots as from the spider's toxicity. A maid found his body the following day.

The years had been kind to Susan. She looked marvelous at sixty-seven. Her shock of gray hair reminded me of a flannel suit, one soft from time and warm no matter how inclement the conditions. Her greenish eyes sparkled. Her skin showed not a day over fifty-five. Except for the hair, Susan stopped aging when *Atrax robustus* sank its lethal fangs into Duncan's throat.

It surprised me she had not remarried. Though Susan still turned heads, she avoided older widowers at Charlie's soirees. Their yachting stories, distilled through martinis and repetition, bored her no end. She parried all advances and found security in the cache of surrounding women. Duncan was her only love.

Enveloped by Manhattan's street noise, I spoke loudly into my cell phone. From years of smiling and dialing, I understood the importance of warming up an audience before broaching controversial topics. "Grove O'Rourke here."

It was okay to call Susan on a Saturday morning. But odd. We had never clicked. I held myself responsible for the mutual dispassion. Life had plucked each of our loves way too soon, and I kept my distance. Affinity through death was way too damaging.

"This is a surprise," Susan replied, cordial but formal.

"Do you have a few minutes?"

"What's on your mind?"

So much for warming up the audience.

"Sam Kelemen asked me for help."

"I'm sorry about Charlie," Susan said.

"Me too."

"What kind of help?"

"Mostly financial," I explained, "with details regarding Charlie's estate and the Kelemen Group."

Susan said nothing. I had expected some observation, some comment no matter how light. Nothing. The mood changed, quickly, instantly. What began as cordial shifted to distant. How had I wandered into off-limits territory so soon?

Uh-oh.

"I found a spreadsheet that showed your investment in the Kelemen Group."

Again, Susan said nothing. Money talk could derail even the most pleasant conversations. But her abrupt change in demeanor bordered on bizarre.

"Susan, I don't want to be intrusive. But is it okay to ask a few questions?"

"Let's start and see what happens," she answered. All geniality had left her voice. Through the receiver I could feel her smile dissolve.

"Did you ever receive audited financials from the Kelemen Group?" I crossed my fingers.

"Of course. I keep all that stuff."

"Do you recall if the financials included a list of the hedge funds in the portfolio?"

"I can check, but I doubt it."

"What makes you say that?" It impressed me that Susan even remembered. So few people paid attention to Wall Street's mail.

Our paperwork will deforest the planet someday.

"I probably would have noticed," Susan said. "I own a bunch of hedge funds." She exuded confidence, sounding like a seasoned viewer of CNBC.

"The spreadsheet said you were up five hundred thousand dollars."

"To the penny," she acknowledged, pleased by the return, unaware of my skepticism.

There's no such thing as an even profit of $500,000.

"Why'd you pull out?"

"Charlie was always sending me letters. Every time I checked the mail, he was there. A note. A letter. A present, like the latest bestseller. There were always invitations to spend time with Sam and him. This may sound funny, but it felt too intimate."

"Too intimate?" I repeated, the Socratic-sales echo used by all top producers to open up prospects.

"Creepy intimate, if you know what I mean. My hedge funds leave me alone. They send computer-generated statements. They send market letters that brag when they're up."

"And snivel when they're down."

"You got that right. Charlie was different. He got too close."

"He wanted to take market share," I pointed out.

"That's not how Duncan ran things," she argued. "His business dealings were more formal."

"The Kelemen Group gave you a nice return." The point was to coax more information from Susan, not to defend anyone.

"Don't get me wrong, I loved Charlie. We made good money over three years."

"But what?" I heard the qualifiers.

"I struggled to get my money out."

Hotel California?

"All funds of funds have lengthy redemption features," I observed. My tone was neutral. My big ears could have been elephant transplants.

"That's not what I mean," she countered. "My other hedge funds have those clauses."

"They surprise some people."

"It surprised me I had to nag Charlie. He wouldn't even start the redemption process."

"What did you say?"

Without skipping a beat Susan Thorpe replied, "I threatened to call you. Then your firm. That's why you're calling now, right?"

Another forged letter.

"Tell me more," I prodded, nonplussed and clinical.

"Charlie promised never to lose a dime. He sold me an option that guaranteed the returns."

Another OTC option.

Translation: "OTC" stood for "over-the-counter." In the world of derivatives it meant a private option negotiated between two parties, usually a brokerage house and an investor.

"And you needed a letter from SKC proving his ability to guarantee your investment."

"A girl can't be too careful, you know."

"Your letter says Charlie keeps an eight-figure account with us?" I asked, already knowing the answer.

"You wrote it. Why are you asking?"

I was unsure whether to hang up or throw up. "One other thing," I said, not answering Susan's question. "Once you threatened Charlie, how long did it take to get your money back?"

"That's just it," she replied. "Two weeks at the most."

"All of it?"

"Every last dime," she replied. "None of the holdbacks that my other funds use. Kind of odd."

"Creepy intimate," I agreed, borrowing Susan's expression.

When we hung up I stopped walking for a moment and gazed down the sidewalk, seeing everything but focusing on nothing. The forgeries, Susan's threats, and the quick return of capital—it all came together in that moment.

Can it be this simple?

I knew the answer already. It was time to discuss Charles Borelli with Sam Kelemen.

CHAPTER 39

During the sticky summer of 1925 Charles Borelli mulled over Boston's shortcomings. "Those bluenose ingrates can have this place," he told himself. He never much liked the people or the weather. "Pain in my ass," he cursed. "Yankees are colder than their damned winters."

All January and February Borelli had slipped on the sidewalks. Snow slicked the bricks. Frozen pooch piss greased the paths and turned them treacherous.

"I bet a thousand dogs pee against my door every day," he complained, now standing in the buggy heat outside 27 School Street.

Charles Borelli had fallen into a funk. He hated Boston, the people and the dogs that pissed everywhere. "The food sucks," Borelli continued, his foul mood prompting him to decry everything. He considered Boston's most famous dish, "boiled dinners," and grimaced. His paesanos in Rome would never serve that slop to pigs, let alone to each another.

Oh, for the old country. Oh, for a bowl of fettuccine Alfredo, he dreamed wistfully.

"Vaffanculo," he swore, cursing all of Boston but no one in particular. He still preferred his native tongue. *"Vaffanculo"* sounded far more elegant than "Fuck you."

For all the bugs and heat, Florida's white-hot real estate offered a chance to start fresh. That night Borelli grabbed his wife, Rose, and together they fled. They left their home in Lexington forever. He never looked back, not once. He never regretted jumping bail.

Months later an unhappy horde gathered outside the steps of the Boston courthouse. "What was Judge Sisk thinking?" a short man asked. "Releasing a convicted felon," he complained in bitter disbelief.

"While the appeal was pending," another man fumed.

Several members of the crowd talked about baseball, the diversion a comforting panacea. To a man, to a woman, they hated the New York Yankees. Those blackguards had been to the World Series three times since stealing Babe Ruth. The conversations invariably returned to the Italian. Some knew him as Carlo, though it had been years since the fugitive had anglicized his name.

A tall man growled, "Carlo was a rat bastard." His head poked over the growing crowd like the tallest poppy in the field.

"Rat bastard. Rat bastard," the crowd chorused uneasily in agreement. They all agreed Borelli was devious, a criminal without conscience. What had Sisk been thinking? Maybe the summer humidity had boiled the judge's pea brain. How would he rule today? Would he abandon the stay of sentence? Would he listen to the crowd's heated chants outside his office?

Charles Borelli, blessed with good looks and old-world charisma, had not always been a rat bastard. There was a time when Boston had cheered his financial wizardry. The city had toasted his name. Good salt-of-the-earth New Englanders, ten thousand people strong, once invested $9.5 million in the Securities Exchange Company. In 1920 his business had attracted thousands of dollars every day from good Yankee stock.

The early clients extolled their gargantuan returns: "Double your money in ninety days." As word spread, people could not send money fast enough. Boston's police certainly believed. By some accounts Charles worked with nearly 75 percent of the officers on the force.

There was a time when Borelli loved Massachusetts. The New World promised a life of riches for young men that worked hard. In 1903 he had immigrated to America. At first he washed dishes. Carlo, however, refused to toil in hot kitchens forever. He abandoned dishwashing for other pursuits, and eventually his perseverance paid off. Charles bought a twenty-room mansion in Lexington, Massachusetts. He draped big jewels on Rose. He carried a gold-handled cane and dressed in the finest suits, hand-sewn by the tailors of Newbury Street. He hired staff, and his company opened branch offices. He even opened a small outpost in Rhode Island, the state that Cotton Mather had contemptuously labeled "the sewer of New England." It was a dreamy time for an industrious thief.

During those heady days Charles Borelli went by another name—Carlo K. Ponzi. He never aspired to become a felon. In 1919 Ponzi had no idea the world would one day scorn him as the father of a scam. He fancied himself an arbitrageur. Carlo identified, quite by accident, a risk-free trade born from the inefficiencies of exchange rates and international commerce. He noticed it was possible to redeem postal coupons, purchased for a penny in Spain, for six cents in the United States. Ponzi dreamed of investing millions and earning a nickel for every penny ventured. No matter there were only 27,000 postal coupons in circulation. No matter the maximum profit was only $1,350 at five cents per coupon.

Ponzi told everybody about postal coupons. He promised to double investors' money in ninety days. He told friends and a former boss, certainly all the bartenders at his favorite speakeasy. He offered to double the collection plates for the good fathers at St. Paul's. "Just give me ninety days."

He cut Protestants in on the deal, too. Carlo was a nondenominational con. He told his butcher as well as Rose's new hairdresser, and she told everyone else. He even told the playful redhead from the bar. *The bubs on that girl*, he thought salaciously. Ponzi mesmerized his flock of sheep, and they invested frenetically. They could hardly wait to reap extraordinary returns from promissory notes issued by the Securities Exchange Company.

Ponzi did something brilliant. As new investors arrived in droves he repaid early backers with incoming funds. He returned every cent of principal times two. Even the most avaricious drooled. "Double your money in ninety days."

The capital markets had never been this kind. Ponzi's posse, from the priests to the redhead with the big bubs, delighted in their windfalls. They became walking, talking testimonials to the brilliance of the immigrant arbitrageur from Italy. "Double your money in ninety days." It was like free money from heaven.

Windfall profits spawned an orgy of greed. The blue-collar folk invested whatever they could scrape together. They bought discount notes with face values of $5 and $10. The rich folk, while generally more cerebral, were just as greedy and no less gullible. They calculated $10,000 today would grow to $160,000 by year-end. Rich and poor alike flooded into room 227 at 27 School Street and traded bags of cash for Ponzi's promissory notes.

At times the premises overflowed with marauding bands of investors. Carlo often asked cops to stand guard outside his doors. No wonder 75 percent of the police department invested. The boys in blue listened to all the stories, overheard all the calculations. It seemed all of Boston had overdosed on the aphrodisiac of avarice. Everyone wanted a piece of Carlo's action.

"No problem," Ponzi promised. Unlike today's hedge funds, the Securities Exchange Company never employed a soft close. Simple math forced Carlo to raise ever-increasing sums. It was the only way to sustain the house of cards.

"Who needs postal coupons when people throw money at me?" he once asked no one in particular.

Investments made no difference. Records would later show Carlo Ponzi had only purchased five shares of a telephone company. For that matter he never bought any of those twenty-seven thousand outstanding postal coupons. As long as he repaid a handful of investors from time to time, the new money arrived in buckets.

Ponzi had his own needs of course. He could not work for free. The endless schmoozing required too much time and energy, not to mention cash. Carlo had already scoured enough dishes to fill a lifetime. He would never again slog over suds and settle for a laborer's pittance. To hell with that noise. Why not skim some jack for himself? Someday he would pay everybody back.

I'll buy a used battleship from the U.S. Navy, he dreamed, *turn it into a floating mall, and sell American goods.* It seemed the patriotic thing to do.

In the meantime he needed a house and fine clothes. He needed that watch from Shreve, Crump & Low. He planned to engrave his initials on the back of the timepiece. Rose needed her baubles, and then there was that redhead with the great bubs. She needed something special. When Carlo's scheme finally unraveled, trustees of the court found that his needs totaled $1.5 million in total assets. It was a monstrous sum in those days.

The courts never recovered all $9.5 million deposited with the Securities Exchange Company. Most investors received about a third of their original stake. That third took eight years to find as court-appointed receivers worked feverishly to wring out dollars wherever they could. Carlo had spent money like a drunken sailor. He hosted lavish parties and scoffed at Prohibition, uncorking only the finest bottles of French

Bordeaux. He hated that rotgut wine his friends drank at the speakeasy. It tasted like potato vodka cut with fermented cranberries. But where had all the money gone? Had it really disappeared down the gullets of New Englanders drunk on wine and good times?

Many years later, while the world waged war in Europe and Asia, Ponzi sat alone on a stool inside a grotty Brazilian bar. He could not drink the wine in this godforsaken place. Instead, he slugged down his cold beer and slammed the dead soldier on the wooden counter.

Three stools over, a big-butted hooker appraised him carefully, considering whether she could toss the sixty-something drunk. He was only five-two after all. *No money. Not worth the hassle*, she decided.

Carlo returned her stare. He sighed wistfully and remembered his past life on the edge, the frenetic pace of robbing Peter to pay Paul. By and by, his thoughts trailed to Rose and her letter from two weeks ago. "It was fun while it lasted," he remarked to the prostitute. "Best show in Massachusetts since the Pilgrims landed."

He's daft, the big-butted hooker concluded. She said nothing. With every ounce of vacuum in her one remaining lung, she drew from an unfiltered cigarette. When she exhaled, a blue smoke ring crowned the funny old man's head.

Charles Borelli may have been the king of Ponzi schemes. It was Charles Kelemen who perfected the scam. Charlie solved the problem that had plagued every Ponzi since Carlo the first. And the pupil became the professor.

Robbing Peter to pay Paul was a scheme that always ended badly. The flow of new money inevitably slowed. There was never enough as exiting investors clamored for the gargantuan returns they had been promised.

"Double your money in ninety days."

Today's SEC will live forever. But the Securities Exchange Company sowed the seeds of its own collapse by accepting $10,000 on Day 1. In effect Ponzi had promised to return $160,000 by Day 365. Multiply that commitment by a hundred investors, by a thousand investors, by ten thousand investors and the pressure to raise money must have been overwhelming. The bookkeeping alone was a nightmare, especially without computers. There were no real investments, just lifestyle. It was that way with all the Ponzi disciples who followed.

Charlie's fix was simple. He used the redemption language of hedge funds to ply his trade. Lockups, redemption notices, and the like—they made it harder for investors to exit and minimized the frenzy of raising new money. The legalese bought Charlie the time to dupe Betty Masters, pay Susan Thorpe, and skim some money for himself.

Damn him.

Those cuts on Charlie's arms made sense now. Nobody had been torturing him for information. The wounds weren't the by-product of someone seeking a confession. I knew what had happened.

Charlie swindled the wrong person.

The realization was far from comforting. If anything, it distressed me further. I could almost predict what Fitzsimmons would say. "Well, chowdahhead, here's how it looks. You ran a Ponzi scheme with your best friend. Nothing like a letter from SKC to give investors confidence. But something snapped. I'd say Sam Kelemen was that something. Didn't you say she's smoking hot?"

Charlie's dead. Money's gone. What am I missing?

CHAPTER 40

Growing up in the land of might-could manners was a mixed blessing. Pro: I learned to ladle out generous helpings of syrupy respect no matter what the day brought. Charleston gave me the tools to become a top producer, the grace to speak like an ambassador even when "Eat shit and die" was the right thing to say.

Con: I hated conflict, Wall Street's one constant. Our industry encouraged skirmishes. Clients, money, and investments—we wrangled over everything. Warring with Radio Ray was learned behavior. I preferred to avoid both hostilities and tough questions that put people on edge.

Walking down Columbus Avenue, I was all Wall Street and no Charleston. Lucky for Charlie, he was dead. I wanted to pummel his face. The discussion with Susan Thorpe had pissed me off. It was not the letter per se, not the fact that Charlie Kelemen had signed my name to yet another testimonial.

It was the horror. Future discoveries would only confirm that Charlie Kelemen had no conscience. All his acts of kindness had been a sequel to the Trojan horse.

"Carlo" Kelemen never saved helpless widows or battered women. That sociopath never rescued anyone.

What kind of asshole would scam Fred Masters?

Charlie forged what he needed from me, specifically the endorsement of a nonexistent eight-figure account. I wondered whether he had manufactured the financial statements from Crain and Cravath. No one from the firm had ever called me back.

Why'd you do it, Charlie?

Like Ponzi, Charlie had lived large, all the parties, the food, and the French wine. He had even hired a driver. If I was right, Charlie had never legitimately paid a tab in his life. We had his investors to thank for underwriting the good times. He duped his wife, her family, and his friends. He fed on deception and shared the table scraps with us.

The Jeffrey Dahmer of finance.

The phone rang, cutting through my anger. In the blackness of that moment, I decided it was Mandy Maris. Just my luck, the press would arrive and make life miserable.

What's she want?

But the caller ID on my BlackBerry said, "Unknown number."

Not her, I decided. We weren't scheduled to speak until Monday anyway.

"Hello."

No answer.

"Can you hear me?"

Still no answer. We had a connection. Traffic sounds filtered through the receiver, and I sensed a presence.

"Call me back. Or lock the keypad on your cell phone." I hung up, assigning no significance to the call. We all had our stories about accidental dials from cell phones. My conclusion was a mistake, only there was no way to know at the time.

Instead, I focused on Sam Kelemen. She could confirm the Ponzi scheme beyond any doubt. All I needed were Charlie's tax records. They were probably lying around the house somewhere. More pressing questions were beginning to shape my thoughts, though. Charlie's little racket pissed off somebody. Sam, however oblivious, was his wife and a beneficiary of the fraud.

What does Sam know? Does Charlie's killer blame her, too? Is she in danger?

Awash in the muggy heat that Saturday afternoon, I simmered outside Sam's town house in Greenwich Village. It would be one thing to tell her about Charlie. It would be another to dig deeper.

What do you know, Sam?

"Fertility drugs make some women a little crazy," Evelyn said years ago. We still had not conceived Finn. "You'd better hope we never need the help. There's no telling what I might do." Her brown eyes dilated. They turned saucer wide, as Evelyn feigned drug-induced lunacy.

The memory gave me pause. Had Sam, finally pregnant, turned ditzy from a cocktail of hormones and pharmaceuticals? I could almost hear Evelyn scream from the grave, "Sexist pig." My cynicism gathered momentum anyway. How could Sam be so oblivious to

Charlie's Ponzi scheme? He never could keep secrets from her.

She knows.

Helen and Walter Wells, Sam's parents, had been among the first to invest in the Kelemen Group. It was ridiculous to assume Sam had colluded with Charlie. She would never tolerate the con. She would never allow Charlie to fleece her folks. Sam was a victim, like Betty, Lila, and all the other investors, including her parents. Charlie had left her vulnerable, no income and two months pregnant.

She doesn't know.

What would she tell her parents now? "Mom, Dad, I have something to confess. Charlie was a pathological liar. He stalked our friends and stole your life's savings."

Probably not. It sounded way too clinical. Not enough emotion. More likely, she would start with "rat-bastard husband" and end with "rot in hell."

She would have exposed Charlie long ago.

Sam greeted me at the front door absent any such rancor. She looked stunning in her tight blue jeans and crisp blue blouse, still no hint of a baby on the way. We cheek-cheek kissed hello.

"Always the Southern gentleman," Sam said, easing her embrace. She suddenly frowned. "What's wrong, Grove?"

The question jarred me. I never could hide my emotions. People killed me in cards.

"Bad news?" she asked.

The truth will flatten you.

I scanned Sam's home anxiously. The brownstone felt different than last Monday, though the change was hard to pinpoint. Everything looked the same: the octopus chandelier, the $125,000 Oriental rug, and the fourteen-foot painting. Somehow Charlie's presence was fading, his memory already inching into oblivion.

"The news could be better," I finally answered, unsure where to start, Ponzi scheme, closet homosexuality, or my new fears about the killer. Right now, I would have traded the decision for a cramp.

Why does the house seem so different?

"Tell me everything," Sam coaxed. "Did you hack Charlie's laptop?" She stroked my hair, a friendly touch, not provocative. Her blue eyes, the Siberian-husky gaze, reassured me.

" 'Pleaser.' "

"What?"

" 'Pleaser' is the password."

"Oh. Where's the laptop?" she asked. "I'd love to look through his pictures."

Not if he downloaded them from his favorite Web sites.

"The police have it."

"Why'd you give it to them?" There was an edge to Sam's voice.

"I mentioned the computer to Fitzsimmons, and he got all pissy. They picked it up from my office."

"I wish you hadn't said anything." She sounded annoyed.

"I backed up all Charlie's files on an external hard drive."

"I'd love to get a copy." Her tension eased.

"No prob."

"Did you find anything?"

"You might say that. How were things with Charlie?"

I immediately regretted my question. Not because it would out Charlie. It would out Sam's half-truth. According to Crunch, she knew all about her husband's dalliances. Yet she had dodged my question when I asked, "You don't suppose Charlie was having an affair?"

Now she continued to equivocate. "Charlie adored me. What else is there to know?" Her response bothered me—too flirtatious, too gamey. I was more serious.

That dog doesn't hunt, Sam.

Looking into her cupboard, she pulled out a huge crystal wineglass and abruptly turned serious. "What makes you think we had issues?"

"The history on his browser."

"What was it?"

"Gay porn."

Long way from Charleston.

"I see." Sam absently grabbed a bottle of cabernet from the kitchen counter. She poured and pondered.

Crunch was right.

Sam handed me the glass, nearly spilling the red wine. She didn't use a corkscrew to open the bottle, which made me wonder whether she had been drinking.

No way. She's pregnant

"Sam," I finally said, emboldened by the wine, "would you level with me?"

"What do you mean?"

"Your marriage sucked. And you know it."

She glowered. Unblinking and feral, Sam looked ready to pounce. "Are you here to talk about my marriage?"

What happened to the mild-mannered art history major?

"I wish you'd been more open last Monday."

"I don't know what to say," Sam replied, fiddling with her bra strap. "I thought you were helping me with the Kelemen Group, not investigating my bedroom."

"There's more, Sam."

"I'm listening," she replied, bracing for the worst.

"Okay," I said heavily, holding her eyes with mine. "I'm about ninety percent sure Charlie was running a Ponzi scheme."

She blinked. Her blue eyes pierced mine. I saw anger, not horror. No doubt she was thinking about her parents, the venerable Mr. and Mrs. Walter Wells from Boston, still venerable but out 2 million bucks.

"What do you mean, ninety percent?" Sam asked.

"I need to see your tax files to be absolutely certain."

"Why?"

"Nobody declares stolen money as income," I explained.

Thank you, Law & Order.

"Our money is gone?" she asked, tugging her bra strap furiously, almost pleading for me to confess an error.

Damn thing's going to snap.

"I don't know. Let's check the 1040s." I settled her hand and squeezed it reassuringly.

Sam led me upstairs to the home office. She said

nothing, as the stairs of the Greenwich Village brownstone groaned from our weight. The risers had probably begged for mercy under the lumbering steps of her 230-pound husband.

Black-and-white photos of Charlie's posse, AWOL from the society pages of *The New York Times*, lined the office walls. Almost everyone in the pictures wore tuxedos or evening gowns. Many held tumblers of scotch and flashed toothy grins for the cameras. Betty and Sam sandwiched hard against Charlie in one photo, and all three howled at the lens. It had been a great moment, like many others.

Why does the house seem so different?

I searched for my favorite shot. It was seven or eight years old, one of the few taken outside. A fishing captain, with three days' stubble and enough wrinkles to make prunes look taut, bunched in tight against Sam, Charlie, Evelyn, and me. We had chartered his boat. That day the old salt guzzled peach schnapps and regaled us with marlin memories from his "storied" career. Neither the peach schnapps nor the fish tales had comforted us on the open seas then, but I liked seeing Evelyn now.

Sam caught me lingering. Perhaps she read my mind. She rubbed my shoulder, her touch a cease-fire to earlier hostilities. The near caress said, *Let's get this over with.*

"Our 1040s are in here." Sam opened the bottom drawer of an old office file. Mottled grains, black from time and abuse, occasionally interrupted the rich mahogany patina. The file looked like a trophy from one

of Charlie's Saturday afternoon forays. He had exqui-
site taste, and Sam knew just where to look. She handed
me a thin folder. "I came across this file while looking
for bank records."

The Kelemen tax return bore no likeness to the filings
of the wealthy. There were no K-1s or supporting attach-
ments. There were no fat exhibits designed to make IRS
agents go away. The couple had not even itemized deduc-
tions on Schedule A. The whole world itemized. The ad-
justed gross income, line 37 of the 1040, startled me.

Sam saw my double take. "What did you find?" she
asked.

"You reported fifty-three thousand dollars in income last year." In that instant I erased any lingering
doubts about Charlie's innocence. The image of Fred
Masters, the star of home run derby, haunted me.

Game over, Carlo.

"Damn him," Sam howled. "Charlie spent fifty-
three thousand dollars a month."

He had help.

Spending $53,000 a month took effort. And Charlie
"Carlo" Kelemen was the master. He shopped compulsively and bought expensive gifts bordering on the ab-
surd. He once presented an air conditioner, a massive
window unit that cranked out 12,000 BTUs, to his host
in Georgia. "Their guest bedroom is hotter than road
tar in July," he had complained to Sam. No doubt her
estimate was right.

"There are probably no assets at the Kelemen Group,"
I finally said. "Investor money paid for all your things."

"Oh, come on," she objected. "My parents invested."

Then Sam slumped like a marionette with its strings cut. She slid evenly, her back to the wall, and plopped hard against the wooden floor.

Charlie duped her, I decided.

Seated, she drew her knees to her chest. The protective fetal position shielded Sam from my words and Charlie's secrets. I sat and put my arm around her, suddenly the ambassador of kindness and sensitivity.

Or hard-nosed shit. I piled on the supporting evidence. It was the only way to stiffen her resolve. Sam's troubles were just starting. "Take a look at this." Reaching into my pocket, I unfolded Lila Priouleau's letter as well as the "Investors" spreadsheet. I told Sam the whole story: my misgivings about redemptions, the forged testimonial, and the conversation with Susan Thorpe. I spared no detail.

"What should I do?" Sam asked.

"I'd start by hiring a lawyer. Popowski can refer you to the right litigator."

Sam looked at me curiously. "Why do I need one? I haven't done anything wrong."

"No, but Charlie did. People will be pissed," I said, displaying the spreadsheet for emphasis. "They'll sue, everybody except for two. Maybe."

"My parents?" Sam ventured.

"Right."

"But why me?"

"I don't know which is worse, losing money or feeling stupid because somebody flimflammed you."

"Why me?" she repeated.

"Vengeance. Charlie's gone, which makes you the

target. The courts may force you to sell all your posses-
sions: paintings, Oriental rugs, and even your jewels."

"I can't find my jewels."

"Oh, right."

We sat in the silence underneath all those pictures of
good-time Charlie. We sat for a long time and said
nothing. We broke our silence only once, and I was the
person who initiated the conversation. "I'll take care of
calling the police."

"Why are you calling them?"

"The people on this list all had a reason to feed
Charlie to the sharks."

"Is my name there?" she asked angrily, her voice
oozing menace.

"Don't go there," I scolded. "And there's one other
thing."

How do I tell her?

"Which is what?" she asked.

"I wonder if Charlie's killer thinks you were involved?"

Sam grabbed my shoulder, hard and urgent. She bore
into my eyes, and it seemed her moist blues had never
looked more beautiful. "What do you think, Grove?"

It's a no-brainer.

"There's one thing about old-school Yankees," I replied. "Money never motivates you. It's always something else. I bet that's why Evelyn and you were such
good friends."

In that instant she released her grasp, perhaps comforted by the memory of her friend, my wife. Sam and
I sat for a long time in Charlie's office, our backs against

the wall, figuratively and literally. It was only after a lifetime of silence that I realized what had changed.

The dogs.

"Where are Un, Deux, and Trois?"

"On their way to Boston," she replied. "To my parents."

"Really?"

"They were too much."

Sad. I loved how the three dachshunds lined up in a
row, sat bolt erect on their haunches, and hammed for
food. *So fragile,* I thought, considering Sam's upheaval.
Fifteen days ago she had been rich, however artificial.
Now she had no money and would soon face a slew of
lawsuits. My fears about Charlie's killer, I decided, had
been an overreaction.

*All the vengeance in the world won't get the money
back.*

CHAPTER 41

There was no bike race on Sunday. I woke before six A.M. anyway, immediately alert and mad as hell. Clarity was grinding my brain into hamburger. One person dominated all my thoughts.

Fred Masters.

In my head I saw only Fred. There was Fred swinging at a softball, Fred laughing when I hit the deck, and Fred waving good bye. How could anyone with a conscience hurt him? How could anyone embezzle his hall-of-fame mother? Betty had scrimped and scraped for the day when she was gone.

Kelemen looted that nest egg. He gorged his fat face on $3,500 dinners with her money. The 1040, specifically the adjusted gross income of $53,000, confirmed the Ponzi scheme and with it my realization that Charlie Kelemen had cheated his friends. He disgusted me.

A colostomy bag in wingtips.

Charlie had no interest in Fred. His offer to help was crap. Charlie studied Down's syndrome for one reason—to bilk Betty for $250,000. That money repaid Thorpe.

And Susan's money probably paid for the octopus chandelier, the $125,000 Oriental, and who knew what else.

Charlie's offer at Virgil's haunted me more than ever. "Why don't you join me at the Kelemen Group?" he had asked over lunch. "I need people to grow the business."

Jon Stewart has the word for that train wreck. "Catastrofuck."

My thoughts intermittently returned to Sam. She was broke, vulnerable, and disillusioned. As soon as I briefed the police, news would spread like fire. Investors in the Kelemen Group would react with first disbelief, then horror, and finally fury as details came to light. They would go ape shit.

Who could blame them? Charlie had stolen their money and preyed on their trust. They had dropped their guards, greed suffocating reason. I could hear echoes from another era. *"Rat bastard. Rat bastard."* Investors needed a scapegoat. They would sue, and Sam would lose everything as court-appointed trustees liquidated the Kelemen plunder. She was collateral damage on the come, another victim of Charlie's chicanery.

There was no way to bury the story. Charlie Kelemen had flimflammed friends and family. He had targeted a young boy with Down's syndrome. Charlie's crimes bordered on the satanic, and soon the sordid details would fill newspapers across the nation. *The New York Times* would run a terrific exposé on their front page and seal his status as Wall Street's anti-Christ. And the *New York Post*—they were something else.

Mandy Maris will have a field day.

Sam would pay the price. Reporters might measure

their words at first. They might chronicle a young widow's grief. Inevitably, the media would go for her jugular.

The wilderness is always calm before a slaughter.

"Is the widow an accomplice?" That would be the question on everyone's mind, the one asked by reporters, the one inviting a guilty verdict from the court of public opinion. I had already reached my decision. Sam Kelemen, friend and emotional nurse, was no con artist. She was a victim, and she was helpless.

After leaving her town house, I had debated whether to tell the police. The revelation of a Ponzi scheme would ignite Sam's problems. It would be impossible to defend her. Telling the police would start her dance with the press, her fifteen minutes of shame.

So what. I had no choice. Charlie Kelemen had pissed off the wrong person. Someone on the "Investors" spreadsheet had discovered the crime. Whoever it was had the motive to murder Charlie. I no longer believed Sam was in danger. She had no money, no jewels, and nothing of value for a defrauded killer.

Fitzsimmons and Mummert need to know anyway.

That Sunday morning I decided the police could wait a few hours more. It was still early, and I did my best thinking on a bicycle. Thirty, maybe forty miles, I would hammer out the distance before waking up Boston's finest. I wondered whether Fitzsimmons and Mummert had even stayed in town over the weekend. I needed to think and pedal hard. The cocktail of speed and lactic acid would focus my mind and make me more articulate.

* * *

Living alone fuels eccentricities. Consider my case. Around 6:30 A.M. I talked to my bicycle: "Let's roll, Colnago."

The July air, still fresh from an overnight rain, hinted at the fierce humidity to follow. Traffic, the City's daily regimen of driving anarchy, had not yet kicked into gear. Yellow cabs were nowhere in sight. With a city sleeping and New Yorkers still recovering from Saturday night, it was a great time to start riding. Motorists would multiply. Their impatience would surge as the day progressed.

The only moving vehicle was a creamy green Vespa. The color, though metallic, reminded me of my mother's key-lime pie. As the scooter buzzed down Central Park West, its driver looked cartoonish. He was huge and ripped, his monster pectorals bulging through a black polo shirt. The diminutive scooter labored under the hulking weight above, its engine whining like a pesky mosquito.

For just a moment I laughed at the incongruity. No other vehicles navigated the streets. The tranquility, early morning and empty city, proved comforting as the mosquito engine drowned in the distance.

With a twist against the pedal, I snapped my cycling cleats into place and headed south toward Seventy-second Street. The park felt safe inside. It was closed to autos on the weekends, and there were few potholes on the well-paved roads. There was little need to stay vigilant, no ruts to fold $800 bike wheels like origami. Central Park was the perfect place to wake up and get the heart pumping. My favorite loop started in the park and included a spin around the West Side of Manhattan.

At first I pedaled with a slow, measured cadence, no more than sixty-five turns of the crank every minute. The pace was just fast enough to fold comfortably into the flow of Central Park's traffic. Joggers to the left. Riders to the right. My carbon handlebars, padded with blue cork tape from Cinelli, felt like warm handshakes from old friends.

Up ahead a mini-peloton of cyclists wore blue spandex togs. I hit the gas and raced alongside. All their jerseys screamed "Italia" in bold white letters. The last rider in the pack rode a silver-black Serotta with Dura-Ace components, brakes, crankshaft, and wheels.

"Nice bike," I volunteered, falling into the ad hoc camaraderie that unites all cyclists. We loved our bikes and reveled in the shared experiences of pain, flat tires, and bad dogs. There were no strangers among our ranks.

"Thanks," Italia said.

We passed the Guggenheim, visible through sweeping foliage on our right, and then veered west. The road tumbled, the steep descent abruptly ending my conversation with Italia. Every cyclist in the pack concentrated, tucked aerodynamically, and barreled downhill with the wind whistling in our ears.

At the base I waved good-bye, said, "Arrivederci," and pulled right to the park's exit. Italia touched his helmet and saluted farewell.

Pedaling hard on 110th Street, I stood out of the saddle and pulled against the handlebars, rocking the bike side to side to gain leverage. British cyclists called this motion "honking."

As I raced west toward Riverside Drive, my thoughts returned to Sam. Would she inherit civil liability from her dead husband? It was a legal question, and I had no idea. Would investors in the Kelemen Group sue Sam? Or would they sue Charlie's estate? Did it make a difference? I planned to call Popowski on Monday. He would know.

My Catholic side said Sam bore responsibility for the aggrieved investors. She had profited, however reluctantly, from Charlie's wrongdoing. My humanitarian side disagreed. Sam was a victim, not an accomplice. Charlie screwed her.

More figuratively than literally.

Charlie's secrets saddened me. Sam and he had been so good together. She had the right to piece her life back together. I worried about her ability to provide for a baby while soldiering through adverse legal judgments.

What a mess.

The streets stirred with growing anticipation of a new day in the July sauna. Drivers grew more agitated under the rising sun. Horns wailed at irregular intervals. Every now and then, car brakes screeched and overpowered the *whoosh, whoosh, whoosh* of my twiggy bicycle tires.

Traffic had gone into labor, perspiration-soaked cabbies the picture of pre-delivery histrionics. They rolled down their windows, yelling expletives in choleric tongues from other countries. They pushed their yellow cabs forward, squeezing through the streets, relaxing upon occasion, screaming, and finally breaking free from the jams. I stayed alert, no desire to become their focal point.

The key-lime Vespa from earlier that morning pulled alongside. The man in the black polo shirt wore sunglasses that wrapped around his curly black hair and tanned face. The look said Europe, 100 percent Euro chic, probably Rome or Paris. His features were too dark to say Copenhagen.

Key Lime, a human refrigerator teetering atop a tiny rig, belonged on an American muscle bike. Something heavy and chrome would do, something like a Fat Boy from Harley-Davidson. He throttled the engine and scooted ahead, his improbable acceleration surprising me. He turned right onto Riverside Drive. It was my route.

At the Riverside corner of 110th, a dozen or so people sat on park benches worn by time and rubbed smooth by countless bottoms. Overhead, a thick spray of leafy boughs sheltered guests from the sun's rays. The park was no more than a sliver in size. The lush garden separated my one-way access road from Riverside's two-way traffic on the other side. Like other cyclists, I appreciated the highway's configuration for its safety and scenery. Fast northbound traffic stayed in the two-way lanes to the west of the park. Slow-moving vehicles stayed on the access roads to the east.

Between 117th and 118th, a red Hummer wallowed against the curb like a beached whale. Though parked, the SUV dominated the road. It jutted obnoxiously into the street, making passage difficult for other cars on my narrow lane.

Odd.

For the third time that day, I spied the green Vespa. It was not moving. Key Lime, who had stopped in the middle of the street, was straddling his bike and talking to someone inside the Hummer. It was weird to spot him so many times. People in New York City caught your attention once and then disappeared forever into the urban bush. Ordinarily, I would have forgotten Key Lime and his Vespa. Not today.

The Hummer's open door reached far into the street. No way a car could pinch by. It was narrow even for a bicycle. I braked gently and slipped between the SUV's door on one side and the park's hedges on the other. The driver behaved as though he owned the lane. Other vehicles had to wait.

Not my problem.

I was on a bike. Squeezing past the two-man conference, I called in my friendliest voice to Key Lime, "Nice Vespa."

The guy in the Hummer flipped me the bird. His resemblance to Key Lime made my skin crawl: same wraparounds, same slick black hair, and same refrigerator torso. The two looked like twins, though their sunglasses made it impossible to know just how identical they were. One thing was clear. They creeped me out.

What's your problem?

Hummer Guy sneered like there was something personal between us. Key Lime mimicked his partner, and together their twisted faces radiated contempt. I had no idea who they were or why the hostility. Was I reading something extra into an ordinary day in the life of a New Yorker?

"Fuck you, Steroid Boy," I snapped, perhaps a little too loud. That's the thing about belligerence. Nobody ever thinks. Words just erupt.

Wrong thing to say.

New York City was not the kind of place to tell a stranger, "Fuck you, Steroid Boy." Even a Bronx cheer, the local dialect, was risky. The twins, enormous and militant, smacked of genetic experiments gone haywire. The odds sucked. Two gorillas would trounce me. And my bike was no help. Colnagos lost to Hummers every time.

I shot ahead and gained speed with each turn of the crank. A car door slammed, the loud thump a signal to pedal faster. The Vespa's distinctive motor buzzed awake. A larger engine roared to life. My anger turned to dread, and my spine tingled.

They're chasing me.

Fear fed my legs. No looking back. One guy, and I would have stood my ground and gotten my ass kicked properly. Size always trumped guile in street fights.

At least it's respectable, mano a mano.

But there were two of them. Maneuverability was my only advantage. Building speed with each down-stroke, I chanted, "Dig, dig, dig."

Veering left, I accelerated past a car turtling right. An old woman clutched the steering wheel just a few inches from her nose. She evaluated her right turn as though solving a geometric proof.

Keep deliberating.

Somehow her indecision slowed both the Vespa and the Hummer. I didn't look back. At 122nd my access lane folded into the main road. Riverside Drive turned into a two-way street. Grant's Tomb appeared just ahead on the left. My instincts directed, *Break for the park.*

Not a chance. There were too many oncoming cars, a real fluke for Sunday morning. There was no way to cut left across traffic. I stayed straight, tucked into a cyclist's crouch, and pedaled hard as the road bent and descended. Lactic acid racked my calves. The twins could still catch me. My chest pounded. My knees swore hell to pay later.

Past Grant's Tomb at the base of the hill, Riverside Drive turned into a bridge spanning about eight city blocks. The majestic Hudson drained past New York City into the Atlantic. No time for sightseeing. My cyclometer registered thirty-seven miles per hour, fast for a bike but no match for a Hummer or Vespa.

There was nowhere to turn. I sprinted for the opposite end of the bridge. It ended at 134th Street, just under a huge billboard. Halfway across the bridge, the roar of the SUV returned. The earlier surge of cars had disappeared. No witnesses. I glanced back over my left shoulder. The Hummer trailed by eight bicycle lengths. It was closing fast.

No chance to outrun the SUV. I pedaled anyway. There were no side streets on the bridge, no escape through better maneuverability. I pedaled harder, sucking air in snatches, uncertain what to expect when the Hummer caught me. My breakaway was failing.

The red SUV thundered two feet from my left. The gap was hostile, too close on the open road. The red SUV inched right another six inches, toying with me. I stayed straight. I had ridden in tighter pelotons before.

I can do this.

Hummer Guy rolled down his window and sneered in heavily accented English, "Who's the asshole now, Bicycle Boy." He sounded European.

I snapped my head straight and cranked, daring to watch only from the corners of my eyes. *You made your point*, I thought. *Now go fuck yourself.*

No such luck. The Hummer inched six inches closer. It was only a foot away, okay for cycles in a peloton but not okay for gas-guzzling SUVs with deafening engines. "What's your problem?" I raged.

The Hummer veered right another seven inches. Only five separated us. Scary and tight, there was not even an inch to veer right. The downstroke of my pedal would catch the raised curb. I would crash and break a collarbone. Maybe worse.

Sweat poured from my forehead. Sun crème washed into my eyes and stung like hornets. My vision blurred. I couldn't steer straight like this forever. The tight squeeze eliminated any room for error.

I hit the brakes. My Colnago stopped fast and straight. The SUV roared past. It was no match for the lightning response of a bike. My eyes begged for help, tearing and smarting from the sun crème. I pulled off my sunglasses and shoulder-rubbed my eyes, desperate for relief.

The Vespa's motor whined behind me. I remembered

Key Lime and forgot my eyes. Something closing fast. A flash of motion from behind. I ducked instinctively. The move was good. Not good enough.

Key Lime clubbed the back of my head. His balled fist slapped my brain like a hard grounder to the hot corner. A cycling helmet helped some, but not much. My eyes filled with tears, pain rather than sun crème. Stars everywhere.

"Mother of gator shit." It hurt. It really hurt. Teetering on the verge of blackness, I shook my head and somehow managed to stay conscious.

The Vespa and Hummer stopped no more than twenty feet ahead. Key Lime spoke to his twin through the SUV's window. A Mercedes passed to my left. I waved violently, anxious to make him stop. The driver honked at the Hummer and Vespa instead. He passed to their left and continued north on the raised bridge of Riverside Drive.

Still foggy, I was growing more alert with each second. Up ahead, Hummer Guy dangled something out the driver's-side window. Key Lime grabbed it.

What is it?

Then, I understood. It really had been a mistake to say, "Fuck you, Steroid Boy." He handed Key Lime a thick, chunky chain.

Futile to continue north. The twins had the advantage. They'd catch me on the wide road. They'd work me over with that chain. There was no way to make the billboard or the side street below, no way to get around Key Lime and Hummer Guy.

Failed breakaway.

I pushed away from the curb and started to honk, rocking back and forth in a desperate sprint. My only chance was to race the Vespa and Hummer south. Perhaps I could evade them. Turn off the road at the end of the bridge and they would give up the chase.

Perhaps nothing. I glanced over my shoulder. Key Lime was closing fast. He throttled the Vespa with his right hand. He swung the chain lariat-style with his left. His lips twisted into a sick smile, his expression both smug and sadistic. Hardly the good guy, Key Lime looked like the Lone Ranger in his wraparound sunglasses. He poised, ready to strike.

I pumped hard, but my legs were no match for the Vespa's horses. The moped accelerated faster. Closer, closer, Key Lime pulled closer. He cocked the chain over his head ready to rain blows any second.

My lungs begged for mercy. *Shut up*, my brain screamed back. No time for pain, I pedaled faster and ignored my burning, aching lungs.

Instinct took over, cycling tactics now my weapon. For years I had competed against stronger riders. Some possessed more natural talent. Others juiced. Strategy had become second nature, sometimes my only way to keep pace.

I veered hard right. Key Lime could not overtake me from that side. My bet was simple. Swinging the heavy chain from left to right would be awkward. The weapon's trajectory, across the body while driving at thirty miles per hour, might destabilize the moped. The goon might even hit himself.

My thighs burned. My head throbbed. My heart

crashed against the walls of my chest. It felt like the Goodyear blimp had gone off course. I had no idea where the Hummer was. Not important.

Key Lime gassed the Vespa with his right hand and pulled alongside my left. He swung his weapon from two feet away. I ducked as the chain sang through the air. The motion rocked the moped, forcing his throttle hand to slip. I thought Key Lime might fall, but he recovered. Bummer.

He edged right and tried to mash me against the curb. I braked hard. He scooted past, his momentum driving him forward.

Key Lime turned. I stopped. We squared off. He had the advantage. This time he could charge from his left. There would be no ungainly swings across the body. The big man snarled. His anger sounded like the growls of a hound gone berserk.

That was it. Every cyclist carried makeshift weapons to stave off bad dogs. My water bottle was still full, half frozen from a night in the freezer, and heavy as a rock.

The Vespa barreled toward me. Key Lime stood and whirled the chain clockwise over his head. His muscles rippled underneath the black polo shirt. I threw the bottle with all my might. It caught him squarely in the Adam's apple with a sickening thud. World Series pitch or a lucky strike, it was a bullet not seen since the days of Sandy Koufax. The bottle bounced forward and skittered back to me along the pavement.

Key Lime dropped the chain instantly. I thought he would keel over. But he stayed upright. He whizzed past me and traveled north another fifteen feet before stopping in front of the Hummer. He clutched his throat and gasped. His wheezes sounded like he had swallowed a rusty harmonica. Hummer Guy stared daggers through the windshield but did nothing for the moment.

From under the billboard at the north end of the bridge a paceline of cyclists appeared. At least a dozen, they were barreling south, closing on us fast. Italia, my friend from earlier that morning, led the charge of riders. I had never been so happy to see men in blue spandex.

Hardly weekend warriors, they looked more like the cavalry coming to my rescue. I turned and pedaled hard to gain speed. The paceline caught me, and I folded into the comforting vacuum of their slipstream. There was an angry shout from behind us, something that ended in the word "asshole."

But I never looked back. I cycled home, looking over my shoulder all the way, wondering who hung up on me Saturday morning.

CHAPTER 42

On Monday futures indicated the market would nose-dive at the open. Between hurried gulps of coffee and monster mouthfuls of bacon, egg, and heart-attack sandwiches, PCS advisers readied themselves for the coming onslaught. The talking heads from CNBC and Fox Business fed every investor's fear. "Financial stocks have yet to see the worst," one reporter panted into the camera. "The bears smell blood."

Yeah, mine.

The market held no interest at the moment. Down 200 points today, it would probably soar 200 points tomorrow. "They're circling the carcasses," the reporter continued. I didn't care what the bears ate so long as it wasn't me.

It was my day to address problems. They started with Patty's play for Jumping JJ. Somehow, someway, Lady Goldfish would get hers.

Fish rot from the head down.

There were also SKC's lawyers to consider. I had sparred with the business prevention units before. I had no grand plan, but frankly, strategy was never my thing. I preferred to be in the shit fighting my way out. Action beat analysis paralysis every time.

The twins from Riverside Drive made me forget Patty's maneuvers and Charlie's forgeries. They dominated all my thoughts. There was Key Lime swinging the chain. Hummer Guy flipping the bird. There was my spectacular pitch and Key Lime holding his throat, gasping for air. The two gorillas gave DNA a bad name. It was my day to deal with a new problem. What do I tell the police about yesterday's bicycle incident?

Self-defense.

I had not called the police on purpose. What would they say? What would I say? "There's something you should know, Fitzsimmons. I threw a frozen bottle at the twin with the chain. Hit him in the neck. The last thing I saw was blood and shit all over the place." Talk about unintended outcomes. The police might arrest me for assault and battery.

A fly buzzed my face.

No wonder I feel like a stiff.

Only it wasn't a blowfly, nothing from the Calliphoridae family that lays eggs on dead meat. Over the weekend a fresh hatch of fruit flies had established the most annoying air supremacy. Vast squadrons, flecked with ten thousand red eyeballs, patrolled our skies. They scouted for yogurt cups and dive-bombed garbage cans for discarded fruit. Intermittent "ughs" erupted around the floor when their legions flew up the occasional nostril or two. One fly refused to leave me alone.

Several cubicles over, Patty Gershon swore into her phone. She caught my eye and smirked, raised her arm, and tapped her Bulgari wristwatch in an exaggerated manner. Today I was to call JJ and initiate joint coverage.

No way.

"Hey, Boss," Annie called, slipping inside my mind as only she could. She held a large, clear glass container. A paper cone rested on the lip of the container, pointy side down. There was something brown inside.

"What's in the jar?" I asked.

"A banana slice. I think we should start a catch-and-release program," she chirped, too much cheer, too early in the day. Her sparkling blue-green eyes betrayed something devious.

"What are you talking about?" I looked to Chloe for help, an explanation, anything. She quoted stock prices to Fletch, a client, and gave me a thumbs-up.

"The flies, Boss, the flies. I want to catch and release them," Annie said.

"What for?"

"It's what you do with trout, right?"

"Why bother?" We had better things to do than play games with fruit flies. I needed to ready myself for Gershon. No doubt our fight would start in front of Frank Kurtz and escalate from there. I held my tongue, my self-control stemming from Charleston manners, habitual obsession with Annie, or distractions from yesterday.

Key Lime. Hummer Guy.

"Radio Ray asked me out for drinks," she explained. "Third time in two weeks, and I need to send him a signal."

"What's that got to do with anything?"

Annie inched forward as though sharing a national secret. "Catch and release, Boss."

"I don't get it," I vented with growing exasperation.

"Catch and release," she repeated. "Catch and release." She gestured with her hands and spoke with exaggerated enunciation. She drawled the way Americans drawl to foreigners, hoping loud and annoying prolongation will somehow translate English for those not fluent. She looked at me quixotically, stifling her tendency to raise her eyebrows when delivering punch lines.

Suddenly, I understood and managed a chuckle. Annie planned to relocate the fruit fly epidemic upstairs to Radio Ray's floor. It was brilliant, but not enough to chase my funk. "Too funny," I observed in a flat tone lacking conviction.

Annie rubbed the crease over her upper lip and looked at me, puzzled. The gesture surprised me. Evelyn had had the same nervous habit. Annie's smile disappeared, headed west like the sun. Her face clouded with concern. "You okay, Boss?"

"Yeah, fine."

"What's bothering you?"

Chloe, talking on the phone, snapped her fingers and interrupted before I could reply. She pointed to a news flash scrolling across the television monitor overhead. It read: "Brisbane to buy Jack Oil for $140 per share, a premium of 68 percent."

No wonder JJ went dark. He was protecting inside information and avoiding any leaks.

"Yes," I cheered. At $140 per share, JJ's 2.3 million shares were worth $322 million in aggregate. Added to the other $200 million I managed for him, JJ was now worth $522 million.

Career client.

Patty Gershon stared at me while talking on the phone. Her eyes narrowed into slits. Her lipstick shone redder than usual, the blood color of fresh slaughter. She had seen the news, too.

How will she spin this with Frank and the bankers?

The answer arrived sooner than expected. My phone rang. The LCD screen, like a miniature movie marquee, announced Frank Kurtz was on the line. Without a moment's hesitation, I switched to my friendliest make-happy voice: "Frank, I just saw the news."

"Grove, I need you in my office." He hung up. That was it. He never said, "Please." He never said, "Good-bye." There was no hint of civility, just a few dictatorial words followed by a dial tone. He could have said "Screw you" with more warmth.

"Here we go," I muttered into the dial tone.

Gershon got to Kurtz.

"Guys," I said to Annie and Chloe, "the fruit flies need to wait."

Walking past Estrogen Alley, I avoided Patty. No such luck. She ended her conversation and returned the receiver to its cradle. I could hear her footsteps, sense the venom of her gait, and feel eyes knifing me in the back on the way to Frank's office.

Showtime.

CHAPTER 43

Gus, the PCS rent-a-cop, was speaking with Frank's assistant outside the office door. He saw me but averted his eyes. It didn't take a bloodhound to smell trouble. Security people seldom patrolled during the day, except of course on Friday afternoons when people resigned.

Kurtz sat with his arms folded, his agitation unmistakable. He eyeballed my entry. Had he smiled, his face would have shattered and crashed to the floor in weighty chunks. He fiddled with a Cohiba and reached for his double-blade guillotine.

Too small for a neck.

A pudgy man sat in a guest chair to the right of Frank's desk. He had a baby face, wavy hair a touch long for the workforce, and brown eyes. I judged him to be fresh out of graduate school. Poisonous vibes wafted all through the room.

Who died and threw this party?

Gershon barged in through the door behind me. Her perfume billowed after her. The scent was probably Chanel but reminded me of burp smells from fish-oil tablets. Patty started to speak. Frank cut her off. "You ever hear of knocking?"

"You saw the news, Frank. Somebody competent would have chased the deal between Brisbane and Jack."

"Patty," he stated with authority.

"O'Rourke was asleep at the switch," she continued, undeterred by Frank's effort to wrest control. " 'Wait till Monday,' " she whined sarcastically, mimicking me. "This guy just cost Banking twenty million dollars in fees, Frank. Sutherling is ripshit. Me too."

"We have something to discuss that doesn't concern you, Patty."

Not a good thing.

The words sounded ominous. I almost wished Gershon would stand her ground so we could argue over Jumping JJ. Instead, she blinked and said, "I see." Looking over her shoulder, she announced, "To be continued, O'Rourke."

It was no time for pleasantries, but I extended my hand to the pudgy visitor and introduced myself. "Grove O'Rourke."

"John Diaz," he mumbled, and added something about working with our internal legal department. I was half listening and decided he looked more like a "Baby Face" than a "John Diaz" anyway.

"What's going on, Frank?"

"Sit down," he ordered. Kurtz stopped and waited. The Monthly Nut, usually quick to back down, expected me to comply. His authority had never been more absolute. "Here's how it is, Grove. The Legal Department wants you to take a leave of absence until we sort things out. We all agree it's for the best."

How is ripping out my gallbladder a good thing?

"That's crazy." I couldn't believe my ears. This meeting—Kurtz, Baby Face, me—had nothing to do with JJ and the deal between Brisbane and Jack Oil.

"That reference letter is the problem," he continued. "Everybody has questions about your relationship with Charles Kelemen."

"Are you firing me?" I asked, still not believing my ears.

Kurtz leaned back in his chair, calm, resolute, increasing the distance between us. "We all hope you will be cleared, Grove. We want you back."

"That doesn't answer the question," I snapped. "Are you firing me?"

"We need to do what's right for the firm."

"Give me a break," I barked. "I gave you Charlie's letter. Why would I expose my involvement in a Ponzi scheme? It makes no sense."

"What Ponzi scheme?" he asked.

"That's why Charlie forged the letter."

"What do you know?"

I told Frank and the lawyer about Charlie's 1040, Susan Thorpe's letter, and the $53,000 in gross income for the Kelemens. I poured my guts out, confident the truth would vindicate me.

It didn't. Frank considered the story for a moment and asked, "Were you involved?" His alarm was growing.

"Fuck you, Frank. You've known me eight years. You know better."

"We can't put the firm at risk," Kurtz replied. "Besides, it's just a leave of absence."

"This isn't right, Frank. 'Leave of absence' is what management says when they don't know how to fix a problem. You and I both know it."

"We gave your reference letter to the police," Baby Face said. "They can check if the signatures match," he offered helpfully, trying to defuse my mounting anger.

"Thanks for your fine work," I replied, all sarcasm and Southern molasses.

"Look, I'm trying to protect you," Baby Face replied defensively. "We haven't decided whether to report this incident on your U4."

Is that a threat?

He was referring to the form that brokerages filed with regulatory organizations like the SEC. Compliance departments logged customer complaints through U4 forms. The "dings" followed advisers everywhere. There was even a public Web site where prospects could perform background checks. My U4 was clean, a matter of pride. But it was becoming less important by the second.

"What does he mean, Frank?"

"You know the drill," Kurtz replied. "We report damages greater than five thousand dollars. That's a rounding error on what the Priouleau family stands to lose."

"They're not even clients, Frank."

"We're not sure it makes a difference," Baby Face stated. His voice sounded clinical, matter-of-fact.

"You won't find the answer in your comic books," I

snapped, seeing red, not thinking. So much for avoiding conflict. The lawyer shut up and seethed.

"That's not helpful," Kurtz warned.

"It's not meant to be helpful," I rejoined, my anger swelling. "We all know where this is going. You're laying a paper trail." The two men straightened in their chairs, bolt erect. "You're trumping up U4 charges to cover your ass and lay the groundwork to fire me."

"It's not like that," Frank objected.

"The hell it's not. What are you doing about my clients until I sort this out?"

That's when Baby Face made the one observation guaranteed to turn every top producer postal: "They're SKC's clients." In that moment he morphed from in-house attorney to human hemorrhoid, a walking, talking flare-up.

I wanted to punch his face. They were my clients. I made the cold calls. I suffered through the rejections. Not the firm. No one ever hung up on a slick television ad from SKC.

"Who forgot to flush you, Rook?" I asked, and turned to Frank.

The young lawyer lost his cool. He stood, fists clenched. His size surprised me. He kept rising and rising. It seemed he would never stop. In his chair he had simply looked pudgy, baby fat everywhere. Now he looked immense, about six-four and 250 pounds. "I've had enough of you," he thundered, a crusader with hurt feelings fresh out of law school.

He's big. He's soft. I can take him.

"Sit down," Frank ordered Baby Face, the walls reverberating around us. The Monthly Nut fussed with his double-blade guillotine, clipping nothing over and over again.

The fidgeting distracted me. "Stop playing with that damn thing, Frank. You'll cut your damn finger off." I peered at Baby Face and appraised his chin.

Shovel hook or haymaker?

Kurtz watched nervously, sensing an undercurrent of violence. "Grove, don't do anything you'll regret."

"This is bullshit, Frank. It's not right."

The room grew silent, and Kurtz declared a temporary cease-fire. "We want you back after this blows over."

"Then why is J. Edgar Hoover prowling outside?" I immediately regretted the jab. Gus, the guard, was just doing his job.

"Be nice," Kurtz warned. "We need to discuss your clients." Baby Face shifted uncomfortably in his chair. He recoiled at the word "your."

"I'm all ears." My words came out bitter and hostile. There was another emotion. It was pain. SKC had turned on me.

"I want Patty Gershon to handle your business while we sort things out."

"Over my dead body," I scoffed. "You're kidding, right?"

"I don't see the problem," Kurtz replied evenly.

"She eats her young. That's the problem."

"Grove, she's experienced. She's good at her job. She identified a twenty-million-dollar opportunity with Jack Oil. You didn't."

"She'll swallow you whole and spit out your zipper," I replied. "She'll blow up my business."

Magnetic principles never worked on Wall Street. Likes attracted. Opposites repelled. Brokers found clients with personalities similar to their own. A nice broker meant nice clients. A jerk meant jerkettes. Call it broker's instinct. Call it what you want. I knew Patty would scare my guys away. She emitted too many predatory vibes.

"She'll do just fine with at least one client," Frank countered.

"Who?"

"JJ," he replied. "She speaks Polish."

"Go ahead, Frank. Put Patty in charge of my business." I was bluffing. My heart was racing. Poker was never my strength. "Just remember what I told you come bonus time."

"Then who do you have in mind?" he asked, dropping his guard, doubting his decision.

The bluff worked only because my revenues, a big slice of the department's income, suddenly looked precarious. My "book" would atrophy with the wrong adviser. So would Frank's bonus. He knew the game.

I shared Frank's anxiety, but for different reasons. All brokers distrusted other Wall Street insiders. Money killed alliances in our industry. Colleagues took checks and morphed into competitors all the time. Given the choice, I'd rather lose a molar than trust someone with my clients.

"Annie and Chloe do an awesome job," I offered after some hesitation. "My clients love them. They can handle it."

"No," he ruled without hesitation. His eyes bore into mine, his message clear: *Don't negotiate.*

His body language spoke more diplomatically. It offered hope. He uncrossed his arms, and the defensiveness faded away. He held his chin between thumb and forefinger, a gesture that said, *We can work this out.*

"I'd like to give Zola a shot," I said. "We had lunch this week. Annie and Chloe like her, and I was thinking about asking her to join our team anyway."

"She's inexperienced," Frank countered. "She hasn't even passed the Series 7."

Baby Face fat-butted into our debate. "Frank," he said, "you don't need to negotiate. Grover is taking a leave of absence." It irked me when people used my full first name. It reminded me of the Mad Russian.

Kurtz glowered at the young lawyer and extended his right hand, palm side down. He lowered it six inches, a precise, deliberate motion. Loosely translated, the gesture said, *Go suck on a cork.*

"Zola's taking the exam now," I reported without looking at the lawyer. "She'll pass. She can call my allies for help."

"And who would they be?" Kurtz crossed his arms again, snapping the double-blade guillotine in one hand. The defensive posture was not a good sign.

"Cliff Halek."

"Halek's in another division. He doesn't know our business. Besides, there's no way I'm sending some newbie to a managing director for help. It sends a bad message to other parts of the firm, Grove."

"Cliff will help Zola as a favor to me. I don't care if he's in Derivatives or not. He's forgotten more about the capital markets than most PCS boneheads will ever know. Plus he has a secret weapon."

"And that would be?" Kurtz leaned forward to ask the question.

"He can smell bullshit a mile away."

"I don't know," he resisted feebly, and gnawed on his unlit cigar.

"Look at the alternative."

"Which is?"

"Let's assume Patty doesn't horrify my clients. I'm not ceding the point. But I'll humor you for the moment." I paused to underscore my next comment. "If Patty Gershon ever controls any of my revenues, there'll be no living with that woman. Every time you two disagree, she'll go over your head."

"Let me worry about that," he scolded sharply.

I took the shot and delivered my knockout punch. "She generates revenues, and you don't. She'll get her way, Frank."

Kurtz said nothing for a long moment. He glanced at SKC's lawyer. Baby Face shrugged.

I piled on. "Let's see, Frank. By my calculations JJ is worth five hundred and twenty-two million dollars this morning. At a half percent, that's two-point-sixty-one million every year in fees. And that's just JJ, Frank. I have other clients. Do you really want to ask Gershon's permission every time you need to take a piss?"

The scare worked. Frank surrendered with one word: "Uncle." I had him pinned.

My victory was short-lived. Baby Face ordered, "Grover, you need to leave the premises."

I scowled my best go-play-in-traffic face at him. The glare felt good. It changed nothing. And I knew it. "Frank, may I get something from my desk?" The request almost sounded contrite.

"Sorry, Grove. We'll send what you need."

"Damn it, Frank. I've been here eight years and you're treating me like John Fucking Gotti. I need to get something. And it's not some damn trade secret, either."

"Okay, okay," he acquiesced.

"Thank you."

In better times Frank and I would have shaken hands. Not today. We both held back, our tension filling the room like smog. I had become a pariah to Frank. My touch was toxic, poison that jeopardized his bonus and his career. He no longer regarded me as a top producer. Right then and there, I realized that there was yet another axiom in my industry.

Six: There is no tenure for top producers. We can fall from our pedestals any time, hard, without warning.

Frank rose and ushered me to his office door. He moved slowly, keeping a safe distance between us. His body language said, *I'm taking a seven-hour shower thirty seconds after you leave.* Kurtz, ever the professional, expressed concern nonetheless: "Grove, I hope this thing is temporary."

"Frank, you don't think I'll be back. Do you?"

"I'm not sure," he said.

Baby Face looked doubtful.

"Let's go," I said to the guard outside Frank's office. Behind my back Frank's photo lineup of financial rogues mocked me. Or perhaps they were welcoming me to the club. John Paul appeared ready to grant absolution.

Everyone stared as Gus escorted me to my desk. The brokers, sales assistants, and operations people scrutinized me from all angles. Their mouths, all half ajar, beckoned the fruit flies like Venus flytraps. I felt humiliated and ashamed. It was a perp walk in progress, and there I was scuffling off to jail in handcuffs and leg irons. No wonder suspected felons hid from the cameras on the evening news. It would have been comforting to pull a jacket over my face. My head tingled, a sure sign I was going flush. That was the problem with fair coloring. I never could hide my emotions.

My colleagues saw something other than a criminal. They hailed me like a conquering hero—Julius Caesar of PCS. One broker exclaimed, "Not you, Grove!"

Another said, "It's not Friday. Did you screw up your calendar?"

Scully, the world's loudest stockbroker, said, "Put in a good word for me." I had no idea what he meant.

The pregnant women around Estrogen Alley parted like the Red Sea opening for Moses. But it was Lady Goldfish who surfaced, not Charlton Heston. She looked me square between the eyes and asked, "Where are you going, Grove?"

The lights finally went on. The office thought I had taken a check to join the competition. Scully had asked me to put in a good word, hoping for a big check, too. It was almost funny.

But it wasn't. "I guess this settles the JJ matter," Patty added. She was already fighting to keep JJ's business when I moved to another firm.

"Knock yourself out, Patty." In that cheerless moment my swagger would have impressed Winston Churchill.

Chloe focused on me as I approached our work area. She whispered hoarsely into her receiver, "I have to go."

Annie jumped up from her chair and confronted me with the quickness of a linebacker. "Where are we going?" she demanded anxiously, her allegiance clear.

Chloe huddled from the other side.

"There's no check," I whispered, my voice low so it would not carry. "You may hear some awful stuff about me, but none of it's true. We'll be fine." The words stuck in my throat. I had no idea what would happen.

Annie said nothing at first. She was trying to make sense of what was happening. Finally, she whispered, "Call us from the outside."

"And tell us what to do," Chloe finished.

"I need you to take care of things here."

Gus touched me on the elbow. "I'm sorry, Mr. O'Rourke. It's time to leave."

I made the receiver sign with my thumb extended, pinky held out, and three middle fingers closed. "I'll call you. Zola will be joining you. Make sure to help her."

That was it. I grabbed my briefcase and the picture of Evelyn and Finn from my desk and followed the guard. On the way to the elevator, the brokers in my office stood. Some clapped. Some patted me on the back. I felt their envy, their hunger for a big payday. Scully boomed, "Attaboy, Grove." Damn, he was loud.

We passed Casper, oblivious as he clipped through the commotion. *Plink. Plink. Plink.* I snatched those damn nail clippers from his hand and hurled them into a wastebasket. The cheers, the clapping, once dull, erupted into Malthusian ovations.

To this day I have no idea what possessed me next. Maybe it was denial, my refusal to believe the turn of events. Maybe it was delusion. Kurtz's sentence would never become public, right? The whooping and hollering bellowed across the PCS boardroom. I turned, raised both arms to the floor of cheering stockbrokers, and pretended to be Lance Armstrong, a victor on the Tour de France podium. I was perpetuating the myth of a fat check. I was embracing the enthusiasm of every Judas Iscariot out there.

They'll chase my clients the moment I'm gone.

That's when the joke ended and my world exploded. The ovation stopped abruptly. The jaws on every face dropped. The expressions changed from praise to something new. I saw revulsion and disgust. I saw loathing on every face, save one.

Patty Gershon beamed from ear to ear. She smirked at something behind me. From her grin I knew one thing from for sure. It was trouble, and I feared the worst.

My fifteen minutes of shame are here.

CHAPTER 44

Detective Michael Fitzsimmons hoisted his badge for Gus. But every stockbroker on the floor saw it. "Boston Police," Fitzsimmons boomed at decibels worthy of Scully.

Mummert eyed the rent-a-cop uniform and added, "We'll take over from here. We need O'Rourke." There was a short brunette behind them, also in plainclothes. She didn't look familiar. I assumed NYPD.

First Crunch. Now them. Our reception security is for shit.

In the spellbound silence of the room, I heard Gershon gloating. Rewording Miranda for Estrogen Alley, she trumpeted, "You have the right to turn over all your clients to me." Someone giggled a nervous rattle but only for a second. PCS advisers were riveted to *Eyewitness News* unfolding before their eyes.

"Now's not a good time, fellows."

"What makes you think you have a choice?" Fitzsimmons bellowed. He rolled his head round his shoulders. His neck popped like sizzling bacon.

My Charleston savoir faire had long since vanished.

I came out swinging and promptly got decked. "Glad to see you guys brought backup." I nodded toward the woman in plainclothes.

"She's not with us," Fitzsimmons announced.

"We thought she worked here," Mummert clarified. That's when my face hit the canvas. I knew who she was.

"Mandy Maris," the brunette woman said. "I'm with the *New York Post*, and I have an appointment with Grove O'Rourke."

The letter, the twins, and the fight for Jumping JJ— she slipped my mind.

"You need to reschedule," Fitzsimmons growled.

"I've been waiting a week for this story," Maris argued. "What's your interest in O'Rourke anyway?"

"You're interfering," he retorted.

At that moment Kurtz and Baby Face emerged from the office of good and evil. "What's this all about?" Kurtz demanded.

"Boston Police," Mummert explained.

"The *New York Post*," Maris proclaimed, trying to upstage the two officers.

"Holy shit," Scully bleated from several cubicles back.

"Do you have an appointment?" Kurtz asked her.

"With O'Rourke," she replied, pointing to me.

"He's busy," Fitzsimmons corrected.

Baby Face, who had seemed so naive before, calculated the odds and took command. "What's your name, ma'am?"

"Mandy Maris."

Mandy Fucking Maris to be precise.

"We'll get you an interview, Ms. Maris." Baby Face eyed Gus, and they graciously ushered her in the direction of SKC's PR department. The pudgy lawyer worked her like an ambassador.

I underestimated him.

Maris called over her shoulder, "The Kelemen story runs Wednesday."

What story runs tomorrow?

"Do you need a conference room, Officers?" Kurtz offered.

"That won't be necessary," Fitzsimmons replied. "We're heading over to a station."

I never asked, "Do you have a warrant?" The question would have been too embarrassing inside a room full of stockbrokers drooling over my clients.

The two officers and I headed for the elevators. The last thing I saw was Patty Gershon sidling up to Kurtz. Scully and Casper slithered after her, a department full of hooded cobras right behind. I think one of them hissed at me.

CHAPTER 45

All things considered, the day sucked. SKC had just evicted me. Two officers were escorting me away from a building that had been my corporate home for eight years. And Patty Gershon, arch nemesis and primordial cutthroat, was upstairs stealing clients.

That's only half of it.

Scully, Casper, and others were scavenging for Gershon's spit-backs. Mandy Maris, the brunette in plainclothes, was somewhere inside our offices chronicling the rise and fall of a top producer. What was Baby Face saying to her?

Bad-hair day.

Kurtz could never control Gershon, no matter what he agreed. She was probably on the phone with JJ now: "Congratulations on your deal."

Brown-nosing in Polish.

"Did you hear about Grove?" she would ask. "He left the firm. Gee, it's awful how he gouged you on all those trades. You mean you didn't know? Oh my."

There was also the matter of reputation, of innuendo

and the thousand cuts of hearsay. Rumors would tarnish my name. I could already hear the whispers and see Mandy Maris's words in print. I still wasn't sure why the unexpected visit from Fitzsimmons and Mummert. But I had a good idea, and it wasn't pretty.

Losing clients is the least of my problems.

It felt strange outside, the Midtown chaos surreal. During trading hours there was never enough time to venture along the sidewalks, to lose myself in the daily portmanteau of tourists and employees. I barely had enough time to break for meals, and here I was perp walking over to the precinct on Fifty-fourth and Eighth.

What do Fitzsimmons and Mummert want anyway?

The two officers reminded me of those other myocardial migraines, Key Lime and Hummer Guy. I had not reported anything to the police. Perhaps the twins reported me, and the dynamic duds from Beantown already knew. They were guests of NYPD after all. My omission suddenly felt dirty.

"Listen," I burst out, not thinking. "That guy was swinging a chain at my head. That's why I threw the bottle."

"What bottle?" Fitzsimmons asked.

"What guy?" Mummert followed.

They don't know.

The two officers stopped walking and waited for an answer. Fitzsimmons stretched his neck in a big, round orbit. Mummert cleaved to the side of our building, his ferret eyes locked onto mine. The tag-team intimidation worked. I confessed to the fight. Had they asked, I probably would have copped to the Lindbergh kidnapping on the spot.

Fitzsimmons challenged me first: "How come you didn't file a complaint?" It was more accusation than question.

"Yeah, how come?" Mummert pressed.

"I was upset. Okay? I didn't get their license plates. Okay? I have issues at work. Okay?" The staccato excuses rained like hail.

"Do your issues have anything to do with Lila Priouleau?"

"A letter?" echoed Mummert.

"You know about that?" Their knowledge caught me off guard.

Then I remembered Baby Face's attempt to be helpful: "We gave your reference letter to the police. They can check if the signatures match."

"Word travels fast in a police station," Fitzsimmons replied, confirming my hunch.

"It's not my letter."

"Our people say it's your signature," the big officer leered, all doubt and hang-the-jury suspicion.

"Photoshop works magic."

"Maybe so," Fitzsimmons agreed. "You can tell us about it at the station."

My cell phone rang and saved me from saying something stupid. The ring tone, set to the highest volume, trumpeted the *Pink Panther* theme. A few tourists laughed as they walked past. I was glad Fitzsimmons and Mummert were wearing plainclothes. Otherwise, the three of us would have attracted attention.

"Will you hold this?" I asked Mummert, handing him my briefcase.

Cliff Halek was on the phone. "Annie told me what happened."

The interruption annoyed Fitzsimmons. He scowled and tilted his head, first to the left, then to the right.

"I can't talk, Cliff. I'm with the police."

"Did you hit somebody on the way out?" he asked, surprised by the mention of police.

"No time to explain. Call Kurtz. Tell him you'll help Zola Mancini run my business. Don't take any shit. If he objects, go over his head. Crush him. I need to go."

"Call me later," he replied, and clicked off.

Fitzsimmons prompted, "As you were saying."

My cell phone interrupted, yet again. The *Pink Panther* theme had never sounded so annoying. It was Annie. "Did Cliff call you? What should we tell clients?"

"He called. I can't talk."

"What's going on, Grove?" Annie never backed off when she wanted something.

"I'll explain later." I hung up cold-call style.

Wish I hadn't done that to Annie.

"Maybe you should turn that damn thing off," Fitzsimmons ordered, grinding and cracking as he rolled his head round and round.

"Maybe you should fix your neck."

Wrong thing to say.

"Don't be a wiseass." Fitzsimmons touched me on the elbow with his left hand and gestured west with his right. "Let's go," he ordered. "You were telling us about the letter."

"Lila faxed it last Friday."

"Why is it important?" he asked as we walked.

"Cash Priouleau insisted Charlie demonstrate his financial strength."

"What for?"

"Her family invested ten million with Charlie, and they paid an additional one-point-two-five million for his guarantee."

"And your letter proved the victim had the cha-ching to make that guarantee," Fitzsimmons observed.

"It's not my letter. How many times do I need to tell you?"

"Whatever."

"It's not whatever," I flared up angrily. "Charlie's fund of funds disguised a Ponzi scheme." There it was. I had just exposed Sam's flank to cover my own.

"What makes you say that?" the big officer asked. Before I could answer, he scolded, "And why didn't you tell us sooner?" His questions sounded like the reprimands from my high school nuns.

"I wasn't sure until Saturday."

"That left you all day Sunday," Fitzsimmons objected. "Our work is never done," he added sarcastically.

"If you recall," I protested, "some failed steroid experiment tried to whip my head with a chain on Sunday."

"We'll get back to that," he countered. "Now, what's the problem at your office?"

My head was swimming. Fitzsimmons kept changing the subject. "SKC asked me to take a leave of absence."

"Were you fired?" he asked.

"Given the heave-ho?" Mummert clarified needlessly.

"No," I stated with more outward confidence than internal conviction.

"They didn't waste any time running you off the premises," Fitzsimmons observed dryly. "What do you mean by leave of absence?"

"It means, Detective, that financial scams make for bad public relations. My shop, the venerable Sachs, Kidder, and Fucking Carnegie, is distancing itself from me."

"Nice mouth," Fitzsimmons observed. Then, he threw another curve. "What's your relationship with Sam Kelemen?"

I stopped short on the sidewalk. The questions had just turned dangerous. "Do I need a lawyer?"

Neither of the officers answered my question. Instead, Fitzsimmons volunteered, "We know you wired her seventy-five thousand dollars."

"How do you know that?"

"Your firm told us," Mummert said. "A guy from Legal."

SKC's lawyers watched everything, including wire transfers. "What difference does my wire make?"

"Let me spell it out for you," Fitzsimmons snapped, "Tina Turner style."

"What's that mean?"

"Nice and easy."

"Like the song," Mummert explained.

"Maybe you guys should write for Leno."

"You won't see *The Tonight Show* where you're going," Fitzsimmons scoffed. "The television is off long before eleven-thirty."

"What's that supposed to mean?"

"We have a dead husband," he explained, "who happened to be your best friend. We have a letter that says Charlie Kelemen walked on water. And that letter has your signature on it. We have a widow. She's hot as balls, and you wired her seventy-five thousand dollars. And now come to find out, we have millions of dollars missing, a Ponzi scheme. All this makes you an interesting person, and I'm trying to understand the links between the victim, his widowed bride, the seventy-five thousand dollars you wired her, and of course . . . your letter. Understand?"

"It's not my letter."

"Your fingerprints are all over this case. So far you haven't volunteered much information to Yours Truly. Get the picture?"

"Am I a suspect?"

"Either that or a material witness."

"More suspect than witness," Mummert clarified.

At the east corner of Fifty-fourth and Eighth, I turned north in the direction of my condominium. But the two officers blocked my path. "Let's go down to our clubhouse, pour some coffee, and talk," Fitzsimmons instructed.

"I don't care for doughnuts."

"Do you hear that, Mums?" Fitzsimmons looked at the other officer. "We have a comedian."

"Yeah, a comedian," he chorused.

"I'm through talking."

"We can do this the easy way or the hard way," Fitzsimmons threatened. "Mandy Maris might need a few quotes for her story."

"That's the way it is?" I asked.

Fitzsimmons held his hands out from his sides, palms open and facing me. He smiled and cracked his neck again.

CHAPTER 46

Inside the station house Fitzsimmons and Mummert grilled me. They played every trick of interrogation, used every technique authorized by the Geneva Conventions to prod confessions and wring out information. They cursed. They screamed. They pouted. They banged their angry fists on the table. They gassed up on Coke, coffee, and chocolate, any kind of caffeine. Around 12:30 P.M. they ate chips and sandwiches, even though there was no food for me. They threatened. They scoffed. They huffed, and they puffed, and they scowled and rolled their suspicious eyes every time I answered a question. They jeered. They sneered. They labored like bulldogs to intimidate me. And for the better part of three hours, they met their match.

I work for a large NYC brokerage firm. I deal with this shit every day.

At times Fitzsimmons and Mummert treated me like a witness. Other times like an accomplice. Each man alternated between good cop and bad. It was an uneasy rotation, for they both preferred the darker, nastier role. In the end only one thing rattled me.

* * *

"Are you going belly to belly with Sam Kelemen?" It was hardly a question. Fitzsimmons accused more than he asked.

"Am I sleeping with her? Is that what you mean?"

"Locking crotches and swapping gravy," Mummert explained. "Crotches and gravy."

My face reddened. "That's it. I'm calling my lawyer." The officers waited while I stirred a venom cocktail: two parts outrage, one part shock, and a big splash of kiss my ass.

No one moved at first. No one said anything. We just sat there. The officers looked at me. I looked at them. The sweep hand on my watch ticked off fifteen seconds. Fitzsimmons cracked the knuckles of his meaty hands.

Glad it's not the neck.

The clock on the wall ticked off another thirty seconds. Mummert's chin jutted at an imposing angle, more ferret-like than ever, as he chewed a hangnail. Forty-five seconds equaled an eternity inside a silent room full of nervous tics.

I finally pulled the cell phone from my pocket, brandished it like a sword, and said, "My attorney. Can you hear me now?"

"Go ahead," Fitzsimmons encouraged with a sneer. "Lawyer up. Mandy Maris will love what she hears from us."

"Right. You can tell her how we sat down in a big conference room and I repeated myself over and over again. Skipping records make for a great story." I expected Fitzsimmons to roll his head and crack his neck, but the big man spared his vertebrae.

He went for my jugular instead. "Let me set the scene, chowdahhead. Wall Street wizard questioned in death of best friend." He paused to ensure my attention. "Here's where it starts to get interesting." He rolled his head for dramatic effect. "Did a lovers' tryst end in murder? Questions abound regarding broker's behavior with bewitching, beguiling widow."

"Be hard not to bang," Mummert quipped on cue.

"Over at the *New York Post*," Fitzsimmons continued, "they're a rolling ball of whoop ass when it comes to innuendo. Stuff that would never fly in Boston." He yawned and looked at his nails. "Even a Harvard man can be tempted by money."

"And one nice piece of ass," Mummert added.

"I wonder what your clients will think," Fitzsimmons sighed disingenuously.

"Your clients," Mummert echoed.

That was it. "Why don't you pour yourself a steaming cup of shut the fuck up?" I snapped at the weasel-faced officer.

"Oh my," Fitzsimmons soothed or taunted or both.

Mummert started to say, "Oh my," but he thought better of it. He wilted under the weight of my piercing stare.

"You know," Fitzsimmons said, "I bet they read the *New York Post* in Nome, Alaska."

"All the news that's fit to print," Mummert added.

"Wrong newspaper. And I'm not your guy."

"I wonder how the Eskimos will see it," the big officer countered. "The morning paper, a few logs on the fire, tales of scandals from the far reaches of Wall Street. A stockbroker who won't cooperate. The story beats mushing the dogs all day."

"Okay, okay. I get it."

"I thought you would see it my way," Fitzsimmons said. "Let's go back to the beginning. How long have you known Sam and Charlie Kelemen? What do you know about their marriage? When did you first suspect a Ponzi scheme? Did Sam Kelemen know about it?" And so on.

"Your interest in me makes no sense," I protested more than once. "There were five hundred people watching me when Charlie died. Why don't you investigate the people who invested in Charlie's fund of funds?"

"Leave the sleuthing to us, Harvard Boy."

I hate that expression.

Three hours after the police interrogations first started, I walked out the front door of the Fifty-fourth Street police station. I felt like the star of an Alfred Hitchcock movie, an innocent man unjustly accused. My cell phone reported twenty-three messages in voice mail.

Meandering, my head in a listless fog, I headed up the West Side toward my apartment. The streets blurred until I passed the Star of Bombay, an Indian restaurant on Eighth. Three or four union men were striking outside, picket signs, the whole ball of wax. They chanted raucously, "Bombay is not okay."

One of them jammed a yellow flyer into my hands and repeated, "Bombay is not okay, brother." The page showed a turbaned man, presumably the owner, looking grotty and severe. Cartoon rats encircled his photo. Underneath, the union detailed its grievances.

Everybody has issues.

My focus turned to Cliff Halek. We spoke nearly every day. Our work required constant communication because of the business I generated for his team—zero-cost collars, prepaid forwards, and all the other hedges for large blocks of stock. Cliff was one busy guy, in great demand among PCS advisers. How long would it be before we had nothing further to discuss? Our friendship would fade into nothingness.

There was Annie. She had been dancing through my thoughts as of late. Her stories, her looks—I had been falling for her winsome charms. Once I was a statistic at SKC, just another broker who had come and gone, how long would it be until Annie forgot me?

What about Jumping JJ and Frank Kurtz and Radio Ray? What about all those meals stinking up the trading floors and festering in our cans after lunch? Continuing north, I considered the most devastating loss of all. In my job I managed ideas, not people. Now there was nothing to fill the recesses of my mind, nothing to prevent me from dwelling on Evelyn and Finn. My island was sinking faster than Atlantis.

As the chants of "Bombay is not okay" faded behind me, I understood how the union felt.

CHAPTER 47

Back in the safety of my condominium, away from the corner of Fifty-fourth and Abu Ghraib, Fitzsimmons's warning reverberated through my brain. *Don't be a chowdahhead and take a trip somewhere. We wouldn't like it.* His meaning was clear.

They think I'm dirty.

There was also the worst of Mummert to consider. *Crotches and gravy, crotches and gravy.* His refrain rumbled inside my head like bad lyrics from a British rock band. He watched too many police shows, the ones where the spouse is always guilty.

Sam has nothing to do with Charlie's death.

It was late afternoon. I fixed coffee and promptly splashed Kenya Bold all over my starched white shirt. "Damn it," I cursed to the dead quiet of the condominium. Then I knocked my calculator to the floor while pulling a laptop and photo from my briefcase.

Not my best stuff.

Moments later Windows cycled through its start-up. The blinking lights cautioned me to steer clear of the computer lest I knock it over, too. The calculator rested safely on my desk, next to the picture from PCS.

Over a year.

That was the last time a photo of Evelyn and Finn had appeared in my apartment. The awareness gave me hope. It reinvigorated me with a dark kind of solace.

Glad they don't have to see this shit.

Step one was to call Sam. Some help I had been. Her money was missing, and I had done nothing to recover it. Confused and conflicted about what to do, I remembered the worst fact of all.

It's not Sam's money.

The Ponzi theory only heightened police suspicions. They identified Sam as a "person of interest." Mummert remarked during our interview, "It's always the wife." My wife's best friend didn't need that kind of help.

Sorry, Evelyn.

Fitzsimmons had instructed me to send the "Investors" spreadsheet. His urgency made no sense. "Why? You have Charlie's computer."

"Our techies haven't hacked the files yet."

"The password is 'pleaser,' " I had announced triumphantly. It was the wrong thing to say, exulting over a lucky guess the wrong thing to do.

Fitzsimmons asked, "How do you know?"

"Yeah, how?" Mummert echoed. "Did he tell you?" The officers and I circled this topic for the next twenty minutes.

The phone rang and extricated me from these recollections. "Hello."

After two or three seconds of silent eternity, a strong, steady, caring voice boomed into the receiver, "Where have you been? What's going on, Grove?" There was no "hello" or friendly introduction, though I could feel the gush of relief. The caller added with a hint of anger, "You never returned my calls."

It was Annie. She probably left twenty-two of the twenty-three messages on my cell phone. I had not listened to any of them.

"Sorry."

Her tone absorbed me for a moment. She always called me "Boss." She always walked the fine line between playful and deferential. Not this time. She was different, commanding, no monkey business. There would be no mention of fruit flies or Radio Ray.

Annie's voice drew me close, forced me to forget the Boston police. I hit the send button on my laptop. The "Investors" spreadsheet zipped off to Fitzsimmons's mailbox.

Time to move on.

"Compliance Nazis are scouring the place," she reported. "Kurtz has been rifling through your desk since you left. Your files, your drawers, everything. He kept asking us about Sam Kelemen. We said you had dinner with her at Live Bait."

"Answer all his questions. I have nothing to hide."

"Kurtz told us not to call you."

"What did you say?"

"Think I care what he said?" Hearing the irreverence, I glanced at Evelyn. "I'm calling," Annie continued. "Right?"

"Where are you?"

"The office. Level with me, Grove. Have you done something wrong?" Suddenly, our age difference of eight years no longer existed.

"Don't call me from the office," I barked, not answering her question. "They monitor calls."

Annie barked back, "You think I'm stupid? I'm on my cell." She dropped her voice several notches, less aggressive and more conspiratorial. Us against them. "Besides, what can they do?"

"Fire you. Let's start with that."

"Who cares," she snapped. "Now answer my question. Did you do something wrong?"

"Not a damn thing. I'm helping two friends."

Sam Kelemen. Betty Masters.

Annie went silent. For a long, lingering moment Evelyn and Finn stared at me from the photo. In a sudden storm of mental war games, memories of my family's brief life span versus disquiet about the future, I decided that Annie did not believe me. I was wrong.

"I know you didn't do anything wrong," she finally said. "I just wanted to hear you say it aloud. Now, what are we going to do about this?"

We?

"We are not doing anything."

"I'm helping," she argued. "You don't have a choice." She had probably been the kid on the block who defied neighborhood bullies.

No matter her words, Annie's voice still betrayed fear. It could have been fear about money. Broker teams shared their payments from fees and commissions.

Annie and Chloe received a base salary from SKC. They made even more money from their percentage of team earnings. If I blew up, they would lose the bulk of their incomes.

Annie's angst had nothing to do with money, though. She had already jeopardized her job by calling me. And she knew it. There was something else in her voice.

"Tell me what to do," she pressed.

"You can start by avoiding me. Charlie forged my name on a reference letter. That letter helped him swindle friends and his wife's family. SKC and the police both think I'm involved, which makes me a leper."

"Hey, Grove," Annie declared evenly.

"Yeah."

"Shut up."

This "shut up" was different, not the valley-girl kind I had heard so often among her cabal of twenty-something friends. This "shut up" was the real thing. It was more of a "listen up."

"You're innocent. Nothing else matters."

"I'm damaged goods, Annie. Kurtz will have a fiasco on his hands once the story gets out."

"I'll help."

"No."

"You don't get it, Grove."

"Get what?"

"Ever since Gus escorted you out the door, I've been afraid of one thing."

"Which is?"

"Trust," she replied, her voice faltering. She had ventured into uncharted wilderness.

"What do you mean?"

"I need you," she explained, "to be right."

"Right?"

"To be the good guy, Grove." Somewhat exasperated by the need to clarify, she added, "Okay? Do you get it?"

She even thinks in stories.

"Annie, I know what it means to lose respect. I lost mine for Charlie." Digging deep, rummaging through feelings long out of reach, I added, "It would kill me to lose yours."

"Don't worry, Boss." With that word, "Boss," I knew her misgivings were gone. I had recouped her trust beyond any doubt. It was the boost I needed.

"There's a way for me to prove I had nothing to do with Charlie's scam. I just don't know how. Not yet anyway."

"Why don't we go to Goldman Sachs?" she suggested brightly. "Joe Lindmann is always trying to recruit you," she said, referring to the head of Goldman's PCS.

"He wouldn't come near us right now. I'm toxic. What does Kurtz want you to tell clients?"

"He didn't say."

"You're kidding, right?" I wasn't surprised, not really. Kurtz's oversight was classic, the habitual behavior inside brokerage firms. Top producers considered customers first. Managers considered politics and kissed asses first.

"Typical Kurtz," Annie observed with wisdom beyond her years. "We have the clients covered. We're saying you took a few days off." She added, "It's true, too."

"Perfect. Has JJ called?"

"No."

"He probably won't given the deal between Brisbane and Jack. If he does, tell him to reach me on my cell. How about Zola Mancini?"

"She stopped by. She's moving her stuff here in the morning."

"Make sure she coordinates with Cliff."

"Gotta hop," Annie interjected. "Drive-by," she explained.

"Duck," I said.

"Drive-by," in our world, referred to Kurtz's patrols around the floor. He left his office sporadically to take the pulse of PCS brokers at work. "Check your Black-Berry," she added tersely. "I think the compliance Nazis turned it off. And one other thing."

"Yeah."

"Fight for your job, Grove. I'm in your corner."

The line went dead. Evelyn smiled from the photo.

CHAPTER 48

Annie was right. No e-mails had arrived since 11:17 A.M. There should have been at least seventy or eighty new messages, breaking news, internal research, anything. There was nothing, and I could not help but see the irony. The IT department never hustled to fix day-to-day computer glitches.

Show me the door and tech buzzards start picking five minutes later.

I dialed Mancini. She answered, "Zola," and her husky tone almost made the name redundant. Her distinctive voice would be a powerful asset on the phone.

She sounds confident. Good sign.

"Did you pass?" I asked without introducing myself. SKC gave brokers one chance to pass the Series 7, a regulatory prerequisite for selling securities. Fail and you were fired.

"Ninety-seven."

"Great score, but you studied too hard. Anything above seventy is overkill."

"Thanks. I think." With that, our banter evaporated. "Frank briefed me," she said. "I don't like your trouble."

"Me either. I assume your instructions are not to contact me."

"You called me," she said. "Fuck 'em." There was no hesitation, no end to Zola's defiance. She had already joined the union of suffering brokers against the world. It was only a matter of time before Zola became a top producer.

"I need time to sort things out. And you need to trust me." The knot in my stomach tightened.

"What can I do?"

"Play the game. Tell Kurtz whatever he wants to hear. When clients call, jump on the line and introduce yourself as my new partner."

Makes it harder for Gershon.

"Is this where we say 'I do'?" she asked wryly, marriage vows the PCS metaphor for partnership.

"You're perfect for this business," I observed. "If you need help, talk with Chloe and Annie first, then Cliff Halek. And stay away from Patty Gershon. No matter what she offers, no matter what she says, stay away from her. That woman can suck a raw egg and leave the shell intact."

"She already approached me."

"What'd she say?" I asked, trying to hide my alarm.

"Your U-4 will be thicker than *Crime and Punishment*, with all the dings and everything."

Bet Patty never opened the book.

"What else, Zola?"

"She said you two agreed to joint coverage of Josef Jaworski."

"Gershon's doing a landgrab," I corrected.

"I knew she was lying."

"How?"

"Too big a bitch. There's no way you'd work with her."

Zola's definitely top producer material.

"What else did Patty say?"

"That she met JJ at a party. That I should bring over some portfolio statements so we can prepare for a meeting."

What meeting?

"Damn her." Patty was already making her move. I wondered whether she had reached JJ.

"What should I do?" Zola asked.

For a moment we were both quiet, the silence atypical of people who talk about the markets for a living. "Stall," I finally replied. "I need time to think. Say yes to everything, but put off delivery of the statements until next week."

"You know Gershon. I can't delay forever."

"Do your best."

"Is there anything else?" Zola asked, trying to be helpful.

"Well, there is one other thing," I said tentatively.

"Which is?"

"Don't call me until I sort this out. If I call you again, hang up. I have no idea what's ahead. And I don't want to fuck up your career."

"Hey, Grove." Zola paused and waited, a clear demand for my undivided attention.

"Yes?"

"I'm in. I'm with you."

"Like a wingman?"

"Hey now." She laughed and hung up.

Zola had sounded convincing. But she stood to win whether I cleared my name or not. She knew it, too. She was street savvy and recognized that a share of my revenues had fallen into her lap. Not a bad start for a newbie. I immediately brooded over the decision. Charlie's legacy made me second-guess everyone and everything.

Instead of checking my twenty-three voice mails, I called Sam. "It's me."

"Hi." She went silent.

Had I interrupted something? My career depended on reading people's moods instantly. Sam's perfunctory "hi" sounded all wrong. "Did I catch you at a bad time?"

"I'm meeting someone." There was no hint of goodwill.

"Have the police spoken with you?"

"They came yesterday and asked about us."

"Us?"

"Yeah," she shrieked. "Us."

"Tell me." Inadvertently, I had truncated the classic line salespeople use to probe prospects: "Tell me more."

Why the anger?

"They focused on the seventy-five thousand dollars you wired. They think we're sleeping together."

"Piss on them."

"The exact expression escapes me. It was something about going belly to belly."

"Piss on Mummert. Piss on Fitzsimmons. The whole lot as far as I'm concerned. What else did they ask?"

"Whether you had any business dealings with Charlie, like referrals, that sort of thing."

"What did you say?"

"I told the truth. Charlie hid our financial affairs from me. I have no idea what he did or with whom."

"Good answer." It would have been nice to get a stronger testimonial—a statement from Sam that Charlie and I had no business relationship. But I endorsed her honesty.

"I have to go," she announced. "I'm not sure we should be talking with each other."

"Why?"

"This suspicion is so complicated."

I could almost see Sam through the receiver, fiddling with her bra strap as though it were a rosary.

"Sam, I'm only trying to help," I soothed.

"I don't know what to say," she said. "I'll call you. Okay?"

Prospects had blown me off. But it had been years since a woman tossed me aside. *Damn, Sam.*

It took a few seconds before the realization dawned on me. "Do you think I wrote that letter for Charlie?"

"I don't know. I have to go," she said. Abruptly, a dial tone jarred my ears. It sounded like police sirens en route to a crime.

Sam's hang-up stung. The afternoon shadows peeked through the windows of my empty condominium. I had failed her. All that money, $75,000, and no questions asked. My wire, my attempt to help, bought five minutes of phone time and a curt hang-up. It also provoked police suspicion. My questions had scared Sam away. Why had she gone cold? It made no sense.

When there were snags at the office, I worked the phones. I called clients and traders, even Radio Ray, to resolve issues. My instincts screamed for me to work the phones now. "Start dialing, smiley." But after the conversation with Sam, I could not bear further rejection. Nor could I bring myself to call Betty Masters with an update. I had my own problems and cycled through voice mail instead.

Annie left six messages, not the twenty-two I had suspected. The first was a simple: "It's Annie. Call me." Her voice escalated in alarm with each communiqué. "Where are you?" led to "I'm worried sick." She even threatened: "I'm sending sniffer dogs." And so on.

Halek had called while walking the streets of Manhattan to an appointment. I could hardly make out his words. Traffic noise eviscerated any hope of a comprehensible message. Only a few words survived: "Don't worry." Angry horn. "Kurtz." Screeching brakes followed by the crunch of metal against metal. "Dumb as an unplugged computer."

Alex Romanov's message surprised me the most. Where did he get the number to my cell phone? Annie or Chloe had not given it to him. That much was certain.

His voice mail was succinct: "Charlie's notes didn't arrive. Should I send a runner over to your place?"

I wondered what Romanov meant by "your place," the office or my home. What did he know? Eventually, he would learn about my forced leave of absence. Word would spread.

Before long Gershon and a handful of other top producers would bellyache to Kurtz, resurrecting gripes
and settling old scores: "You owe me, Frank. I'm always
taking one for the team." They would interrogate the
boss with skills worthy of Fitzsimmons and Mummert:
"If Grove is coming back, why was he escorted out the
door?" They would gossip without shame. They would
broadcast their opinions everywhere, almost like posting
verbal editorials.

I could hear Scully, figuratively, not quite literally,
even though he was the world's loudest stockbroker:
"Let me get this straight, Frank. You're turning Zola
loose on Grove's centi-millionaires. She's a rookie. Are
you crazy?"

Casper kept detailed notes on all PCS clients—not
just his. Who are they? How much money do they have?
Which brokers cover them? He even recorded what
stockbrokers confided during passing conversations.
That way, he could ask for handouts when people left:
"Grove told me all about the client, Frank." I once caught
Casper jotting reminders on a linen napkin during a top
producers' dinner.

Nail-clipping vulture.

Romanov probably knew about my forced exile. The
thought prompted me to pull the red folder from my
briefcase. Actually a stylized bicycle bag, my black
leather satchel served as a dump for all things tedious.
It contained "not-now" items ranging from medical
claims to expense receipts. Good thing Charlie's folder
made the cut. Otherwise, the red file would be at the
office and beyond my access.

Romanov's request could wait until the morning. Instead, I looked for the pages where Charlie had scrawled "31.12" and "30.11." I still had not reviewed Rugged Computers, the stock next to those scribbles. That was the problem with the "not-now" satchel. The stash usually gained in size and weight. My black hole of procrastination sucked papers, management memos, everything into its hungry void. I only dealt with the paperwork when it became too heavy to haul back and forth to work.

What had gone through Charlie's mind? I found the page with his notes, inspected it briefly, and reached for the Hewlett-Packard 12c. Whenever I looked at numbers, my calculator morphed from circuitry to security blanket. I punched the 12c's buttons as though they would reveal hidden secrets. Unfortunately, the display had changed. Commas were periods, and periods were commas.

The 12c did that at times, particularly when dropped. In the parlance of Hewlett-Packard, its display had gone from "U.S. mode" to "non–U.S. mode." That's why commas were now periods and vice versa. I hated this quirk. I never could remember how to fix it, which was a problem because the inversions bugged me. It was always necessary to dig through the instruction manual to fix the readout.

I studied Charlie's notes and then the LCD display. Somewhere inside the fog of personal irritation, it occurred to me the two numbers did not look like stock prices. Even though securities were now priced in decimals, we still thought of shares in fractions—a throwback to the old pieces-of-eight thinking that had ruled Wall Street forever.

First trader: "I'll throw in my dog for an eighth."

Second trader: "I'll give you a steenth." A steenth was one-sixteenth.

There were no dollar signs, either. Everybody used dollar signs. Romanov's words repeated over and over inside my head: *If Rugged Computers hits anything north of twenty dollars, I'll own Bermuda.*

They're something other than money.

I scrutinized "31.12" and "30.11," trying to identify a pattern. It would have been easy had they been Fibonacci numbers, the numerical sequence named for Leonardo of Pisa. Looking at the Hewlett-Packard, I suddenly realized what the pattern was.

"Jesus, Mary, and Joseph!" is the exclamation my mother would have used.

I went with my old standby; "Fucking shit."

Charlie had been working in "non–U.S. mode." The numbers weren't stock prices. They were European-style dates. Probably trade dates. How could I have missed something so obvious?

What happened on November 30 and December 31?

CHAPTER 49

That night I shed my suit and slipped into khaki shorts, flip-flops, and wrinkled button-down. It was the neo-tribal dress of a modern hunter-gatherer foraging the Upper West Side for the ultimate plate of carbs. My belly said one thing. With the right comfort food I could swallow troubles and everything else on my plate. My brain said another. All the pasta in Manhattan could never cure my problems.

Hungry and drained from the day, I slogged over to the trendy cafeteria in the basement of the Time-AOL building at Columbus Circle. Dozens of cuisines taunted my nose with their savory smells. The smorgasbord of bright colors and exotic spices, some complementary and some in competition, reminded me of trading floors at high noon. I wandered from one food cart to the next surveying the alternatives from kitchens across the globe. They were all tempting. It was impossible to choose.

Twenty minutes later I stood at the checkout counter plate in hand. The girl at the cash register, chunky beyond her years, looked first at my dinner and then at me

"That it?" she asked, not bothering with a verb or hiding the disapproval in her voice. She sounded Southern.

"Yes," I replied flatly. Ordinarily, I would have asked about her accent, Southern but not from Charleston.

"Two pounds of garlic mashed and gravy. That's disgusting."

"I had a bad day."

"If you eat that," she observed, "it's gonna get a lot worse, honey." She punched the keys of her cash register.

"I'm coming back for a pint of Belgian chocolate ice cream. If that's okay with you, honey." I immediately regretted punctuating the sentence with "honey." It sounded assoholic.

"Real bad day," she observed, shaking her head from left to right.

Twenty minutes later, true to my word, I returned to the checkout line with ice cream. But when I dug into the Belgian chocolate back in my condominium, the cashier's warning proved right. The "garlic mashed and gravy" promised there would be hell to pay if I continued on the present course.

I traded the ice cream for ice water and began an evening with Charlie's file and Internet Web sites that offered financial information. Access to Bloomberg, the mother of all subscription databases, would have been much better. I considered taking a cab to LaGuardia. The airport offered free access to Bloomberg terminals.

Are they inside or outside security?

I could not remember, so I stayed home. Eventually, a number other than Charlie's scribbles flagged my attention. The printout showed that Alex Romanov owned 9.5 million shares of Rugged Computers. It was a big position. The absolute number, even for a fund the size of MRI Capital, shocked me. How had I missed 9.5 million shares before? That number could make MRI Capital an "affiliate."

In the vernacular of securities regulation—legislative tyranny to some—an affiliate is a director, corporate officer, or anyone who owns more than 10 percent of a company's outstanding stock. I am no lawyer. But I consider affiliates to be people with access to material, nonpublic information. I use the word interchangeably with "insiders," which sometimes draws fire from those who argue semantics for a living. Who cares? I know enough to keep my guys out of trouble.

The SEC regulates affiliates. It forbids them from profiting on inside information, which is like buying lottery tickets and knowing the winning numbers in advance. The penalties are stiff. Cross the line. Go to jail. Serve hard time as the prison's bend-over bitch in residence. This deterrent is simple and effective most of the time.

The SEC also requires affiliates to disclose their trades publicly. The CEO of Company X, for example, must report his personal buys and sells in Company X stock. All investors, from investment club grandmothers to Wall Street wizards, can see insider trades by visiting Yahoo! Finance or other Web sites with financial data

The decisions of senior management, 10 percent share-holders, and other affiliates hang like damp laundry in the gale of public scrutiny. Who sold? When did they sell? How many shares? At what price?

At issue is whether insiders possessed material, non-public information prior to their sales. If an insider sells shares one day and the stock tanks the next, there are questions you have to ask: What did they know? When did they know it? Did they profit illegally?

Sitting at my desk, I doubted Romanov would ever allow himself to become an affiliate. Why take the risk? Most hedge funds disdained publicity. They invested stealthily, away from those who would otherwise regulate their activities or copy their market moves.

There were exceptions. Some hedgies, like the share-holder activists, hogged the limelight. They made sport of managerial ineptitude and skewered underperforming managers on the pages of *The Wall Street Journal*. Not the Mad Russian. He preferred to operate in the shadows. He kept his mouth shut about triple-digit returns until his gains were secure.

There was good reason. Romanov bought volatile stocks. They traded "by appointment" in Wall Street vernacular, only a few thousand shares per day. News could send prices flying or wipe out paper profits in short, cruel flurries. All it took was one large order, buy or sell, just one person to copy an investment decision and blow the economics.

According to the industry rule of thumb, Romanov could trade 20 percent of a stock's daily flow without moving the share price. He could sell fifteen thousand shares, for example, of a stock with an average daily volume of seventy-five thousand. Any more would crush the price. It would take sixty-seven days to "lose" a block of 1 million shares.

Translation: "Lose" is special jargon from hard-boiled traders. It's how the film-noir wannabes of Wall Street say "Sell."

Losing a block of a million shares over sixty-seven days brought risk. Word might get out. For Romanov, a heralded money manager, the last thing he needed was to tip off other investors. They would follow the lead of the next Warren Buffett, overwhelm demand with sloppy sell orders, and erase MRI's gains amid the torrent of falling prices. In these cases "lose" reverted to its more traditional meaning.

It made no sense for Romanov to become an affiliate. His disclosures, mandated by the SEC, would take just three days to "hit the tape" and become public knowledge. Other investors, assuming insiders had better information, would sell: "What do they know we don't?" Nobody wanted to hold falling shares or hot potatoes.

So much for sixty-seven days and MRI's triple-digit returns. Based on my assumptions, Romanov could only sell forty-five thousand shares of a million-share block before other investors noticed his actions. Just three days of trading. Given the 20 percent profit participations, the swings in Romanov's personal fortunes could be huge.

He can't be an affiliate. But 9.5 million shares is too big a number.

Romanov had once said, "I concentrate my bets. I

never own more than fifteen stocks at a time. That's how I generate my kind of returns." His words reeked of arrogance then. My gut said something was wrong now.

It took only a few clicks to find Rugged Computers in Yahoo!'s finance section. The "key statistics" page did not show total outstanding shares. The "profile" page, however, contained a link to Rugged's Web site. The company had issued a total of 44 million shares.

"What are you doing?" I asked aloud. With 9.5 million shares, MRI owned 22 percent of the company. Romanov, in control of more than 10 percent, was clearly an affiliate.

I clicked back to Yahoo! The Web site often showed insider transactions. Bad news: Yahoo! provided no information about Rugged's insiders. It was disappointing but hardly a surprise. Access to micro-cap information was often sketchy among free Internet services.

Good news: Yahoo! offered historical prices. I clicked once, and Rugged's trading activity filled the screen. Prices and volume numbers dated to August 13, 1996. History that far back was more than necessary. I just needed Rugged's trading statistics around November 30 and December 31 of last year.

Maybe it was broker curiosity. Maybe it was a complete waste of time. Maybe I could still hear Annie's voice inside my head: *"Fight for your job, Grove."* Whatever the reason, my instincts suspected the link between Kelemen and Romanov might help. I was searching for a buried fact, any shred of information that would dispel questions about my involvement with the Kelemen Group.

Damn that Charlie.

Rugged Computers had been an excellent investment. On December 29, 64,436 shares traded and closed at $4.50—a gain of 32 cents from the $4.18 close the previous day. On December 30, 67,492 shares traded and closed at $5.10. On December 31, another 75,008 shares traded and closed at $5.50. The stock had gained $1.32 or 31.6 percent in just three days.

The turnover statistics, however, smelled fishy. Rugged's shares traded less than 7,500 shares on most days—one tenth of my 75,000-share example. Volume had totaled 206,936 shares on the last three days of December, unusually large for the stock but tiny by market standards. Using the highest closing price during those three days, $5.50 per share, the value of 206,936 shares barely exceeded $1.1 million.

Peanuts.

With $800 million under management, Romanov easily possessed the power to buy every single share that traded. The $1.1 million would hardly dent his fund. MRI could run up the price of Rugged Computers simply by purchasing blocks of stock. The SEC had coined a term for manipulation of this sort. They called it "marking the close."

Did Romanov buy stock on December 29, 30, and 31?

He certainly had the incentive. He received his 20 percent profit participation based on the book value of the portfolio at year-end. No way had MRI purchased all 206,936 shares. But the $1.1 million outlay would have been an awesome trade in theory. MRI's total block of 9.5 million shares had appreciated

more than $12.5 million. Assuming there were no
losses elsewhere in the portfolio to offset the gains,
Romanov's 20 percent profit participation totaled about
$2.5 million.

Why did Charlie care?

The November 30 date puzzled me even more. Most
hedge fund managers waited until December 31 to calculate their profit participations. The reason was more
than simple industry convention. Investment agreements
required audits in advance of payments to money managers. It would be too expensive and too time-consuming
to audit results more than once a year. The only values
that counted were the closing prices at four P.M. on the
last day of the year. Forget stomach-churning lows or
euphoric new highs earlier during the year. The audited
numbers determined how much investors kept and how
much money managers took home.

It made no sense to manipulate stock prices thirty
days in advance of an audit. The gains might not hold.
Consequently, I expected little action from Rugged
around November 30. I was wrong. The shares had
gained nearly 21 percent during the last three trading
days of November, again on light but higher-than-
normal volume.

Why did Charlie care?

I instinctively fished the subscription agreement out
from the red folder. Ordinarily, these documents were
death in print. The legalese suffocated business funda-
mentals. The countless disclaimers contained too many
warnings about risk, too many references to forward-
looking statements, and too many repeats of Wall Street's

favorite standby: "Past returns do not guarantee future results."

It would be easier if lawyers printed just one simple statement in bold red letters on all covers: **"You can lose your ass if you invest in this piece of shit."** Investors would think twice before putting their money to work. That night, the agreement was anything but boring. I scoured the pages.

My curiosity paid immediate dividends, specifically, a clause on page seven. MRI calculated performance fees on a monthly basis. If the fund appreciated $5 million during November, for example, then Romanov would earn $1 million. The document required an annual audit for the year ending December 31. But audits were unnecessary to pay monthly performance fees to the Mad Russian. Share prices on November 30 mattered just as much as share prices on December 31. This payment mechanism struck me as unusual.

Hedgies can negotiate anything.

Romanov had the incentive to manipulate Rugged's share price on either November 30 or December 31. But the link between the Kelemen Group and MRI Capital still eluded me. It was hard to think objectively. My best friend had betrayed me. I feared my imagination had run amuck.

"Romanov marking the close," I muttered. "No way."

CHAPTER 50

The best ideas in life are unpredictable. Brilliance arrives without warning. Sometimes, genius accompanies duress. All too often the catalysts behind inspiration are impossible to identify. Careers would be so much better if creativity came with on-off switches. It makes me sad I have no control over my best thinking.

The alarm clock from hell said 10:15 P.M. Monday had sucked, and I was ready to hit the sack. It would be impossible to sleep, though. I was doomed to another night of raise, lower, raise, lower.

What's Ron Popeil selling?

SKC called my exile "a leave of absence." In polite moments I called it "termination." Right now it felt more like a Serbian war crime. Eight years of service made no difference. SKC tossed me out on the street in less than ninety minutes.

I had money to weather the storm. Unlike other advisers, I avoided big mortgages and recurring expenses. Fortunes changed too quickly in my business. Losing a monster client could easily wipe out $200,000 or more in take-home pay.

Am I really safe?

All my money was at SKC. I knew a broker who left PCS for a big paycheck from another firm. Twelve months later he was squabbling with the brokerage over his signing bonus, and they froze his assets pending arbitration. I made a mental note to wire all cash to my bank account at Chase first thing in the morning.

So what if it sets off more alarm bells.

I had been exiled less than twenty-four hours, and Annie's words were again reverberating through my head: *Fight for your job, Grove.*

She was right. If I was gone too long, if too many questions went unanswered, my clients would leave of their own volition. Today, SKC had run me down, run me over, and wrung me out.

They won't freeze my assets. They know I'll sue.

A few seconds later I refuted my own argument. SKC paid retainers to every law firm in New York City, a strategy designed to thwart angry advisers. No lawyer could take my case. The good ones were boxed out by conflict-of-interest protocol.

As I brushed my teeth I considered Kelemen and then Romanov. I asked myself, over and over, sometimes aloud and sometimes in silence, "Why did Charlie care?"

The link between the two won't save my job.

That was when a wicked, wonderful burst of clarity hit me from nowhere. The idea offered hope. It was too late to call Halek. I called anyway. His answering machine picked up. "Do your thing at the beep."

"Shit," I said, and hung up.

Charlie cared, all right. Not just a little. I bet MRI Capital consumed his every waking moment. Now it was consuming mine.

CHAPTER 51

"Hey, it's me."

"Nice message on my answering machine last night."

"Yeah, sorry."

"Let's see," Cliff Halek said into the receiver, "you've fled the country, and now you're calling from a safe house in Rio."

There was no humor in his voice, no levity whatsoever. I knew better. "Cute. I need your help."

"No shit," he declared.

"Cliff—" I started.

He cut me off with words blasting from his lips the way pinballs ricochet off electric bumpers. "Zola called. We're meeting later this morning." Tilt. "We're setting up procedures for your equity portfolios. No changes without my approval." Tilt. "Why didn't you return my calls yesterday? What's happening now?" Tilt. "Zola didn't know much, and Kurtz didn't say jack."

"Thanks for running the portfolios," I said, knowing my clients would be safe. "You spoke with Kurtz?"

"For thirty seconds," Cliff answered. "He thinks you stole a bunch of money. He's scared of column-six risk."

Cliff was referring to the front page of *The Wall Street Journal*, where for years the sixth column had featured stories about Enron, Tyco, and WorldCom. It served as the epicenter for articles about bad business behavior.

"Kurtz is an ass," I countered, "and he's wrong about me."

"The lawyers got to him," Cliff continued. "Right now, he won't take a leak without their green light."

"Will you check something for me?" I asked brusquely.

"Will it make me an accessory?" he shot back, half joking. I noted the concern in Halek's voice, not for himself, but for my career.

There's the problem, I reflected in silence. *It's the taint of Charlie Kelemen. SKC will wash its hands of me, of anything to do with a Ponzi scheme.*

"Are you in front of a Bloomberg, Cliff?"

"Of course."

"Pull up Rugged Computers. The ticker is R-C-O-M."

"Okay. R-C-O-M, equity, go," he announced like a sportscaster delivering play-by-play commentary for Bloomberg keystrokes. "Now what?"

"Go to the 'Ticket Writing and Holders' section and tell me who bought or sold the stock recently."

"Okay," he said. I waited. I waited. I waited. "It says, 'No insider transactions available for these settings.'"

"Shit," I cursed absently. "I thought Bloomberg reported insider trades for all companies."

"Not the small ones," Cliff explained. "Why are we doing this anyway?"

"I hoped Alex Romanov's name would pop up."

"No way," Cliff objected instantly. Everybody on Wall Street had read the financial press. "It's not Romanov's style. He wouldn't buy enough stock to become an insider."

"He owns twenty-two percent of the company." For a moment the phone went silent. "Are you there, Cliff?"

"Yeah, hang on. I'm checking something."

I wondered how people in our industry had communicated before computers existed. It was always, "Hang on," while somebody performed a calculation or surfed the Web for an answer.

"Bloomberg doesn't show the trades," Cliff continued thoughtfully, "but it shows the major holders. Romanov's name isn't listed anywhere."

"You're kidding. How about MRI Capital?"

Again, silence. "No, nothing," Cliff reported finally. "Where did you get twenty-two percent?"

"I have a printout that shows MRI owns nine-point-five million shares."

"Then I'd say your boy is fucked. He didn't file a 13(d) with the SEC."

Section 13(d) of the Securities Exchange Act of 1934 gave owners ten days to notify the SEC when they established 5 percent positions in public companies. The law also required them to disclose their holdings to both the issuers and the exchanges where shares traded. The penalties for noncompliance were stiff: criminal sanctions, disgorgement of profits, or both. Clearly, a 13(d) violation spelled trouble for Romanov, especially given his intent to manipulate prices. The violation would expose him as yet another rogue from the capital markets. It would put MRI out of business.

The cheaper the hood, the fatter the mouth.

"I didn't even think about 13(d)."

"Romanov doesn't strike me as the kind of guy to fuck around with the SEC," Cliff observed skeptically.

"I know. That's what bothers me. But my printout says he owns nine-point-five million shares."

"Why wouldn't he file?" Cliff challenged. "It doesn't make sense."

"It does if you're cheating. I can't prove it, but I think Romanov's marking the close. Filing would expose him."

Cliff whistled first and then objected. "No way, Grove. I don't buy it."

"During the last three days of December, two hundred and six thousand, nine hundred and thirty-six shares of Rugged Computers traded. And the stock appreciated thirty-one-point-six percent. Typically, three days of trading total twenty-two thousand, five hundred shares."

"You're kidding."

"Unfortunately, there's no way to prove MRI bought any of those two hundred and six thousand, nine hundred and thirty-six shares."

"That's a problem," Cliff agreed. I heard conflict in his voice. He wanted to believe. He also wanted to identify a crack in my reasoning, anything to end the nonsense. Alex Romanov was the next Warren Buffett, not some thug marking the close. There had to be a better explanation.

"Any suggestions?" I asked.

"Let me think about it," Cliff replied. I realized he had no clue how to trace the trades to Romanov. Before I could respond, Cliff asked, "What's this printout you keep referencing?"

"I found it in a file that Charlie kept on MRI. It's either a spreadsheet or something Romanov printed off the Web. Maybe a printout from a prime broker where he custodies his securities."

"How would Charlie get that printout?"

"No clue."

"What makes you think it's legit?"

"Romanov wants it bad."

"You told him about it?"

"I told him Charlie kept a file on MRI. Romanov keeps asking me to send it over to his office."

"Why?"

"That's what I say. I didn't think twice about his requests until you mentioned 13(d). Now I understand. Charlie's file is the only link between Romanov and nine-point-five million shares of Rugged Computers."

"I'm not sure about that," Cliff argued. "Word gets out. You can't hide nine-point-five million shares of a thinly traded stock."

"Yes, you can. Romanov trades with every broker on the Street. A buy here, a buy there. No shop has the complete picture. I bet he uses different firms to hold his shares."

There was a long pause. Cliff finally broke the silence. "Grove, we've been friends for how long?" he asked carefully.

"About eight years."

"Right. And in all that time, I've always been straight with you."

"What's on your mind?" Cliff still had reservations.

"You may be right about Romanov. But I don't care. Forget about MRI and take care of yourself. You need a lawyer. And frankly, I don't see what any of this has to do with the forged letter."

"I can explain. But I need your help to prove it."

Cliff asked his assistant to reschedule a conference call. Then he focused on our conversation. "Let's start at the beginning, Grove. What do you have?"

Thirty minutes later Cliff understood everything. At first he balked at my request. Then I said, "It's the only way for me to save my job and come out clean. No guilt from association."

"I'm in," he promised, friendship overriding reluctance. But the hesitation lingered in his voice.

"Don't flake out on me." My words were half warning, half plea.

"I still think you should talk to the firm first."

"No way, Cliff. Lawyers fuck advisers. I didn't trust the business prevention unit before, and I sure as hell don't trust them now. Besides, Romanov won't know what hit him."

"Things are starting to heat up around here," he said. "Gotta go." Dial tone.

I dreaded my call to Betty Masters, crossed my fingers and hoped for the answering machine. But she picked up on the first ring. "Hi there," Betty chirped in a voice full of caffeine and good humor. I could almost see her dazzling white smile through the receiver.

"Do you have a few minutes?"

"Is everything okay, Grove? You sound stressed."

"It's nine A.M. and I already know how a salmon feels at the end of the day."

Tension replaced her good cheer. "Does it have anything to do with Fred's money?" she asked anxiously.

"Yes, I'm sorry to say."

"Don't sugarcoat it," she ordered. "How much are we down?"

"The market's not the problem, Betty. The Kelemen Group was a sham. Charlie was running a Ponzi scheme. He cheated you. He cheated all his investors."

"Not Charlie," she gasped.

"Fred's money is gone."

For a long insufferable moment, a pregnant pause from purgatory, we both remained quiet. Betty finally asked, "Can Sam pay me back?"   .

"I doubt it. She has no idea where Charlie kept their money. He conned Sam. He conned her parents, too. They invested big bucks in the Kelemen Group."

"But Sam and Charlie acted so rich. The parties, the dinners, the jewels," Betty countered.

"All purchased with investor money. She has no cash. Right after the funeral I lent Sam money just to keep her afloat."

For a moment Betty weighed her words. "Sam's dirty, Grove," she hissed. "All my money," she cried. "Fred's money." And that was when she blew. "They paid my decorating fees with Fred's money. Fred's money."

"What do you mean she's dirty?" I asked, knowing the answer. Hunting season had opened on Sam Kelemen.

"She knew, Grove. Charlie could never hide anything from Sam. She probably helped."

"If Sam knew," I argued, "she deserves an Oscar."

"Don't be naive, Grove. I'm an expert on dysfunctional marriages. Husbands and wives try to hide things. But stuff always turns up in the wash."

"Not this time," I disagreed. My reservations were mounting deep inside.

"I don't buy it," Betty yelled, her anger a jolt of decibels. I jerked the phone away from my head, protecting my ears from further blasts. For a moment Betty softened and said in an apologetic tone, "Grove, I'm just thinking about Fred."

"I understand."

"Do you think I'll get my money back?"

"I don't know."

"What should I do?" Betty asked.

There was no alternative. I advised her to do the unthinkable: "Get a lawyer."

"Tell me something I don't know," she returned. "Sam Kelemen is dirty."

The words made me cringe. It felt like I had betrayed Sam. "There may be someone else involved." It was my last desperate attempt to save Sam from Betty's growing wrath.

"Who?" Betty asked.

"I can't say yet. I should learn more during the week."

"Grove, just help me get back Fred's money."

We said good-bye. Neither of us had the stomach or inclination to continue. Betty was assessing her loss. I needed to call Romanov and insist on giving him the red folder in person. He might not like it. But he would meet, all right. There was no doubt.

That one comment bothered me: *Sam's dirty, Grove.*

Betty had to be wrong. Sam had not helped Charlie with the Ponzi scheme. She had no idea where he banked. But I still could not erase Betty's words from my mind.

Sam's dirty, Grove.

Rifling through the red folder, I hoped to find a clue, an answer, something to help Sam, anything to prove Betty wrong. Sam had treated me like a leper during our last phone call. So what. It would take more than one bad exchange to undermine my loyalty. Sam had been such an important friend to Evelyn.

Nothing.

I found nothing except for my note on the back cover of the red file. That day at Charlie's office, I had noticed the name Pinckney in his Outlook calendar. There were Pinckneys all over Charleston. According to my note, Charlie had a doctor's appointment tomorrow.

My next decision surprises me even now. Why I did it I will never know. Had I been more thoughtful, I never would have called Nurse Pinckney. A call was way too intrusive. Deceased or not, Charlie's medical affairs were his business. Not mine. At the time, however, a call made all the sense in the world. In Charlie's vernacular, I was a "pleaser." Canceling his doctor's appointment seemed the courteous thing to do.

On the second ring the receptionist answered, "Manhattan Fertility Clinic."

Thirty seconds later, the hell of Muzak on hold, I heard soothing sounds of stretching syllables. "This is Nurse Pinckney. May I help you?"

"I'd know that accent from anywhere. You're from Charleston." It was impossible to continue until we played the do-you-know game. It turned out we both knew Bubba Condon, a kid from Bishop England High School I had not seen in years.

Rita, Nurse Pinckney's first name, finally asked, "So, Grove, why'd you call?"

"It may be silly."

"Fertility problems are a way of life," she said kindly. "Would you like to make an appointment?"

How would I know? I haven't slept with a woman for eighteen months.

"Actually, I want to cancel one."

"Really?"

"Charlie Kelemen was a friend, and—"

"It's just horrible what happened," Rita interrupted.

"I thought you might know already. I wanted to err on the side of caution by calling."

"That's sweet. Nobody called, but we all saw the television reports."

"You haven't heard the good news then?"

"What good news?"

Odd.

"Whatever you did for Sam, it worked."

I remembered Sam's words from Live Bait, as though it were yesterday: *The fertility drugs kicked right in. And wham bam, hello, Sam.*

"Sam wasn't the problem." Rita immediately checked her outburst. I was not a family member. Sharing the Kelemens' medical information had been a mistake.

For a moment neither of us said anything. Then the nurse's words registered like a magnitude-seven earthquake. "Charlie was impotent?" It took all my self-control not to say "firing blanks."

"I've already said more than I should."

I refused to overlook the slip. "Rita, you don't know me from Adam. And I apologize for putting you in an awkward position. I'm in serious trouble, though. I may lose my job, and I have problems with the police. When I called you, I never expected to learn anything personal about the Kelemen family." I paused to let my words take hold. "What you just said may fix my problems."

Perhaps it was the sincerity. Perhaps it was the sound of a familiar accent, one Charlestonian to another. Whatever, I will always be indebted to Rita Pinckney for her response.

"Sam's pregnant?" she ventured, still deliberating about how to respond.

"Yes."

"You didn't hear this from me," she announced.

"Hear what?" I confirmed.

"Do you remember the name of that Catholic school on Coming Street before it merged with Bishop England High School?"

"You mean Immaculate Conception?" I asked tentatively. Then her meaning registered. This time I could not hold back. "Charlie was firing blanks?"

"I have to go."

CHAPTER 52

"Now you want to talk?" Mandy Maris demanded over the phone. "Weren't you the one who called me a cobra fucker?"

"Guilty as charged. I have this thing about the press."

"So it seems. The Kelemen story runs tomorrow."

I had just finished speaking with Nurse Pinckney. The back-and-forth with Maris could not have started worse. The *New York Post* had its deadlines, no matter what bodies were left behind.

Hard to court favor from somebody you called a "cobra fucker."

"Mandy, I treated you like dirt. I'm sorry. There's probably no way to take it all back."

"I'm not changing a comma."

"Don't blame you. And don't touch the periods, either." Dealing with the press suddenly felt like selling— agree with the objections and reposition. "But let me ask one thing."

"Okay."

"How come you didn't print anything about the police coming to our office yesterday?"

"We decided it would make a bigger splash in to-morrow's feature."

"My involvement with the beautiful widow, Sam Kelemen? And of course, my involvement with Charlie Kelemen's death?"

"You catch on fast for someone who never talks to the press," she confirmed. "I'm kind of busy if you don't mind."

Now for the bait.

"Wouldn't the Ponzi scheme make a bigger splash?" I asked innocently, replaying her words.

"What Ponzi scheme?" She was all ears.

"You get the exclusive under one condition."

"Which is?"

"Hold any reference to me until Thursday."

"Not happening," she stated. "I can get details from Kelemen's investors. Patty Gershon already told me everything I need to know about you."

"You spoke with her?"

"She called Monday afternoon," Maris replied. "What did you do to piss her off?"

Don't say it.

"Patty has her own agenda. And Charlie's friends don't know what I know, Mandy. The other half of the story plays out tomorrow. You can be on the scene thirty minutes before any of your competitors have a clue."

"Only the references to you?" She bit. "What do I need to do?"

"Be at your desk at noon tomorrow. At twelve-thirty you'll get a sign where to go."

"What's with the cloak-and-dagger? How do I know you're for real?"

"You don't. How do I know you won't print nasty stuff about me?"

"I need something to convince my editor."

Thirty seconds later we wrapped up. I sealed either a deal or my fate. It still wasn't clear. I had two more calls to make, one to Romanov and one to my secret weapon.

I hope this works.

CHAPTER 53

As far back as I can remember, the Red Flame has been slinging hash near the corner of Forty-fourth Street and the Avenue of the Americas. Crowds jam into wood-veneer booths throughout the day. The menu features scrambled eggs, meat loaf, bacon, and potatoes fried a dozen different ways. It's a place where hyper-tasking New Yorkers savor comfort food combos, oblivious to the snap, crackle, pop of their arteries with every grease-laden fork.

"Surly" is not listed anywhere among the entrées. But the waiters shovel up king-sized helpings of attitude at no extra charge, and the busboys hover around the Formica tabletops as if they cannot wait to clear dishes and send patrons packing. I eat at the lunch counter sometimes, more for the clamor of the crowd than the flavor of the food.

The Red Flame was the perfect place to meet Romanov. There would be plenty of people around when we spoke.

* * *

It was Wednesday, the second full day of my forced exile from SKC, another twenty-four hours for Gershon and others to poach clients. On Tuesday Romanov had agreed to pick up the MRI folder in person. But the arrangement annoyed him.

"Can't you just send a runner? Some of us work, Grover."

No question Romanov's remark had been a dig. I held my tongue and kowtowed into the receiver. Deference, it seemed, would be the best way to catch the Mad Russian off guard.

At 11:40 A.M. a mishmash of tourists and executives began filing into the Red Flame for an early lunch. About two-thirds of the booths were already full. Twenty minutes more and a crowd would stand until tables became available. Three thin men, black tank tops and backs turned toward me, sat at the counter in the rear of the diner.

Good thing we got here early.

The greeter bunny, a short woman with Mediterranean features, pointed to an empty stool next to the men. "No," I said, and asked for a booth at the front of the greasy spoon. "Someone is joining me."

The hostess flashed a wan smile that may have said, *No problem.* More likely it was, *Fuck you.* One never knew at the Red Flame.

She handed me a menu, crusted with petrified ketchup, and gestured toward a booth sandwiched between a family with three small children on one side and an executive huddled over a portable computer on the other.

It was perfect. I could see the door and almost everything inside the restaurant.

The trans-fatty smells of bacon cheeseburgers and French fries hung heavy in the chill, air-conditioned climate of the small diner. The scents failed to soothe my nerves. And I was not the least bit hungry. Tense and impatient, I fidgeted with Charlie's red folder and occasionally peeked at the guy behind me with the computer. Over at the counter the three amigos in black laughed and hooted.

What's so funny?

A little girl, much to her parents' annoyance, stood up on the bench seat and turned to face me. She hid her eyes with both hands and played "Now I See You, Now I Don't." I joined the game, first covering my eyes and then moving one hand to the side in order to see. The girl's laughter pealed through the room. And for a moment, I forgot all about the Mad Russian.

Romanov broke the spell. He showed at noon, right on time. His punctuality always impressed me. Late arrivals were the norm on Wall Street, and through the years I had grown to believe they were premeditated. It was a matter of style. Tardiness implied big deals, more important quests for money, elsewhere. Some executives, in my opinion, ran late just to telegraph their importance. Not Romanov. Whatever his faults, tardiness was not one. He arrived promptly and planned not to hurry.

Alex wore a gray pin-striped suit, matched with a white shirt and a tie the perfect shade of blue. He circled toward my table with disarming elegance. He moved like a prizefighter stalking an unranked opponent from a smaller weight class.

When I stood to shake hands and say, "Hello," I noticed Romanov's companion for the first time. I blinked once to make his escort disappear. It didn't work. Sam strutted behind him, no longer a shrinking widow, but feral and haughty in her heels.

What's this?

I had not bargained for Sam. There she was. Her stinging blue eyes commanded my attention. They had gone Arctic cold. Never before had she looked more Siberian husky than now.

Not this.

Sam's presence unnerved me. I missed Romanov's clasp when we shook hands. He grabbed my fingers by the middle knuckles, rather than the palm, and shook my hand like a dead fish in all its ignominy.

I hate when that happens.

Romanov's broad smile made a cameo appearance. Sam tilted her face for a perfunctory peck, and it seemed in our hasty bump of cheeks that a real Siberian husky would have offered more warmth and affection. Her sudden reserve reminded me of Betty's words. *Sam's dirty, Grove.*

"Sam, I didn't expect you." I spoke with every ounce of good humor in my body, hiding profound disappointment. The plan had already gone off track. No one intended to confront Romanov in front of Sam.

What is she doing here?

Sam read my thoughts. "Alex and I are having lunch."

"With me, I hope."

"Sorry, Grover," Romanov said, rolling his *r*'s to the point of annoyance. "May I have the file?" he asked, glancing at the red folder on the booth tabletop. "We have reservations at Le Bernardin." He spoke with the regal bearing of someone who hates bacon cheeseburgers piled high with pickles, mushrooms, and onions.

No wonder he bugs me.

"Le Bernardin has the best fish in New York City," I observed. "Do yourself a favor, Alex." I waited for my words to register. "Call them and cancel."

The command, audacious, terse, powerful, would have impressed any drill sergeant. Sam snapped to attention, her eyes opening wide with shock and awe. Romanov's jaw dropped, just for a second. When he recovered, his lips sealed in taut contempt.

Romanov sat. Sam sat. I sat. For a while the three of us sat and said nothing, sitting and suffering in our increasingly uncomfortable seats. Romanov finally demanded, "What's on your mind, Grover?" He rubbed his knuckles, like a boxer massaging his fists before the title match.

"I want to review your portfolio," I said sarcastically.

"Let's go, Sam." Romanov scooted along the booth, reaching for the red folder, as he readied to leave. "Grover, we don't have time to play games."

With the palm of my hand, I smacked the folder down against the counter. Hard. The thump, flesh against cardboard and cardboard against Formica, rang out over the clamor of the diner. At the counter several yards away, the three men wearing black glanced in our direction.

Sam recoiled before lashing out, "Grover, what the hell is your problem?" She scooted across the bench, moving more quickly now.

"Grover"? She never calls me that.

I ignored Sam and yawned for effect. "Alex, you can speak with me. Or you can speak with the SEC. I don't care either way."

They stopped scooting. Stone still. "This is interesting," Romanov parried. "I'm listening." He smiled broadly, inviting me to take a shot.

"I'm glad we agree." I pulled MRI's printout from the red folder. "Look at the two numbers Charlie scribbled, thirty-one-point-twelve and thirty-point-eleven. I thought they were share prices, but Rugged Computers hasn't traded over six dollars in years."

"Would you give me the CNN version?" Romanov growled.

"They're not stock quotes, Alex. They're dates."

"So?"

"So, Rugged's trading looks odd on the last few days of November and December."

"What do you mean, odd?" Romanov asked, feigning boredom and looking at his watch.

"Alex, you're absolutely right," I started, the sarcasm building in my voice. " 'Odd' is too delicate. 'Manipulated' is the better word."

Romanov glared. No boredom now. His black eyes punched holes into me. He clenched his fists and relaxed, clenched and relaxed.

"Large blocks traded at the end of those months," I continued. "They moved the stock price up twenty-one percent in November and thirty-one percent in December."

"I hope you understand what you are saying." He rubbed his right fist.

"Oh, I understand all right. You own nine-point-five million shares of Rugged Computers. See the number." I pointed to the portfolio printout in order to confirm the veracity of my words.

Alex looked and listened without expression.

"Your shares, Alex, equal twenty-two percent of the company's outstanding stock. And you didn't file a 13(d). You got a problem."

Romanov never blinked. He spoke softly and evenly, his voice in control: "Come on, Sam. Let's leave Sherlock Holmes to his lunch." He motioned to get up. I was losing. He was not biting.

"Sit down," I barked. "I'm not finished." Across the aisle four people stopped eating midfork. They gawked at us. I leaned back, lowered my voice, and stated, "Charlie knew."

Sam squeezed Romanov's shoulder, gently, tenderly, and beckoned him to sit. Her eyes narrowed, cold, hostile, and callous. Flecks of blue peeked through the tight slits. That look, the scorn, the steel, told me everything. I saw guile and cunning. Sam had never been wily at Wellesley. She was prone to forgetting dates. Nor had she been devious during marriage. There was no need. Charlie showered her with attention and presents, anything to stave off the private demons that accompanied his secrets. If anything, Sam had always been open and innocent.

That's why Evelyn liked her.

In that look I saw a survivor and a schemer. Sam had forged an alliance with Alex Romanov. She made her bed. Her eyes, the cobalt razors, told me everything. Her pregnancy was anything but an "immaculate conception." Charlie was sterile. She was carrying the Mad Russian's baby.

"What do you mean Charlie knew?" she asked, tugging at her bra strap.

"Charlie had his own problems. Didn't he, Sam?"

Romanov replied for her: "What are you saying, Grover?" He stopped rubbing his fists. He put his elbows on the table, folded his hands loosely in the shape of prayer, and rubbed the tip of his nose with both index fingers. He glared venomously over the cathedral of digits.

Turning back to the Mad Russian, I said, "Charlie didn't start out bad. I doubt he ever intended to cheat anyone. At the beginning, that is. But his mistakes consumed him. That's the problem with Ponzi schemes. There's never enough money. However you disguise them, fund of funds or high-interest notes, they always collapse. Right, Alex?"

Romanov said nothing. He watched impassively. No emotion. Sizing me up. Checking for weaknesses. Circling, a boxer ready to jab. He finally asked, "What does this have to do with me?"

"Charlie wanted out," I replied. "He needed a windfall. All the scrambling to find new investors took its toll."

Susan Thorpe threatened him.

"Is there a point here?"

"You were the exit, Alex. You have the big returns." Impersonating his voice, I said, "We are maniacally obsessed with value."

"You don't like MRI's sales pitch?" he sneered, his words vocal acid.

"Triple-digit returns hide plenty of sins. Charlie could invest with you until he accumulated enough money. He'd probably show gains, ten percent, maybe even twenty. Who knows how much? I know one thing. The gains he reported would be less than yours. That way he could build up cash to pay investors."

"Nice theory, Grover. But your facts are all wrong. Charlie never put a dime into MRI."

"Maybe not, Alex. But Charlie found you out."

"There's nothing to find out."

"Give me a break. Charlie was no member of Mensa. Me either, for that matter. But he sniffed out your twenty-two percent position in Rugged Computers."

While the SEC was out to lunch, I added mentally.

"Too much television, Grover."

"You're marking the close, Alex. Charlie knew it. He wanted a piece of the action. That's when things got out of hand."

"Too much *CSI*," Romanov said.

"I prefer *Law & Order*."

Every top producer understands body language. The skill makes us good at our jobs. And we universally agree that eyes reveal what prospects think. Eyes are the first to betray discomfort or even deceit. Sam had the look before, the cobalt razors. Now Romanov blinked. With that involuntary flutter, he confirmed my instincts were right.

"The police can figure out who actually tossed Charlie in the tank," I continued. "But three things are for sure. You planned it. You killed him just as sure as the sharks ate him. And you're finished."

They stared speechlessly.

"Was it worth it, Alex?" I asked, cocky on the outside, not so on the inside.

Sam spoke instead: "Let's get lunch, Alex."

No wonder they want fish, I thought, remembering the aquarium sharks.

"Yeah, Dad," I taunted, "let's get lunch. But if I were you, I'd bag Le Bernardin and find some shashlik. You want to start baby out right." Shashlik was a type of shish kebab popular in countries that had once comprised the Soviet Union. I nodded at Sam's belly, playing my ace.

"I think you're confused, Grove," said Sam, still fiddling with her bra strap.

"Rita might say otherwise."

"Who?"

"The great thing about Charleston," I replied without answering Romanov's question, "is that we stick together. It's cliquish as hell down there. But leave town and we're all brothers and sisters."

"Who's Rita?" Romanov snapped.

"Rita Pinckney was in Charlie's Outlook. Tell him about your nurse, Sam. You weren't the problem. You lied about the fertility drugs."

Wham bam, take that, Sam.

Romanov observed without emotion. Fear welled in Sam's eyes. She never could handle confrontations.

"Rita and I are buddies," I continued. "I got the life story: Bishop England, College of Charleston, and she lived in a carriage house on Hasell while attending the Medical University of South Carolina. No toothpaste in the tube, Sam. Charlie was sterile."

"She told you that?" Sam asked.

"Sperm out of luck."

"Be quiet," Romanov counseled Sam, his words succinct, clipped, and careful.

"Hey, it's my job to open people up. It's what advisers do."

Sam said nothing and averted her eyes. Her left hand rested on Romanov's shoulder, a subconscious effort to absorb his strength. Weak body language, according to the strategy handbook of all top producers, was a clear signal to probe further.

"Was Alex worth it, Sam?" I wanted to shake her. "Were you getting even? For the way Charlie liked boys? For the way he pissed through your parents' money? I never heard you say no to all the jewels."

"I told you, Grove. They're gone." The shaky timbre of her voice sounded like she might crack.

Romanov, gazing out the window, interjected calmly, "No more, Sam. It's under control."

This time I turned to the Mad Russian. "What? Are you tossing me in a fish tank, too? You're finished."

"Perhaps," he acknowledged, and cocked his head, looking at me through hateful black eyes. "Perhaps not."

In the din of the diner, blinded by the moment's fury,

I had not seen anyone approach. Two strapping men now loomed over our table. I recognized both instantly, Key Lime and Hummer Guy. Bile and breakfast, the backwash of terror, scrambled the words in my throat.

"You remember my friends, Yuri and Viktor," Romanov asserted more than asked.

The one who had ridden the key-lime Vespa scowled. He said nothing. He still had a welt from the frozen water bottle.

"Grover, push over for Yuri," Romanov commanded, "and let's finish our talk."

Yuri screwed his face into a sanity-challenged smile and stuck it close to mine, cocking his head at an odd angle. Invasive. Aggressive. I thought our noses might bump. His warm breath, a moist mixture of secondhand garlic and something raising hell with his digestion, bullied back the kitchen odors. I flinched from either stench or proximity to his face, probably both. Yuri grinned smugly, aware that halitosis had just kicked my ass. He pulled away and squashed awkwardly into the booth, shaking the tabletop with his barrel chest as he slid across the bench.

"Are you sure Borscht Breath will fit?" I pronounced "borscht" to sound like "boar shit."

"I wouldn't upset Yuri," Romanov warned. "You'll pay later."

My heart threatened to thump out of my chest. It was time to slow things down.

Our waitress, AWOL for the last five minutes, arrived with order pad in hand. Service was that way at the Red Flame. She surfaced just as the executive with the laptop squeezed past Viktor, the one-man traffic jam previously known as Hummer Guy. Next to him, the waitress and the executive both looked tiny. "Have you decided?" the woman asked.

"No," Alex replied flatly.

"What do you mean?" I protested in a voice loud enough for other diners to hear. "I'm starved. I'll have the mozzarella sticks, two cheeseburgers deluxe, a Popeye salad, and your plate of twenty-one fried shrimp. Medium rare on the burgers. Extra pickles. And hold the tomatoes. If you could hustle some potato skins and stuffed grape leaves in the next few minutes, I'd be thrilled. Got any grits?"

The executive looked back over his shoulder and turned in full, a double take for the ages. He flashed the thumbs-up sign. It looked like a nonverbal celebration of my appetite. I knew better.

The waitress did not write. Instead, she asked, "You sure?" She spoke in a monotone, no surprise in her voice but loads of exasperation. She was a veteran, battle tested through the years by demanding diners. She had seen and heard everything. "You sure?" she repeated, cocking her ear to be certain.

"You're right," I chirped. "Make that three cheeseburgers deluxe."

"With wheels?"

"No. We're eating here."

Something hard and blunt jabbed my hip. Dull pain dashed from my right side over to the coccyx, up through the spine, and landed in my brain, where it instructed my mouth, *Shut up.* I winced but did not gasp.

I looked down to see Yuri ramming a pistol into me under the cover of the table.

He grinned. His expression confirmed the message from my hip: *Shut up.*

Romanov instructed the waitress, "Make his order to go. Nothing else."

"Whatever." She turned and left.

Looking at Yuri's pistol, I wondered whether the confrontation had been smart. The gun, though small in his meaty hand, looked like a damn bazooka. He jabbed harder, and I winced again.

CHAPTER 54

Ira Popowski had instructed his secretary to hold all calls. He sat alone in his office, surrounded by degrees cluttering the walls: Princeton, Harvard, and Columbia. Stacks of paper occupied every square inch of flat surface. It looked like a cat-five hurricane had filed his legal briefs. He remained oblivious to the chaos, his eyes riveted to a computer. Its screen barely peeked over a pile of family foundation documents.

"You should have called me," he muttered under his breath. The images, three people, then five, were grainy and distant. He recognized Sam Kelemen. He would have known her anywhere. He heard every word from the group. And the conversation angered him.

Several blocks away in the hallowed halls of SKC, Annie recognized the back of my head. She would have known me anywhere, my red hair and triangular noggin. She leaned forward, her blue-green eyes plastered to a flat-screen monitor.

"What possessed you?" she asked incredulously.

Zola watched over Annie's shoulder. "I can't believe

it!" she exclaimed hoarsely, the words rumbling from her throat. "MRI's investors are toast."

Chloe removed her headset. She peered directly at her computer display, concentrating hard not to miss anything. "Oh" whooshed from her mouth. She had never really intended to speak. The word just happened. She cupped her mouth, both hands stifling further outbursts.

The phone rang on Chloe's line. It rang on Annie's line. It rang on Zola's line. It rang and rang and rang. Somebody wanted to trade. No one answered. No one cared.

On the same floor but at the opposite end of the building, Kurtz eyed his twenty-one-inch displays, two of them, one on top of the other. The huge screens could show stock quotes, Excel graphs, CNBC, Outlook, photos, Google, Adobe documents, and Bloomberg all at once. No cramping. No fussing with window sizes. The massive screens could hold everything comfortably. Kurtz gaped at the Web images in the right corner of the bottom screen and listened intently to the words pouring from his computer speakers.

"Call them and cancel," he heard. The words caught his attention. *He would recognize my smart-ass repartee anywhere.*

"What were you thinking?" He cut nothing but air, over and over with his double-blade guillotine.

Downstairs in Derivatives, Cliff Halek's chair sat empty. A small crowd huddled around his computer some gawking in silence and some babbling at what they saw. Inevitably, gallows commentary consumed the group.

"Ten dollars," a tall, rangy trader proclaimed, "somebody throws a punch." Disheveled, he could use a nap, a haircut or a comb, and a meal.

"Even odds?" the trader to his right asked. He was negotiating. He knew the drill.

"Even odds," the rangy one confirmed.

"You're done on ten dollars," said the second, sealing the deal.

The rowdy crowd of onlookers heard something about "Boar Shit Breath." And seconds later, the screen went dark.

"We'll never know about that punch," the rangy trader lamented.

"Oh, we'll know," the second trader disagreed, "That's O'Rourke. Don't you recognize his Southern accent?" He paused and added, "Y'all," gratuitously.

"Where the hell is Halek, anyway?" someone asked in the crowd. With that, the Derivatives team succumbed to their nature. The bitching and kvetching began. It was the only way to trade.

At precisely 12:30 Mandy Maris saw the cover of a restaurant menu on her screen. Somebody had written the address in bold, black Sharpie letters. She knew the Red Flame. She wrote down the location anyway.

Rising from her desk, Maris exhaled and said, "I owe you, Grove."

* * *

Over at the Midtown North Precinct, Fitzsimmons and Mummert watched a computer screen in astonishment. Like Maris they jotted down the address, seconds before the Web transmission went black. They froze.

Fitzsimmons was the first to speak. "That chowdah-head will get himself killed."

Ordinarily, Mummert would have echoed the sentiment. But the phone rang. He snatched the receiver from its cradle. As he listened, his eyes grew wider and wider from what he heard. "Yeah . . . Yeah . . . Got it . . . See ya."

"What?" Fitzsimmons demanded.

"That was a guy named Halek. He arranged the webcast we just saw. He stopped transmitting because all hell's about to break loose."

"Let's go," Fitzsimmons roared.

CHAPTER 55

Everything was proceeding to plan. Cliff, the executive with the laptop, had given me the thumbs-up. Our secret webcast from the Red Flame would bring the police soon. No doubt, Halek had already called them.

Did he see the gun?

Bullshit. Nothing was right. Sam and Romanov had not confessed to anything on camera. Nor had I anticipated the two big men, who confirmed my suspicions. Romanov, Yuri, Viktor, and even Sam had played a role in Charlie's death. But confirmation was no consolation. Yuri jacked his piece halfway through my hip. And Viktor hovered over me, ready to mop up the mess.

"Alex, tell your goon to put the gun away," I said, doing my best to sound tough. Inside, my heart beat like a drummer with the hiccups. Confronting Romanov belonged in the hall of fame for stupid ideas.

"Yeah, right," Romanov snorted. "You and your lunch are going for a ride."

"Don't bet on it," I bluffed with fake conviction. "I'll make a scene and the cops will come."

"Be my guest. Viktor and Yuri know how to handle

messy situations." Romanov smiled broadly, and I finally realized just how prescient his nickname, the Mad Russian, was. Charlie had been right about everything. Romanov gestured to Sam, who was feigning disinterest. They started to leave.

"Sam, what the hell have you become?" I asked. Her answer made no difference. I was stalling until the cavalry arrived.

"I don't know what to tell you," she replied. Sam's growing discomfort was palpable. Her eyelids drooped to half mast. Her jaw slackened. Her head quivered with a side-to-side motion. It looked as if she were stifling a sneeze, but I knew better. Sam was struggling inside. What they had done to Charlie. What they would do to me. She deliberated for a second or two, before her eyes narrowed into slits. She made her decision—the wrong one.

I pressed anyway, attacking because there were no alternatives. "How many bodies do you need, Sam? Charlie? Me? Who's next?"

"Charlie screwed my parents," she announced, her voice flat and unfeeling.

"I was the one who told you, remember?"

"All we ever wanted, Grove, was for you to find bank accounts. That's it," she snapped. "But you couldn't leave well enough alone."

"What the hell does that mean? I wired you seventy-five thousand dollars."

"Nobody asked you for money." Sam squeezed Romanov's shoulder ever so slightly.

"I was never a threat."

"You're one now," she countered, "just like Charlie."

It all made sense in that moment. Charlie was the first to discover Romanov's scam. He could have exposed the Mad Russian—disgracing the hedgie and forever ending his ability to print money. Now I threatened Romanov's fund and Sam's love affair or financial support or whatever she saw in him. Charlie's missing bank accounts, if they ever existed, had become irrelevant.

Who's your sugar daddy, Sam?

"What about your baby?" I asked.

"*Our* baby," she corrected, and caressed Romanov's neck with the casual intimacy of lovers.

"Good luck arranging play dates from the cell block."

"Won't happen," Romanov scoffed.

"You're too convenient," Sam said.

"Convenient?" Repeating key words had always been a sales technique. I never thought it would buy time and stave off an execution.

"When you disappear, investors will assume you stole their money and skipped New York City." Sam spoke clinically, with no indication of inner turmoil now. "Do you really think anyone will sue a helpless widow?" She batted her eyes and pouted, externally the picture of innocence, internally all fangs. "There's also that letter with your signature. It points to you. And SKC."

"It's not my letter."

"You'll never prove it, Grover." She shooed my words with a dismissive wave of her hand. "I can sell all my belongings and nobody will say a thing. You're my get-out-of-jail-free card."

"How much is left?" I asked. "I thought your jewelry was missing. Or was that another lie?"

"With the exception of my wedding ring," Sam said, "I can't find any jewelry. But there's the silver, the paintings, the Oriental rugs, and a few other things." She smiled conspiratorially. "It's a start to fixing things with my parents." She squeezed Romanov and added, "Alex can help, too."

"What? Support your folks and feed you Beluga caviar over in Brighton Beach?"

"Something like that."

Romanov, growing tired of the conversation, interrupted, "Come on, Sam. Let's go."

"There's one more thing," I said, addressing all four captors.

"And that is?" Romanov asked.

"Do you see that guy with glasses by the cash register? The one who was sitting behind us?"

"Yes. So?"

"He runs Derivatives at SKC."

Romanov instantly went on the defensive. "What's this about?" Yuri jammed the gun into my side, harder. Viktor cracked his knuckles. "Don't get his attention," Romanov continued. "Don't say a word."

"Not a word," I said hoarsely. With the barrel of the gun, Yuri rolled skin against bone. Excruciating pain.

"I'm glad you understand, Grover."

"I don't need to say anything, Alex. You already did."

The Mad Russian's eyes narrowed. He grabbed my shirt just under the collar and jerked me hard across the tabletop, his face just inches from mine. "What do you mean?"

"My friend is also a computer geek. Did you notice his laptop?" I asked. "It had one of those built-in cameras rolling the whole time. We also had an industrial-strength microphone. Alex, what did you say about Yuri and Viktor?"

Not enough for a life sentence.

I smirked anyway, and Romanov's cool veneer vanished. He reached back, cocked his right arm, and threw a furious punch of scarred knuckles. His quickness surprised me. I barely slipped to the left, but his hand grazed hard against the right side of my head. The glancing blow stung like a flicked ear in subzero weather.

Forgetting the gun, I popped Romanov with a quick jab to the nose. The blow stunned him, blood immediately trickling from his left nostril. It stunned me, too. I hadn't thrown a punch since eighth grade. The contact felt good.

Romanov recoiled to strike again, but a voice boomed through the room and arrested his movement. "Sam! Alex! Grove! Yoo-hoo!"

Crunch, all biceps in his black tank top, stood next to Viktor. The hairdresser looked like a gay David, either sizing up Goliath or asking him to dance. Crunch had emerged from his hiding place at the lunch counter previously undetected by Romanov and Sam.

It was Crunch's turn to steal the show. He grabbed Viktor's face with both hands and said, "My, but you're a big boy."

Before Viktor could react, Crunch kissed him full

on the lips, head-butted the site of the kiss, and kneed him in the balls in one fluid motion. The big man collapsed under his own weight, gasping hard and sucking for oxygen. Crunch landed a second knee on Viktor's face as the big man went down.

Yuri reacted like a load. Still wedged in the booth, he stood awkwardly. His fat and flesh flapped against the Formica. The back of Crunch's left hand whipped hard against Yuri's face before he could raise his gun. The big man's nose exploded like Old Faithful upon impact. A red geyser of blood and snot sprayed everywhere. With a quick motion Crunch grabbed the back of Yuri's head. Crunch smashed Yuri's face hard against the tabletop. One, two, three times. The dull thuds ended just as quickly as they had begun. The two men lay soaking in pools of their own blood. Crunch had taken less than four seconds to neutralize them.

All around us the diners scattered. A woman screamed, "Oh my God," as others scrambled to exit the Red Flame.

Romanov blinked at Crunch and considered whether to throw a punch. Crunch sensed the deliberation. "Would you like to make it a trifecta, sweetie?" The hairdresser, with the storied military past, batted his eyes suggestively and cocked his hip provocatively. Romanov relaxed his fist, put both hands on the table, and capitulated.

We could already hear shrill sirens from the approach of police. A few brave souls outside the diner, sensing the imminent danger was over, stared into the Red Flame through the picture windows. I grabbed Yuri's gun and gave it to Crunch. He ejected the clip of bullets like a pro, gently placed the gun on the ground, and stood on it as we waited.

"May I get out?" Sam asked. "I need to use the bathroom."

"You can pee at the precinct," Fitzsimmons bellowed from several yards back. He strode to our table like the cavalry to the rescue. "We need to ask you a few questions, Mrs. Kelemen."

"A few questions," Mummert said. For once I appreciated the officer's echo. Crunch bent over and carefully handed the pistol to Mummert.

"Am I under arrest?" Sam asked.

"We'll figure that out down at the station," Fitzsimmons replied. He turned and called out, "A little help over here, fellows." Four officers in blue uniforms started moving Yuri and Viktor. Another officer cuffed Romanov and led him outside.

Sam shrieked at Fitzsimmons, "Don't even think about putting handcuffs on me."

Crunch, surrounded by a sea of blue uniforms and his two clones from the salon, eyed one young patrol man. "Officer, do you need any help?"

Cliff Halek joined Fitzsimmons, Mummert, and me. "That was monumentally stupid," Fitzsimmons scolded. "Who are you?" he barked at Halek.

"Cliff Halek. I sent you and dozens of people the link to the Web site," he explained. "Grove and I work together."

"How did you set up a webcast in here?"

"Did you ever hear of Foster Cam?"

"No."

"Probably not," Cliff acknowledged. "Let's just say, I've had lots of practice."

Fitzsimmons grunted, "Oh."

His caustic response bugged me. "Whatever happened to 'thank you'?" I asked.

"Listen, chowdahhead," Fitzsimmons commanded. "We've been watching Alex Romanov for about a week now. So has the SEC. He's been linked to a cleaning service that puts listening devices inside CEO offices. We're onto him. And you didn't sign that reference letter. Our experts said it was a Photoshop cut-and-paste deal."

"Then why'd you grill me so hard on Monday?"

"We didn't get the handwriting results until yesterday," he replied.

"Just doing our job," Mummert added.

Cliff and I walked outside the restaurant. The police had already cordoned off the restaurant and a crowd had gathered around the barriers. Onlookers craned their necks to look inside the Red Flame. "Let's go back to the office," he said.

"What about the leave of absence?"

"We can work things out."

Outside and beyond the barricade surrounding the Red Flame, Annie ran into us. Literally. She barreled through the growing crowd and smacked into me, her body pressing against mine. I nearly fell over from the impact. Annie did not say a word. She just hugged me, long and hard. She hugged and hugged. Her sobs trembled against my chest.

Then she pulled back, balled her hand into a fist, and boxed my chest like a girl. The blow carried none of

Romanov's malevolence. Forget the knuckles of pain. Annie struck with her wrist bent, and it surprised me she did not hurt herself. "Don't you ever do that again," she cried as she pulled away.

"I may need to press charges for that," I said, and pulled her back.

Annie looked at Halek sheepishly from the folds of my embrace.

"Hey, Cliff," I said.

"Yeah."

"About going back to the office."

"Yeah."

"There's a reservation for two over at Le Bernardin we plan to commandeer. You okay with that?"

"Totally fine with it," he said. "See ya."

As the shrill screeches from midday traffic assaulted our ears, it seemed the sticky heat of New York City had never felt so wonderful. That's when Mandy Maris called my name from nowhere. "Grove, about that exclusive?"

"Mandy, can you mop with the police until after lunch?"

"No way," Annie overruled. "Grove, it's about time you treat our friend to lunch at Le Bernardin. Right?" she asked Mandy.

"Nothing better than fish," the reporter confirmed. And the three of us walked over to the restaurant, where we would tell stories and drink wine.

CHAPTER 56

Frank Kurtz reached me first thing Thursday morning, his voice laden with remorse. "We need you back, Grove. Are you coming in today?"

"Can't. I'm scheduled to debrief with the police."

"Afterwards?"

"Who knows?" I replied coyly, toying with him. "SKC may not be the right place for me."

"Tell me what you want," he pleaded. "Let's smoke some big-assed cigars and work things out today."

The idea of big-assed cigars turned my stomach. "I don't know, Frank."

Kurtz may have seen an opening. Perhaps my voice softened. He persisted, "I've given a great deal of thought to Zola since our discussion on Monday. You were right. You guys can ring the cash register together."

"We can ring it over at Goldman Sachs," I countered.

"But I'll help here."

Investment banking leads. Here come the bribes.

"Listen, Frank, it's the principle. Where was all your loyalty Monday morning?"

"You think anybody cares about you over at Goldman?" he argued.

Touché.

"Come back to the office," he said, sensing his words had found their mark. "We'll work this out mano a mano." Kurtz prevailed. I agreed to meet at PCS on Friday.

Thirty seconds later I dialed Jumping JJ to assess Patty's damage. My job and reputation were secure. But Gershon, like any other stockbroker, would call the client and angle for revenues. She'd say something to JJ, invent an excuse for joint coverage. There was no limit to her monkey business with a $522 million account in play.

"That's a sweet deal you cut with Brisbane, JJ."

"Now you know why we couldn't speak last week," he explained.

"You had your priorities," I said. "A multibillion merger trumps zero-cost collars all day long."

"Where are you calling from anyway?" he asked. "I don't recognize that number on my LCD."

"Home."

"Vacation?"

"Not quite. Are you sitting?"

"I'm all earlobes," he said in his Polish accent.

"Over the past few days, I helped the police unravel two large investment frauds."

"Does this have anything to do with all the messages Patricia Gershon left for me?" he interrupted.

"Yes and no. Did you talk to her?"

"No time. Besides, I wanted to speak with you first."

You're the best, JJ.

It took me a full fifteen minutes—no further interruptions—to brief JJ about the Kelemen Group, MRI Capital, and my forced leave of absence from SKC. What I did not expect was the ferocity of JJ's negative reaction to Gershon.

"Let me get this straight," he said. "She knew about our deal last week, because of something Baker said?" Baker was the CEO of Brisbane, the company acquiring Jack Oil.

"It was nothing explicit," I confirmed. "But Patty's smart. And they've been working together for years. She put two and two together. It happens all the time."

"Baker will be pissed, Grove. When I tell him, he may pull his account."

There's a reversal of fortune.

"Why? I don't understand."

"We've been working on this merger for six months. Leaks jeopardize deals. She should have kept her mouth shut instead of telling everybody at SKC."

"I don't want to blow up her business, JJ."

"And I don't want to work with her, Grove. It's taken me six years to break you in," he joked, ever the Jack Nicholson of Warsaw.

"Well, there is one thing you can do."

At 10:30 A.M. I entered the police station at the corner of Fifty-fourth Street and Eighth Avenue. Inside a battered conference room appointed in 1950 Stalingrad chic, Fitzsimmons and Mummert took their cues from

Martha Stewart. Doughnuts, coffee, orange juice, the whole shebang. I answered their questions about the Red Flame, the Kelemen Group, and Sam's tryst with the Mad Russian. And they answered mine. We worked like a team piecing together an intricate puzzle.

"Would you like some more coffee?" Fitzsimmons offered.

"I'd kill for some."

"That's probably not the right thing to say around here," he laughed.

"Something you'd hear from a chowdahhead," I agreed.

Almost reverentially, Fitzsimmons asked, "What made you call that nurse?"

"Southern manners. I was canceling his appointment."

"Great work," Fitzsimmons observed, and cracked his neck.

"Great work," came the echo.

I put my arm on Mummert's shoulder and said playfully, "Don't you ever have an idea for yourself?" The ferret blinked, and I asked Fitzsimmons, "Is Sam's tryst with Romanov important to your case?"

"Could be," the big man equivocated. "We're holding Mrs. Kelemen on conspiracy-to-commit-murder charges."

"Charlie's?"

"No, yours. Those two huge perps—"

"Viktor and Yuri."

"Right. You're lucky you didn't end up in some meat wagon with your oatmeal splattered all over the place."

"Oatmeal?" I asked.

"Brains," Mummert explained.

"Got it. Hate the visual."

"We have your statement," Fitzsimmons continued, "about Mrs. Kelemen's threat. Specifically, 'when you disappear . . .'"

"Too bad that comment wasn't on your webcast," Mummert observed wistfully.

"What do you mean?"

"He means," Fitzsimmons started, "that it's her word against yours on the conspiracy charges. She'll probably make bail any minute now. And I doubt the charges stick."

"Can't you do something?" I asked, more surprised than thoughtful.

"We can't turn those two big guys. They don't speak a lick of English."

"Bullshit. One of them said, 'Who's the asshole now, Bicycle Boy,' the day they attacked me."

"'Nyet' is all we get," Mummert replied.

"Romanov?" I asked.

"Lawyered up," Fitzsimmons said, and added, "He's too smart to say anything."

"What about Charlie's death?"

"We've got squat."

"You've got motive. Sam was sleeping with Romanov. He's the father."

Both officers listened attentively. Their eyes betrayed none of their thoughts.

"Sam, Charlie, Romanov," I said, "that's a three-way

from hell if you ask me. It's a safe bet there was plenty of tension."

"Keep going," Fitzsimmons prodded.

"There's the money. Sam's parents lost two million bucks. Doesn't bode well for family congeniality over Thanksgiving dinner."

"Keep going."

"There's Romanov. Somehow, Charlie discovered MRI Capital was a scam. But he didn't care about marking the close or the illegal eavesdropping. Triple-digit returns would repay everybody who had invested in his fund of funds. The problem, however, was that Charlie miscalculated. His knowledge threatened everything Romanov built."

"Keep going."

"What else do you need?" I asked, exasperated now. "I'm positive Viktor and Yuri chummed the water, tied the cart to Charlie's leg, and chucked him in."

"Won't stick," Fitzsimmons countered. "Nobody saw Viktor and Yuri there."

"Damn burkas," I cursed.

"Bingo," Fitzsimmons said, shaking his head.

"I'm telling you, Romanov planned it. I saw guilty all over his kisser in the Red Flame yesterday."

"Won't stick," Mummert echoed.

"They're not walking, are they?" I asked, suddenly alarmed.

"They're doing time," Fitzsimmons soothed. "It's just a question of what charges we can get them on."

"How do you think Charlie got the printout of

Romanov's investments?" Fitzsimmons asked, changing direction.

"Charlie just knew how to get information. It wouldn't surprise me if he got the printout through Sam somehow."

"I don't buy it," Fitzsimmons countered.

"He knows plenty of private eyes. If he had suspicions about Sam, he probably used an agency to follow her."

"Do you have any proof?"

"No. But a few years ago, Lila Priouleau had a problem with her ex-husband. Charlie convinced Cash Priouleau to hire some private eyes, and they put together all kinds of pictures showing the ex with his mistress."

"You getting this, Mums?" Fitzsimmons asked.

"Every word," Mummert replied, scribbling furiously.

"Do you know which agency he used?"

"No clue. Talk to Lila Priouleau. She can get it from her dad."

"We've got lots of questions for her anyway."

"Yeah, lots," Mummert echoed.

"What do you mean?"

"We pulled his bank records."

"And?"

"He wired sixty thousand dollars to her."

"Why?"

"You're the Wall Street wizard. You tell us." Fitzsimmons stood up from the table, hitched his thumb under the big belt buckle, and walked over to pour more coffee.

"Fellows, I don't have a clue. Maybe he repaid a loan."

* * *

That afternoon I passed the Star of Bombay on the way home. The union was still striking. "Bombay is not okay. Bombay is not okay," the three representatives chanted. They all wore jackets and ties.

I told one man what I wanted. "No, brother," he said. "We've got our principles."

"Understood," I said, "but how much would it take for you to consider my request?"

A second striker joined our discussion. "Three hundred would get my attention. I probably wouldn't do it for three hundred dollars, but I'd listen."

A few minutes later, the four of us agreed to five hundred dollars.

CHAPTER 57

The next morning I assembled all my innate diplomatic skills and mustered every bit of inner self-control. The surrounding histrionics required a cool hand, the deft, ambassadorial touch of Henry Kissinger. Such were the joys of SKC's politics.

With somber and weighty tones, I measured every word as though global détente hung in a precarious balance. "Fuck you, Frank."

"You're right. I deserved that," he said. Every picture in his office hung askew, the pope, Fastow, Ebbers, and Kozlowski.

"Are you going to take that?" Patty asked incredulously. Suddenly she was a modern Joan of Arc rescuing the man she had ridden so hard.

"I feel like shit," Frank said, and reached for the wooden box on his desk.

I ignored Patty and thundered angrily at the Monthly Nut, "Eight years, Frank, and you bolted at the first hint of trouble."

Gershon slapped the humidor's lid shut. The resounding thump silenced Frank's response, as though

Bluto had stolen Popeye's spinach. "Frank, don't let him pull that crap," she swore. "O'Rourke fucked up. He was napping, and it cost us a twenty-million-dollar banking assignment. Do you really want the junior varsity advising a firm client what to do with five hundred and twenty-two million dollars?"

"Give me a break," I replied to Patty. "You cover the CEO of Brisbane. He sure didn't hire us for an I-banking assignment."

"Listen, Frank," she threatened. "If you can't make the right decision for SKC, then maybe we should get Percy on the line. He'll know what to do."

"Call him," I said. "Knock yourself out. Our CEO really wants to mediate a turf battle." I added sarcastically, "Bet it does wonders for everybody's career."

As Frank looked at Patty, his phone rang. He hastily grabbed the receiver, a makeshift life buoy offering safety from a sea of broker discord. "Yes," he said. "Who?" he stammered. "You're kidding." Frank paused, listened, and then added, "Tell him to bring it in."

Patty, annoyed at the interruption, persisted in her harangue: "Frank, can we please focus on our business with Jumping JJ? I'm not here for my health, you know."

I almost told Patty, "Piss off," on behalf of Frank.

But the Monthly Nut spoke first. "There's a messenger here with a delivery from Jack Oil."

She looked daggers at me and accused, "What's this about, O'Rourke?"

A short, lean man walked into Frank's office. He wore a gray shirt that advertised "Arnold's Bicycle Delivery" just over the pocket. Underneath the company title, his name was embroidered in cursive. It said "Perry." The red stitching added a nice touch to his uniform.

Perry looked at the three of us, his eyes asking for direction. I gestured to Frank with a sweep of my arm. "Sign here, Boss," the messenger instructed Frank while handing him a pen, the delivery manifest, and finally a sealed envelope.

Perfect.

Frank signed. Patty sighed. Perry left.

"Maybe we should call Percy," I baited Frank, who was staring at the return address.

It said "Office of the Chairman."

Patty smelled a setup. "O'Rourke called JJ, Frank. Don't you get it?"

That was when Gershon first grasped the war for Jumping JJ was over. I had been covering JJ for six years. We opened accounts together and enjoyed a good working relationship. Patty had not delivered the $20 million banking assignment, which would have been the only way for her to wrest control of my client. Outnumbered, outgunned, out of gas, she did what any top producer would have done to save face. She attacked, ranting and raving, bitching and whining, accusing and blaming, clinging desperately to the belief that decibels produce results when all else fails.

"It's unprofessional," Patty screamed. "He went to the client, Frank. He's airing our dirty laundry."

Frank ripped open the envelope, where he found a letter folded in thirds. He opened it, glanced at the contents, and announced what we all knew: "Jose Jaworski."

"Read it, Frank."

"No," Patty countered. "I don't want to hear it."

" 'Dear Mr. Kurtz.' "

"Why didn't he write me?" Patty complained. Frank's menacing look silenced her.

When did Kurtz grow a backbone?

He started over. " 'Dear Mr. Kurtz, I am writing to commend PCS and the outstanding character of your investment representatives.' "

Patty twirled a lock of hair impatiently.

" 'In particular, I would note—' "

"Stop right there," Patty interrupted. "O'Rourke set JJ up. I can't stomach the self-flattery."

Where's that industrial-strength muzzle when we need it?

Frank stared daggers into Patty, a heartbeat away from telling her, "Shut up." Patty pouted in silence but twirled her hair manically. " 'I would note,' " Frank repeated, " 'that Patty Gershon is an outstanding reflection on your organization. We met at a function recently, and her breadth of market knowledge impressed me enormously.' "

"Hah," Patty screamed in premature triumph. "I told you he wants joint coverage." She crossed her legs and smirked in my direction. She pumped her arm victoriously.

"There's more," Frank cautioned.

" 'I understand that issues of coverage arise in brokerage firms,' " he continued. " 'Although Patty impressed me enormously, I am well served by Grove O'Rourke and his team. I do not wish to make any changes at this time. Accordingly, my assistant knows to screen out her calls. Yours sincerely, JJ.' "

Who would have guessed this hard-charging CEO, a man who had once tap-danced on a conference room table to wake up a money manager, could be so tactful? His letter sounded like the work of a young diplomat from inside the State Department.

Patty blanched, struggling to save face, considering how to respond. Frank said, "There's a P.S."

"There's more?" I asked.

"It says: 'Please have Ms. Gershon contact my new colleague, Mr. Baker.' That sounds like a problem," Frank observed.

"Let me see that," Patty said, reaching for the letter, reading furiously. Even her Ferrari-red lips seemed to drain of color.

"It sounds more like a stay the fuck away from my client."

"Knock it off," Frank intervened. "It's clear what the client wants. JJ belongs to Grove." I could almost hear his gavel striking the bench.

"It's not over," Patty threatened, and stormed out of Frank's office. She clipped the doorjamb as she exited, and Frank's photos shuddered on the walls.

We watched Patty leave in all her goldfish fury, an angry swish of the tail. When she was out of earshot, Frank extended his hand and said, "Welcome back, Grove. Now let's get to work."

"Well, there's one other thing, Frank."

"Name it."

"It's amazing what people remember," I started

"The moments that define lives. I wonder how people will remember me. The broker that exposed Alex Romanov? Or the broker tangled up in that new and improved Ponzi fraud?"

"It's over, Grove." Frank tried to sound reassuring.

"I'm not sure about that. Bill Buckner had a career worthy of the Hall of Fame, but everybody remembers how the ball went through his legs in game six of the 1986 World Series."

"Your point?" Frank asked.

I handed him a sealed 9.5-by-12-inch mailer.

"What's this for?" he asked.

"Just make sure you get it on the right wall." I left Frank sitting among the pope, Andrew Fastow, Bernie Ebbers, and Dennis Kozlowski.

It was Friday, and the weekend exodus began. As strategists headed for their choppers to the Hamptons, as traders abandoned their LCD displays, as I-bankers booked their car services, as secretaries padded about in their lace-up sneakers, as brokers banged messages into their BlackBerrys, as Casper clipped, as Scully boomed, as newbies charged purposefully to the designated bar, as PCS colleagues welcomed me back, as Estrogen Alley sulked, as Chloe talked into her headset, as Annie gathered stories, and as Patty Gershon fumed in angry silence—they all spied the most curious thing upon exiting the building. My three union brothers from outside the Star of Bombay.

The trio brought their inflatable friend, an eighteen-foot union rat. Planted outside the building's entry door, the rat stretched its creepy talons over all those who walked underneath. The hateful red eyes looked phlegmy, the fangs a touch bloody. The pointed snout, all whiskers and monster teeth, would give anyone the creeps. The rat was by no means a loveable product from Disney animation.

No one chanted, "Bombay is not okay." This time, the noisy strikers had packaged a special ditty for Patty. Somehow, their commotion slowed the weekend break-away. A small crowd gathered to hear the singsong slogan:

> *"Gershon, Gershon, rich and rude,*
> *We don't like your attitude."*

CHAPTER 58

Three weeks have passed since the big sit-down in Frank's office. This morning, Lila Priouleau called with disturbing answers to the questions troubling me ever since my last tête-à-tête with Fitzsimmons and Mummert.

Our lawyers had instructed me to avoid contact with anyone from the Kelemen Group fiasco. That included the Priouleaus, great prospects notwithstanding. For a brief period it seemed the family might sue SKC. Lila had played rough in those days leading up to the Red Flame. She harped over and over, "It's just business."

Lila never threatened SKC, though. And her family backed off when I proved Charlie's letter was a fake. Baby Face didn't care. He said, "Stay away from her."

Not in my lifetime.

Lila was part of my past, a link to memories of Evelyn. I could never shun Lila. Our friendship had been good. I didn't care what the lawyers ordered. And truth be told, the curiosity was killing me. She and I had not spoken since our night at the gym.

What was that $60,000? I wondered, remembering

how Fitzsimmons had asked about Charlie's wire transfer to her bank account.

Lila's first words on the phone were not "Hi," or "How are you," or "I'm sorry." She was unequivocal. There was no hesitation in her voice. She reported anxiously, "I am so fucked." She seldom swore like that.

"What's wrong? You sound awful."

"The police are investigating me."

No surprise there.

"The district attorney may press charges."

"Whoa, Nellie," I spit back in shock without an ounce of frivolous inflection. "Better start at the beginning."

Lila Priouleau lost $2 million. Her dad, Cash, lost another eight. Including the premium they paid for Charlie's put options, the family is out $11.25 million in total. That sum is all the money in the world for people like Betty and Fred Masters.

An $11.25 million loss, however, will hardly make paupers out of Priouleaus. No one likes losing money. Cash Priouleau hates it more than most. But I can almost hear father and daughter chant in unison, "It's no big deal."

The Priouleau family was worth $120 million in the late 1980s. Assuming their investments compounded at 10 percent per annum, the family is probably worth $800 million today. No doubt their holdings are scattered across trusts, real estate, hedge funds, traditional money managers, and all the other accoutrements of great wealth. Somewhere in that mix is a bond portfolio, and I would guess it totals at least $200 million.

The interest income from municipals would wipe out losses from the Kelemen Group in about a year.

The really grim problem started with Cash's business. Or I should say his industry. Car guys are characters. They were the ones who always made trouble during high school. Got loud and got drunk. As adults they still run in packs. During dozens of annual car conventions, Cash became quite close to a dealer from San Francisco and one from Chicago.

Through the years the three men traded investment ideas. A hedge fund here. A real estate deal there. It was only natural that Cash tell them about Charlie Kelemen and his fabulous fund of funds. As the interest in San Francisco and Chicago grew, Lila made the introductions.

"They each lost one-point-five million dollars," she reported during our phone call. " 'Pissed' would be an understatement."

"Are they suing? Is that the problem?"

"Part of it," she replied. "The four of us held a conference call last week. The guy from Chicago asked us to cover their losses."

"All three million?" I asked. "What did Cash say?"

"He said, 'It's just business. You're big boys. You knew the risks.' "

"That probably triggered some fireworks."

"You got that right," she agreed. "The guy from San Francisco threatened to fight our family through the Mercedes front office. He said we'll lose our dealership."

"That's a civil matter. Why are the police and district attorney involved?"

"The Kelemen Group seemed legit, so I told Charlie we wanted two percent for making the introductions."

That explains the $60,000.

"He paid you a referral fee?"

"It's just business," she replied defensively.

"You're being charged with some kind of securities violation, I presume. You don't have a Series 7 license?"

Our industry is meticulous about licensing and obtaining the right credentials to sell securities. For a moment my thoughts drifted back to the 97 Zola had scored on her exam. I was not sure whether referral fees required a Series 7.

"Our lawyers think they can handle the licensing issues," Lila said. "But Charlie and I traded e-mails back and forth while we were negotiating the sixty-thousand-dollar finder's fee."

"I know where this is going. You deleted the e-mails." Unfortunately, my intonation sounded somewhat accusatory. Not by choice. The words just came out that way as I grasped what Lila had done.

"I got scared when we discovered the Kelemen Group was a fraud," Lila protested, feebly trying to justify her actions. "It was just business." She lacked conviction, and the weight of her admission crashed our conversation like an anvil.

"I don't mean to sound insensitive," I said carefully, "but maybe you shouldn't tell me any more. Advisers don't enjoy the finance-guy equivalent of attorney-client privilege."

*   *   *

At one point during our conversation, I had asked Lila, "How can I help?"

"Maybe you can say something to your friends at the police department," she replied.

She was referring, of course, to Mandy's story in the *New York Post*. Fitzsimmons had told the press, "Grove O'Rourke provided the links to Wall Street that busted this case wide open. He's been a good friend to the police force, and we're grateful."

I called Mandy after the story ran, thanked her for putting such a positive spin on my role. In my attempt to bury the hatchet, I even teased her, "To think, I once thought your full name was Mandy Fucking Maris."

"That's funny," she said. "Fitzsimmons tells me your middle name is Chowdahhead."

Glad she didn't print that.

It may be too late for Fitzsimmons and Mummert to help Lila, though. The damage is done. When Lila and I finished speaking, I agreed completely with her assessment. If anything, "I am so fucked" understates her problem.

I am not a lawyer. Most of the law I know comes from column six of *The Wall Street Journal*. From what I have read, however, it is a monumentally bad idea to destroy documents relevant to pending legal investigations.

In 2002 Sarbanes-Oxley updated the government's laws on document retention. It is a criminal offense to destroy all the text missiles we send back and forth "in contemplation of" a federal "investigation" or "administration of any matter." The penalties include fines, up to twenty years in jail, or both. E-mails rank among the top items not to destroy, even if you have not done anything wrong. The lawyers call this destruction "constructive interference." It sounds like the kind of offense where the courts would throw away the key.

I doubt Lila cares about fines. I know she is not stewing over money. If Cash covers the other dealers, the family's aggregate loss will equal $14.25 million. It is a great deal of money. And I don't intend to make light of the sum. But the money is the least of the family's worries.

The twenty years caught their attention. Big-time. I am scared sick for Lila. I am scared sick for her daughter. If Lila goes to jail, how will her absence affect that poor little girl? She has already been through her mother's divorce from Osama bin Trailer Trash.

I hope the family finds a way out, but I am not optimistic Fitzsimmons can or will help.

It's worth a try anyway.

The legacy of the Kelemen Group strikes me as darkly ironic in one sense. Years ago Charlie saved Lila from Hurley's beatings and those purple welts on her rib cage. More recently, Charlie left her to battle through a murky, unsettling future. Lila may well spend the next five years fighting the courts. And in the end, jail time is a real possibility, no matter how good her lawyers are.

She is so fucked.

CHAPTER 59

My world changed the day Annie, Mandy, and I ate lunch at Le Bernardin. It improved remarkably during dessert. Mandy exited with a pad full of quotes, leaving Annie and me to explore new territory.

Annie no longer calls me "Boss," and that's just fine. The label bothered me. It sounds pushy and overbearing, too corporate ladder for my taste. Besides, the title no longer fits. Annie works for Cliff Halek these days. By all rights he should be "Boss."

Cliff said yesterday, "I prefer something more tribal. 'Chief' has a nice ring to it."

Yeah, right.

Nothing, not even "Chief," will ever replace Halek's real title. He is "SKC's Smartest Man."

Annie's departure means we can date in peace. There is none of that psychobabble from Human Resources, no need for me to worry about a hostile work environment. We spend all our free time together.

I worry about our relationship. It's not my eight years on Annie. It's my baggage. I've been ridden hard and put away wet. My wife, my daughter, well, there are things I'm still working out.

Evelyn's jewelry may be the first step. I dropped it off with an appraiser last Monday, everything except for the engagement ring. I could never use her baubles to romance someone else. So I'm meeting with Popowski tomorrow. We're setting up a trust for Fred Masters and funding it from the sale of Evelyn's jewels. Betty will resist when she learns. But I won't take no for an answer.

When I confided my plan to Annie, her eyes brimmed with tears. My heart sank. "Did I say something?" I asked, fearing the worst.

"No, Grove," she said, punching my arm. "Sometimes you don't understand anything." She smiled radiantly and hugged me hard. My throat swelled. It grew fat inside from all the affection.

I am completely out of practice.

This past week Annie and I went out every night. One night to Shun Lee, one night to a gallery in SoHo, and one night to a chick flick. Annie thought the movie was trite. I bawled like a baby. That's why I stick to films with car chases and no dialogue.

Words spoil the ass-kickings.

Madame Rosa, neighborhood psychic and local whack job, read our palms last Sunday and stated, "The spirit is strong around you. Would you like to contact friends from the other side?"

We presumed she meant dead people and almost walked out of her shop. No way were we conjuring up the memories of Charlie Kelemen. Instead, I asked,

"Can't you just read our palms? Tell us we have long life lines and all the standard stuff?"

Spending time with Annie is great. I'm trying hard not to blow my good fortune. We do stupid things together. It beats all those research reports every night in the solitude of a deserted office. No more sifting through prospectuses with CNBC's talking heads blabbing in the background. The other night she mentioned law school and asked my opinion about Columbia, Fordham, and NYU.

"They're okay," I said, not endorsing the concept, not really.

"What do you mean?" she bristled, suddenly angered by my lack of enthusiasm.

"I think you should consider a graduate degree in journalism, like Columbia's program. You're a born storyteller." That reply settled things down, and Annie's exploring both options. I'm glad.

It still mystifies me why we took forever to "hook up," as Annie says. For the record, the expression is not my favorite. "Hook up" sounds like something you do with laptops. Maybe that's the point. So many times I had savored Annie's perfume, her smile, the way she dressed, simple yet provocative, and the way her hips swayed while walking. Her golden-blond hair glowed like Big Sky sunshine. But it was the big personality I loved the most. Who else could have conceived a catch-and-release program for fruit flies?

Our impromptu lunch at Le Bernardin pushed us over the edge. As Annie worked through her sorbet and me through some kind of chocolate bombe, she asked,

"Are you asking me out again? Or do you need to fight somebody at the Red Flame first?"

"You're not seeing anyone?"

"What makes you think that?"

"You said 'love you' to somebody on the phone the night after Sam and I had dinner at Live Bait."

"My sister."

"Oh," I replied. "What about all those weekends at the beach?"

"Four girlfriends," she explained. "We share a summer rental in the Hamptons."

"You set up my date with Sam at Live Bait," I observed. "Why?"

"Proof of concept," she replied. Her breezy confidence reminded me of first years at Harvard Business School.

"What do you mean by that?"

"Grove, you're always telling clients that competition is a good thing among companies. It legitimizes their product offerings. When I set up that date with Sam, I realized why you never asked me out. You never asked anybody out." She raised one eyebrow, an expression stuck somewhere between flirtatious and all knowing.

"Got it. You seemed really upset the day after Live Bait. Do you remember?"

"Oh, I was upset, all right," she confirmed.

"Why?"

"I wanted to be your date," she said shyly, and grabbed my hand across the table.

When I told Chloe that Annie was leaving our team and we were now dating, she replied, "It's about time,

Grove. I remember the way you eyed her going for coffee."

My face turned crimson red, and for a moment I said nothing. The two of us stood in silence, Chloe grinning and me just abso-fucking-lutely mortified.

"Oh, stop it," Chloe finally said. "I'm not telling anyone. Annie makes you laugh. All of Wall Street will breathe easier when you lighten up." She was Solomon wise underneath that airplane-sized headset.

I owe Chloe. Head down, she held our team together for the last six weeks and, in some ways, the last eighteen months. She steered clear of office gossip and kept our clients happy, Jumping JJ in particular. Chloe is easy to overlook: quiet, focused, not as playful as Annie, checking on her children during spare moments, always be-domed with that stupid headset. I may buy her a new one, something lightweight and state-of-the-art. No one works harder, especially now that I am mothering back.

Patty Gershon was the first to notice my abbreviated work schedule. She accused me of "broker burnout" last week. Frankly, I was glad to hear her scream, "Hey, O'Rourke. Thanks for coming in today." Our fight is over for the time being, though she must suspect I hired the Union Rat.

Gershon, Gershon, rich and rude,
We don't like your attitude.

Zola Mancini agreed to become a junior partner on my team. We cemented a fair deal, easier now that my troubles are behind me. We are still learning how to work together. Zola may be a newbie, but she is 100 percent firecracker. She speaks her mind, even if it means zinging me from time to time. And I am no walk in the park. Top producers have answers for everything. Remember? It makes me fucking insufferable at times.

I never took calls from recruiters in the past. Now I do. The folks over at Goldman are anxious to meet. Morgan claims to have a better mousetrap. Merrill Lynch is waving big dollars. "Grove, we're different," or "Grove, we'll take good care of you," or "Grove, you can make us better."

All I can say is "horseshit." Not aloud, of course. Not to Goldman, Morgan, Merrill, or any of the other shops. I have no desire to piss them off. For defensive reasons I listen to everybody. You never know when your firm will toss you out on your ass. Or when competitors will become your new employers.

Someday, I may even take a competitor's check. The reason has nothing to do with the quality of corporate services. Or products for that matter. Goldman touts all its proprietary offerings, which I regard as little more than fees searching for an excuse to exist. The reason is all about survival. Wall Street's allegiances are ephemeral. Deals change. Friends become enemies, and enemies become friends. Our coalitions are convenient. Our genealogical roots all trace back to Brutus. If there is a threat, any shop on Wall Street will sacrifice brokers without a second thought. Anything to make the problems go away. Someday, it may be in my best interest to join another shop. Why not take their check?

Deep down, I know Frank Kurtz was right the day I agreed to return. "You think anybody cares about you over at Goldman?" he had asked. "Goldman" could just as easily have been a blank. Fill in the name of any investment bank. Your choice.

Frank Kurtz apologizes weekly. All his expressions of remorse, all his bloody olive branches, have little to do with guilt. When my name cleared, his number-one problem disappeared: loss of revenues. He needs my fees to make his budget.

"Grove, it's good to have you back," he said upon my return. "Let's grab dinner and kill a bottle of red after work one night. Smoke a few Cohibas."

Call me cynical, but I eschew the cabernet school of people management. During our dinner he teased, "Did I get the wall right? Maybe you belong next to Kozlowski and the rest of the crew?"

He was referring, of course, to the glossy black-and-white photo of me. I had given it to him after Patty stormed out of the room during the big sit-down. My portrait hangs next to Pope John Paul. And frankly, I am pleased with the product. The pope and I look good together.

With a bold Sharpie I had signed: "Make sure your people stay out of trouble, Frank. All the best, Grove." It was not conceit driving my demand to hang this picture. Rather, the picture was a reminder to Scully, to Casper sans clippers, to Radio Ray if he ever shows his commission-clipping face on this floor, to Patty and her cronies from Estrogen Alley, to people visiting Frank's office, and to all those who might otherwise besmirch my name and reputation. I played no role in the Kelemen Group.

Crunch cut my hair last week. He was the friend Sam had charged with bringing Un, Deux, and Trois to her parents' home in Boston. He never delivered the dogs, though. The three hang out in his salon with crustaceans all day long. I'm happy the dachshunds have a good home. Crunch said he might design a new logo around the dogs.

One thing still gnaws at me. Sam's jewels are missing. The trademark baubles, like the blue-green peacock brooch and the diamond cluster earrings, all vanished. Gone.

I asked Crunch, "Any ideas where they might be? Did Charlie pawn them?"

"No clue, honey," he replied, and snipped away.

I won't be looking under any rocks, though. As a runaway son of Charleston, a Southern boy just trying to find his way in the wilds of New York City, I "might could" leave you with a final axiom. It's probably the most important one of all.

Seven: Top producers stick to their day jobs.

THE GODS OF GREENWICH

CHAPTER 1

December 11, 2007

"I want my money."

Jimmy Cusack gazed out the window of his office in the Empire State Building. Most days he savored the southern view of downtown Manhattan. To the east was Goldman Sachs, its Broad Street headquarters an impregnable fortress in the world of finance. To the west was Lady Liberty, her harbor a vast cluster of skyscrapers rising from the sea. New York was a city that attracted great fortunes—and epic brawls to manage them.

There were times inside his hedge fund when Cusack could taste the adrenaline. He reveled in the rush of competitors waging war from their granite towers, New-Age monuments that celebrated the triumph of capital. There were no ceasefires sixty-one floors below. The struggle to win clients never stopped, and the ethos was "kill or be killed" among soldiers suited in the battle rattle of Armani pinstripes and Gucci loafers.

Today was no ordinary day. Those four words, "I want my money," haunted Cusack's thoughts. Gone was the crooked smile. The creases around his lips, sometimes mistaken for a good-natured smirk, had long since vanished. His eyes a bitter blue, Cusack's face resembled the dark clouds outside his bluff of sixty-one stories.

The ambush was cold and ruthless. "Here's how it is," the lead investor said. "Tomorrow morning, James, you'll get a FedEx. Not the afternoon delivery, but the one at ten. Inside are eight redemption notices. Each one is signed and notarized, ready to go. I want my money. So do my friends who invested in your fund."

"Who else wants out, Caleb?"

"Everybody I put in."

"Not Whitney," insisted Cusack.

"Yes."

"What about Gould?"

"Everybody," Caleb repeated. "By my calculations, our stake totals one hundred and twenty million dollars."

"You agreed to a lock-up," argued Cusack. "We're talking eighty-five percent of what I manage and—"

"My lawyers say your documents are a joke."

"You talked to Ropes & Gray?"

"What difference does it make? Just get us our money, James."

"That the way it is?" Cusack sounded hard, but he was wobbling inside.

"My hands are tied."

"Yeah. To an axe."

"I may run for governor, James. I can't ask my buddies for contributions, not when they're losing their shirts at Petri Dish Capital or whatever the hell they call your hedge fund."

"And you think pulling your money is smart in this market?"

"Not open for discussion."

Nearly six hours had passed since then. The markets were closed. The sun was setting. And Cusack racked his brain for a Hail Mary solution, a glimmer of hope, anything to save his business from redemptions that would leave him with less than $20 million to manage.

It could take years to replace $120 million from Caleb and his fellow deserters. Until then, revenues from the remaining $20 million would not pay the light bill. Cusack had no cash left to fund operations. He had gone "all in," Texas hold 'em style with every chip in the pot.

With the grim reality of Caleb's words unfolding, Cusack lacked his characteristic focus. His thoughts drifted from New York's office towers to the "Irish battleships" of his youth, the three-family homes of Somerville, Massachusetts.

Jimmy had always been the scrappy kid with promise. Long ago he traded membership in Somerville's blue-collar CIA—Catholic, Irish, alcoholic—for a career on Wall Street. He was thirty-two and Ivy-educated, a graduate of Columbia and Wharton. His pedigree included a one-year Rotary Fellowship in Japan and five years at Goldman Sachs. He was his family's hope for the future, the son, the entrepreneur his parents had backed.

Those were yesterday's dreams. Cusack's money-management business was going down. It was taking on water through a *Titanic*-sized hole in the hull, the lead investor's words tearing at him still. "Nothing personal, mind you."

Caleb, you made it personal.

"And we expect you for Christmas dinner, James."

CHAPTER 2

Wednesday, December 12

The following night a biting wind roared down the street named Hverfisgata. It gusted through doors and windows, through all the nooks and crannies of the stark buildings that lined the street. The air smelled of salt and sea and the damp wrath of Arctic squalls. The windchill registered icebox-cold under the dark Icelandic sky.

Seeking cover, three Americans from Connecticut ate dinner inside Hverfisgata's 101 Hotel. The men relished their hiatus from the trading floors of Greenwich, where drip bags of gloom emptied into the markets. Their trip to Reykjavik was no boondoggle. The three had focused on business all week.

Their back-to-back meetings, insufferable at times, resembled a funeral procession of Icelandic bankers and low-ranking bureaucrats. The marathon tête-à-têtes about liquidity and leverage were benumbing. But they paid off. The fieldwork confirmed their instincts and gave shape to a scheme that had been percolating for months.

Hafnarbanki, Iceland's most celebrated bank, was vulnerable to financial attack. Headquartered ten miles south of Reykjavik, the bank had borrowed forty-five billion dollars. It was too much debt, more than twice the size of Iceland's entire economy. Much of that forty-five billion came from overseas. If European depositors lost confidence and closed their accounts, Hafnarbanki would collapse under the weight of its financial obligations. It was a bank on the brink.

All it needed was a little push.

Not one of the men discussed their scheme, not at first, not during the main course of bloody lamb. They were pros, wizened hedge fund veterans and far too wily for premature celebrations. Counting money jinxed trades. Backslapping was gratuitous. They could already taste each other's silent dreams anyway. They could almost touch the expectations of a sure thing that would net them tens of millions.

It was not until after dinner that the three relaxed, after a $15,000 "vertical tasting" of 2001, 2002, and 2003 Screaming Eagle Cabernet Sauvignon. After the wine located self-control switches on two men, a conga line of port chasers turned all three faces beet-red. They split the tab and moved to the hotel's sleek bar, where conversation turned to their business in Iceland.

"Tomorrow," announced the tallest money manager, the one with the Stanford MBA, starter wife, and four kids, "I'm shorting Hafnarbanki at twelve hundred."

"Tall" believed Hafnarbanki's price was about to crash. His plan was to borrow stock and sell at 1,200 Kronur right away. If Hafnarbanki fell to 500 Kronur, he would buy at the lower price, return stock to the lender, and book a tidy profit of 700 Kronur per share.

"I'm in," agreed the second man. He had a Napoleonic build, MIT degree in math, and hot-action mistress. "When we're finished, these Vikings will know Hafnarbanki as Bank Hindenburg."

"If you ask me, it's more of an H-bomb," scoffed Tall. He ordered three more ports. "Cy, what do you think?"

"That you two have mouths like billboards. Keep your voices down." Cy was the most sober and the most alert, the money manager with a history degree from NYU. He smiled Joe Biden–bright, his good mood at odds with instinctive caution.

"Hey, we're with you, Cy," soothed Napoleon, raising his glass for the others to clink. "We can't lose, right?"

Cyrus Leeser grew up in Hell's Kitchen, where he survived Irish Catholic kids and eluded "poison people." Outside his family's apartment on West 54th, the heroin addicts were forever scratching through life in search of scag or the five way—a cocktail of heroine, cocaine, methamphetamine, Rohypnol, and alcohol. He made it to college, graduated, and began a steady, if unremarkable, career as a stockbroker with the "thundering herd." Leeser left Merrill Lynch in 2000 and co-founded LeeWell Capital. That was the beginning of his spectacular rise.

Most estimates placed Leeser's net worth around $75 million. Some hedge fund insiders argued it was more. He owned a sumptuous estate and was married to Bianca Santiago, best-selling author and his trophy wife of sixteen years. He was an accomplished pilot, a philanthropist, and father, a guy proud of twin daughters attending Andover, the elite boarding school. He ran big money and recruited new investors every day, vowing never to set foot on West 54th again.

"The only risk," Napoleon suggested, "is that three hundred thousand people live in Iceland. And they're all related."

"It's like some kind of Nordic Appalachia," Tall agreed. "Webbed feet and shit."

"These cousins can band together," Napoleon continued, "buy stock, and prop up Hafnarbanki's share price."

"Don't say the name of the bank," warned Cy. "What is it you don't understand about keeping your voice down?"

"You worry too much," scoffed Napoleon. "We're performing a community service."

"How so?" asked Tall as another round of drinks arrived.

"By shorting dumb money so it goes away." Napoleon clinked glasses with Tall and raised a toast, "To Hafnarbanki."

Cy winced as he noticed a bookish man a few seats down the bar.

Furrowed brow, sleek black glasses, Siberian-blue eyes—Siggi Stefansson pretended to read his novel. The Americans annoyed him: the bottomless drinks, the clinking of glasses, the laughter that occasionally rocked the bar. It was all he could do to concentrate.

Siggi cursed the tallest foreigner under his breath. Then he cursed his girlfriend Hanna, who always ran late. The Icelander was forever sitting in bars, alone, reading books and drinking himself into drunken stupors with people he didn't know. Or drinking with Ólafur. His second cousin was a regular at every gin mill in downtown Reykjavik.

Siggi could not help but eavesdrop, especially because the three Americans were discussing Hafnarbanki. He deposited his money there. It was the pride of Iceland, a national treasure, a legacy from a few fishermen who abandoned their nets in the 1930s for the glory of international banking.

The Americans almost seemed giddy. Siggi closed his book, taking care to dog-ear the page, and sipped his Guinness. He studied the man named "Cy," who shushed the other two men from time to time.

Cy was in his late 40s with deep crow's feet and basset-hound eyes. He was an imposing figure: muscular build, five foot eleven at least, and jet-black hair that lopped over his ears and touched his shoulders. He spoke little. But he conveyed power. Siggi judged Cy to be a man who could handle himself in any bar whether drinking, fighting, or womanizing.

The other two Americans, however annoying, intrigued him. Drunk or not, they sounded smarter than most tourists. He heard the word "short" every so often, but he was not sure what it meant. Their toast seemed friendly enough:

"To Hafnarbanki."

That was when Leeser caught Siggi's eye. "Are you

from Reykjavik?" the long-haired American asked. He was all smile and bleached teeth. He spoke in a disarming manner, as though asking for directions.

"Yes." Siggi pushed his black glasses up from the bridge of his nose.

"Come on down and let me buy you a drink."

Leeser prided himself on one skill. He could read people. As a kid the talent helped him duck punches, both on the streets and inside his apartment which was a hell all its own. Within thirty-five minutes, Cy was convinced he knew everything about the bookish Icelander with the craggy face and wavy blond hair.

Siggi was the youngest of three children. He was thirty-four and engaged to be married. He had been dating his fiancée for nine months and three days. He reminded the American of a young Michael Caine.

Cy knew Hanna's name. He knew her studies were a source of conflict. Siggi wanted to get married right away. But Hanna's law degree came first as far as she was concerned. Planning a wedding, Hanna argued, was out of the question given her course load at Reykjavik University's School of Law.

Leeser's interest in the Icelander had little to do with affability. It was all about damage control. Cy wondered what Siggi had heard, whether he was a threat. Ferreting out information, though, required finesse. The American gave a little to get a lot.

At one point, Siggi asked, "What brings you to Iceland?"

"I run a hedge fund."

"I don't understand much about them," Siggi confessed.

"Few people do," Cy replied in his most disarming, empathetic voice. "In my opinion hedge funds have three things in common. We manage money. We usually charge twenty percent fees on profits. And we're less regulated than other financial institutions, because we each work with limited numbers of wealthy investors."

"But what do you mean by 'hedge'?"

"Fair question, Siggi. 'Hedge' is a misleading word. It makes us sound like money managers who protect against downside risk—in the same way landlords insure buildings against fire. I do. But not everybody does. Like I said before, hedge funds manage money for wealthy investors."

"Well, that leaves me out," Siggi noted, his voice wistful. "I have no head for stocks and bonds anyway."

Cy relaxed. And then he discovered a bonus. Siggi owned a small art gallery, two blocks away. The Icelander traveled extensively, spoke fluent Russian, and catered to an exclusive clientele of eastern Europeans. This discovery thrilled Leeser, a true lover of art, a collector with eclectic tastes. Cy covered both his home and office walls with emerging masters from everywhere.

"Would you like to see my gallery?" Siggi offered. "We can go when Hanna gets here."

"Not me," Napoleon replied. "I'm going to bed."

"Me either," agreed Tall. "Cy's your guy. He wants to become Stevie Cohen."

Tall was referring to the founder of SAC Capital Partners. Cohen, a billionaire and king among hedge funds, owned the greats. His collection, worth $700 million by some estimates, included masterpieces by Eduard Munch, Pablo Picasso, and Andy Warhol.

"I'm small-time compared to Cohen," Leeser added in a wistful, self-deprecating way. "Maybe one day."

Siggi and Cy could have yakked about art all night. But Leeser stayed on plan and forced himself to learn more about the Icelander, to ensure the art dealer was no threat.

Cy knew Siggi was a happy drunk, incapable of holding his liquor. He knew the names of Siggi's parents, not to mention his older brother and sister. He knew the Icelander felt a special affinity with his second cousin. There was only one detail Cy missed.

Cousin Ólafur worked for Hafnarbanki. He was the Managing Director of Strategic Development, the senior executive charged with mapping out the bank's competitive strategy. When hedge funds attacked, his job was to mow them down.

CHAPTER 3

Wednesday, December 19

"You're taking too long."

"Do your job, and let me do mine." Rachel Whittier clicked off her cellphone, annoyed by his pressure. Who needed it? She had never failed her employer before. Two, maybe three more years of this aggravation, and she would tell him to take a hike. She would have enough cash and could stop moonlighting forever, or at least until she moved to Paris.

"Get your boots," a deejay advised over the radio. "There's a blizzard coming."

Rachel gazed out the window of her Park Avenue clinic. All morning the squalls had threatened. Now avalanche-white nimbostratus clouds were dusting New York City with snowy powder. It was only a matter of time before they launched a full-scale assault.

The storm would snarl traffic. The taxis would skid on rutted roads, windshield wipers slapping this way and that. The cabbies would swear and spit and smack each other's fenders, while pedestrians slipped on unsalted sidewalks and scuttled from store to store. But Rachel's green eyes blazed with gelid detachment, trancelike, in a nether zone.

She was blasé about the holiday craze in New York City. She ignored Christmas decorations and the Salvation Army ringing their hand bells on Fifth Avenue. Today was the day. It was time to go.

Rachel charged out of the break room, down the marble-lined corridor, and found Doc in reception among towering ferns and back issues of *People* magazine. New York's foremost plastic surgeon, fiftyish and too Hollywood for her taste, was braving the elements to grab lunch.

"I'm taking the afternoon off," she announced. "See you tomorrow."

Rachel was not asking. She was telling. She owned Doc. He was the one who prepared collagen syringes for her treatments. He was the one who bought lunch whenever she asked. Doc was the boss, the big biscuit in the pan. But he said, "Yes," no matter what came out of her mouth. And she doubted her honey Texan accent was the reason.

"Christmas shopping?" Doc inquired, ever the obedient dog with tongue hanging out.

"You're on my list." Rachel flipped her golden-blond hair and spun round to retrieve a purse and winter coat. She could feel Doc ogling her from behind, his eyes tracing the starched white blouse and cup of her white skirt. He appreciated her sway. She appreciated her power, the ability to milk desire for control.

Inside a private consultation room, which housed

the staff's closet, Rachel appraised her figure in a full-length mirror. She approved the fullness of her breasts. She cocked her head slightly to the right, unconsciously rubbing a raised puffy, round scar on the back of her right hand. For a moment she scrutinized her thin hips, wondering if she had put on weight.

The moment passed. It was time to get started. She was starved, already savoring the hunt.